KATHR... ... ...
ing *Th...* ... ...n
works of ... ...er
Knot. She lives in New York. Her website can be found at
www.kathrynharrison.com

Visit www.AuthorTracker.co.uk for exclusive information
on your favourite HarperCollins authors.

From the reviews of *Envy*:

'Her novels have pushed into areas of forbidden desire in
ways that are always enjoyable as well as disturbing. In a
world that has almost lost its taboos, Harrison still provides
a daring sense of pushing against boundaries'
NATASHA WALTER, *Guardian*

'Intense and sometimes unbearably moving . . . Compelling
and genuinely disturbing' *The Times*

'A dark and brooding novel . . . Particularly impressive is
Harrison's ability to write about sex in a way that is explicit
and revealing but never prurient' *Mail on Sunday*

'A darkly dazzling tale' *Daily Mail*

'A splendid study of modern American life' *Observer*

'A marvellous writer, one of the best at work today.
Harrison is unflinching, however difficult her material. Her
characters are complex, her dialogue razor-sharp and her
range – moral, historical and geographical – is unparalleled.
Few authors of serious fiction are so daring' *Daily Telegraph*

F/2068481.

County Council Library

2068481

COUNTY
LIBRARY

'An exquisitely handled novel, beautifully paced and emotionally engaging. Many of America's best novelists have focused on the threat to the family in recent years, including Philip Roth, Joyce Carol Oates and Jonathan Franzen. Harrison deserves her place among them'
Scottish Sunday Herald

'Kathryn Harrison is a wonderful writer... Spellbinding'
New York Times

'A juicy story of psychosexual suspense'
Wall Street Journal

'*Envy* is full of Harrison's astute, often mordant powers of physical and psychological observation... The fact is that Kathryn Harrison is one of our more earnestly impassioned and intellectually engaging players. Long may she run'
Elle

By the same author

FICTION

Thicker Than Water
Exposure
Poison
A Thousand Orange Trees
The Binding Chair
The Seal Wife

NON-FICTION

The Kiss
Seeking Rapture
Saint Thérése of Lisieux
The Road to Santiago
The Mother Knot

KATHRYN HARRISON

Envy

HARPER PERENNIAL

London, New York, Toronto and Sydney

Harper Perennial
An imprint of HarperCollins*Publishers*
77–85 Fulham Palace Road
Hammersmith, London W6 8JB

www.harperperennial.co.uk

This edition published by Harper Perennial 2007
4

First published in Great Britain by Fourth Estate in 2005

Copyright © Kathryn Harrison 2005

PS Section copyright © Sarah O'Reilly 2007, except 'Sin Boldly' by
Kathryn Harrison © Kathryn Harrison 2005

PS™ is a trademark of HarperCollins*Publishers* Ltd

Kathryn Harrison asserts the moral right to
be identified as the author of this work

A catalogue record for this book
is available from the British Library

ISBN-13 978-0-00-721662-8
ISBN-10 0-00-721662-9

Set in Janson with DIN display

Printed and bound in Great Britain by Clays Ltd, St Ives plc

This novel is entirely a work of fiction. The names,
characters and incidents portrayed in it are the work of the
author's imagination. Any resemblance to actual persons,
living or dead, events or localities is entirely coincidental.

All rights reserved. No part of this publication may be
reproduced, stored in a retrieval system, or transmitted,
in any form or by any means, electronic, mechanical,
photocopying, recording or otherwise, without the
prior permission of the publishers.

This book is sold subject to the condition that it shall not,
by way of trade or otherwise, be lent, re-sold, hired out or
otherwise circulated without the publisher's prior consent
in any form of binding or cover other than that in which it
is published and without a similar condition including this
condition being imposed on the subsequent purchaser.

for Kate Medina

In those years I had a great need to be seen.
And when one succeeds in seducing someone,
one also succeeds in being seen.

—LARS GUSTAFSSON,
  The Death of a Beekeeper

ENVY

Will leans out of the driver's-side window toward his wife. "It's not too late to change your mind," he says.

Her dark glasses show him the houses on their side of the block, greatly reduced and warped by the convexity of each lens. The fancy wrought-iron bars on their neighbor's windows, the bright plastic backboard of the Little Tikes basketball hoop one door down, the white climbing rose, suddenly and profusely in bloom, on the trellis by their own mailbox: it's as if he were studying one of those jewel-like miniatures painted in Persia during the sixteenth century; the longer Will looks, the more tiny details he finds.

"Did you remember to bring pictures?" Carole asks.

He points to an envelope on the seat beside him. "I mentioned the pool at the hotel?"

"Several times."

"Babysitting services? Pay-per-view?"

"Come on, Will," Carole says, "don't do this to me."

"Do what?"

"Make me feel guilty." Her bra strap has slipped out from the armhole of her sleeveless dress, down one shoulder. Without looking, she tucks it back where it belongs.

"You know I'd make it up to you," he tells her. She smiles, raises her eyebrows so they appear above the frames of her sunglasses.

"And how might you do that?" she asks him.

"By being your sex slave."

She reaches behind his neck to adjust his collar. "Aren't you forgetting something?" she says.

"What's that?"

"You already are my sex slave."

"Oh," Will says, "right." The errant strap has reemerged, a black satiny one he recognizes as belonging to the bra that unhooks in front.

Carole ducks her head in the window to brush her lips against his cheek, a kiss, but not quite: no pucker, no sound. For a moment she rests her forehead against his. "I just can't deal with it. You know that. I can't talk about Luke—not with people I don't know. And the same goes for your brother." She pulls back to look at him. "If you weren't such a masochist, you wouldn't be going either."

I'm curious, Will thinks of saying. *It's not as simple as masochism. Or as complicated.* Carole steps back from the car door.

"See you Sunday," she says, and her voice has returned to its previous playful tone. "Call if you get lonely."

"Oh, I doubt that'll be necessary." Will turns the key in the ignition. "I'll be too busy connecting with old friends. Blowing on the embers of undergraduate romance . . ."

"Checking out the hairlines," she says. "Seeing who got fat and who got really fat."

Will glances in the rearview mirror as he drives away, sees his wife climb the stairs to their front door, the flash of light as she opens it, the late June sun hot and yellow against its big pane of glass.

Something about the cavernous tent defeats acoustics: the voices of the class of '79, those Cornell alumni who made it back for their twenty-fifth reunion, combine in a percussive assault on the eardrum, the kind Will associates with driving on a highway, one window cracked for air, that annoying *whuh-whuh-whuh* sound. He moves his lower jaw from side to side to dispel the echoey, dizzy feeling. Psychosomatic, he concludes. Why is he here, anyway? Does he even want to make the effort to hear well enough to engage with these people? Everyone around him, it seems, isn't talking so much as advertising. Husbands describing vacations too expensive to include basic plumbing, referring to them as experiences rather than travel, as in "our rain forest experience." And, as if to demonstrate what good sports they are, wives laughing at everything, including comments that strike Will as pure information. "No, they relocated." "Ohio, wasn't it?" "The kids are from the first marriage." "She fell in love with this guy overseas."

He tries to picture the women's workaday selves: quieter, with paler lips, flatter hair. Still, on the whole they're well preserved, while the men by their sides look worn and rumpled. Receding hairlines have nowhere else to go; love handles have grown too big to take hold of.

"Hey!" someone says, and Will turns around to a face he remembers from his freshman dorm. "David Snader!" the face bellows to identify itself. With his big, hot hand, David pulls Will into a crushing hug. "Where you been!" he says, as though he'd lost track of Will hours rather than decades ago.

"Hey!" Will pulls out of the sweaty and, it would appear, drunken embrace.

"Are you here alone?" David asks him. He blots his forehead with a handkerchief.

Will nods. "Carole—my wife—she wasn't up for a long weekend of nostalgia with people she's never met before."

"Same here. Same here." David gives Will a companionable punch in the arm. "Where's Mitch?" he asks, and Will shrugs.

"Didn't make it. At least not as far as I know."

"Oh yeah?" David squints. "You guys not in touch or something?"

"Not at the moment."

"Well." He punches Will's arm again. "Guess that makes sense. All the travel. Media. Price of fame."

Will produces the rueful smile he hopes will convey that his estrangement from his famous twin is no big deal. Unfortunate, of course, but nothing hurtful or embarrassing. He's about to ask David about his wife and whether or not they have children, when David lurches off into the crowd. Will fills his cheeks with air, blows it out in a gust. David Snader is the fifth person in one hour to have approached him to ask not about Will or Will's work, his family, but about his brother, whose career as a long-distance swimmer has given Mitch a name as recognizable as that of, say, Lance Armstrong or Tiger Woods. Not that any of these alumni were his friends. Will and David hadn't even liked each other. But still.

He goes to the bar for a glass of red wine. If he's going to drink, he might as well rinse a little cholesterol out of his arteries. He's just replacing his wallet in the inside breast pocket of his blazer when he looks up to see someone else bearing down on him, Sue Shimakawa, with whom he'd shared an exam-week tryst, if that's the right word for abbreviated coitus in the musty, rarely penetrated stacks of the undergraduate library. Punch-drunk from studying chemistry for a few hundred hours, on a dare Will had asked Sue to have sex with him, prepared for a slap, or for her badmouthing him later or laughing at him in the moment, anything but what he got: her accepting his invitation with a sort of gung-ho enthusiasm. She had one of those bodies Will thinks of as typically Asian: compact, androgynous, and smooth-skinned, with pubic hair that was absolutely straight instead of curly, the surprise of this discovery—along with the panic induced by having intercourse in a potentially public place—enough to eclipse other, more inclusive observations.

"Will, Will, Will," Sue sings at him. "I was hoping to see you!" She has a man in tow, a sandy-haired giant at least a foot and a half taller than she. "Meet Rob. We have five kids, if you can believe it! Five!"

Wow, Will is about to say when Sue turns to her husband and says, "Rob, this is Will Moreland, an old fuck-buddy of mine."

Whether Rob is mute or only, like Will, horrified into silence, he thrusts his big, freckled hand forward without saying a word. The two men shake, silent in the clamor all around them, and then each drops his hand to his side and looks at Sue to see what might happen next.

"Rob's a debt analyst," she says.

"Really!" Will exclaims.

"Yes."

They all nod.

"Hey, hey," Sue says. "How about that brother of yours, huh? We're major fans. Major."

"He has had a spectacular ride." For once, Will is relieved when the conversation turns to his brother.

"Oh, I don't know. There's heaps of athletes that are celebrities."

"Of course, yes," Will says. "I know that. I just—"

"Is he here?"

"Here?"

"At the reunion. Here at the reunion."

"No. I'm afraid not."

"Oh, too bad. I really wanted to catch a glimpse of him."

Me, too, Will thinks as Sue and her husband move off. Having not heard from his brother for fifteen years now, during which time Mitch went from being known in the world of elite swimmers to being known by just about everyone, Will fantasized that Mitch might actually show up. If he's honest with himself, the hope of seeing his brother was at least part of what persuaded him to attend the reunion—especially after he'd learned that Andrew Goldstein, the one friend with whom he'd kept in touch after college, wouldn't be coming because his wife's due date fell on the same weekend. Not that seeing Mitch would be pleasant or, Will imagines, anything less than traumatic, but he's fed up with having to manage his private anguish even as he's forced to admit sheepishly to friends, colleagues, neighbors, and now alumni that he's no better informed about his brother's latest stunt swim—as Will has come to think of them—than the average reader of *Sports Illustrated*.

"Hello," says a voice behind him, startling Will out of what Carole would call one of his social desertions, when he becomes a spectator rather than a participant. He turns in the direction of the flirtatious tone he almost recognizes. As for the face: arresting, angular, unforgettable. Thinner than she used to be, but no less substantial—she looks concentrated, a distillate of her younger self.

"Elizabeth," he says.

"William." She tilts her head to one side, lifts her eyebrows. "Were you looking for someone?"

"You, of course. Who else?" Will unbuttons his shirt collar and loosens his tie. "Do you think I didn't scour each of those e-mail bulletins listing who was planning to attend, hoping—hoping against hope—to see your name?"

"Can it be?" Elizabeth says. "Has Mr. Fatally Earnest developed a sense of humor?"

"Only in extremis."

Elizabeth glances around herself. "I guess this qualifies," she says.

"Actually, I was just looking over the crowd. Seeing what generalizations I could make about the class of 'seventy-nine."

"And?"

He shrugs. "I don't know that I've had enough time to study my impressions. You?"

She shakes her head. "Insufficient data," she says.

"Data? That's a clinical word."

"I'm a clinician."

"Oh, right. I'd heard you'd gone on to med school." Having read her bio in the reunion book—studied it would not be inaccurate—Will knows also to which school Elizabeth went, when she got her degree, and where she now works. But he's not going to give her the (false) impression that he's still pining for her. "Where'd you end up—what school?" he asks.

"Johns Hopkins." Elizabeth pauses, Will suspects, to give him the opportunity to compliment her for having been accepted by a top-flight med school. He dips his head in an abbreviated bow of congratulation. "I was in dermatology," she continues, "then I specialized."

"I thought being a dermatologist was specializing."

"It is. It is up to a point. I went further, into burn treatment. I'm the program head at Johns Hopkins. We get patients from all over. Medevacked." Another pause. This time Will holds up his glass as if to begin a toast.

"So," he says, "no clinical observations whatsoever?"

She takes a sip from her drink. "The usual midlife stuff. Sun damage mostly, keratosis, a few carcinomas. But you probably weren't talking pathology, were you?" She looks around the big tent, shrugs. "Standard nip and tuck," she says. "Eyes. Neck. This isn't exactly a B-and-C crowd."

"B-and-C?"

"Botox and collagen." She draws her eyebrows together as she turns her attention back to him. "You?" she asks.

"Nah. Well, not collagen anyway. Maybe some Botox when I hit fifty."

Elizabeth ignores this. "I was wondering what it is that you do," she says.

"I'm a shrink."

"Really?" She smiles a faintly condescending smile. Will remembers this about her, the superior manner she wouldn't get away with were she less attractive.

"Really," he says.

"You look the part."

"Do I? How?"

"Oh, you know, the beard, the glasses. And you always did have those deep-set eyes that make you look thoughtful. How's Mitch?" she asks, moving efficiently through the expectable topics. "Is he here? I don't have to ask what he's been up to."

"He didn't make it, I'm afraid."

"Is he avoiding you?"

"What's that supposed to mean?"

"Nothing," she says, but she looks at him diagnostically, he thinks.

"Can I get you another drink?"

"Sure," she says. She hands him her glass. "Gimlet," she tells him. "Vodka, not gin."

"Why don't you grab that table before someone else does?"

When Will returns, Elizabeth has taken off her shoes and is sitting with one leg tucked under herself. She's one of those women, it strikes him, who will remain indefinitely athletic and limber—a woman like his wife, actually.

"So," she says. "Were you at the tenth?"

He shakes his head. "I was getting married. You?"

"Nope. Traveling."

"Somewhere good?"

"Cape Town. A conference. I managed to tack on a few days." She takes a sip from her glass, frowns, stirs it with a finger. "What have you been up to for the last twenty-five years, William? You didn't submit one of those what-I-did-over-summer-vacation reports. How come?"

"I don't know. Missed the deadline, I guess."

"Still married?" she asks.

He nods.

"She's not here?"

"She hates reunions."

Elizabeth smiles. "Me, too," she says. "Kids?"

"Two. Boy. Then a girl." He takes a breath. "The boy died," he says, amazed as always at how the words just come out. *The boy died.* Like any other little sentence. The boy climbed. The boy jumped. The boy ate his dinner.

"Oh, William. I'm—I'm so sorry. I had . . ." She talks through the hand covering her mouth. "I had no idea."

"No. How could you? That's the real reason I didn't send in the bio. I couldn't get around that one piece of news."

"When? When did he . . . when did it happen?"

"Three summers ago. An accident at a lake." Will looks at her and she looks away, briefly, then returns her eyes to his. "It's . . . we don't need to talk about it," he says, and he takes a swallow of his wine. "Among the things I didn't anticipate about death was how awkward a subject it is. Just mentioning it is the equivalent of a terrible gaffe, like pouring your drink on someone or inadvertently exposing yourself. An inappropriate nakedness. You just can't . . . people can't get past it. But, well, I find it equally impossible not to bring it up."

Elizabeth slips back into her shoes and stands. "I have an idea. I'll go to the women's room. I think it's over there." She points in the direction of a nondescript building, he can't remember what it is, a library maybe. "It'll give us an intermission, sort of. Then you can . . . we can . . . well, we can start over. Or not. You decide."

Will watches her move through the crowd, nimble and quick, as if she's trained for this specific topography, the congested party. Alone at the table, he finds the level of noise around him almost intolerable, one voice indistinguishable from another, punctuated by bursts of loud, alcohol-fueled laughter. He's glad to be slightly drunk himself; it makes it easier to move on from Luke to another topic.

"I want to ask you something," he says when Elizabeth sits back down in the chair opposite his. She inclines her head very slightly in a gesture of assent, nothing so unequivocal as a full nod. Her face is untanned, the freckles she had in college gone, bleached away perhaps, and her eyebrows are thicker now, almost lush. They balance the new, more tense and defiant line of her jaw.

"You left me in 1979." Will stops to consider what he's just said. Context, context, he warns himself: college reunion, level of blood alcohol, his tendency to make interpersonal missteps in Carole's absence. Anger, too, still there, not quite burnt out. A mistake to ignore it, even if it is a given. It seems Elizabeth's ability to provoke him, to knock him off-kilter, hasn't diminished. If anything, it's more intense, just like the rest of her. Ironic that she'd become a dermatologist. She'd always had a personality like a rash, itchy, chafing, the kind of woman who just won't let you get comfortable. A waiter moves among the tables, gathering abandoned glasses onto a tray.

Elizabeth brushes her hair back with obvious irritation. "We're not—that's not what we're going to talk about, is it?" she says.

"No," he says. "We're not."

"Okay, good. Look, I'm sorry. But . . ." She's shaking her head. "I don't want to talk about our breaking up when we were, what, however old we were twenty-five years ago."

"You were twenty-one."

"Not quite," she says.

"And I was twenty-two."

"Twenty-two," she agrees.

"And then you married."

"I did."

"You had a child."

"Yes."

Will nods. "I read your bio," he says. "No pictures, though. Did you bring any? Any pictures of her?"

"No. Well, I have one, but it's back in my room."

"She's how old?"

"Jennifer?"

"Jennifer."

Elizabeth produces her hands from under the table and places them together below her chin, palms and fingers aligned as if in prayer. A pretty gesture, it makes him wonder if she prays, goes to church, believes in God. Did she used to? He can't remember. "Oh," she says, nodding. "I get it. I get it now."

"Get what?" he says.

Mouth closed, she looks as if she might be holding her breath, counting to ten so as not to lose her temper. Her face is every bit as arresting as it was when they were students together. More so, because the passage of years has scrubbed at her features, worn away whatever flesh once softened the angles of her jaw and of her cheekbones, revealing a face that is fierce as well as fragile. The fierceness was always there, of course, but now it announces itself. Her good looks are the opposite of the girl-next-door's, the opposite of Carole's.

"William," she says. "You can't . . . you think Jenny is—" She stops. She separates her hands and leaves them open, with their palms up. "I'm not going to say it," she says.

"Is she?"

"Is she what?"

"Were you pregnant when you left me?"

Elizabeth smiles, not warmly, and drops her hands. "I left you the summer we graduated, in August. Forgive me if I don't recall the exact date." Her voice is sharp with sarcasm, enough so that it seems to twang. "I married Paul on September eleventh. Jennifer's birthday is February sixth."

"So you were pregnant when you married Paul."

"Yes."

"And you were pregnant when you left me."

"Possibly."

"So is she mine or Paul's?"

"Well, really, William, who knows? Maybe she's Tom's or Dick's or Harry's. Maybe I was sleeping with any number of people." Elizabeth tosses one arm out as if to include all the men in the tent.

"I'm not judging you," he lies. "I just want to know if you know who her father is."

Elizabeth tips her head up, eyes on the tent canvas overhead.

Veins show green through the white skin of her throat. Oddly sexy, Will thinks, feeling desire awaken. She looks back at him. "Paul is Jennifer's father," she says.

"Because it would be easy enough," he continues as if she hasn't spoken, "to find out if she's Paul's or, well, whoever's."

"I suppose that's true." She gives him a stare of transparently manufactured patience, an expression intended to convey its opposite. Having lost whatever goodwill she once bore him, she's eager to terminate this unfortunate meeting.

"So, have you?" Will presses.

"Have I what?"

"Have you ever had the tests done to see—"

"Look," Elizabeth says. "I'm sorry for what's happened in your life, Will. Truly. I'm sorry for you, sorry for your wife, sorry for your daughter. I admit that I have no idea the pain your family must have suffered. But what you and I had, a college romance, a relationship that's been over and done with for twenty-five years, it can't . . . there's nothing left of that, nothing that could—"

"This isn't about Luke."

"Of course it is."

"No. I just . . . when I saw your page in the reunion book, the bio, the year your daughter was born, I mean, how could the thought not have crossed my mind? How could—"

"You lost a child. Now you want to find one."

"That's a little reductive, wouldn't you say?"

"Absolutely. But can you give me an alternate explana—"

"Elizabeth. You walked out on me. Possibly, you were pregnant with my child. Jennifer was born on—"

"Jenny is twenty-four years old. What's the point of talking about biological paternity now, after another man—Paul—has been her father for all her life?"

"Because. I want to know. I'd think she would, too. And you."

"Seriously?" Elizabeth says. "Surely not seriously."

"Seriously." As he repeats the word, Will realizes that this is in fact what he wants. What he seriously wants. Suddenly, nothing seems more important than learning this one fact. He watches Elizabeth shake her head briskly, as if to dislodge what she's heard.

"But you're . . . you're interested. Is that what you're saying? You're not, you can't be asking me to have this, this thing done."

"Yes, I am."

"No."

"Yes."

"Why!"

"I told you. I want to know."

"*You* do."

"Yes. *I* do."

"But so what? In terms of my life and her life, so what if you want to know? Information like that—it's pointless now. It would only confuse Jenny. Who knows? It could disrupt her education, compromise her understanding of herself. And to what end? To provide you solace? Illusory solace, because it's not going to fix anything, not really."

"But paternity does matter. And I'm not asking for anything to be 'fixed,' whatever that might mean."

"What then?" Elizabeth lays both hands on the table, palms down. She leans forward. "What could possibly be the point?"

"I want to know, that's all. Jennifer doesn't have to. You don't have to. I was thinking . . . well, here's an idea." Will feels his cheeks tingle with surprise at what he's about to say. As if it weren't wine he'd been drinking but a far more potent disinhibitor, a solvent not just for common sense and restraint but whatever keeps a person from voicing everything that pops into his head. "Give me a strand of her hair. You could take it from her brush, tape it to an index card, and mail it to me. Then I could find out. I would know, and that would be it. I wouldn't tell you. I wouldn't tell her. Not unless you specifically asked me to share the results."

Elizabeth stares at him, looking genuinely incredulous, her mouth ajar. "That is very, very perverse," she says.

"What is?"

"Asking me, her mother, to take—steal—her hair."

"It's not stealing."

"It is. It is stealing."

"How can it be stealing if the thing stolen has no value?"

Instead of answering, Elizabeth closes her eyes, long enough that he finds himself studying her face, the mauve skin of her eyelids, her pale mouth and cheeks. She could do with some color, a little lipstick or something, but she's always been too proud to wear makeup. Too assured of herself, one of a minority of those who suffer from high self-esteem.

"It does have value," she says at last, in the measured tone she might use on a retarded adult, someone with the critical capacity of, say, a six-year-old. "Identity has value. Who your parents are is information with value. Obviously it has value to you, enough that you're attempting to convince me to perform an act of, of . . . we won't call it stealing if that offends you. We'll call it, what? How about voyeurism? Like taking a picture of someone who doesn't know you're there, hiding with your camera. You want to peer inside my child, find out what, exactly, she's made of, *who* she's made of, and you have the nerve to ask me—her mother—to be an accessory to this act of voyeurism." Elizabeth is still leaning forward over the table as she speaks, articulating each word with angry precision. "Besides," she says, "why should I believe you when you say you won't do anything with the information? You say you won't tell her, or me, but why should I believe you?"

"I'm trustworthy, Elizabeth. You remember that."

Elizabeth snorts. "Says who?"

"Well, I'm not deceitful. Not like you."

"What!"

"You left me knowing you were pregnant with my child."

"That's . . . that's your fantasy, William Moreland. Your presumption. Not my deceit."

"Prove it."

"Why? Why should I?"

"Because you owe it to me."

Elizabeth gives him a narrow-eyed smile, a look of unambiguous hostility. "I don't owe you anything," she says in a voice that matches the expression.

"Yes. Yes, you do. You do owe me something."

"What?"

"The truth."

"No, I don't." She shakes her head.

The last thing Will wants is to create a scene, and yet he can't stop himself from raising his voice. "You do!" He slaps his hand on the tabletop, not only summoning the attention of those seated nearby but startling himself. What's wrong with him? It's a clinical something, but what? This isn't the only instance, of late, that Will had caught himself struggling to come up with a self-diagnosis. "You do," he says again, less loudly but just as emphatic.

Elizabeth looks at her wristwatch. "I'm going to leave," she says, and she stands.

"Wait," he says. "Just finish this conversation."

"It is finished."

"The honorable thing is to help me find out what I need to know."

"Why? Why do you need to know? What difference will it make? No. Forget that. I know what difference it makes. It's what I said it was. You lost one, you want to find another. But it's too late to find Jennifer, even if she were yours. She's grown up. And"—she points at Will's chest—"can you tell me why is it that men always start talking about honor when they're losing a . . ." She doesn't finish.

"A what?"

"Whatever," she says.

"As a human being, not a friend or an ally but just another human being, don't you think it's fair—I won't say honorable—for me to know if she's my child?"

"She's not. She is not yours. She's hers. She is her own person."

"Fine. Agreed. But she may be a person who is closely, physically, related to me. And one day she may want to know that. For her own well-being she may want genetic information about her father."

Elizabeth shrugs.

"In any case, she doesn't have to know. I want to know, but she wouldn't have to."

"Fuck you," Elizabeth says in a low voice. "Fuck you."

"She wouldn't. Why would she?"

"Because," Elizabeth says. "Because."

"Because why?"

"Do you really not understand that you are being astonishingly stupid?"

"Why would she have to know?"

"Because she's a person, her own person. Not your person or even my person. She belongs to herself."

"Yes, but she, she didn't invent herself, she—"

Twice Elizabeth goes up on the balls of her feet and then slowly lowers her heels, the habit of a woman who's had to come up with strategies to offset the fatigue of standing for much of a workday. Hands on her hips, oblivious to the people, quite a number of them by now, staring and listening, Elizabeth glares at him for what feels like a long time. "I have one thing to say," she says.

"What?"

"You are an excellent example of why it is that people think shrinks are nuts." She snatches her purse, a little black one, from where she's hung it on the chair. She drops it over her head, the long strap crossing her chest like a bandolier, and walks swiftly away, slipping back into the crowd like a new penny dropping into a dark well. He sees a flash of her red hair and then nothing—she's gone.

Will stands, eager to quit the company of people before whom he's behaved so, so . . . how has he behaved?

Badly, that's how. He's behaved badly, stupidly, possibly hurtfully, certainly unadvisedly. He feels the arrival of one of those red-wine headaches, the kind that make it imperative to walk carefully lest he jar it up a notch on the pain scale. And there's no minibar in his room at the hotel, no ten-dollar first-aid kit with Band-Aids, antacids, and two headache pills in a single-serving envelope. If there is a God, the front desk will dispense Advil. If there isn't, he's going to have to walk to a convenience store.

It's just guilt—please make it be a simple case of guilt—but along with the headache, Will feels an increasing sense of dread, or something like it. Foreboding. Not that Elizabeth didn't make it clear that there wasn't a chance she'd respond to his insane (Nuts! Nuts! What the fuck was he thinking!) request. Still, he can't shake the idea that what he's done belongs to the potentially costly rather than simply embarrassing brand of foolishness.

He will write her. An e-mail. He'll say he's sorry, that he's dropped the whole thing.

t must be the conversation with Elizabeth, Will thinks when he wakes, the room dark, a silver seam of light dividing the curtains. It must be that, because he can't remember the last time he dreamt about Luke.

In the dream, his son had been taken up to heaven.

The boy was white and luminous. He looked as solid as if he were sculpted from marble. Yet light leaked from his body. Every breath streamed and flickered from his lips; every hair on his head was incandescent, a halo of sparks like those thrown off a welder's torch. He was sitting in profile at the top of a fantastically beautiful and treacherous staircase, a staircase chiseled into the face of a cliff formed of glass or of ice, each glistening tread steeper than the one below.

Even from a distance, Will knew that his son was alive, and he began to climb toward him. Having no tools that might on earth prove useful—no pick, crampons, or rope—he willed himself upward, ascending slowly and with an effort that made him gasp and choke. Perhaps he sobbed in his sleep?

The stairs were slippery; they got taller and taller; the uppermost flight almost defeated him. F/206 8481.

When he at last reached the top, the light was so intense, he couldn't lift his eyes. It was only by cupping his hands around his face that he could see at all. Even so, the light penetrated, filled his head,

COUNTY
LIBRARY

informed him that he had reached Luke not because he was strong enough or good enough but because it was inconceivable to him that he would not. Separation from his son was an outcome he was unable to imagine. He had to tell Luke he loved him and not to miss him too badly, not to grieve. He didn't want anything to worry him.

But when at the sound of his voice his son began to incline his face toward him, showing Will its familiar and cherished contours, a face polished and burnished and shining with love—not only his father's but his mother's and his sister's, his grandparents', his uncles', aunts', and cousins', his teachers' and his friends', the love and longing of so many people for this one child—when Luke began to look his way, another boy stopped him, a boy taller and older than his son, a boy Will didn't recognize. The boy put his hand out and touched Luke's cheek to prevent him from turning in the direction of Will's voice.

You must not look at him, the older boy said.

And Luke answered, *But it's my father.*

Luke struggled against the older boy, who Will understood had been assigned to show his son the ropes and prevent such mishaps as the one that had occurred. Because Luke did see Will, just for a moment. Still, it was long enough that his face registered horror.

The older boy said accusingly, *See!*

And Luke asked, *What's happened to him! What's happened to him!*

Nothing, the older boy said. *It's just that that's the way he looks to you now, because he is only mortal.*

Luke sobbed, his face in his hands, and the older boy bent to comfort him.

And Will fell from heaven back to his bed, not down the stairs he ascended, but falling as a man falls from a plane, without a parachute, dropping through space at fatal speed, yet with time to see, and the vision of a god.

At first the city appeared as it would through the window of a jet approaching La Guardia, a tidy arrangement of lives, block after block, with an occasional landmark by which it was possible to orient himself. But then he was closer; he could find his own neighborhood and then his roof among the others on his block, the particular house toward which he was plummeting. What a mess it was in! Cracked façade and derelict rain gutter, two missing storm windows and an inadequately patched leak, broken satellite dish, snarls of TV cable and a useless antenna, its arms askew, like the ribs of a broken, stripped umbrella. Could this really be his house? How was it that Will had allowed it to crumble into such a state of disrepair?

Fast though he fell, Will could see into the rooms of his home as if peering into lidless boxes. There was his wife, and with Carole was Samantha. His mother, his father, and his brother. Neighbors and patients, current acquaintances and people he hadn't seen for decades, even children with whom he'd gone to elementary school—faces he couldn't summon when awake. How small everyone appeared and, like slides from a holiday long past, how nearly transparent. Worse than their smallness was the tiny warmth and throb of them, the insectlike brevity of human life. Unbearable—unspeakable and obscene to be spirit trapped in matter, the bodies we worship and fear, exalt and punish, the flesh that grants every pleasure and ushers in our grief. How awful to be given these sublime and flimsy houses for our souls and then to witness their decay. How monstrous.

The idea of it—flesh—gathered into a fist, or a blow, something that struck him hard on the chest, hard enough that he woke facedown and mouth open, unable even to gasp. As if, in truth, he had fallen from a great height back to earth and hit with a wallop, the dream knocked the breath out of him.

All you, he would have said, were he speaking with a patient about that patient's dream: fragments of you, aspects of you, possible yous, impossible yous, incarnations of you, the you you were, the you you may become, your wishes, your fears, your . . .

But the people he saw as he fell didn't feel like him. And he didn't want the dream Luke to be taken away. He didn't want to have to make his son into, say, a part of himself that looked aghast at another part of him.

What had Luke seen? What did his son see in his face that so frightened and repelled him?

The blue numbers of the digital clock shift from 11:08 to 11:09. He's slept much later than usual, and his body feels stiff and achy, as if in the aftermath of a fever. Will considers the coffeemaker on the dresser, a little basket beside it filled with packets of sugar, artificial sweetener, and nondairy creamer. Eight O' Clock coffee in Christmasy-looking envelopes of tinselly red and green. He tears one open. The ground coffee is packed in a round, white filter, like a doll-sized cushion. He puts this, along with water, into the coffeemaker, and it begins brewing with a congested noise. The contents of the orientation package he picked up the previous day are spread over the table by the window—venue maps and drink vouchers and announcements of added or changed weekend seminars, a seven-page schedule of events that conjures visions of exhausted alumni, some with canes and walkers, lurching from breakfast meetings to round-tables to picnic lunches to step singing (*What is step singing? Could it be singing on steps? Which steps? Surely not those big stone library steps*); memorial services; guided tours of advances in veterinary science; panels; lectures; and God knows what else. The only important thing in the package is the *Class of 1979 25th Reunion Book*. Big black letters on a glossy red cover. Cumbersome and unwieldy as a phone book, it has torn its way out of its shrink-wrap, crumpled and mashed its self-congratulatory cover letter.

Here is the story of your class—your struggles and your triumphs, your journeys from promise into fulfillment . . . Who writes this drivel? Will balls up the letter and drops it in the trash can. Along with all the other members of Cornell's graduating class of 1979, Will had been invited to contribute his dispatch from midlife—*Dear William More-land, We want to hear from you!* And Will had drafted and redrafted and drafted once more his condensed (*No more than 500 words, please!*) autobiography, dividing himself into professional and personal; into husband and father; into brain, body, heart; into year twenty-three, year twenty-four, year twenty-five; into grad student, intern, resident, private practitioner; into citizen and consumer; into into into. There were any number of ways to dismantle himself, but how was he to reassemble his parts into a narrative, a string of words from here to there?

By default, Will became one of the 687 members of his class who didn't contribute to the reunion book, 89 of those having died, 161 "missing," and the rest like himself, he guesses, unable or even unwilling to account for themselves in the form of an essay or a timeline or a résumé illustrated with photographs of children, pets, vacation homes, and fancy cars. Unlike his brother's résumé, rendered in ten-point type to accommodate all his accomplishments, Will's is two lines long: his name followed by what few facts the university has acquired about him since graduation. Ph.D., Psych., Columbia University, 1986; Married to Carole Laski, June 28, 1989; Children, Luke Michael, March 30, 1990; Samantha Jane, October 10, 1996. Member NAAP, APA, NYPA.

So there he is: educated, employed, married, the father of two children. And, like most men within his experience, either as a friend or psychoanalyst, a man transformed by fatherhood as he could not have been by any school or career or woman. Take the arrival of his daughter: wet and naked, arms thrown wide with the shock of her first breath, still tethered to her mother by a glistening rope of blood.

Even now, this moment, how clearly he can see it, the blue and purple vessels bound together in an almost iridescent membrane, slippery and hot—the heat of it against his palm. He cut as directed and then found he didn't want to let it go. Wasn't it a thing too splendid, too holy, even, to burn in a hospital incinerator?

Eight years, almost, since that day, and yet even a familiar glimpse of his daughter can still catch him off guard, grab him with the force of a hand at his throat. The intensity of her concentration when she skips rope, for example, and the way her skinny arms cross at the elbows when she does some of her fancier moves. Through the turning circle she jumps, over and over, the scuff of shoes against pavement alternating with the light slap of the rope. The elastic comes off the end of her moving braid, and her hair, after a few turns of the rope, comes undone and flies up with every jump. She smiles and shows him the completely unexpected beauty of the gap between her teeth. Coming home from work, he finds a smudgy greeting underfoot, chalk hieroglyphs on the sidewalk in front of their house. How many times in a single day can he bear to be shown what is at once too valuable to surrender and guaranteed to be taken? She is flesh of his flesh, a small and perfect creature who is all promise, no regrets or disappointed hopes. He is her father. That her life will have its portion of unhappiness and ill fortune seems impossible, a species of crime, a wrong that must be righted.

Is Carole prey to thoughts like these when she watches their daughter in a school play, when she counts her years in cake candles? Will doesn't think so. The woman he married isn't inclined to melancholy; she neither speculates about what might go wrong nor dwells on what already has. She loves him, even as much as he loves her, Will believes, but she isn't romantic or even sentimental; her boundaries are definite; she has thoughts she will not share and assumes the same is true of him. A blessing, in that certain of his preoccupations are those that might alarm a wife. His sexual fixation, for example, which is beginning to feel too big to keep inside his head. Was there even one woman he encountered the previous evening, one upon whose body he allowed his gaze to linger, without seeing himself— seeing her—well, without seeing what he saw? Even were he to re- member one, the act of calling her back before his mind's eye would disqualify her: she wouldn't get away a second time.

He wants to believe that love can't make mistakes, but what he knows is that it's like water, assuming the shape of the vessel, always imperfect, that holds it. He's not a blameless father or a perfect hus- band, and though he's made a career of listening to other people's problems, he can't always respond with patience and insight. He does bear witness: this is a role as old as childhood, as old as his conscious- ness of his brother's suffering. He opens old wounds and binds up new ones, strips away defenses, shores up egos. To be paid for the work he craves seems marvelous to Will, a reason to give thanks—but to what, to whom? Because he's also a tortured agnostic, suffering spasms of private, even desolate, self-examination. Alert to coinci- dence and unanticipated symmetry, to aspects aligning in patterns, almost readable, he sifts, sorts, and turns the pieces, lays them down and picks them up in what amounts to an endless game of mental solitaire, occasionally drawing close to something that comes out neatly and looks like a grand and universal plan, a sequence of details in which, as the saying goes, God resides. Summoned to his door by a pair of canvassing Jehovah's Witnesses, Will not only accepts the literature they press into his hands, he reads it. Accosted on his own corner by a canvassing flock of young Lubavitchers who demand to know if he's a Jew, he stammers in confusion, receiving the question as a challenge to him, him in particular, rather than the proselytizer's customary preface. He's not so much godless as God-bereft.

Armed, of course, with distractions from existential anxiety.

Apart from sex, there's real estate: he's landed. He's even a landlord, if only incidentally and only as a means of managing the debt they carry on their home. A personal trainer who works at a local health club rents the top floor of the brownstone they were lucky enough to buy before the market recovered, a now mostly fixed fixer-upper, with bay windows, an ornate cornice, and a stained-glass skylight: 138 Lincoln Place, in the historic district of Park Slope, named for streets that descend gently from the long, lush meadow and ball fields of Brooklyn's Prospect Park. Both his own and Carole's school loans long behind them, Will is paying down the mortgage, each month chipping away at the principal, reduced now from the $475,000 they borrowed to $280,000. They've lived on Lincoln Place for thirteen years, long enough that the rent for the upstairs apartment at last covers the monthly mortgage, a fact that thrills him, allowing him to tear open statements purely for the pleasure of seeing that his last assault on the principal has been recorded, even if it's no more than a few hundred dollars. It's nothing he could have anticipated, but their mortgage bill has become the single piece of mail to which he always looks forward. Each time he checks the principal, he translates his most recent subtraction from what they owe into its material equivalent: a pocket door, one of the original chandeliers, the parlor's crown molding. Checks made out to him by his patients are welcome, but oddly, they don't inspire the same feeling of accomplishment. Brick by brick, he is making himself and his wife the owners of these four soaring and dignified stories faced with a milk-and-coffee-colored stone that no longer exists in nature, brownstone having been quarried into extinction many years before he was born.

But Will didn't—couldn't—articulate any of what he knows about himself, his essential self, in a five-hundred-word essay. Not any more than did the alumni who submitted their brief, sanitized promos, admitting none of the missteps or misfortunes or unfulfilled longings that might have added texture to their whitewashed autobiographies. No one wrote in to say he'd lusted after his neighbor's wife, and then married her. Or that he'd suffered all his life from gender dysmorphia and was now a woman, no longer Joe but Joanne. Or that, in the wake of her daughter's diagnosis of schizophrenia, she'd fallen into a profound depression that was cured only when she walked out, left her family, abandoned them because, after all, how much was a person expected to endure?

Will scans each page of the reunion book and flips to the next, skimming over advanced degrees and promotions; residencies and relocations; awards and more awards; marriages and births; travel to Turkey, to Tuscany, to Majorca, to Machu Picchu, the Galápagos; marathons, triathlons, thrills of victory, agonies of defeat; PTA committees and car-pool purgatories, these last not so much complaints as advertisements disguised as complaints: *Look at our children; are they not the ultimate wealth and accomplishment?*

Many of the photographs are reproduced from holiday greeting cards, families carefully arranged around sparkling trees, hair combed, eyes bright. Without conscious intent Will finds himself lingering on the faces of those few who admit a family misfortune, looking for evidence of losses on which they don't dwell but make curious asides, rather like sneezing: quick, helpless convulsions that interrupt a text or are bulleted absurdly within the résumé format. These references are abbreviated and in every case weirdly upbeat, their authors clearly having determined to present a hard-won silver lining rather than the lowering black clouds of fate: "Lost my brother to cancer in 1993, and learned a lot about how strong I am!" "Our daughter Kyla, 12, has cystic fibrosis and she is Awesome!!! She is doing Great!!!" "Two brain surgeries, 1999 and 2001—if anyone out there is suffering unexplained neurological symptoms or has been diagnosed with NMH, e-mail me! I love to share!" After each of these plucky announcements, followed by at least one exclamation point (a few decorated with little happy-face icons, as well), the afflicted's life story veers without transition back into the mundane.

This is what Will has come to understand as his problem: transition, an obstacle on the page as in reality, because he insists on it, and there are unbridgeable divides in a life. Things don't add up; they don't segue; they follow chronologically, one upon another, without obeying the more important logic of meaning and sense and, well, acceptability.

"Not this year," he said to Carole when she asked about their Christmas card the November after Luke had drowned. For the ten previous years they'd sent out a photo greeting, not without a guilty, sheepish irony (at least they'd hoped irony was the evident subtext) because both he and Carole understood and intended to acknowledge that such cards were inherently obnoxious, even if, to them, irresistible. So they hadn't dressed their best or used a perfect vacation shot but instead posed in their everyday clothes, each wearing a goofy Santa hat, Carole with little if any makeup, the kids' hair unbrushed, Will looking effortfully (and thus less than completely successfully) candid. And they trusted that this casual, studiedly haphazard quality would be taken as an apology for the cards' inherent bragging—*Please forgive us our pride, the pleasure we take in our two perfect offspring. Overlook, won't you, the vulgarity of our publishing their inestimable worth. Our living golden calves—how beautiful they are! Our sacred objects! You must understand that we cannot help ourselves. We can't not exult.* Will shudders with the recognition, feels the flesh crawl on his neck. How foolish to flash a target at the jealous gods—to not merely disregard but show off the chink in their armor. *Aim here! Here where we presume our divinity and yet are most mortal!*

"No," Will said to Carole. "Not this year."

"Why?" she asked.

"Why!"

"Yes, why?" Carole set her coffee cup on the table and looked at him in that unnerving way she has, her eyes wide with what appeared to be genuine curiosity.

"Because . . . because . . ." He remembers spluttering in outrage, in the face of her calm. "Because one of us is missing! One of us who was in last year's card is gone!"

"Dead," she clarified.

"Dead. Yes. Yes. Dead."

Carole nodded. "Well, everyone knows that. All our friends, they know about Luke. And we could maybe acknowledge him with a, I don't know, something on the—"

"Like what! R.I.P? His initials? His dates? Like a gravestone? A little gravestone in the mail! Happy holidays, and in case you forgot, our son drowned last summer! But don't let that bother you—go ahead and have a wonderful new year!"

"No, that's not—"

"I'm not going to do it."

"You aren't letting me talk. I think we should. For Samantha."

"Why for Sam? It's not as if it's good for her. It's sad for Sam."

"It's sadder if we don't."

So he caved. He tried to arrange his features into an acceptable expression, an expression of what he couldn't say. He's never looked at the photograph Carole picked and had reproduced above their greeting. Two hundred copies. *Peace on Earth*, they probably said, as in years past. Even now he can't figure out what kind of artifact that particular photo greeting might be, or the level—

depth?—of its bad taste. Or maybe it wasn't in bad taste. Maybe it was just what Carole claimed it was: an impossible response to an impossible situation. Apparently she doesn't get stuck there, at Impossibility, the way he does. There is no conceivable transition, so she doesn't insist on it. She's pragmatic in that impressive, fearsome, and always surprising way that women are, the way they preside with equal industry and competence over tea parties and deathbeds.

At home, in the magazine basket by the couch, is *Yoga Journal*, a publication that continues to resurface from under the others because both of them thumb through it, Carole as a disciple, Will as a bystander at once fascinated and incredulous. "A Vedanta Paradigm for Transforming Negative Emotions," the most recent cover promises. Will has reread this article several times, attempting to translate phrases like "the classical citta-vitri-eroding yogic approach" into psychoanalytic terms. But he gets tripped up by discussion of topics like "heart energy" or "the consciousness that has no content" and ends up casting it away in irritation.

He did attempt to recap the last twenty-five years for the reunion book, but he couldn't leave out the drowning, nor could he tell it. What was the previous sentence? What was the one that followed? Will began a letter over and over again, getting no farther than a paragraph before he deleted it from his computer file. According to an online survey, to which 37 percent of the class of 1979 responded, 41 percent of the 37 percent are more spiritual compared with when they graduated, 9 percent less spiritual, 50 percent about the same. Forty-seven percent of them have achieved about what they expected to achieve, 28 percent have exceeded their life expectations, 20 percent are a little disappointed in themselves, and the remaining (unaccounted-for) 5 percent are, he guesses, either apathetic or in despair. Sixty-four percent of them are on their first marriages, 19 percent have remarried, and while the autobiographical dispatches indicate that a few alumni have lost a spouse or a child, no statistical breakdown of tragedies is included in the survey. Nine percent have earned a Ph.D. Forty-one percent choose relaxing vacations, 18 percent cultural, and 25 percent adventurous; 3 percent don't vacation at all. Eighty-two percent claim reading as a favorite pastime, 31 percent "creating," whatever that means.

Perhaps it means gardening or knitting or drawing or, like Sally Henderson, building the world's largest freestanding structure made from discarded plastic bleach containers. Will looks carefully at the picture of Sally standing next to the door of her bleach-bottle tower. Her smile is more rictus than evidence of pride, baring her teeth against a looming threat. Haven't studies of evolution demonstrated that a smile is the pallid descendant of primate rage? A warning of aggression? Will flips quickly through the book, trying to see smiles separate from faces. Are any of these people happy, really? And if they are, how can one tell?

11:57 by the digital clock on the television set. He's missed the ecumenical Sunday service, and if he doesn't hurry, he'll miss brunch in the big tent, as well.

What was it that Luke had seen? he wonders, head bent under the shower's needling spray—the white and shining and exalted Luke of Will's dream. Was it a thing worse than grief, something degenerate and disgraceful, that a child can't allow his father?

The boy in the dream: Will knows he's no more real than a wish, or a fear. And yet, he might ask himself, of what else are we composed?

S o why didn't you stay the whole weekend?" Carole asks him when he comes to bed. "I thought you were looking forward to this thing." The way she says the word *thing* betrays her feelings about reunions, that they are all, without exception, events to be avoided whenever possible.

"I was going to stay. I'd made plans to meet up with a couple of guys, maybe even play some racquetball after the picnic. But, I don't know, after the main attraction, the cocktails and dinner thing on Saturday . . ." Will trails off. He should tell her about running into Elizabeth. Instead, he finds himself talking about Mitch. "After the hundredth person approached to ask me about my famous brother, I got a little tired of the whole thing," he says. Carole makes the face she always does when he mentions his brother, something between a wince and a frown.

"That must have been crummy."

"Well, I should have known. Prepared myself. I guess I was so wrapped up in my own fantasy of his appearing that I didn't consider the more likely scenario."

"Where'd they hold it?" she asks, having apparently decided to move them along to a less loaded bedtime topic. "They'd have to use a basketball court or something for a reception that big."

"There were tents. A separate tent for each class."

"Tents? Ick."

"You don't notice when it's crammed with people. And at least there's fresh air."

"Yes, you do. You do notice." Carole wrinkles her nose. "Even if it doesn't rain, they still have that dank, tenty sort of smell, like old sneakers. Aside from the temporary, makeshift feeling of a Red Cross relief effort."

Will shrugs. "The other thing was, after I'd mingled and reconnected and seen how much hair the men had and if the pretty girls had grown up to be pretty women, and who'd gotten married more than once, or twice, and who'd turned out to be gay, and all the rest of it—after that, it seemed like the next day's activities would be sort of redux. Like those picnics the day after a wedding, when everyone just wants to go home."

"Uh-huh," Carole says, picking up her book. She turns the page.

"So, instead, I hung out at the hotel and watched triple-X movies on pay-per-view."

"Yeah?" she says. Will pulls the book from her hands. "Hey! What are you doing!"

"You're not listening to me."

"Yes, I am."

"What did I say, then?"

"That you mingled and it was . . . it was like a picnic."

"No. I said I left and watched triple-X movies at the hotel."

She looks at him. "You did?"

"No! I just said that to see if you were paying attention."

"I'm sorry, Will," she says, and she moves closer to him. "I know a way back into your good graces."

"Do you? How?"

Carole slides one hand under the waistband of his pajama bottoms.

"Yeah?"

"Yeah. But first give me back my book."

"You don't need it. Not now."

"I want to mark my place." She pulls her hand out of his pants, lets the elastic go with a little snap, but instead of returning the book, Will lifts it high out of her reach. "Give it," she says, "or I'm downgrading you to a hand job."

"What? No way!"

Carole makes a grab for the paperback, and Will rolls out from under her, keeping it out of reach. He opens to a random page, reads aloud in a voice of breathless suspense.

"'Glatman jerked the ligature around Christine Rohas's slender neck. His knee in the small of her back, he pinned her to the ground, facedown in a field where, only hours before, the local peewee championship was played. Swiftly, he bound her ankles and through the loops threaded the end of the rope trailing from her neck. One brutal tug, and . . .'" Will closes the paperback to consider its lurid cover, which promises *sixteen pages of shocking photos!* "I really don't see how this can compare to my report of who from the class of 'seventy-nine went bald and who didn't." Carole lunges, and the fitted bottom sheet springs off one and then another mattress corner as she tries to wrestle his arm down.

"Now, how is it that you can square something like this with higher consciousness and feminism and yoga and all that?" he asks, holding the book far above her head. Carole gets up on her knees, but as soon as she pries one hand off the cover, the other has it fast.

"I don't," she says.

"Stop it. You can't pull hairs out of my arm."

"Why not?" Accidentally, Carole kicks the bedside table, toppling a stack of exemplary reading material: professional journals,

novels chosen by her Thursday book group, *New Yorker*s of varying
vintage, arts and education sections pulled and saved from the *Times*,
all lying untouched. The books she actually reads, with titles like
Hillside Stranglers, The Greenriver Killer, Beauty Queen Slasher, she
keeps hidden from view, on the top shelf of her closet—enough true
crime to fill two banker's boxes with the rape and murder, or murder
and then rape, of young women—cheap paperbacks whose covers
bear snapshots of the victims taken in happier times, on holidays and
at high school graduations, mementoes from a family album. "Basically, this is porn," Will says, paging through the photo insert.

"Okay, it's porn."

"Otherwise, why hide it?"

"Because it's not for children, obviously. It's not for Sam to see."

"Meaning unsavory. Subject to parental censorship."

"Yes. I admit everything. Now give it."

"Lowbrow. Do you admit to lowbrow?"

"Yes."

"You'd die of embarrassment if your book group caught you?"

"I don't know that I'd die."

"You wouldn't like it."

"I wouldn't like it. Let go, Will, you're tearing the cover."

He lets her have it. Lying on his side, he props his head on one
elbow. "They don't turn you on, do they?" he says.

"Sexually, you mean?" Carole looks at him, raises an eyebrow.

"Sure. You know, sex so radically sexy it's fatal."

She shakes her head. "Disappointed?"

"A little. What about recipes? I thought women liked to read
recipes."

"Boring."

"Romances?"

Carole turns out the light. "Don't you think I deserve a secret vice?" she says, sliding her hand under his T-shirt and stroking his chest. "A teeny-weeny vice that doesn't hurt anyone?"

"No."

She tugs on the waistband of his pajama bottoms, and Will lifts up, off the bed, slides them down. "I want you to have big fat vices. Give in to your basest impulses."

"Do you?" She pulls her nightgown over her head. "What do you imagine those impulses might be?"

"Hard to say." Will shudders as her mouth touches him. The hairs on his arms and thighs lift his skin into gooseflesh at the wet heat of it, that shock of pleasure that never wears off. "Probably nymphomaniacal."

"Huh," she says, substituting hand for mouth. "You don't think that secretly I might be a compulsive shopper? Or, um . . . let's see, a gambler? A glutton maybe?"

"No. Not for food, anyway."

"Why not?"

"I can tell that you're a sex addict," he says, "by the way you can't let more than a few seconds go by without taking me in your mouth again." With his hand on the back of her neck, Will guides his wife's head back to where he wants it.

Will waits for his father at Molyvos, a Greek restaurant in midtown with a tiled floor and walls the color of terra-cotta. It's not the quietest place, but the lunchtime crowd has started to thin, and the layout makes for a lot of small corner tables, a sense of privacy if not calm. Will prefers to have his back to the wall, but he takes the chair and saves the banquette for his father, who gives his shoulder a hello squeeze before he slides in.

"So," he says. "How's Carole? Sam?"

"They're good. Sam's loving this crazy tai kwon do class we put her in. Spends hours bowing to herself in the mirror. Carole's working too many hours—big surprise. There's some sort of grievance developing between the union and the district, but her position probably won't be affected by whatever changes are made. If any changes are made."

"So she did sign the contract?"

Will nods. In addition to her private practice, Carole has recently taken a job with District 15, screening children for speech disorders. Four mornings a week, she administers diagnostic tests at either P.S. 321 or P.S. 282 in Park Slope, or at P.S. 8, a progressive elementary school in Brooklyn Heights. No retirement package, but benefits that include health insurance at a rate much more affordable than what he can get through NAAP.

Will waves the waiter away. "We need a few minutes," he says. He points at a book in his father's upper-left-hand pocket. "What's that?"

His father pulls out a paperback copy of *Frankenstein* and asks Will if he's read it.

"A long time ago."

His father frowns. "I wasn't expecting it to be so sad," he says, thumbing through the pages. "I'd stop, but you know how I am. Can't walk out of a bad movie. Can't cancel a trip to the beach because rain's forecast."

"Where are you?" Will asks him when he doesn't look up from the book. "What part?"

The two of them meet once a month, just to see each other, keep up. Sometimes they talk about books they've discovered, movies they've seen, and Will is often surprised by his father's choice of reading material. Last month it was *Zen and the Art of Motorcycle Maintenance*.

"Just finished volume two," his father says, and closes the book. "The monster has killed Frankenstein's son. And he's requested a female companion as hideous and deformed as himself, so that he can make love to a creature that won't turn away from him in revulsion." Will's father closes his eyes for a moment. "Isn't it curious that such a tragic figure would have become, a hundred years later, a kind of joke? A hulking, green bungler with big boots and bolts in his neck. A figure of derision. Not capable of an act as focused as a hateful, vengeful murder."

"Why are you reading it?"

He shrugs. "I don't know. I was in the bookstore, looking through the classics because, you know, I skipped so many. I picked it up, put it back on the shelf, ended up coming back to it when nothing else caught my eye. Something about the cover, must have been."

He holds it up, but the picture's too small for Will to see clearly from across the table, and his father hands it to him. It's a reproduction of a painting—six people gathered around a table and above them, on a pedestal, a white bird trapped inside a glass globe. Will turns the book over to read the fine print on the back cover. "A detail from 'An Experiment on a Bird in the Air Pump,' a painting in the National Gallery," he tells his father. No date is given for the work, and Will has never heard of the artist, Joseph Wright. The bird is caught in an unnatural position, one wing extended, perhaps broken, and a tube attaches the sealed glass globe to a sinister-looking apparatus. The whole scene is lit dramatically so that a flood of yellow light picks out certain details and leaves others in darkness, as in a crucifixion by Caravaggio, for example.

"Doves usually represent the holy spirit, don't they?" Will asks his father.

"Guess so," he says. "Distressing, seeing an animal trapped like that." The waiter returns and Will's father points to a line on the menu. Will leans forward, trying to see what he's chosen.

"What are you getting?" he asks him.

"Dolmades?"—*dole maids*—"Is that how you say it?"

Will shrugs. "Grape leaves," he says. "With rice inside and something else, I'm not sure what."

Across the table, his father is patting the many pockets of his sportsman's vest as if to remind himself of their contents, a gesture that has become habitual, even compulsive. Once he'd sold his veterinary practice and discarded his lab coats, he created what is in effect a new uniform: the khaki vest with numerous pockets, all of which he fills; wide-wale, navy blue corduroy trousers; and a fishing hat that looks like an upside-down flowerpot. The hat might be funny on another man—on anyone but his father—and Will has himself to blame for the vest. After he complained to his mother that he and Carole were receiving too many of what they'd begun to refer to as his father's "booty calls," his mother bought the vest so his father wouldn't have to carry his cell phone in the back pocket of his trousers, into which he'd jam the thing and then sit on it while driving, inadvertently putting pressure on whatever button he'd programmed to speed-dial Will's home number. Whoever picked up would hear the thrum and whoosh of highway travel punctuated by random throat clearings and sometimes the strains of whatever song was playing on the local oldies station. "Dad!" Will would yell. "DAD!" But his father never heard the tiny voice coming out from underneath him, and once Will had answered the phone, he found it difficult to hang up and sever the connection. Though his father was oblivious to his phantom presence in the car—or perhaps because he was oblivious—there was an unexpected intimacy in having been summoned to ride along with him, invisible and undetected, returned to his ten-year-old self, happy to be with his father, no matter how workaday the errand.

"So," Will says to him after the waiter has left, "I talked with Mom."

"Oh," his father says. "And?"

"She told me it's that woman you met at the gallery. The one who bought all those prints."

"Yup."

"You're living with her?" Will asks.

"I like the city."

"I didn't ask you how you felt about New York. That's not—"

His father smiles. "I know." Silver hair and laugh lines have made Will's father improbably handsome, more so than either of his much younger sons, more than when he himself was younger and women already found him irresistible, so that they'd linger in the exam room, schedule appointments for healthy animals, drop by the clinic with questions about dewclaws or ear mites or housebreaking, whatever they could think of. Will remembers his mother being good-humored about this, but then, his father hadn't given her reason to be jealous, not back then. Or at least he hadn't as far as Will knew.

His father plays with a rubber band on his wrist. "I spend a few nights in town, then go back home."

"What about Mom?"

"She's busy enough that she doesn't seem to take much note of where I am."

"Is that what this is about? You feel like she's not paying attention to you?"

"She's not. But that's not what this is about." The waiter sets their plates before them, and his father picks up his fork. "Your mother and I have been married for nearly fifty years," he says. "You don't think we've paid attention to each other the whole time, do you?"

"I guess I'm just trying to figure this out—what it means."

"Does it have to mean something? I like spending a few nights a week in the city. I like spending time with Lottie."

"Lottie?"

"Charlotte."

"She's good company?" Will says. "What do you talk about?"

"Nothing much. We rent movies. DVDs. She has a good setup. Big screen. Like a little theater, almost."

"She's rich, Dad," Will says. His father nods, chews. "But that can't be—" Will is suddenly aware that he's pinching the skin over his Adam's apple, pulling at it absentmindedly as he does sometimes while concentrating, especially on something that bothers him. "There must be something else," he says.

His father looks at him, raises his eyebrows. "There is."

"Oh, God," Will says. "Don't tell me this is about sex."

"I didn't introduce the topic."

"It is about sex?"

"Will," his father says. He puts his knife and fork down and leans forward over his plate. "I take it your mother told you I was having an affair. Doesn't that imply that it's about sex?"

"But . . ." *You're seventy-four*, he was going to say, his mind already jumping to Viagra, and then to one of his patients, only two years older than Will, who uses a cocktail of Viagra and Cialis, each prescribed by a different physician, neither of whom knows about the other or that the man doesn't even have a problem with sexual performance. "My happiness," the patient had said when Will challenged him, "is predicated on my getting this reward. The only time I feel really good, really alive, is when I'm getting laid. And everything I do, all the effort I put into my career, my wife, my kids—it's all about earning my right to have relations with as many ladies as possible."

"As many as possible," Will repeated. The man nodded.

"I feel okay about that," the man said. "I work hard. I couldn't work any harder. I feel I'm entitled." He looked at Will. "Who's getting hurt?" he demanded, and then he answered himself. "No one, that's who."

Across the table, Will's father is smiling. "Will," he says, "I'm not asking for your permission, or your advice, or congratulations. Let's talk about something else. Let's talk about you. How's work?"

Will shakes his head. "I have a problem," he says.

"Yeah? What sort?"

"I'm not sure. I'm trying to figure it out." His father tilts his head to one side, frowns. *Come on*, the expression says, *get to the point*. Will draws a deep breath. "For the past month or so, every time I'm in session with a female patient, I end up, I don't know, having this, uh, physical response to her. It's weird. Nothing like this has ever happened to me before."

"Physical meaning sexual?" his father asks, and Will nods.

"As if she were the most desirable woman on earth, and I the most sexually starved man. Makes no difference what she looks like."

"Huh," his father says. "So what do you do?"

"What do I do? Nothing, of course."

"Not with your patient. I mean, what do you do about dealing with the problem?"

"Check in with Daniel, I guess. I've made the appointment."

"Daniel, your what's it called, trainer?"

"Training analyst," Will says. "Basically, the mandate is that any time an analyst experiences feelings that are inappropriate or that might compromise the relationship between him and a patient, he goes back to his own analyst. Whoever it is he sees when a situation like that comes up."

"Countertransference," his father says, nodding.

"Right. But countertransference is a neutral term. It isn't necessarily wrong or even untherapeutic. Just sometimes."

"You see Mitch?" Will asks to change the topic. His father wrinkles his forehead in an expression of something that looks like apprehension. "On TV," Will clarifies, and his father shakes his head.

"When was this?"

"Sunday last. CNN, I think. Some filler show called *People in the News*."

"Oh?" his father says.

Will nods, watching his expression. "Same old, same old." His father doesn't answer, and Will frowns at him. "It still bugs me, you know it does, his turning his back on all of us. I can't square it. Coming after . . . after he was . . . well, after that toast at the rehearsal dinner."

His father waves a hand through the air. "Let it go," he says, as he does whenever Will drags Mitch into their conversations. *Let it go. Let him go. Give it a rest. Do yourself a favor: let it go.* But how?

Will doesn't say anything, remembering his brother the summer they were at camp together in the Adirondacks, both of them thirteen, an age he associates primarily with the onslaught of wet dreams. He sees Mitch's long body moving underwater, white, ghostly, aimed toward the dock where Will was standing, his face breaking through the surface. He came up out of the water and onto the dock in one motion, already more graceful and at ease in water than on land. It was an all-boys camp they attended that summer, and some of the campers teased Mitch about his birthmark, a port-wine stain that colored more than half of his face purple, but it had been Will whom this angered. Mitch was stung, he must have been, but whatever pain he felt in the moment seemed to fade. Or rather, Mitch faded, he became increasingly vague and distant—in Will's memory it's as if he is out of focus, an outline blurring into the background—while Will seethed with rage he couldn't control. Like two people long married, he and Mitch had developed a tacit, if not unconscious, symbiosis, one in which Will bore their humiliation, both the shame of his twin's disfigurement as well as the imperative to respond to insult. For his part, Mitch represented their capacity for patience and long-sufferingness. Superficially, he did.

That summer, Will got into fights on his brother's behalf and, after bloodying a boy's nose, was given formal warning by the camp director. A report of his misconduct was sent home to their parents, and in reparation for the nose, he'd been denied an afternoon of tubing on the river, instructed to spend those hours composing a letter of apology to the owner of the nose and another letter to the nose's mother and father. As he remembers it, he had to write about a dozen drafts of each before he was able to purge the letters of recriminations against the boy he'd punched, and it required an extraordinary act of will to actually form the word *sorry*. Then, not an hour after he'd presented the letters to the director, he overheard a kid call Mitch an ugly douche bag and, before he knew what he was doing, had attacked him. The camp director called their parents to ask that they pick Will up; he was expelled.

Mitch was encouraged to stay, but the twins left together, and though there was little discussion of what had happened, it was that summer, before eighth grade, that Will and Mitch and their parents became aware of what should have been apparent for some time: his and Mitch's mutual, even symbiotic, maladjustment. Because Mitch had to bear the birthmark physically, Will had assigned himself its psychic burden.

"Hey," his father says, "where'd you go?"

"Nowhere. Actually, I was thinking about that summer I got kicked out of camp."

"What about it?"

"I don't know. I guess it was the beginning of my being aware that things between Mitch and me were pretty seriously screwed up. That I didn't respond to people on my own terms, or for my own sake, because I'd fallen into the habit of empathizing with Mitch. As if nothing were happening to me, not really, or not independently. I know, I know," he says, seeing his father's expression. "You've heard this before. And what's the use in going back over it? I just wish the two of us had talked more. Or at all."

His father is still shaking his head, as if the very fact of his other son is baffling, unknowable. "I guess nothing else gives him what he gets from swimming," he says. It's not unusual for Will's father to make non sequiturs, voicing only the last in a series of thoughts.

"What's that?" Will asks.

"I don't know. Beauty, maybe. Excitement. Simultaneous fulfillment of his life and his death wishes." Will says nothing. His father pulls a credit card from his wallet. "This one's mine," he says, and he lays the card on the check, motioning to the waiter. "What's the word for the death wish? *Thanatos*? *Eros* and *thanatos*? Life and death?"

Will nods. "What else are you reading, Dad? *Frankenstein* with a little Freud on the side? A dash of Ferenczi?"

His father smiles as he signs the receipt and slides out from the banquette; he stands and his napkin falls from his lap onto the floor. Will picks it up and lays it on the table. He looks at his watch. "You want to walk a little ways? I'm running early."

"Sure. Samantha still seeing that woman?" his father asks, alluding to Laura, the child psychologist.

"No, no. She hasn't gone since last spring."

"Yeah? That's good, no?"

"I think so. It's hard to say with kids. It's, not as if Luke's death won't stay with her for all her life. Inform who she becomes. But for all that, she doesn't appear unhappy. I'm always looking for symptoms, of course, signs of depression, anxiety, but she seems okay. Genuinely okay. I see her in the school yard. She skips, giggles, plays with the other little girls. She's the president of their jump-rope club. In two years she's going to set a world record, she says, but she doesn't have to start practicing until she turns nine."

"Sounds normal to me," his father says.

Will points to *Frankenstein*. His father is patting the book through his pocket. "Is this classics thing an attempt to suck up some culture so you have something to talk about with, with—what's-her-name, Carla?"

His father grins at him. "Charlotte," he says, "and we don't need things to talk about."

"Nothing?"

"Not much."

They stand just inside the restaurant door, looking out at the people on the sidewalk, the taxis, the buildings that look like walls of glass. A thick fog swirls down the avenue. "It's very strange," Will's father says, "having sex with someone other than your mother. I hadn't done that in, well, decades."

"Forty-nine years," Will says. "Almost fifty. A half-century. Golden anniversary coming up."

His father smiles his disarming smile. "I'm not sure if the sex is better," he says. "Maybe it's just different. One thing—it's reacquainted me with my body, sort of yanked me back into it, like I haven't been for as long as I can remember. Started trimming my toenails with attention. Flossing my teeth. Upgraded my underwear."

"How's Mom feel about it?"

"You know, Will, she's very happy being a businesswoman. She likes it a great deal."

"So much so that she doesn't care if you're cheating on her?"

After Will's father sold his veterinary practice, and perhaps in response to his having embarked on a new, solitary career as a photographer rather than settling into leisure with her, Will's mother transformed herself into a dervish of housework, not so much a woman as one of those tornadoes that blew out of a bottle of, what cleanser was it? Mr. Clean?—something advertised in the late sixties, when he and Mitch came home from school on winter afternoons and watched too much television. Not that she'd been uninterested in hygiene before, but her commitment had ebbed as much as it flowed, never reaching an obsessive standard. But, having scrubbed their house in Ravena until there was no carpet left to pull up, no floor to strip or tub to scour or window to wash, she turned her attention to other people's homes, creating a business, overnight it seemed.

Heaven Help You is the name of Will's mother's cleaning service; her business card includes a graphic of an antic mop wearing a halo. She'd started out with two young women and now employs twelve, sending them forth in teams of three, charging one hundred dollars an hour and clearing 20 percent of the gross. Will went back to his hometown some months after she'd established herself, and the whole place looked cleaner to him. As if his mother's frenzy for order and cleanliness had penetrated as far as the town council, there were new litter barrels on the corners, and a shining yellow street cleaner came by, spraying water on his bumper as it turned its massive brushes against the curb.

As they exit the restaurant, Will's father reaches out and touches him gently on the chest. "Cheating implies that I'm being dishonest. I'm not. I asked her permission."

"You're kidding." They walk out into air heavy with moisture.

"No, I'm not. I'm not kidding."

"I guess I missed that part."

"Oh? What part did she tell you?"

"I don't know. How many are there?"

Will's father doesn't answer this.

"I called to talk to you," Will says. "She gave me a number in Manhattan, and when I asked whose it was, she said, 'Your father's girlfriend's.'"

"Huh."

"I tried to get her to talk to me, but no dice."

"She thinks you blow things out of proportion."

"So she told you it was fine with her if you went ahead and had an affair?"

"What she said was she trusted me to determine how important it was for me to do this. And that if I decided I really did need to, then she accepted that."

"*Need* to?" Will asks.

"Okay—want to."

"And is there parity? If Mom decides she needs or wants to explore sex with another man, is that all right with you?"

"Of course. I'm not a hypocrite." Will's father stops walking and looks up at the slice of sky over the avenue, a luminous gray band. Already his vest is covered with a layer of fine droplets. "I don't think she's all that interested, though."

"That's lucky." Will manages to say this without sounding peevish. It must be that he's feeling guilty for having facilitated his father's entry into the art world, and thus his arrival at infidelity to his mother.

After a period of trial and error that he now calls his apprenticeship, Will's father had come to Brooklyn with a shirt box filled with what he judged were the best among his photographs, and asked Will if they could go together to a gallery in Manhattan.

"I don't think it works that way, Dad," Will told him, not wanting any part in what he was sure would prove a disappointment.

"Well, how does it?"

"You can't just walk in off the street. I'm sure you need an introduction or something, a—"

"Maybe," his father said, and he smiled. What did he know? the smile said. He was a retired veterinarian. But Will lived in the city. He must know someone, didn't he?

Yes, actually, the mother of a friend of Luke's, yet another someone eager to inoculate herself against whatever it was that had fallen upon Will and his family. She'd gladly do a favor—*Anything! Just ask!*—to address the difference between them, the fact that her child was living and his was not. An editor at *Art News*, she knew a number of gallery representatives, and in a gesture akin to throwing salt over her shoulder, she took the box of prints into her clean hands. Will could assure his father, she told him, that she would be responsible for their handling.

To Will's astonishment, within a few months, his father's work was picked up by a small gallery on Greene Street, his photographs mounted, framed, and hung on a freshly painted wall, celebrated with an opening announced on creamy, deckle-edged invitations and catered by attractive, hip young men and women who carried trays crowded with glasses of champagne, caviar rolled into tiny blini, and slices of honeydew wrapped in prosciutto sliced so thin it was almost invisible.

Henry Moreland was an instant and happy success, his work favorably mentioned in *Art News* and *Photography*, his show recommended by *Time Out*, embraced not just because he was old but because he was a retired animal doctor. Having been a humble sort of savior, a man who'd never cultivated connections in the sniping New York art world, never sucked up to anyone or done anything to invite spite, Will's father was forgiven his talent. Gracious at the opening, he introduced Will's mother—wearing a new dress and salon-styled hair—to people she would never see again, among them the woman with whom he'd embark on an affair. Will and Carole had watched all this from where they stood, on the party's periphery, grateful to have Samantha between them, the necessity of answering her questions, of collecting her half-eaten hors d'oeuvres and finding her a cup of water that didn't sparkle, of wiping up her spills and asking her again to please not point, not even at people whose clothes were designed to awe and confound.

The crowd of flushed celebrants; the trays of filled champagne flutes; the indecipherable praise; the little cards that read "Price available upon request": none of this was what Will's father had imagined for his old age. But, on the other hand, as his modest smile implied, it wasn't unwelcome.

"Dad?" Will says now, as they stop for a red light, "when you're working, taking a picture or printing it, do you ever feel something's being revealed to you? That your consciousness is heightened—augmented, maybe—by a force outside of your own intellect? That you understand something you hadn't before?"

His father looks at him. "I don't know. I can't tell what you're talking about. Do you mean something to do with God?"

"It wouldn't have to be. It could, but it wouldn't have to."

They walk in silence for a block, then cross Forty-seventh Street. Ahead are the bright lights of Times Square, mesmerizing, each neon shape bleeding into the fog and creating its own aura of color. So many more giant screens than there were even a few years ago, it seems to Will. On the side of one building a series of portraits appear, each for a second or two. He watches to see what the monumental faces are selling. Insurance of some kind, life insurance, or health. Or maybe it's financial planning, mutual funds. Beyond them, he can just make out the shadowy outline of 1 Times Square, the building on top of which the glittering New Year's Eve ball slides down a flagpole, its audience, five hundred thousand strong, counting down the seconds to their lists of resolutions, or at least to clean slates. Will has never understood why a giant disco ball is the country's chosen symbol of time moving forward, and shouldn't the big orb go up rather than down? So un-American to descend. America was all about upswings and bootstraps and mind-over-matter, a confidence so profound—or was it blind?—it ensured the country would always be out of step with the rest of the world.

"Are you talking about inspiration?" his father asks. "Whether it comes from within a person or from without?"

"I don't know. What's inspiration?"

His father frowns thoughtfully, says nothing.

The photographs his father takes mystify Will. Whenever he visits, he looks at his father's most recent work, going slowly through the images, many of which he can place in the town where he grew up: benches he's sat on, signposts he's swung from, mailboxes and sewer covers and barber poles. But no sculptures or fountains or fancy weather vanes; his father prefers the artless and unassuming among possible subjects, and points his camera at things that stay put. There are no people and no animals, not even trees that aren't incidental, blurred background. Only objects, humble objects strangely transformed by his father's vision. It must be the light, Will has decided, the angle of the sun, the time of day, perhaps a filter that removes light waves of a particular length. What else could elevate a seemingly inventory art into a catalog of yearning? Even a lamppost looks as if, unfulfilled by life as a lamppost, it's on the brink of evolving into something else, something truer and brighter and realer. By virtue of a silent, invisible intent, it seems to shimmer, caught just at that moment before it disappears, changes, becomes another thing, or a nonthing—animate, potent, and unexpected.

Or maybe it isn't a function of light; maybe it's just projection. Maybe what Will sees is his own need to believe in a father who has the ability to alter the world around himself, or, at the least, to show Will what a new, illuminated world might look like.

"Well," his father says, "aside from painting and music and what have you, aren't you asking the old God question? Whether or not God exists outside of faith? Independent of our faith?"

Will looks at him. "Weird how as you get older you find yourself less and less certain of anything."

"Just wait," his father says. "You have no idea."

"Mom believes in God, doesn't she?"

His father shakes his head. "That's a very private question," he says. "I don't think I've ever asked her directly."

"Carole does. Or maybe she doesn't. She seems at peace with life, with herself. Not like me. I think she might be what they used to call a secular humanist. Brimming over with unaccountable optimism.

Even after Luke. Even now, when every day brings more evidence of how many messes we've made that we can't undo. Environmental damage. Terrorism."

His father nods slowly. "Sometimes," he says, as he steps onto the curb, "when I print a picture, I see that I've photographed what I didn't know was there. Whatever it is, it's something I looked at without seeing. So I'm surprised, I feel something's been given to me. But by whom? What?" He looks at Will. "There's a quote I came across. I can't get it out of my head. 'The unconscious is God's country.'" He folds his arms over his chest, frowning. "That's the reason I've been reading up on it—Freud, Jung. What do you make of it?"

"What's the context?" Will asks. "Who said it?"

His father makes a swatting gesture. "I can't remember. What I want to know is, is it true? Do you, as a psychoanalyst, someone who's always mucking about in there, think it's true?"

Will frowns. "Well, the unconscious would be the place from which irrational fears and hopes, dreams—"

His father interrupts. "Whoever it was, that's not what they were talking about."

"You didn't let me finish."

"I know where you're going, and it's a little more mysterious than that."

"No, you didn't let me finish."

"All right. I'm listening."

"Okay. This is the only way I can answer. I've thought about Luke's continued existence. I don't mean my wish that he live on, but the conflict—the discontinuity—between his presence within me and his absence in the world. I've ascribed that, that disparity to the unconscious. My unconscious. I know that Luke's . . ." Will stops, unable, for a moment, to speak. When he does, the first few words come out choked. "I know he's dead," he says, reaching for his father's arm.

"But only when I'm awake, conscious. In my unconscious, Luke lives. The realness of him in my dreams is, is so . . . I wake up, and the bed, the floor, my wife, my own hand—nothing has the . . . the reality, the incandescent life of the child in my dreams. My unconscious.

"So," Will says, "maybe that's an example of the unconscious being God's country. A place of life after death. Of resurrection. Reunion with those who die before us."

His father nods, looking up. "Heaven," he says. "Just as it's always been promised."

T he responsible thing to do—he tells himself every day—would be to take a leave of absence.

Instead, Will has done the opposite. As if to foreclose opportunities for reflection, the danger of too much time spent exploring his own psyche, he's expanded his caseload to make a total of nineteen weekly patients as well as one daily and five thrice-weekly analysands to whom he listens and comments. Comments appropriately, despite whatever alarming, inappropriate sexual scenario is unspooling in his head. Even comments wisely, if he is to believe one fervent letter of thanks.

Denial? Defiance? The exhausting prospect of having to refer all his patients to other therapists, either temporarily, meaning he could look forward to returning to all the compounded distrust and anger his abandonment inspired, or permanently, meaning he'd have to start over and build a new practice from scratch? No matter the reason—and perhaps it's as simple as the inability to imagine himself not working—Will continues on as he has been. "To hell in a hand-basket" is the phrase that pops into his head, one of his mother's tidy dismissals, an announcement that she's "washing her hands" (there's another) of whatever mess it is.

He knows its cause, or at least what he assumes has forced the development of his own lust into a drive he can no longer govern or contain, a drive that has pushed him beyond the boundary of what he used to recognize as himself. He can even guess, within a few days, the night of this catalyst's arrival. Carole was sitting across from him at the dining room table, dinner long over, Samantha asleep, plates stacked in the sink. He was looking at the table's surface, watching the arc of moisture left by the sponge as it evaporated, disappeared, looking at this rather than at his wife's face when he asked her, "Are you *tired*?" Because it was at this moment that he decided it was time: a decent interval had passed. Or if not decent, then bearable. What exactly was the sexual etiquette of mourning? All he knew was he'd waited as long as he could, hating himself for the calculation and for possessing desire that was unkillable, and therefore indecent.

Hesitant, afraid of causing insult, he didn't ask the literal question but couched it as one of their oblique invitations for intercourse, that is, Are you *too* tired?

Carole looked at him. "All right," she said, taking no trouble to conceal that this would be what they call a mercy fuck, an indulgence of his need, a gift she could afford to give him.

No, not afford. *Afford* belonged to the past, before the accident, when minor questions seemed to have answers of consequence. *What restaurant? Which movie? Shower or bath? A walk to the park? Window-shopping along the avenue? White wine? Red?* That it had once been worth considering such choices seemed marvelous, a matter over which to marvel. "All right," Carole said, and he guessed this was because it didn't matter to her what they did or didn't do. What could be given to her? What could be taken away? Nothing that would return them to the consideration of minutiae.

But they hadn't made love since the morning before Luke drowned, and Will felt an awkward and uncomfortable something growing between them, a film of alienation that was almost tissuelike, thickening with every passing hour, acquiring that much more substance. Soon this membrane would be opaque; soon he wouldn't be able to see beyond it to his wife on the other side. He went up the stairs behind her, eye level with the back of her tanned thighs, feeling his gratitude. She would open herself to him. He could follow his body and disappear into hers. For a little while he could.

Carole undressed. She flipped back the covers and lay down without turning off the light. "Did you want it on?" he asked, because she didn't usually.

"If you do." She turned onto her side to face the window, and Will couldn't see her expression. He bent down to pull off his socks and got into bed carefully so that it didn't jounce or creak, drew toward her to embrace her from behind. She turned onto her stomach.

"Do you want to do it that way?" he asked, after a silence.

"Yes."

"You don't want to start the other way?"

"Not really."

So he entered his wife from the back, which he liked—he liked it just as well as any other way, better sometimes—and when he asked, a few minutes later, "Do you want to turn over?" again Carole said she didn't.

She was on her hands and her knees, and he bent over her damp back, reaching to touch her. But he'd barely brushed her pubic hair when she moved his hand. "No?" he said, and she shook her head. He stopped moving; immediately his erection started to ebb inside her.

"Well, will . . . will you do it?" he asked, and she touched herself with her own hand. Obediently, she worked her way toward orgasm.

Carole could deny it, but Will understood the meaning of her silent compliance. It was a judgment against him. Against any organism so primitive that it could take comfort in flesh, against a bereaved father who chose this brief oblivion, who allowed himself a comfort he didn't deserve.

Except *deserve* was his language, not hers. So perhaps she was right: he was unfair, he projected his disgust onto her, he craved punishment as much as he did sex and cleverly manipulated her into a vessel for both. He'd scripted her as his monolithic mother, was that it? The great force who gave and who withheld, who soothed even as she condemned. And Carole was indulgent enough to act this out.

"Oh God, Will! Shut up! Won't you please, please just stop?" she says when he drags her down after him into one of his psychoanalytic rabbit holes, refusing to plummet with him through his bottomless, convulsive guilt.

Whatever it means, it did begin that August evening, their new one-position sex life, unvarying to the point of ritual. Ritual and seemingly irrevocable, as conclusive as a burned bridge, Luke's death the obvious divide. Did this have to be an issue? Did he have to make it into an issue? Were he to accept without deconstructing the shift, he might grow used to it, complacent even. Many husbands—he can think of several—would celebrate a wife who took care of her own pleasure and left him to concentrate on his. But increasingly, Will found this hard, very hard. And the fact that she still went down on him but wouldn't let him touch her, neither with finger nor tongue— so that there could be no parity (not that anyone was measuring, except of course they were, people always did measure everything, especially love and acts of love)—and the disparity made it, well, it's hard to say it made anything worse, in that whatever might include blow jobs can't be *worse*, but it did make it more pointed: their having lost their balance.

That first night—a real first night in that losing Luke had changed them, not returning them to virginity but bringing them to a different state of clumsy self-consciousness and second-guessed gestures, of lacking the skills needed to make it turn out right, the fear of wounding or offending or simply asking too much of the flesh: What could it do? How far away could it take them? How much comfort could it hold?—after Will came, he rested his forehead on her back for a moment. Then he pulled out from her, and she lowered herself silently onto the bed. Beside her, he felt his erection shrivel.

Now the heavier caseload is not only failing to dampen his obsessive fantasies, it may even be encouraging them. Too often Will comes home in the dark to dinner eaten in solitude, to sex without conversation—sex with a sleepy (sometimes almost sleeping) wife, followed by however many laps of CNN it takes to put him to bed. Addicted to its repetition of headlines and looping tape feed, the astigmatic crawl of reprocessed information at the bottom of the screen, he finds it almost reassuring that news desks recycle crimes and atrocities. Apparently there aren't yet enough to fill twenty-four hours of broadcast.

For as far back as he can remember in his professional life, Will's days had proceeded, one after another, like the pages of a book, a text he found readable, sometimes engrossing, above all comprehensible. It was a book he understood. Then, abruptly, this orderly narrative—*his* orderly narrative, the book of Will—gave way to a wild scribbling of urges.

No, that's not true. It may seem he's come apart all at once, but it's an alignment—a compounding—of fractures, none of them new: estrangement from brother; death of son; reinvention of father. All versions of himself, if he can get away with such a Will-centered universe. Well, yes, of course he can. Inside his own head, he can. And why stop there? Why, when father, twin, and son cover all the tenses—past, present, and future? No wonder he was so . . . so whatever he was at the reunion. He's ceased to exist as an extension of himself.

Fuck! Yes, he's obsessed with sex. How else could he escape the inside of his head, where every thought refuses to be fleeting and instead waits its turn to be hyperarticulated, edited, revised, and then annotated like some nightmare hybrid of Talmudic commentary and Freudian case study? How else to jump out of his own skin except by fantasies of getting into someone else's?

In the course of one session with the depressed forty-something accountant, the one with the shapeless khaki skirts, Will was transformed from attentive analyst into what his mother must have meant by *sex maniac*, a term he hasn't heard her use for many years and one he used to find ridiculous, associating it with tabloid papers and true-crime magazines and foolish women who read about rape and secretly dream of it as overly zealous lovemaking. The accountant was sitting across from Will in the black leather chair that matched his couch when suddenly he was standing above her and she was on her knees begging to suck his cock. Not really, of course, and neither did they move on to frenzied, acrobatic-bordering-on-tantric sex.

Except that they did in his head. In his head they did.

He's used to the more or less constant nano-porn that buzzes through his male brain without overcoming or even disrupting the sequence of his thoughts. This is a fact of his mental life. But the new preoccupation is something different, leaving him at the mercy of ultralustful thoughts featuring whoever sits in the chair opposite his, or, worse, lies on his couch so she can't see that he is staring at her breasts. Objectively speaking, not one of the women he treats is as beautiful as his wife, not nearly. But whose fantasies are objective?

On his once rigorously exacting fuckability scale, on which even the iconic Pamela Anderson or J. Lo rated 9, every woman is now awarded 10 out of 10. Fat, thin, old, young, short, tall, dark, fair, flat, stacked: a perfect score depends on nothing more than being female.

The accountant, the grad student, even his training analysand. The menopausal one with too much money. The ASPCA officer, a typically misanthropic animal lover with white dog hair on her black sweaters. The archetypally unfulfilled tax lawyer who arrives for each session with a new missionary plan, off to Africa to adopt AIDS babies one week, bringing birth control to India the next. The lesbian who, having at last moved in with her partner, has decided she probably isn't gay after all. The bride-to-be who has not told her betrothed that she is infertile because her fallopian tubes were badly scarred by pelvic inflammatory disease contracted while she worked her way through college as a stripper who sometimes traded sex for money. The buxom one, who in the old days would have rated a good 7.5, maybe 8, and who makes everything that much worse by letting her snug skirt ride up her thighs and asking outright, "I am attractive, aren't I? I mean I do look good enough, don't I? Be honest with me, please. I know you're my therapist, Dr. Moreland, but as a man do you find me to be an attractive woman?" And all the rest of them.

They talk; he nods. He says "Oh," says "Hmm," says "Yes, I see what you mean," says "Please, go on. I think we should pursue this," and no matter who she is, no matter how inhibited or crazy or admittedly frigid, she's instantly made over into a sexpot whose only purpose is to gratify his every lustful wish.

At work these fantasies remain upbeat, but when he revisits a scenario later, as he inevitably does in his chronic insomnia, they sour with an almost film-noir relish for bad endings, a narrative free fall he's helpless to stop. It all comes apart in awful, bruising sex, intercourse that amounts to battery, struggles that arise out of the one irreversible law of Will's fantasies: there can be no blind consummations. No closed eyes, no doing it in the dark, no front to back, no sixty-nine, no anything that would prevent eye contact: this is the rule, the one point on which he won't—can't—compromise and the one point she can't—won't—accept.

As the forbidden interaction with his patient devolves from consensual to coerced, what he sees in his head acquires an increasingly sordid cast, transformed from the cheery Kodachrome of *Playboy* centerfolds to the grainy, indistinct black and white of crimes unfolding on the monitor of a closed-circuit camera, acts recorded by a secret, peering eye. Hiked-up skirts and yanked-down panty hose, spread thighs, wet whites of eyes, undergarments strewn on the floor: sufficiently arousing that even after having had sex with his wife Will can flog himself on to a second and sometimes (well, once) a third ejaculation. No top-flight orgasm, that third; it left him feeling dizzy and ruined. But he's forty-seven. Even hard-won prowess infuses him with something enough like optimism that he leaves his bed for a nearby armchair where he can move freely without disturbing his wife's sleep.

Typically, by the time Will arrives at orgasm his imagined partner has suffered the opposite of synergy; she's less than the sum of her parts, or fewer parts than would add up to a person: only lips, breasts, the downy cleft of her ass, the handful of flesh, so soft, inside the top of each thigh. It's only afterward, when he's spent and slumped in the chair, that both body and narrative reassemble. The same woman who began by begging for it reports Will's misconduct to the authorities, not some panel of toothless Ph.D.'s whose idea of discipline is re-analysis with the agenda of shrinking his libido back to manageable proportions, but real authorities, whose power is violence. Nameless, faceless storm troopers deliver him to a barricaded compound far from home and family, a place from which he cannot be rescued. There he is blindfolded, beaten, and stripped of his license, his reputation, his savings—all that twenty years of hard work have afforded him. Bound and gagged, with no expectation of release, he's left to bleed silently.

"Maybe," Will says to Daniel, "maybe I'm having a midlife crisis. What do you think?"

Daniel raises his white eyebrows. "Facile. That's what I think. Besides, didn't you already have a midlife crisis?"

"Did I? I don't think so."

"I was remembering the thing with Carole's sister."

"That wasn't a *thing*. And it wasn't *with*. It was an infatuation. Not consummated. Hardly a crisis. As I remember, I was so unnerved by my being attracted to Rachel that I ignored her to the point that she told Carole she thought I didn't like her. I had to work pretty hard to undo the damage I'd done."

Daniel picks up a heavy Mont Blanc pen from his desk, balancing it upright on the blotter between his thumb and index finger and slid-ing them all the way down the barrel until the pen falls, its end still caught between thumb and finger. He repeats the motion, over and over, and Will watches the way each time the pen falls, it hits the blotter with a little bounce.

"Will," Daniel says, "where did you go?"

"I don't know. Nowhere."

"Nowhere?"

"I guess I was trying to characterize for myself the emotions that go with the fantasies. What I feel. Or what I feel apart from lust."

"And?"

"Well, fear at the idea of being found out, caught in the act. And anger. Angry at myself for being so foolish. For risking so much to satisfy lust. But that anger is rational, after the fact. There's a more basic rage I can't get a handle on. Where does it come from? The lust itself is an angry lust, you know? Passion without tenderness. These are the nighttime scenarios I'm talking about. The fantasies during

the day—the ones that distract me during a session with a patient—
they're pretty uninteresting. Like *Penthouse* 'Forum' letters. Wishful,
silly. But the nighttime stuff, it taps into this anguished rage I can't
unpack.

"I mean, it's easy enough to admit that I'm angry with Carole
about her having restricted our sex life. All those rules that kicked in
after . . . after Luke." Will clears his throat, trying to prevent emotion
from making his voice crack. "I think of it as her not allowing me to
have sex with Luke's mother. Which I understand. I mean I'm not
unaware of how profoundly everything is affected by a loss this . . .
this big."

"Is that her explanation or yours?" Daniel asks, having waited for
Will to compose himself.

"Mine. My explanation. Carole won't talk about it. If I bring any
of this up, she accuses me of trying to turn her into one of my patients."

"Is she talking to anyone?"

"A therapist, you mean? No, no. She doesn't believe in it, not for
herself. She believes in yoga. Yoga classes. Yoga books." Will sits forward in his chair. "Actually, we joke about it, but what Carole reads
about isn't yoga. She'd say I was imposing meaning on what has no
real significance, but she's addicted to this true-crime stuff—sinister,
violent. Lust murders. Women savaged by misogynistic psychopaths.
The kind of guys—you know the profile—whose mothers were pros-
titutes, or their sadistic fathers beat them, or there's a frontal-lobe injury or an organic brain disorder, or maybe it's idiopathic and they're
just evil. Richard Speck. Ted Bundy. Sex and violence inextricably
bound up. And the stories have to be true. He can't be a fictional
monster. She couldn't care less about Hannibal Lecter.

"I get there's a fascination in being witness to a crime. I mean,
probably the interest in most movies, novels, biographies—any

narrative—depends on voyeurism, but this seems, well, maybe self-loathing is too strong a word. But suspect anyway. Driven by unconscious need. Otherwise why read one after another book about women getting raped and stabbed? Dismembered." Will shakes his head. "I think she herself worries they represent a perverse impulse, because she hides them. Even has one of those weird little fabric book-cover things so she can read them unnoticed in a waiting room or in front of Samantha. But she won't admit any contradiction in being a . . . a feminist and a yoga devotee and a purchaser of only organic produce, member of the food co-op, NYPIRG, Amnesty International, et cetera, as well as an insatiable consumer of true crime. With photo inserts of chopped-up women. And yes, I do realize that I've switched the focus from me to someone else."

"How is it," Daniel asks, "that Carole has figured out a way to refuse you sex with Luke's mother, as you say? In that Luke's mother is your wife."

"By arranging things so that I can get off with a female body, her body, but one she won't give a face. For three years now I've had to approach her from the back. She won't . . ."

"Won't what?" Daniel asks when Will doesn't finish the thought.

"She won't let me have missionary sex with her. Won't tolerate any position that might risk eye contact. Won't let me perform oral sex. Or touch her with my hand. She has orgasms, but I'm not allowed to give them to her. It's like I'm some guy who happens to be attached to the dildo she's using."

Daniel looks at Will closely. He's leaning forward over his desk, resting his chin on one hand. "You are angry," he says.

"Yes. Yes, I've said I am. But I keep feeling there's a piece missing from the explanations I've come up with. That it's too easy to assign blame to Luke's death. To call it a catalyst for every problem that develops between us."

"Still, you do find a connection between the violent fantasies about your patients and Carole's controlling your sex life? Limiting your access to her body?"

"Absolutely." Will frowns. "At least I think I do. Now, having mentioned her reading about serial killers immediately after talking about my violent sexual fantasies, I'm wondering if it's . . . if that's entirely coincidental. I guess it is—what connection could there be?—but then I worry that my tendency to insist upon connections leads me to find significance where there isn't any. Create meanings that don't exist outside of my consciousness. You know, the whole God thing."

"The God thing?"

"Yes, yes. The trap I fall into. Looking everywhere for significance. It gets out of my ability to control or direct it, won't remain within the boundary of my work, within my patient relationships. Suddenly, significance becomes signs. And there I am, back to obsessing over the possibility of God. Whether God exists or is merely projection. Whether the significance I find or the signs I see represent nothing more than my wish for meaning, or have a validity beyond my desires and my consciousness."

"Will," Daniel says. "Here's a place where I'm afraid I have to be textbook. Call attention to what you already know."

"Wait, wait." Will holds up his hand, laughing. Almost laughing. Every time he does laugh in Daniel's company he's aware, as he didn't use to be, of how similar it feels to crying. The rhythm of it, the way it tightens in his chest, stretches his face. "I heard it, too. I know what you're going to say."

"Tell me."

"My use of the word *obsessing* to characterize my thinking about God." Daniel nods. "I know, I know." Will's voice assumes the bored tone of rote repetition, with a little twist, a lilt, of self-parody. "What is it I'm trying so hard not to perceive? What is it that my obsession defends me against?"

"Exactly." Daniel replaces his pen in the leather tray next to his pipe stand. Though it's been many years since he's smoked, he keeps his pipes on his desk. Sometimes, while Will talks, he takes one and fiddles with it, using a handkerchief to polish its bowl, or holding it, empty, between his teeth, and Will knows these aren't the idle acts they seem but a conscious attempt to disarm him, to suggest the older man isn't listening as closely as he is.

"Remember when I asked if you considered psychoanalysis a type of conversion experience?" Will says.

"Remind me."

"It was a long time ago, years ago. I'd reached a moment of exultation, very excited about what we were doing because suddenly everything was illuminated. Flooded with light. I couldn't separate my . . . well, it was a form of ecstasy, and I didn't separate it from what would be described as a religious experience, scales dropping from before my eyes, however you want to describe it. And I asked didn't you think psychoanalysis was a religion as much as a science? It was a faith, Freud was a prophet, training analysis the conversion experience—a dramatic, road-to-Damascus-caliber revelation."

"What was my answer?" Daniel says.

"I don't know. I was so delighted with the question—really an observation couched as a question—that if you disagreed with me, I doubt I'd have heard you."

Will and Daniel stand, Will noting, not for the first time, that he and Daniel wear almost identical glasses, rimless bifocals with pewter-colored stems. Daniel fastens the middle button of his suit jacket. He holds his hand out to take Will's. "Next week?"

"Next week," Will agrees, comforted by the promise of speaking with Daniel again soon, even though these sessions don't seem to be helping. At least not with respect to the forbidden fantasies—the fantasies Will wants to forbid. They haven't lessened the frequency or the virulence of his lust attacks at all.

Increasingly, Will worries he'll succumb to what he'd reassure a patient was an innocuous normal outlet, and not the symptom of some monstrous psychopathology. He'd remind the hypothetical patient that even the most civilized gentlemen have their brutal fantasies. Especially the most civilized.

But Will isn't his own patient. He isn't hypothetical. What he is, is afraid. He doesn't feel he knows himself anymore, and it seems only a matter of time before he's no longer daydreaming but acting. Before he becomes the very thing he fears: a portion of unhappiness and ill fortune for the people he loves, the family he wants, brick by brick, to protect.

t was two months or more after the reunion that Will e-mailed Elizabeth to apologize. He hadn't intended to put it off so long, but the wording kept tripping him up; he wrote draft after draft that he never sent. *Please forgive me*, he'd begin, typically, *or at least understand my ill-advised request.* Then he'd pause, delete *ill-advised*, or *foolish*, or *ridiculous*, whichever he'd chosen, put it back in, take it out, try to come up with a better word, fail, continue, *as proceeding from the context. I find such events disorienting, and it seems that a couple of glasses of wine were sufficient to enflame my imagination. You have my word that I will not pursue the matter we discussed. Best, Will.* He'd read it over, change a few words, change the last sentence. *You have my word that, though I remain interested in the question of your daughter's paternity, I will not attempt to contact her.* He'd change it back, delete the letter in its entirety, write another that was, but for a few articles and commas, identical to the first.

Finally, one day, it was already September, after a lengthening pause during which he wasn't so much thinking as staring, he hit the send button.

She hasn't replied. Not after a week, not after a month. Of course, he should never have voiced what was, he understood too late, a fantasy. A mistake to have mentioned anything about hair to Elizabeth. He blew it, and undoubtedly this was for the best. So why does he continue to check the mail so assiduously? Why, after more than a month of silence, is he still waiting to hear from Elizabeth? Thinking about making love to her? Well, not love. *Plank* would be the word. It's with pleasure that he imagines himself planking Elizabeth, changing the expression on her face from one of self-satisfaction to . . . to what? Astonishment. The one indelibly delightful memory of the reunion was the look on her face when he suggested she mail him one of her daughter's hairs.

For most of his professional life, Will has preferred working with women patients, who generally articulate their feelings more intelligently than men and whose emotional lives are more available to examination. But now it's the male patients upon whom he depends for relief. No matter that their progress is slow, their insights infrequent. At least he doesn't want to jump their bones. Three of his five new patients are men who have added their voices to what often strikes Will as the attenuated morality play of his work, a sprawling, incontinent production that could be titled "The Seven Deadly Sins." Replete with crises and lacking a resolution, this drama energetically addresses anger, sloth, avarice, and gluttony, ignores vanity and pride (if he had to choose whether this reflects his particular moment in history or the nature of psychoanalysis, he'd go with the former), and showcases lust.

"I love her," the guilt-riddled womanizer tells him. "I do love her. She thinks I can't love her and screw other women, but she's wrong. And it's not like we don't have great sex. Twenty years, and we're still hot for each other."

"So it isn't a matter of turning to other women for what your wife won't give you?"

"No, it's a matter of . . . I don't know what it's a matter of. But in the moment, when I'm with a woman, any woman, it's as if—this is preposterous, but at that moment I'm convinced that if I don't have sex with whoever it is, I'll never be able to get it up again. So, even though I'm aware that I'm sabotaging my marriage and maybe even my whole family, I can't not do it. It's compulsory, and not just from the point at which I'm in bed with whoever she is, but from the moment the idea of sex with that woman comes into my head. It's like the old expression 'Use it or lose it' has turned into some kind of spell, or curse. I end up screwing all kinds of women I don't even want to, when I don't want to."

He keeps talking even though he's seen Will look at his watch. "I've tried other things—everything," he says. "Acupuncture. Hypnosis. We've gone to couples therapy. Nothing works."

"Use it or lose it?" Will asks. The hour's up, but finally it seems as if they're on to something.

The man nods. "I even hear it in my head," he says. "Well, I hear a lot of things like that, phrases that get stuck in my head."

"Tell me about them."

The man shrugs self-consciously. "Some just bug me," he says, "like that old 'Step on a crack, break your mother's back.' And the other one that always pops up when I walk outside. As soon as I see dog crap, I hear 'Eat shit and die.' Well, obviously I don't act on that, but the words stay in my head. They play over and over until something, I don't know what, distracts me or turns them off somehow. I can't tell you how they stop because as long as I'm trying to turn them off, I can't, you know? They have to stop when I've given up, when I'm not paying attention anymore."

"Are there others of these directives?" Will asks. "Others you can remember?"

"Oh, yes, many of them. There's 'Haste makes waste' and 'A stitch in time'—things like that. 'No pain, no gain.'"

"Sayings, you mean? Aphorisms?"

"Yes. But while most of them bother me by repeating over and over, the 'Use it or lose it' one forces me to act because the idea that it's true, that I will lose it, is so powerful."

"Do you avoid cracks in the sidewalk?"

"I guess I do, yes."

"Do some of these directives occur more frequently than others?"

"No. At least I don't think they do."

"And mostly they stop when you obey?"

"Yes. I hadn't spelled it out that way to myself, but you're right."

Will makes a note. He's allowed the new patient to use up not only the few remaining minutes of his hour—he's never been one for forcing a fifty-minute break-off—but a little of the next patient's as well, and she comes in glaring at him. It's six minutes past.

"Maria," he says, standing to greet her. "Please forgive me. The . . . the gentleman whose appointment was immediately before yours was describing a complicated set of circumstances. You know I don't like to cut people off."

She nods, looking slightly mollified. "It's okay, I guess."

"Please," he says. He gestures toward the couch. "I was hoping that today, as I have a cancellation following your session, we could run overtime. If your schedule allows, that is."

"Yeah, thanks, okay." She hangs her coat in the closet but keeps her purse with her, lies down holding it in front of her crotch. Several times, she has pointed this habit out to Will, as if afraid he hasn't picked up on this self-conscious Freudian allusion. He never takes the bait when she asks him what it might mean, just lobs the question back at her.

"I feel like you're always watching me," she says as soon as she's comfortably settled.

"Yes, I remember. We were talking about that last week."

"No matter what I'm doing—I can be at work or eating dinner or changing my clothes or even having sex, and I get this feeling that if I look up, you'll be standing there. Not saying anything, just watching me. Making your silent judgments." She uses her hands as she speaks and doesn't return them to her purse during pauses but leaves them hanging in midair, above her chest. "Well," she says, "don't you have any response to that?"

"Yes," Will says. "I'm wondering why you think I judge you."

"Because you do. You sit there thinking how purposeless and stupid my life is."

"Why do you imagine me thinking that?"

"Why wouldn't you? After all, whatever I do or feel, I come here and tell you all about it. So you might just as well be there with me. Then you could see exactly how stupid and shallow I am."

"Do you think you might like to have someone with you all the time? Someone to watch over you?"

"Why would I want that?"

"It's not so unusual a wish. People get lonely."

"I'd like to be lonely! I'd like to have a minute to myself. But you make it impossible for me to have any privacy even when I am alone. I told you, it's uncomfortable. It's not something I enjoy. It's like I have a built-in peeping Tom."

"But Maria, it's you who's invented this, the idea of my secretly watching you. And you who imagines that my observations are judgmental."

"Omniscient," she says.

"Omniscient?"

"Yes. Because you're in my head, too, so you can see what I'm thinking."

"Go on," Will says when she falls silent. But she says nothing, and he finds himself feeling impatient. He looks past the couch to the dance studio across the street, through whose windows he sometimes watches the students, children mostly. Today it's a group of little girls about the same age as Samantha, although he can make out a boy or two. Beginners' ballet, he guesses, a lot of antic warming up followed by a halting review of the basics. The teacher, a young woman in black leotard and tights with red leg warmers, stands at the front of the class, holding a position until the three rows of would-be dancers have assembled their limbs in an approximation of her own. Then she goes painstakingly from one child to the next, nudging feet, re-aligning arms, a process that requires her to stoop and squat, patiently doing again and again what she must have done countless times before. From across the narrow street, Will can see her wide smiles of encouragement. Her energy and enthusiasm make him feel tired, even old. What—if anything—distinguishes his work from hers? Does he not spend hours each day nudging and straightening, supporting mostly doomed attempts to approach an ideal from various points of stubborn individuality? After each position, the teacher has the class jump up and down and shake their arms and legs, presumably in an effort to dispel energy and make them pliable enough to attempt the next.

"You're just," Maria blurts, "I don't know. It's what I said—as long as I'm going to tell you, you might just as well be there. In my bedroom." She stops there, and Will is silent, waiting. "It feels the same as when I used to get in trouble and my mother would make me wait in my room until my dad got home," she says.

"What does?"

"Your watching me."

"How? How does it?"

"Because. It just does, that's all."

"Do you think perhaps you're feeling angry with me and would like to punish me?" Will prompts, unusually direct, but over the past five years Maria has proved herself someone who can get stuck on a topic for weeks, marching the two of them over and over the same territory.

"Angry about what?"

"Well, I remember that you were upset with me last September, after I had been away during August. We spoke about your feeling abandoned."

"But why would that make me want you to see into my private life? Stuff like with my boyfriend—stuff that's intimate. I mean, why would I want you to see me naked or having sex?"

"Tell me if this sounds possible," Will tries. "You'd like to believe that my life is boring, empty, and doesn't include intimacies like those you share with your boyfriend."

Maria lies still on the couch, says nothing.

"Wouldn't it be that much more gratifying if I were to witness your interesting life? And know that my own was comparatively barren?"

She pulls her purse up, hugging it to her stomach. It's one of the few times her handling it doesn't strike him as premeditated. "I think"—she takes a deep breath, starts over. "I think maybe I want you to see me with my boyfriend so I can prove to you that I don't have any . . . any of those feelings for you."

Can it be true that all of Will's patients are consumed by the topic of sex? Getting it. Not getting it. Getting it, but not enough of it. Getting it from the wrong person. Getting it but not It. Coming, not coming, coming too soon, coming too late. Coming, but only under certain highly specific circumstances. Fetishism. Priapism. Frigidity. Bondage, humiliation, latex. Has he done this to them? Communicated his disease?

The last appointment of the day is an intake, a tall young woman, leggy like a teenager and decorated with what he's come to regard as the usual assortment of tattoos. She sits sideways in the armchair, her back against one padded arm, her legs over the other. Two stainless steel studs connected by a post sit on either side of the pinch of flesh just above the bridge of her nose. Placed where they are, the little orbs disturb him as might a smaller, brighter pair of eyes between her own pale blue ones, themselves offset by owlishly smudged eyeliner and mascara. She's attractive in a sulky, ill-kempt way, her hair falling unevenly around her face, appearing to have been hacked rather than styled. More likely, styled expensively to look as though hacked. As she talks she chews one of her nails, all of which are bitten to the quick, and armored with silver rings.

"So," she says, "that's it, I guess."

"Where do you meet these men?"

"Bars mostly. Except the one I'm going to do next will be an art-history professor. So I'll pick him up at the faculty house."

"The faculty house?"

"Uh-huh. It's my work-study gig. I waitress there."

Will tries to picture the young woman in a waitress outfit along with the studs, tattoos, and smudged mascara. She doesn't present herself as a person who would take orders politely. "That's unusual financial aid, isn't it?" he asks her.

"It would be, yeah. But it's not financial aid, per se. See, there's hardly any teaching slots in classics; there's maybe five TA's in the whole department, so if you're a doctoral student, eventually you end up with these funky jobs. Quasi-official. The department secretary will hunt something down for you if you're willing to, like, grovel and curry favor. Which is the definition of higher education, basically, at least as far as I can figure. I'll maybe go into teaching if I ever get out of there. I wouldn't need an education degree to get hired by a private school." Speaking about her future, she looks earnest and sober, not the disaffected slacker who threw herself into the chair but a scholarly disciple whose postmodern finery might peel right off, like a Halloween costume, and reveal one of those laurel-wreathed heads from a Roman coin. "It's not as impractical as it seems," she adds. "Classics are cool again. They're making a comeback."

Will nods. "I guess that's what makes them classics."

She raises her eyebrows, and the two studs ascend slightly as well. "Precisely," she says. Her expression suggests that she's taken his comment to have been sarcastic, which it was not.

"Latin?" he asks. "Greek?"

"Latin and Greek. Latin all the way back to junior high. Greek I began as a freshman."

Will leans back in his chair, hands behind his head, fingers laced. It's a pose, at once relaxed and challenging. "Well," he says. "What would you want from this process? From what you've told me, I assume you're considering weekly therapy rather than analysis, which would be a considerable investment with respect to both time and money—analysis is three to five sessions a week. If we were to meet once weekly, our dialogue would still take a psychoanalytic approach, because that's my training. We'd use dreams, fantasies, free association—whatever means by which we can access unconscious rather than conscious material. But one day a week would imply a distinct, comparatively short-term goal, rather than the less narrowly defined and, some would even say, spiritual quest of a true psychoanalysis. And, as I said, more affordable."

"Spiritual how?"

"Spiritual as in the hope for enlightenment. About the self. The attempt to become a more fully conscious being." She nods slowly, eyebrows raised in a skeptical expression.

"Was I, like, supposed to be answering a question?" she asks after a minute or more has gone by.

"I'm hoping we can figure out how to help you. And to that end, I was asking what you want to accomplish in here, talking with me."

"To get over this bullshit, obviously. To escape from this, this, um, this thing, this whatever-it-is that makes me go after these old guys."

"Old guys," Will says, deciding to defer practical arrangements until the end of the hour. "Tell me what that's like," he says.

"What it's like?"

"Yes. What does it feel like to seduce older men?"

She makes a face. "Well, first off, it's not seducing."

"No?"

"It's collecting."

"Collecting?" Will writes the word down.

"It's more like that than it is like anything else. I mean, it's . . . that's the only way I can describe it."

"How does it feel emotionally?"

"Emotionally? You mean . . ." She trails off, looking genuinely confused.

"I mean, are you happy? Sad? Satisfied when the date is over? Frustrated? Do you feel you're courting danger? Overpowered, or do you feel you control the interaction?"

"They're not *dates*. Dates presume, like, a future. These are just anonymous hookups with old guys."

"Okay," Will says. "Can you tell me how it feels to anonymously hook up with an old guy?"

The girl frowns in concentration, but it's her thumbnail she's working on, not his question. After a moment she looks up. "I feel like I'm collecting them."

"All right. Then what does collecting feel like?"

"I don't know, it's . . . I guess I said 'collecting' because for me it's the same as it was when I was a kid and I had this, like, thing for glass paperweights. There was always one I needed to have, and I'd be like—I couldn't really think about anything else until I got it. So I'd babysit or go through garbage cans for soda bottles to, you know, get the nickel deposits, or I'd do chores. Whatever I had to do, to get the money together to pay for it. And then, when I got it, this dumb thing I'd been, like, frantic to have, I wouldn't be so much satisfied as relieved. Because then I wouldn't have to think about how I needed it anymore. I had it, so I could get on with other stuff."

Will nods. "I'm still listening," he says.

"That's it. There isn't any more."

"Would it be fair to say that adding a paperweight to your collection made you feel as though it was in your power, rather than the other way around?"

The girl studies the freshly bitten thumbnail and returns it, briefly, to her mouth. "I guess," she says.

"Did you enjoy them once you had them?"

"How do you mean?"

"Well, did you spend time looking at them? Were there things to learn about them, like methods of manufacture? Different kinds of glass? Did you get into the history of the glass paperweight?"

She gives him a contemptuous, who's-the-crazy-one-here look. "Nooo," she says, drawing the word out. "I kept them on a shelf in my bookcase. I mean, they were pretty, but what can you do with a ball of glass? I wasn't into, like, dusting."

"So it was all about pursuing the object?"

"I guess, yeah."

"And it's the same with the older men?"

"Pretty much. I have sex with one, move on to the next."

She falls silent under Will's gaze. A low-necked pullover reveals the words tattooed on her chest to be Latin—at least he thinks that's what they are—letters like those that adorn the entablatures of monuments and big civic buildings, *U*'s written as *V*'s—MVSEVM rather than MUSEUM. When she sees his eye hesitate on the tattoo she pulls at the neck of her sweater to reveal another line of text under the first.

"'*Quo usque tandem abutere patientia mea,*'" she reads. "It's from Cicero's first oration against Catiline. Except I edited out the name Catiline and used *mea* instead of *nostra*." She gets up to dig something out of her pocket, then returns to the same position, legs flung over one chair arm.

"What does it mean?"

"'How long, pray, will you take advantage of my patience?'"

Will smiles. He likes this girl. "Is Cicero one of your heroes?" he asks as she unwraps a hard candy. A shred of cellophane sticks to its surface, and she tries to pick it off as best she can without fingernails.

"One of my *heroes*? Do people even have, like, heroes anymore?"

She puts her feet on the floor and sits up straight, shoulders back, chest out. "The culture is posthero," she intones in a low, stentorian rumble, her expression dour and condescending. "Media-saturated, brand-conscious, inclined to mock every virtue from courage to modesty. Posthero and pro-rich-and-famous, heroism representing no more than a few coordinates along the arc of celebrity: conferred, questioned, doubted, debunked."

Watching her performance, Will has to suppress his enjoyment of what seems an effortless caricature. "Skip hero," he says. "Is Cicero a historical figure you admire?"

"I guess."

Will leans back in his chair, hands behind his head. "What about the man?" he asks.

"What about him?"

"I'm wondering if both of you expect the same outcome. Does he—whoever he is—know it's going to be a one-night stand?"

"What else could it be? It's not like we know each other. It's not like we've ever met before." When Will doesn't speak, she goes on. "Usually it seems pretty, you know, equal. They talk about what they do, their jobs. Or they say what they think they have to, what's required by the, the . . . well, the situation makes them feel like they should flatter me, I guess, tell me I have a great ass or they like my hair or my eyes. Whatever. It doesn't mean anything. Compliments are just, whatever, something to say while we're checking each other out and deciding, like, what's it gonna be, hook or book." Will raises his eyebrows. "Meaning," she says, "are we hooking up or booking, as in, like, leaving." Again she sits up straight. "*Book*," she intones, "verb, intransitive, to leave hurriedly as if tardy for a meeting of critical importance." Too bad she didn't choose drama over classics, Will thinks, take the opportunity to act out onstage. "It's not about feelings," she tells him. "It's not about how I feel or how he feels."

"What is it about?"

"Nothing. It isn't *about* anything." Her expression is one of exasperation. "You've heard the expression 'operate on a need-to-know basis'?"

Will nods.

"Generally speaking, I operate on a need-not-to-know basis. So it's not that I don't need to know about how they feel—I need not to know. Get it?"

"If it's not about feelings, what is it about?"

"God, is this what it's like having your head shrunk? You have to answer the same questions over and over? I told you, *collecting*. I collect them."

Will smiles in a way that's meant to be disarming. He's usually pretty quick to get a fix on a new patient, but there's something about this girl that he can't quite pin; she's guarded in a way he can almost feel, as if she's sitting on the other side of a pane of glass. "This is what's called an intake session," he tells her. "We haven't even begun the shrinking yet."

"Intake?"

"I ask questions to help me understand why you've come to me, and, if we decide to work together, to help me establish a treatment plan."

"If we decide to *work* together?"

"Yes. Because it is work, and not only for me. Once we begin, you do most of the talking." She looks at him. "Let's go back to the men," Will says. "Once you've picked one out, then what?"

"You know. We go someplace. His place. If he's single. Or a friend's place—that's happened. Hotel, maybe. But I'm . . . I don't do, like, cars."

Will removes his glasses, cleans their lenses with a handkerchief, replaces them on his nose: a little act to diffuse whatever tension might proceed from his watching her talk.

"So we, uh, you know. I take my clothes off, and I'm, like, probably the youngest person they've had sex with for a while, a long time maybe, and they're, well, they're excited. I mean, you know, my boobs are still where they're supposed to be. I've never been pregnant or anything that would make me, you know, stretched out or whatever. I've never lost or gained a bunch of weight." Having offered the kind of material that takes some patients years to approach, the girl looks directly at Will. "I don't know why, but they kind of turn me on, too. There's this, this aspect to their bodies—like they're not trying so hard, you know? They're not these gym rats lifting weights in the mirror. I guess that in the same way my being young makes them hot, I like that they're older. If they have a little gray hair on their chests, that helps. Chub around the middle, not so much muscle, whatever. It seems weird, even to me, but I do like it. Also, I gotta say, they're better at fucking."

Will remains expressionless and deploys one of his hard-on inhibitors, a picture his father took of a broken fire escape hung with icicles. He doesn't know why—it's not as if the photograph saddens or disgusts him—but it's usually effective.

"They have, well, what they have is technique. Experience. Maybe it's just that they aren't impatient. They last longer—too long sometimes, but that's better than having it end before it begins. Guys my age, for them sex isn't any different from, I don't know, takeout. They're, like, frantic, hardly bother to unwrap me. Older guys, they take their time, pay attention to what's going on. Ask—beg—to go down on me. They are, no kidding, total, I mean total, carpet munchers. I mean, like, all of them." Will stops writing. He puts his elbows on his desk, fingers together, tip to tip, looks at her. She's disclosing frank sexual material to distract him from her emotional absence. Either that or she's trying to bait him.

"I've done thirty-seven," she says after another leisurely examination of her bleeding thumbnail. "Thirty-seven so far. I have one picked out for Friday."

"I thought you said you were determined to quit."

She snorts. "Quit? Like with cigarettes?"

"Maybe like with cigarettes. Or any other addiction."

The girl shoots him a look. "Did I, like, miss something here? Did anything happen that might make it easier, or even possible, for me to, what, abstain by Friday?"

Will puts down his pen, folds his hands on his blotter. "For some patients, those who can be honest with themselves and commit to change, the process of articulating that they have a problem and identifying the behavior they want to stop is enough to begin to change."

"Would that be me, do you think?"

"I don't know. I just wondered if you were actively struggling to quit."

"This is my 'active struggle.' You. A shrink."

"Yes," he says, picking up his pen. "Perhaps together we'll figure out what it is you get from these experiences with older men, so that you can discover a different source for whatever it gives you. A source you can live with, satisfy more easily. And less expensively."

"What's that supposed to mean? It's not like I'm paying for anything."

"I was referring to the psychic cost."

The girl returns the problematic thumb to her mouth.

"Doesn't that hurt?" he asks her.

"They're kind of numb, actually." She puts her feet on the floor and leans forward, holding her hands out. A fresh line of blood has formed at the thumb's tip, and other fingers are bitten to the point of injury, as well. What's left of her nails is surrounded by flesh so enflamed that it puffs up around the nail beds. "Pretty, huh?" she says. Looking at her hands, Will feels a strange leap of sexual excitement, as if he's not just imagining but feeling the heat of those fingers on him, and he has to stop himself from reaching out to touch them.

He has to get her out of there.

"I've gotten these infections," she says. "Paronychia. From the Greek. *Para*—beside, *nychia*—nail. Like, really excruciating. You can't imagine. I had to go on antibiotics."

"Have you tried to stop?" He has an erection. It's instant, not the kind of excitement he can dampen. One second nothing, then, presto, all he's thinking is: the next in her collection of old guys.

"Bunch of times. Nothing works. I've used that bitter stuff that tastes, like, bad enough to make you puke, but I bit them anyway. Tried keeping gloves on all the time, and chewed through them. Behavior mod, where every time I went after a nail I was supposed to snap myself with this, um, punishment thing—this strap around my wrist like a big rubber band—snap it really hard, so it hurt, but no. All three at once, still no good." She shrugs. "Another problem to work on."

Will looks at his watch.

"Okay," she says, quick to pick up on the visual cue. "Same time next week?"

"If you're interested in continuing."

"I guess. I mean, can I just see how it goes?" She stands and pulls on her coat, picks up her backpack. "What about the fee?" she asks. "Do you . . . I read on your policy sheet that you have a, like, sliding fee scale. That for students it can be adjusted, um, down." She settles her backpack into place by flexing and quickly straightening her knees to give it a little bounce. "Because my insurance is student health, and it doesn't cover psychotherapy outside of the university. I'm entitled to ten sessions a year from student mental health, no charge. After that, it's, I don't know, maybe twenty-five an hour. But the therapists are dorks. I mean, worse than. Useless."

"How much can you afford?" Will asks.

"You're asking me what the bill is?" She tips her head to one side and frowns. Her puzzlement makes her look much younger, almost like a child.

"Yes," he says.

"Uh. Could it be . . . how about, um, like, fifty? Forty?"

"All right," he agrees. She digs her right hand into her pocket.

"Here," she says. She puts two twenty-dollar bills on the blotter. He doesn't touch them.

"It's customary to pay with a check," he says. "I send you a monthly statement, you mail me a check."

"Yeah, well, I'm sort of between apartments right now, trying to simplify the whole mail thing. I don't, like, have a forwarding address. Not yet."

Will nods. "All right," he says.

This is the moment when, ordinarily, he would stand and extend his hand to shake hers, but he can't. He doesn't have to look down to know that this isn't the kind of hard-on he can hide with a notebook, at least not subtly enough to risk it. He leans forward, hands folded on his desk, trying to appear as if this is his usual manner of concluding a session. "Next week?" he says.

She steps a few feet back from his desk, her hands shoved in the pockets of her brown suede coat. Around each is a dark ring of what appears to be grease, as if she were in the habit of keeping French fries in her pockets. The stained coat; the unkempt hair; the bitten fingernails; the soles of her boots, past repair: all these conspire to make her look like an orphan, a girl who has been not so much brought up as "dragged up," to use a favorite expression of his mother's. Hers is an unexpectedly sexy squalor, though; it makes her seem as if she's not so particular that she wouldn't be game for . . . well, for almost anything.

"Next week?" he asks again as she's walking toward the door.

"Okay," she says without turning.

t's 2:17 in the morning, 2:12, actually, because the digital clock on the dresser is five minutes fast. Will listens to the sound of water running on the other side of the bathroom door, water from the bathtub's faucet, not the sink's, because it's too loud for the sink's. Probably his wife is sitting in the empty bathtub, using her hands to direct water from the faucet to rinse soap from between her legs. "It's not you I'm washing off," she's told him, and he believes her. He thinks he does. She just doesn't like to get up in the morning smelling of stale sex. He gropes around for his pajama bottoms while he waits for her to come back to bed.

"Here's what I do, Will," Carole says when she's next to him under the covers. "What I do is, I don't think about myself. I think about you and Sam and my clients, and about Luke. But not in a way that makes me sad. Because lately what I've been thinking is this. We—and I don't mean us particularly, I don't mean you and me, but people in general—we are so fixated on this idea of a life span, that everyone should live a certain number of years. And it's maybe helpful to try to focus on something different, like that Luke had a good life, a happy life, when you think about it. Nothing much went wrong for him. He liked school. He had friends. He was a healthy, happy boy. He was. And maybe that's a thing we can be grateful for—that even if it was just ten years, they were these ten nearly perfect years, and, my God, Will, there is so much suffering—we see it all the time. You do, and I do, too. For much of their lives people are not happy. And, well"—Carole sighs here, a long and almost groaning noise— "Luke was. He was. Think how much worse it would have been if he'd died after struggling with some terrible illness. After years of en- during pain or . . ."

Carole stops speaking. Will keeps beginning a sentence in his head, a sentence that begins *But* and goes no further. If he looks into the darkest corner of the bedroom, where the streetlight doesn't pen- etrate, the blackness there seems to pulse, as if with a pressure like that of blood, something that shoves the blackness up against his eyes. Carole always assumes that in his wakefulness Will is obses- sively returning to the accident, punishing himself by reviewing it over and over, but in fact he'd been thinking about his brother. While he hadn't allowed himself to admit this—not consciously—if he didn't really expect Mitch to come to the reunion before he'd seen the class book, once he'd found that his brother had contributed a bio to it, he was sure he would see him there.

It's odd, but ever since their estrangement, Will's thoughts of Mitch have tended to summon a particular scene from Stanley Kubrick's *2001: A Space Odyssey*, a movie the two of them had watched together every afternoon they could for as long as it played in Ravena's one theater, spending all the allowance they'd saved, searching between sofa cushions and under car seats for stray change. It's the opening scene that Will continues to revisit, as if it might hold some means of understanding his relationship with his missing brother. In it, a community of apes—hairy, upright animals that have yet to evolve into *Homo sapiens*—are disturbed by the sudden appear- ance of a monolith, and it's this monolith itself that compels and sometimes even upsets Will.

More than once during his insomniac rambles he's found himself picturing, almost seeing, the looming slab in their bedroom, not against a wall or pushed back into a corner but smack in the middle of the braided rag rug Carole bought from an antiques shop upstate. Perfect in its blankness, its refusal of feature or detail, the sinister metal slab stands where it is bound to get in their way, to interrupt, block, and impede them. What can it mean, this fantasy? Will assumes the slab, in its inscrutable quality, represents his brother, Mitch's disappearance having become an emotional stumbling block, one right in front of their marriage bed, so large that it doesn't just stumble but blinds, ruining the view. Or maybe the thing is a kind of clock, a massive chunk of a plutonium-like element whose half-life divides and divides the hours, not so much displaying as emitting time: informing them with time, implanting the correct and true time within them. Aligning their mortal coils with its infinite and inexorable measurement. Maybe it's one of Will's clumsy attempts to represent God—a god, at least—who reigns over everyone, as deaf to one petition as to another. If Will can't always believe in God, he can't not believe in Time.

A car passes. Its headlights slide through the windows and over the furniture, the armchair and dresser, the desk piled with clutter: magazines; professional journals; catalogs; a picture of a house made from dried beans glued on blue construction paper; instructions for the assembly of toys long lost or broken.

"When I think of myself at all," Carole says, after what has transcended an awkward silence to become a more pure kind of quiet, the in-out sounds of their breathing joining and then diverging. "When I do think of myself," she says, her voice low and measured, "it's in a little boat on a wide sea. I'm sitting in the boat—I picture myself from high above—and I have to keep my balance. I have to stay right in the center of the boat so I don't tip." She inhales, exhales, an audible, deep exchange of air. "All the things I do, the district work, seeing clients, taking care of Samantha and the house and you, seeing friends, making dinner, weeding the garden, going to yoga, folding laundry, remembering birthdays, calling your parents—all of it, every piece of my life, is about staying there in the center of my little boat."

"But," Will can't help protesting, "but there is such a thing as a life span. An expected life span."

"I know," Carole says. "I know that."

"So your . . . your choice to focus on, well, let's call it the quality rather than quantity of his years—is this one of your ways of remaining in the middle of your boat?"

Carole says nothing. At the foot of their bed, the monolith on the rug fills the room with time, time too big to be contained by their bodies lying small under the sheet, time that is silent and unbearable, time that is a clock too accurate to tick.

"Did you say a river or the sea?" Will asks.

"Did I say what?"

"Your boat, it's on—"

"Oh, the sea, the ocean. Wherever I am, it's all water. There isn't any shore."

Carole turns from her back to her side, facing the window. "Do you remember when we went to see the Edward Hopper show?" she asks. "The retrospective? It was a while ago, at the Whitney. Maybe in 'ninety-eight. There was a painting I kept coming back to, with a woman standing naked in a room. She's that model Hopper used over and over, the woman with straight, thick hair that falls down her back, past her shoulders. A sort of auburn color, almost red. She has a strong, fit body. Muscular in a way that qualifies her nakedness—makes her less naked, I mean. As if she's clothed by her musculature. You know how I mean? Like women at the health club. I see them in the sauna, and they're not naked. Not really. Their clothes are off, but they've created a kind of uniform out of their bodies. They're so aggressively trained and toned that they've conformed to an established, standard shape.

"Anyway, I got off track. There's a door in the room, an open door in front of the naked woman—we see her in profile—and outside the door is the sea. Water, anyway, but it seems endless, there isn't any shore. Blue, flat but not glassy flat, little whitecaps all over. The water fills the doorframe. It's surreal. No context. No path to the beach. No transition. Nothing. Just water.

"We argued about that painting. You said it gave you the creeps, and I understood what you meant. I assumed Hopper probably meant it to be a painting of, I don't know, something existential. Dread, I guess. Like Sartre's moments—crises—of nausea, the times when he apprehends *thing*ness, or whatever he called it. Our material and therefore decaying presence. But this wasn't so . . . it wasn't so stark as that. It was scary but softer. More eternal." She stops.

"Go on," Will says to her back.

"Oh, yeah, I almost forgot—here's the weird part. A while ago I tried to look up the painting in a catalog. I wanted to see it. And you know what?"

"What?"

"It doesn't exist."

"What do you mean?"

"I made it up. Not on purpose, obviously, since I didn't know I had, but in my head I put two paintings together—one of a naked woman standing in a room with an unmade bed and an open window, and a different painting of an empty room with the doorway filled by the sea. I don't know if they were maybe hung next to each other or if I just . . . if I joined them in my head, the woman and the water. Because I needed them together like that."

"I'm not sure I get what you mean," Will says. "Sorry. Am I being dumb?"

"Maybe just that the image—the one I invented—explains something to me, represents something I don't have words for. All I'm trying to say is that when I'm in the little boat, my boat, I'm on the water from that painting."

"Are you the woman?" Will asks her. "The woman who isn't naked when she's naked?" Carole makes an ambiguous noise, one that might be taken as assent. *Please can't you just admit you're angry with me?* he's about to say when another thought stops him.

"That's the reason why—that's why you don't let me touch you anymore, right? Because you have to be alone. Alone in your little boat. The mistress of your own pleasure. You have to mete it out, just so, know when they're coming, your orgasms, so they don't capsize you. Tip you out. That way you won't feel more than you can handle. Because if it were my hand instead of yours, my finger, my tongue, then you'd be taken off guard." Carole doesn't answer. "Right?" Will prompts when the silence has grown long enough to make him anxious.

"I don't know," Carole says to the window.

"But you're not willing—you won't go back to the way we were, the way we were before?"

"No." She shakes her head against the pillow. "Not . . . not now."

"Why?"

"I can't."

"But why? Why, if it's not on account of your little boat?"

"Oh, Will," she says. "Does it really matter why? Or matter that much?"

He sighs loudly in the way that irritates her, one of what she calls his accusatory sighs. "It matters to me, Carole," he says.

"I can't right now." Carole turns onto her back and aligns herself on the mattress. She takes the duvet and gives it a smart shake so that it flies up and then settles slowly and evenly over their two bodies. "Not right now, Will," she says.

"But 'right now'—what does 'right now' mean? It's been three years."

"I know. I know."

"You're angry with me. You don't trust me."

"No."

"Then it's about intimacy. About your wanting to maintain some kind of boundary between us. A kind of sexual cordon sanitaire, invisible, inviolable." Will is speaking with his eyes closed. "You don't want me to get that close to you," Will says. "Close enough to engage you."

"No," Carole says. "I don't know."

"Why not?" he asks. "Why don't you know? We're talking about you, after all. If you'd just admit you're angry, then maybe we could get through this."

"It was an accident, Will."

"But feelings aren't rational. By definition they're irrational. So it doesn't matter whether or not it was an accident."

"It does to me." Carole turns to look at him. "Will?" she says. "If you're going to lie awake, why not remember happy things? Like all the Little League stuff you and Luke did together. Even when you weren't coaching, I don't think you missed one game. Or that summer you taught him to bodysurf, remember how excited he was? And that fort thing you guys made. Or the time—"

"You know what?" Will says. "Before, when I still hadn't fallen asleep, I wasn't even thinking about Luke. You always assume that when I can't sleep it's because I'm thinking about him, but I'm not, not all the time. Not one time in ten. I think about work. Sex. The stuff around the house that I never get to, like the rain gutters. I think about the old wiring upstairs in the apartment and how I have to call an electrician to bring it up to code. And about getting the tree surgeon to come back and take down that maple before it comes down and breaks some windows. Tonight, before we made out, I was thinking about the reunion."

"What about it?"

"I don't know. It was strange. Self-conscious. Uncomfortable, I guess."

Carole makes a told-you-so sound, expelling air from her nostrils in something that isn't, quite, a snort. "Of course it was strange and uncomfortable," she says.

"I guess I really expected—a part of me expected Mitch would be there. Did you think he'd show?"

"No," she says after a moment. Carole yawns and turns in his arms. "Will?" she says. "Can we stop talking?"

Will pulls her body into his, burying his face in the damp nape of her neck, inhaling that smell that, only an hour after they've made love, gets him instantly hard: part shampoo, part sweat, part whatever chemical recipe of pheromones and God knows what add up to his wife. He kisses her, and her skin tastes salty. "We could do it again," he says. "How about making out again?"

Why did Mitch contribute a page to the Class of '79's reunion book? Perhaps he'd intended to come and then changed his mind? It wasn't as if he needed it for the sake of PR, and yet his bio, organized like a résumé, highlighted all his aquatic triumphs since graduation. No mention of Will or of their parents, and no photographs of a wife or kids; Mitch is unmarried. Will has wondered if his brother has so thoroughly sublimated his libido that he remains a virgin, his poor nuts routinely immersed in water as much as forty degrees below body temperature. Mitch's testicles would do well to permanently relocate somewhere warm, ascend as far as his kidneys, perhaps, or go south to cruise the Caribbean. But this is Will's fantasy. Despite Mitch's awkwardness with girls, it's likely that he enjoys the usual trappings of celebrity, athlete groupies who find his exploits so sexy that he needn't bother to woo them, or even go through the motions of getting to know them.

There's no picture of Mitch in the reunion book, nothing from a family album anyway, nothing that shows his face, just one of him in the water, as well as a small if not exactly modest reproduction of his *Sports Illustrated* cover, a silhouette that reveals how long his torso is, and how comparatively short his legs, especially if measured against arms with a span of more than six feet. "Who is Mitchell Moreland?"

a cover line demands. Mitch has been profiled in *People* and is a routine feature in *Swimming World, Outside*, and some other environmentally concerned magazine, Will can't remember its name. By swimming distances unimaginable to the average person, and selling his exploits to wealthy sponsors and patrons, his brother has raised hundreds of thousands of dollars for the Sierra Club, Greenpeace, Audubon, Flora and Fauna International, World Wildlife Fund, and others, a long list included in small type at the bottom of the page. He endorses products for the Nature Conservancy, and that share of company profits is distributed among charities that benefit endangered marine life. The swimwear company that sponsored Mitch's "Challenge: Bermuda Triangle" pours funds into not-for-profit organizations whose goal is to slow environmental damage, a useful means of diverting attention from this same company's overseas factories that employ children as young as nine and routinely dump pollutants into the Third World's unprotected waterways. The summary of Will's brother's accomplishments makes Mitch seem as if he's his own invention, which, Will guesses, is not far wrong.

In Will's experience, identical twins are either insufficiently differentiated, with a single personality floating, amoebalike, between two bodies, or each goes to great lengths to separate and prove his ascendancy. Through grade school, Will and Mitch were, in retrospect, too close to know where one brother left off and the other began. Like conjoined twins, they shared a vital organ, not the kind filled with blood, but a sensory apparatus that, without substance, processed and secreted emotion. At least this is what Will remembers. Maybe it's a conceit, something he's invented in the wake of his brother's desertion—a fantasy projected backward onto a past that had never held such extremes of intimacy. Odd that the culture would fixate on traumatic false memories, child abuse, sexual assault. In Will's experience, false memories tend to be happy.

He knew he wasn't always or even usually kind to his brother. He used to bait him, looking for a way to shatter whatever it was that connected them. Sometimes Mitch didn't want to fight, and Will would go at him until it was impossible for him to resist. Until it was a matter of losing face. He'd plant himself between his brother and whatever Mitch was doing, knock the book out of his hands, mess up the carefully organized pieces of the model he was building.

"Quit it," Mitch would say.

"Make me."

Around the house they'd run, Mitch on Will's heels. They were evenly matched—of course they were—so it was Will who determined how many laps. Because once they'd begun, once Mitch had lost control and lunged, someone had to win. Finally, Will would slow and then Mitch would get close enough to trip or kick him, to shove him to the ground.

His brother's fists found their mark with enough force that Will heard them from the inside out; the sound they made traveled through his body and arrived on the wrong side of his eardrums. Blows to his back that were so hard they made him cough. Kidney punches he could taste, like metal, a taste that filled his mouth with saliva. He never cried. A couple of times Mitch had gone on hitting him long enough that he thought he was going to puke, but he didn't cry.

Swimming changed all that. Hard to imagine they'd started out with the same measure of raw physical aptitude, which didn't add up to talent, clearly not. Will had never liked swimming, never wanted—needed—it; Mitch swam like someone who anticipated shipwreck. Didn't seem to take pleasure in dominating his opponents, not that Will could see, anyway. Packed his trophies away like dry goods: necessary, uninteresting.

Before Will had completed the course work required for a doctorate in clinical psychology, Mitch, by then an industrial engineer employed by a cranberry-processing plant in Maine, was swimming up to eight hours a day, Saturday through Wednesday. Swimming a forty-hour week. Having qualified for the 1980 Olympics, Mitch didn't get to go to Moscow. In protest of the Soviet invasion of Afghanistan at the end of 1979, the United States boycotted the games. Mitch claimed he wasn't, like all the other athletes, bitterly disappointed. Naturally, he'd wanted the validation of his place among those who qualified, but he was impatient to get on with his single-minded pursuit of a more lonely and remarkable quest, a prize unavailable to ordinary swimmers, swimmers who tested themselves only in the controlled environment of pools.

Sour grapes, Will suspected, but if he was correct in his conclusion, what began as an unconscious strategy to offset dashed hopes became not only vocation but monomania. Without yet knowing what it was he was training for, Mitch began spending entire days in the frigid water off the coast of Maine, so compulsive that he rarely changed his schedule to accommodate bad weather, so focused that he interpreted the loss of his job as an opportunity to devote all his time to what he'd come to understand was his real, perhaps even ordained, purpose. He'd spent so little of his salary over the previous two years that, as he told their parents, he could finance his own sabbatical. And, as though he were blessed by the gods, or by one god— Neptune—before Mitch had run through his own money, the Bar Harbor Oceanographic Society adopted him as a kind of mascot merman whose remarkable stamina they put to use for fund-raising. Sponsors paid by the minute for Mitch to breaststroke, crawl, and butterfly through the cold Atlantic surf. He was a local hero, and then an international one, turned pro after the '84 Olympics, got his Wheaties box, the athlete's emblem of fame, arguably a prize of greater value than the gold medals that buy it. For its part, Post Cereals used his face in profile, concealing much of the purple stain.

For a decade Mitch kept in touch with Will and their parents. Even when he left Maine for bigger, international seas, he came home for holidays, and he continued to correspond with Will, writing him long letters crammed with details of his training schedules, the various diets he undertook to maintain an ideal percentage of body fat. Then, when Will and Carole married, Mitch took off. He came to the rehearsal dinner, and the stag party that lasted into the early hours of the wedding day, but he didn't show up for the ceremony itself.

Since then, something in his parents' voices, or perhaps it was their expressions, always strikes Will as resigned to Mitch's behavior. If asked to describe this quality, he'd say it's a look he'd expect to see on the faces of people who own shares of a company that has tanked, a bought-high-sold-low-let's-make-the-best-of-this-and-move-on kind of look.

"You didn't get a call from him?" Will asked when he and Carole returned from their honeymoon. "A letter? Anything?"

"Nothing," his father said.

At the rehearsal dinner, Mitch, who was to have been the best man, stood to ring his knife against a glass. Once everyone was quiet, he began a toast. "To my brother—older, wiser, and more accomplished than I . . . by eight minutes."

Even in his drunk and overwrought condition, Will was embarrassed by the rancor he heard in his brother's voice. Mitch continued on in the expectable, formulaic vein and made the usual benedictions—he flattered Carole, called attention to Will's undeserved good fortune, recounted boyhood stories. A transcript would show that his words were unremarkable. But his tone stunned Will, who listened closely, straining to catch a note of affection, but there was none. As his brother spoke, Carole looked into her lap. Will reached for her hand and squeezed it.

"You okay?" he whispered, and she nodded, squeezed his hand in return, her face betraying nothing.

Carole was twenty-four when they met, one of those girls, Will is sure, who always seem older than they are. In Carole's case this was because of her serene and unruffled, *unrufflable*, countenance, a look of such profound calm that she still has no need, ever, to hide her feelings—often they don't register on her face. Certainly, they never distort it. Dark brown hair, a distinct widow's peak that imparts a heart shape to a face with a wide forehead and wider cheekbones, large hazel eyes, a straight nose, and a small, if not exactly pointed, chin. Pretty features, but then, as now, what made Carole beautiful was her expression of tranquillity, a calm that didn't partake of late-twentieth-century multitasking, of frantic jabbering on cell phones while scurrying among sidewalk crowds, grimacing down subway stairs, PalmPilot in one hand, *Financial Times* in the other. No, Carole still seems exactly as she used to, as if she's slipped out from between the pages of a Victorian novel, or out of the frame of a centuries-old painting, any wrinkle of trouble or doubt smoothed away by the writer or artist.

Wherever they went together—often as not those grimy, chaotic places where students gather because beer is cheap—her face was immediately distinct from all those around it. Unflushed. Unadamant. She seemed to have nothing to prove, and this made Will want to prove everything; it made him want to fuck her. And immediately, from the first date, they made love a lot. A lot a lot, to the point where dates weren't going out but staying in, and when the Chinese food arrived, or the pizza, or the delivery boy from the market came with eggs and orange juice, whoever answered the door was wearing only a sheet.

From the neck down Carole was lustful and energetic, but Will wonders if on some level he hasn't always been aiming at her face, driving toward it. Not that he wants to rupture her countenance, not at all. He wants to plunge through it, as one would the reflective surface of water. Sees himself come out on the other side knowing what he didn't before. He is changed, while she, she of course remains the same. Like water, Carole's face, where he enters it, comes back together, bearing no trace of him, no more than a ripple that catches the light and then vanishes.

Maybe Will's obsession with sex, his sexual fantasies about his female patients, aren't the formulaic, knee-jerk symptoms he's assumed they are. Maybe they aren't just a manifestation of his guilt over Luke's drowning and his desire to be punished, revealed as a danger, humiliated by his peers. Maybe they're more than an escape route from his hyper-intellectualizing everything. Couldn't it just as easily be that all that sex represents his search for Carole, for the anger that must be there, deep under her skin and therefore something he has to force his way toward, into? Unconsciously, maybe he feels that her refusing to make love face-to-face means he has to reach her, arrive at her anger, through a surrogate twice removed from Carole herself, aggression displaced first into fantasy and then onto an object other than his wife.

And as long as he's training his reductive, psychoanalytical apparatus on himself, wouldn't it all relate to his unflappable mother? As we children of the twenty-first century know, she's the first woman he wanted to enter, or rather reenter, return, regress, revert, relapse, the first whose mysteries he was determined to plumb, whose body was once and ought still to be his.

At the rehearsal dinner Will saw that at last Mitch had become a man with a measure of poise, an ease with people that success had afforded him. But being able to stand, unflinching, before a crowd had required approval that blurred into awe, a counterweight to all that had preceded it. Will listened carefully to his brother's comments, a retrospective that included their years together at camp, their first jobs, and first girlfriends. *Girlfriends*—that word was a surprise. Will was sure Mitch had never had one. Well, perhaps in the context of a twin brother's imminent wedding, he'd needed to invent a romantic history.

Effective therapy for *Nevus flammeus* should be initiated in early childhood, because with time, port-wine stains can darken and thicken, acquiring a pebbly texture. Among birthmarks, they aren't accidents of pigment but vascular abnormalities that affect three of every thousand people. Their cause is unknown; there's no genetic predisposition for these spreading patches of malformed, dilated blood vessels, so close to the surface of the skin that they color it pink or red or, as in Mitch's case, purple.

Used as Will was to his brother's face, it scared him when they were kids. Not during the day when he could see it, but the idea of it would take hold of him at night. In the dark he couldn't stop seeing it grow until it had covered his brother, bled over the beds and into the shadows, splattered the walls and run down the stairs. He'd lie still as a stone, too frightened to go to their parents or even to call out to them. In the morning—he knew this, in his fear he could see it— their house and everything in it, and everyone, their neighborhood, the used-to-be-blue sky, it would all be stained and ruined, and who could stop a thing like that?

Will remembers their parents as having been curiously insensitive about Mitch's disfigurement and can imagine the excuses they might have made about doing nothing in response to the stain, the wound, as he used to think of it, unable to see it as skin-deep. Treatments that existed in the sixties were imperfect. Without the ability to fine-tune or pulse the beam, as doctors can today, lasers were either ineffective or left burn scars. In any case, the cost of what an insurance company would consider an elective, cosmetic procedure was prohibitive; it wasn't as if Mitch were physically endangered by the birthmark.

Although he might have been. Port-wine stains such as Mitch's, which involve the eyelids and forehead, are associated with Sturge-Weber syndrome, which affects vascular tissue in the brain and causes seizures and learning disabilities. But Will doesn't believe their pediatrician entertained such a possibility, if he even knew of it. "Don't borrow trouble," was Dr. Aldrich's favorite expression. He dismissed any fever below 104, interpreted all stomachaches as attempts at truancy, and, most infamously, misdiagnosed a case of appendicitis as stage fright precipitated by the 1965 Christmas pageant. Will and Mitch visited his cluttered office once each year, where they were weighed and measured and where Dr. Aldrich would take Mitch's face in his hands and look at it closely. "Doesn't hurt, does it, Mitchell?" he'd ask, and Mitch would shake his head.

"Not like he's a girl," he'd say to their mother. "If he was, I'd send you to the skin man up in Albany."

Mitch never complained. It was Will who removed the mirror from the back of the closet door in the room they shared, no longer able to stand the sight of his brother's circuitous passage around beds and behind chairs, his face averted from the sight of itself.

According to *Swimming World*, Mitch has participated in scientific studies of cold-water endurance, trials that require him to spend hours in tanks of frigid water, wearing only a swimsuit, his temperature monitored by a "rectal probe." He maintains nearly normal core body temperatures in water that, after several hours, would render the average person hypothermic to the point of shivering incoherence, even cardiac arrest. He's swum in water just a few degrees above freezing and lost remarkably little body heat. So far, the doctors who have studied Mitch don't know what circulatory adaptation allows this, but one researcher's hypothesis is that whatever ontogenic glitch caused the vascular abnormality that resulted in his *Nevus flammeus* is linked somehow to his freakish ability to swim for many hours, even days, in cold water, protected by nothing more than a Speedo, goggles, his own body fat, and a layer of petroleum jelly. If this is true, then Mitch's tragic flaw—his heroic strength that is also a mortal weakness—is an accident not so much of character as of biology.

Twinship was a torment. Will can't remember a time when he wasn't aware of Mitch's discomfort, sometimes even misery, as well as his own. How could it have been otherwise? Mitch could always see how he might look if unmarked, and Will knew what it would be to have his face disfigured. To be de-faced. The birthmark denied them the fun of pranks based on mistaken identity, and saved them the insult of not being recognized as individuals. "War Paint," they called Mitch at school, and "Gobbo," and then, finally, the name that stuck—"Africa."

Irresistible, because there was nothing fanciful about the similarity between the coastline of the continent and the outline of Mitch's port-wine stain. Certain borders, the Atlantic coast of Namibia and South Africa especially, seemed to have been traced onto his face. Cape Town marked the faint cleft in his chin; Angola blanketed his nose. His right eye was at sea, the left was the Democratic Republic of the Congo. His left temple was as pale as Will's, his right was Ethiopia. The purple stain covered 60 percent of his face, leaving only his left ear, eye, cheek, and the left half of his nose and chin un-touched.

It was arresting, Mitch's face. A person of broad and sophisticated taste might even call it beautiful, in that beauty can terrify and ac-cuse.

There was one teacher who didn't permit Mitch's classmates to tease him, but this didn't endear him to Will's brother. Any witness to his plight made Mitch that much less able to pretend nothing was happening. With his flushed face and ill-kempt black suits, Mr. Slaughter might have been a drunk, although none of his students understood this at the time. From U.S. History—the course he'd been hired to teach—Mr. Slaughter strayed east to Europe, Palestine, India, Asia, and beyond, circling the globe until he'd crossed the Pacific and landed back on native soil. He lectured on all topics with equal fervor, never referring to the stack of note cards he held in his hands. Every other Friday he handed out lined paper, and when all the class was sitting at attention, eyes on him, he bowed theatrically—sometimes he did a Shakespearean flourish, sweeping an imaginary hat through the air—and then wrote a date on the blackboard. 1862, 1884, 1918. The test was to summarize what was happening all over the globe during that particular year, old world and new: Europe, Asia, and Africa, the Americas, Australia, India, Russia, Greenland—everywhere.

Not surprisingly, no one succeeded at these tests. No one but Mitch. He earned the one A among all the other C's and D's. Once, to honor his achievement, Mr. Slaughter read Mitch's answer aloud, and what he read wasn't so much an essay as an associative string of facts, some connections apparent, some not, each detail astonishing for its accuracy, and the accretion of so many of them more surprising still. At home Mitch was in the habit of reading the *Encyclopaedia Britannica* for entertainment; without trying he'd memorized names and dates that he recycled into his answer. When Mr. Slaughter came to the last line of Mitch's test, he held it up so that everyone could see the large letter *A* on the top of the first page.

At the ceremony marking the class of 1975's graduation from Ravena High, Mr. Slaughter presented Will's brother with a leather-bound book of his tests, arranged chronologically, about two hundred pages' worth of Mitch's hurried block printing, the pressure of his pen so intense that he could use only one side of a sheet of paper. The cover was embossed with gold letters. "The History of the Modern World" by Mitchell Moreland, it read.

"Can I have this?" Will asked his mother when he found it on a shelf in the bedroom he'd once shared with his brother. It was a guest room now; flowered wallpaper covered over the scuffs and grime of boyhood; the *Apollo 11* decals had been razored from the window panes long ago; but the bookshelf remained, and on it the books.

"What is it?" Will's mother asked, taking it from his hands. She sat at the breakfast table and paged through a few tests. "I suppose," she said, closing the cover. "What for?"

Will shrugged, and she didn't press him for what he wouldn't have admitted—that he was going to read it for clues. Somewhere, embedded in the text, there must be some tiny something that Will's training would allow him to pick out and deconstruct, an answer to the riddle of Mitch that Mitch's own unconscious had hidden among references to war and revolution, the invention of the cotton gin, the birth of Mozart, Dr. Livingstone's discovery of Victoria Falls.

There was no such answer, but Will looked for it anyway, wondering if, in the end, his vocation was going to add up to anything more, really, than his ongoing attempt to understand his brother and the way an accident of biology might form—deform—character. 1830, 1843, 1878, 1902 . . . He combed through one year after another, and when he was done he put the book on the table by his side of the bed, not on top but at the bottom of the pile of things he never gets around to reading. Every so often he still pulls it out, but he's found he can't look at it for long without the risk of becoming ensnared in an hours-long spasm of searching through whatever documents he has of his past—snapshots, letters, his own juvenile diaries that embarrass and pain him, and a lot of other detritus packed in boxes but not put far enough away. All of it has the ability to leave him with one of those headachy hangovers peculiar to a nostalgic wallow, and—depending on how long it's been since he's suffered one of these—he usually replaces Mitch's tome within a few minutes of looking inside, sometimes before he's even opened the cover.

N umber thirty-eight," says the girl with the bitten fingernails. "Very old-school, very houndstooth tweedy. Like, the leather patches on the elbows of his jacket appear to be genuine, as if it didn't come like that but his wife sewed them on for real after he wore holes in his sleeves. He's so central casting that it's actually cute in a kind of avuncular way. I mean, maybe less than sexy to most girls and even a little too Mr. Chipsy for me, but as we've established, I'm turned on by the musty, old, academic type. Even the slightly askew bow tie does it for me. Still, I'm worrying because he's onto his third glass of pinot noir and, well, you know . . ."

"The faculty club serves alcohol?" Will says, intentionally missing his cue.

"Faculty *house*. Yeah. In the fourth-floor dining room. Elsewhere, administration or whoever turns a blind eye on professors going to the bar and buying drinks to carry back to wherever. Besides, it's not as if I'm underage."

"No, I was just—"

"*Anyway*, so I'm counting glasses of wine, and by the time he orders a third, I'm thinking erectile dysfunction, and I start teasing him a little. I say, I can't remember what exactly, something to the effect that so handsome and distinguished a scholar shouldn't be drinking alone. Or maybe I called him a gentleman and a scholar. Whatever I say, it's direct and it's also kinda generic, you know, not too personal, so that if I've, like, miscalculated—which hasn't ever happened, FYI—but if I did, and he's going to get all offended, I haven't compromised myself by saying something too sort of overt. But he's not offended. Not at all. The point is, I've put out minimal effort and already he's very friendly, very chatty, very ha-ha-ha. By now we're close to closing, and remember, this is the faculty house we're talking about, it's not exactly your happening venue. Anyone who has, like, a life is pursuing it elsewhere. Since he's the only diner left in the room, he says, why don't I sit down, I must be tired, no? Maybe I'd like a piece of cake. I can bring it along with his dessert. So I'm like, sure, that'd be nice, and he asks what's best on the dessert menu, and I say mud pie, and he says too rich, so I say apple brown Betty, and he says too sweet. Pear tarts are not his cup of tea. By now I'm wondering, did I go overboard this time? Maybe he's not just older but *old*, and has to watch his cholesterol or his gallbladder or whatever, because now that I'm thinking about it, he did order an inauspiciously Spartan entrée. Not that I'd imagined he was some sort of sybarite epicure, because anyone of, like, gustatory sophistication would sooner suck down a platter of Chicken McNuggets than a faculty house dinner, but I am hoping for a person of appetite because, you know, sex and food, people who like one usually like the other, and this guy's chosen a meal conceived by a, like, frigid nun—filet of sole without any sauce, meunière, tartar, whatever, only lemon. And on the side a dry, make that desiccated, baked potato, and he didn't touch the dish of creamed onions that automatically comes with everything; you can't get rid of them for some reason.

"So, how about sorbet, I ask, and he says too cold. Pecan pie? Too sweet. So, now that we've established that everything's too this too that, I say, very perceptive here, 'Maybe you don't want dessert?' and he says yes, I'm right, just bring him a cappuccino—which, by the way, suck big-time at the faculty house, I don't know why; it's not exactly rocket science, making coffee. Starbucks should bring in a franchise, since there isn't one in a radius of, like, three feet. Anyway, I bring him one, and another for myself, and neither of us mention the fact that it tastes like shit. He drinks his; I pretend to drink mine."

The girl pauses and, when Will doesn't speak, goes on with her story. "By now we've established that he's a professor of Italian Renaissance architecture, and we've tried to move beyond our own 'disciplines,' as he calls them, to an appreciation of each other's, and while he's asking have I seen the Brunelleschi chapel or the *baldochino* or the—whatever it is, it begins with a *B*—while he's asking, I'm making my standard, hello-nice-to-meet-you gesture, surfing one stockinged foot up his inseam, and when I get there, guess what? He's not fifty, not downtown he isn't. Downtown he's maybe twenty, his hard-on is *hard*. So hard I'm thinking, like, whoa, what's this, a strapon? You know, like a fake one? And my next thought is that it may be cliché but it might also be true that many professors are pedophiles. I mean, why else settle for all that work, plus the academic rat-fuck for tenure, and then there's the crummy salary? Intellectual passion? Maybe. But, come on, there have to be perks. Not that I'm exactly a child, or even underage, but institutionally speaking, we could call me the child whereas he's, um, what's it called, in loco parentis?

"The professor stops talking as my foot starts rubbing, and we have a bit of an uncomfortable moment, and guess what? Not a strapon. A palpable retreat from high-impact, crash-dummy rubber to, say, Dr. Scholl's gel arch supports, but it's temporary, nothing so much as a setback. In a minute we're back to playing chicken, which apparently neither of us is. Mr. Crash Dummy is back in the game."

Will opens the imaginary bag of ice he's been holding in his lap, turns it over and pours ten pounds of cubes directly onto his unsheathed and unsuspecting penis, willing it to freeze in mid-tumescence.

"'Have you been keeping up with the film series at the Thalia?' he inquires, Professor Suave—he has to have said this line about a gazillion times—and I answer, quite on cue and even truthfully, 'Berlin Alexanderplatz?' I nod, he nods, we say incisive things about Mr. Fass-binder and other of our favorite self-destructive artistic geniuses. It's a grim little game, the pathetic penny-ante one-upmanship of academe. They say dentists are more likely to commit suicide than people in any other profession, but I dunno, this whoever-commands-the-most-rarefied-cultural-references-wins audition makes me feel like sawing at my wrist with a steak knife. But finally it's over, he wins by two Japanese directors and a Maori poet no one's ever heard of—he could have made him up for all I know—and goes off to pay, while I head for the lockers to change out of my waitress costume. Which, by the way, is not so much Howard Johnson's as it is French Maid, a genuine asset as far as my motives are concerned, and I guess kind of unex-pected in an institutional setting. I mean, we're not talking Hooters, but it does have that naughty, come-hither look. Still, off it goes, except for the tights. I've brought an alluring après-work outfit, a crotch duster, meaning microminiskirt, plus a sweater I've had since ninth grade, a little short so there's navel-ring disclosure, and a redder-than-red swing coat for the sake of high visibility plus mod-esty while walking in dark alleys.

"The too-brilliant-to-live Fassbinder is playing not far from the faculty house. The Thalia's maybe three quarters of a mile the safe way, a little less if you're late and willing to risk your life for culture. And, guess what, Mr. Crash Dummy is wild for culture, can't get enough stimulation, and the shortcut offers a perfect opportunity for the professor to coax Little Red off the primrose path and into the woods. We cross over the green in front of the library, and, big surprise, Professor Hard-on pushes me against what's holding up some giant dead bronze guy for some very eager and, I have to say, clumsy wet kissing before we move on to this sinister little breezeway near the bookstore. Then it's him leaning against a wall and me on my knees eye-to-eye with his trouser button. How I get there is one of those delicate, wordless negotiations, his hands on my shoulders exerting a faint but not ambiguous pressure, me responding with a gradual, is-this-where-we're-going descent.

"Once I'm where he wants me, everything accelerates. A little friendly attention, and Mr. Crash Dummy speeds through the intersection and whams into the back of my throat. A minor episode of gagging on my part, as, having expected a, like, five- or six-second so-nice-to-meet-you-won't-you-come-in prelude, I've been taken off guard by his impetuousness, but I ignore the fact that I can taste pizza dating back to dinner at six and regain my composure to deliver a perfectly calibrated act of fellatio, meaning great rather than good, great rather than pro forma, a few little touches that would imply erotic creativity plus generosity. Then I stand up, leaving Mr. Crash in the cold autumn wind. 'How about shelter?' I ask, not having to feign eagerness. Forget breezeway, it's 'a nipping and an eager air' tearing at my skirt—that's Shakespeare for arctic blast, if you didn't know. Not only am I just about frozen, with aching knees to boot, but I really want to fuck him, I'm no-kidding-around horny. But he can't take me to his place because—well, just because. Why waste time enumerating complications? But, as his office is on a newly refurbished floor of Barnard Hall, perhaps I'd like to see an etching or a Xerox machine or a box of paper clips?

"We scurry off through Low Plaza, me hoping to arrive before my snatch, like, grows stalactites. He fumbles the electronic key, the regular key, the light switch, the security code. Whatever he can get wrong, he does—testosterone impairing cognitive function, no doubt—and the department phone starts to ring. Good evening, sir, campus police. Would you be so kind as to give us the password? Which, of course, the professor has forgotten, if he ever knew it, that is—his mind was meant for better things—so now he's scrabbling around in the bottom of his briefcase for whatever matchbook or gum wrapper on which he's inscribed the code word or whatever, since the alarm did go off at the station and we wouldn't want to trouble an officer on a Friday night when countless degenerate undergrads are jitterbugging naked in adults-only clubs or topping off their iPods with stolen music or snorting their dead grannies' OxyContin or whatever it is they do for entertainment.

"When he finally finds it, the password is, get this, 'Lily Bart.' Kind of a nice touch, I think at first. Later, lying in my own little bed and reviewing the evening's successes, I remember the plot of *House of Mirth* and think, not so nice after all. I mean, is this how it goes: Barnard Hall faculty calls a meeting and decide that the open sesame for their building should be a reference to illicit and, by the way, fatal promiscuity?

"Anyway, too late for regrets. His office is"—the girl looks around at Will's walls and furniture—"I guess it's well appointed, sort of contemporary intellectual, like yours. Black and beige and chrome, and there's some framed Renaissance print thing on the wall." Her tongue appears and explores her lower lip with seeming interest. Will says nothing, recrosses his legs to adjust his thawed erection.

"We don't undress, not all the way. I peel off my tights, he drops his tweedy trousers. And, I can't believe it, but he is actually, really and truly wearing sock garters. I mean, wow. They almost turn me on, that's how gross they are, black and stretchy and, well, anyway, once I get past the shock, we go at it, we do it three ways. One, standing at his desk, my ass on his blotter, legs around his waist. Seems it's inevitable whenever there's a desk around—you do end up taking cues from the office environment. Two, on the brand-new, itchy, Scotchgarded, stain-and-spooge-repellent, blue-gray institutional carpet. I'm the bottom and it's missionary, so his knees and my ass are getting, like, third-degree carpet burns. Three, I'm on top, standard, liberated, attuned-to-her-physical-self female taking advantage of her partner's still rock-hard cock. Altogether I get off about four times: once on the desk, once on my back, then twice astride before I let him have his.

"He's so close, it's one, two, three thrusts, and that's it. He moans, closes his eyes, I stand up and note with satisfaction that when we did it on the desk I left a big stain of squat juice on his blotter. I do not, do not over my dead body, let myself look at him naked and flaccid and wearing sock garters. This, I know, would make me feel worse than desperate; the whole world and all its nearly four billion human occupants would somehow be implicated by the sight of them. It would be one of those unfortunate moments when I have an unanticipated and very much unwanted awakening to how pathetic and ridiculous and indefensible it is to be an example of this disgusting species."

"Why?"

"Why?"

"Yes," Will says. "Why will seeing the sock garters of an Italian Renaissance architecture professor reveal the pathetic and indefensible ridiculousness of being human?"

"You can't be serious."

"I am serious."

"Do you wear sock garters? Tell me you don't. If you do, you're the one who should be having your head examined."

Will says nothing. Within the parameters of this dialogue he wears whatever she thinks he does.

"Well, you've, like, seen them, right? You do know what they look like?"

He nods.

"So, picture these ultra-ultra-white legs with not so much as one hair because, well, I guess because it all gets, like, rubbed off by his pants or something—or maybe it's his age—and on his glabrous old shins are these pervy black socks that are kept up without a sag or wrinkle by sock garters. *Glabrous* is a good word, don't you think?" She looks at Will pointedly.

"Very descriptive."

"Yeah. I looked it up in the *OED* to be sure it was the one I wanted." She smiles at him.

"You looked up *glabrous* before you came here today?"

The girl nods, still smiling. "When I was rehearsing the story for you."

Will folds his hands on his desk. "This is a story you rehearsed for today's session?"

"Story as in narrative, not make-believe. Swear to God." She holds up her right hand, puts her left on an imaginary Bible.

"Why would you need to rehearse?"

"I'm shy."

Will lets this one go and watches while she bites her nail, taking the finger out of her mouth, examining the damage, putting it back in for another leisurely go before continuing.

"What I've described doesn't make you feel suicidal?" she demands. "Picturing that? Shiny old shins dressed up in serial-killer socks and garters?"

"No."

"Well, okay. Fine. Whatever. There's stuff like sock garters and toupées that don't match the person's actual hair color that are just too depressing."

"Why is that?"

"Because they are! Why do you pretend to be stupid!"

"I—"

"In fact, his sock garters are so inclined to inspire suicidal ideation that I ask him to do me a favor, and he says what, and I say take me to the student center and give it to me in a stall. He sits up, checks Mr. Crash to see he's not all gummy with spooge. 'In a stall?' he says, looking more than willing.

"'Yeah,' I say, 'like the women's room, or the men's, I don't care— just so it's public.'" The girl stops talking. "What are you writing down?" she demands when she sees Will noting her use of the words *suicidal ideation*, a term that only someone with experience of psychiatric texts or treatment might use. She sighs dramatically when he doesn't reply, returns to her story.

"'That would be the lavatory in the basement under Kent—the Starr Library,' he says, and I'm like, 'Why there?' 'Because it's open until midnight and guaranteed to be deserted,' he says. 'Stalls for you. Safety for me.' I tell him I prefer the student center. He shakes his head. 'Student center no, Starr Library yes. Take it or leave it.'

"I take it. We pull up our scanties and head over to Kent. I don't know if you remember last Friday, but like, wow, a record low for November fourth. I'm getting head-to-toe frostbite, and it's not as if I'm a girl who wears sensible shoes, the soles are, like, nonexistent. Anyway, we arrive and, as promised, the library is open and empty. Except for the librarian, who's in a vertical coma of boredom, basically, and the bathroom downstairs is suitably vile. Shocking, really, considering tuition, but a place to keep in mind for the future.

"I don't know what it is, my inner gay man maybe, but I am majorly turned on by public toilets—I love metal stall doors with the enamel chipping off the corners, a little rust, dirty words that won't scrub off—you can see where the poor janitor has scrubbed the thing dull trying to get *cunt* or whatever off the damn door, but it's there forever. Words like that—they have a life of their own, don't you think? Also, I love the fluorescent light and even that gross smell of disinfectant. I get all itchy and sex-starved just walking into a public *loo*. Which is what my mother calls it in certain company. Unbelievably pretentious and irritating. I mean, as if! She's about as British as Oprah." The girl checks her watch and buttons her coat.

"It unfolds according to my script: inside the stall, up against the door so the whole thing kind of squeaks and moves, and despite being taller than me and not so young that I can assume buff thigh muscles, Mr. Italian Renaissance is very good on the tricky upthrust. It only takes a few minutes for us both to get off. No sock garters in view, praise the Lord, so we end on a good note. Polite parting in the corridor, a handshake—quite weird—and we're off in opposite directions."

"Weird?" Will says.

"Don't you think?" She stands and swings her backpack up onto one shoulder. "I mean, we've had sex, what, four times in an hour—thrice in his office and once in the lavatory—and he's holding out his hand to shake mine like we've just been introduced at some dread sherry-and-cheese mixer." She approaches the door—it's exactly ten of three—and pauses, apparently struggling with the knob. "Do you mind?" she says. "I'm having this, like, carpal tunnel flare-up."

Will stands to open the door, notebook casually (he hopes, dear God, he hopes) hiding his erection, the fact of it preoccupying him enough that he doesn't see what's coming. Like a cartoon character who steps into the noose attached to a bent-over sapling, *zoing*, he's flying in the air—What's up? What's down?—Will is without a clue.

She's got him with his back to his office door, a hand on either side of his face, her tongue deep in his mouth. He makes an ineffective noise, something between a gargle and a moan, a noise intended as protest but received as encouragement. The tongue does a little somersault, and one hand leaves his cheek, drops down to his fly.

"I thought you'd like that story," she says, her breath warm on his face and smelling like her tongue tastes, of caramel or toffee, something sugary. She rubs him harder, seals his mouth with hers so he can't respond. But what was he going to say? Already he's forgotten. After months of panic over his own barely controlled lust, he's been—he's *being*—jumped by a patient, forced up against his own door, his tongue sucked so hard that it aches at the root, his cock very aware of each one of her moving fingers.

He's always loved dreams—his own, other people's. With respect to analysis, they're invaluable, like having a wiretap on someone's soul. Even the most cryptic yield to examination, and a mere fragment can get a session going. But, as transparent as Will finds his patients' dreams, suddenly he's become clumsy, even dim-witted, with respect to his own. Take the one he had last night, when at last he fell asleep, having told Carole what had happened with the girl without managing to communicate what really happened, which was not that a patient had pulled some highly inappropriate stunt but that he'd been aroused by it.

He'd refused himself the relief of masturbating to dismiss the erection that popped up shortly after he'd made love with Carole—his traitorous cock stirring even before she fell asleep—because there was no way he could beat off without again reviewing the kiss and the feeling of the girl's avid fingers, their tips that seem less chewed now than burned by corrupt explorations. His memory of what she'd done, what he'd allowed her to do, was—*is*—all too pungent: three parts horror, say, to one part intoxication, a scene highlighted as if by a mental klieg light, a thousand watts of attention issuing from some dark corner of his head, trained on the two of them at the door. Familiar clichés apply: she's caught red-handed, he with his pants down.

When he woke from the nightmare—at least he doesn't have to deal with sweet dreams following upon guilty fantasies—he remembered it in detail. Commented to himself that it was obvious, almost formulaic. But then he couldn't interpret it. The longer he tried, the slipperier it grew, until now he finds it's acquired the quality of a koan, a riddle that confounds as much as it compels.

In the dream, he's engaged a third party, an agent to whom he entrusts a sum of money to hire a private investigator. This detective's assignment is to tail Will—Will himself is the object of the hunt—and the detective is to use whatever powers of surveillance are required to mark Will's passage through each day. Spy cameras, hidden mikes, infrared periscopes—the man is outfitted with all the paraphernalia of male paranoia, an array of absurdly compact devices like those that saturate a James Bond movie: potent, shiny, and impossible.

The dream detective makes notes and tapes and photographs. He captures Will as he sleeps, showers, works, as he has sex with his wife and, as this is a dream, with other women as well. When the report comes back, when Will is shown the evidence collected against him, he's shocked by what he sees.

The detective's photographs and videotapes have an unimpeachable authority. Black-and-white, blurred, grainy, they look illicit, as one expects of images that have been snatched. Will stares at them in loathing. Despite the snow on the video monitor, and despite interfering, vertical lines—as if all the action unfolds in a jail cell—Will sees that it is, in fact, his face that leers at him, his features twisted with malevolence. But can this really be how he appears to other people? The man's face is his own, but the sinister expression, the animosity, even hatred, the intent to wreak havoc: it's a person he can look at for only so long.

The pictures frighten and disgust him; he wants to destroy them;

yet he cannot deny that they render the very thing he's paid to be shown: a monstrous and unredeemable someone who must lurk within him, but whom he couldn't find without the help of a private eye.

It's only after he's fully awake, after he's been awake long enough to have left behind the murk of his unconscious, that Will realizes the face in the dream was never more than half revealed. In every image, a dark swath has fallen across the man's features, leaving the right half of his face black. Shadowed, Will assumed in the dream, but perhaps all along the man in the pictures, the man the detective trailed, was the wrong man.

Not Will. Mitch.

Beside Will, Carole sleeps. It's not yet light outside. She's kicked the covers off and is facedown with her nightgown bunched up around her waist, arms and legs spread, showing him more than enough of herself to summon an erection. Apparently, nothing can kill off lust, not his lust. It's always there, undeterred by illness or by lack of sleep, by mourning, by nightmares. And Carole has an appealing butt, plump and defiant, the arrival of middle age halted with— what else?—yoga. Sometimes he feels like he sees it more often than he sees the rest of her.

Not looking into each other's eyes: wasn't this one of the accommodations they made after Luke died, a tacit one? How could they have risked the chance of recognizing it: the other's anguish? But because it had been an unspoken adjustment, not so much a decision as a reflex, they'd never undone it. Just as no one said *let's*, neither has either of them said *it's time we stopped*.

It used to be that Will considered himself among the self-aware, but something—what?—seems to have taken away some essential knowledge he had of himself, his true character. As if there exists a key—Will's key—to his own psyche, a key he once owned and now has lost. He's misplaced it, or someone has taken it. Is that even possible?

He tries the idea out on Daniel. "Does that make sense?" he asks, and receives the standard analytic riposte.

"It only matters if it makes sense to you." Daniel raises his eyebrows, and Will, reading the expression as a request that he continue, goes on talking.

"Well, there are two possibilities—two that I see. Two points at which I might have, I don't know, lost touch with myself, I guess. First, my brother's disappearance, which, since the reunion, has taken on some new weight of significance. I don't know why. But it feels even more personal than it used to. His rejection or abandonment or whatever you want to call it.

"And second, I'm guessing the loss of Luke, also in the past, but the recent past, relatively speaking. I mean, I didn't even feel as if I'd woken up, as if I were genuinely conscious and aware of my surroundings, until a year or so afterward. And he was my son. Myself projected into the future. Not finite. At least not in any way I had to admit. Because in the natural order of things I would die first. His death would never exist for me. It wouldn't be possible to be abandoned by my child, the person in whom I placed my essential self."

"Without your son you discover mortality? Your mortality?"

Will stands up. He shoves his hands in his pockets and looks at the ceiling and then back at Daniel. "Are you ridiculing me?" he asks.

"Not at all." Daniel shakes his head. "Do you think what you've said is ridiculous?"

"No. But I do find it banal. And I wasn't talking about mortality. At least I don't think I was. Certainly, it's a topic that preoccupies me, but just then I was talking about how I'd managed to lose touch with myself."

"Why banal?"

Will sits back down. "Isn't this the crisis of faith I was supposed to have as a kid, when my dog died? The standard-issue if-my-dog-died-there-is-no-God crisis?"

"Who said anything about God?"

Will laughs, at himself, shakes his head. "Touché. I think it must have been me, the guy with the God problem."

Daniel raises his eyebrows, folds his hands on his desk. Hanging on the wall behind him are so many framed diplomas and citations that he has no more space to put any of the newer ones. Instead, he opens old frames and slips one in front of another so that in a few cases two sets of words appear, ghostly writing from the document on the bottom showing through the paper of the one above.

"Forget the key. The idea of a key or something to unlock me. My secret self. I want to come at this a different way. The context for the dream is, I think, my continuing to dwell on the reunion." *The girl, the girl,* Will prompts himself, *tell him what happened with the girl.* But he goes on without mentioning what he was stewing about when he fell asleep. "The context aside from my knowing we would be meeting today, that is. Because I realize that for the last few weeks I've been remembering what I dream the night before I see you, so I can bring it here, like a cat with a dead bird."

Daniel raises one hand, a signal for Will to stop, but his innate politeness makes it a slightly deferential gesture, tentative, like an uncertain student's rather than the person whose name is presented in all those frames above his chair. "You haven't forgotten to be suspicious of those dreams?" he asks.

"Because of the likelihood of their being a defense?"

Now both of Daniel's hands are in the air, palms up and empty. "What might we talk about if we weren't busy deconstructing your dream?"

Will starts to laugh. "Maybe Carole's right. Maybe analysis does depend on masochism."

"Self-absorption."

"Was that the word she used?"

"I think so," Daniel says. "I could look it up."

In years past, before Daniel's wife died, the four of them—Will, Carole, Daniel, and Jessica—often ate out together, arguing companionably around the window table of a Korean barbecue restaurant, a place none of them had liked particularly but that no one disliked enough to sacrifice the ritual aspect of gathering around the same table time after time. They always shared a couple of bottles of wine, and if anyone said something Daniel found interesting or amusing, he'd inscribe it in a notebook he used for that purpose.

Will shrugs. "Don't bother. The part I liked was her idea that psychoanalysis should adopt a symbol like that used by physicians. You remember, instead of two snakes coiling around a sword, there would be only one, swallowing its own tail."

"Right," Daniel says, and he laughs. "She drew a picture for me. In my journal."

"Anyway," Will says, "admittedly, the reunion is over and done with. Well, no, not done with, actually, because it's had so long a fallout. Subjected me to what felt like an interrogation. Which was the reason Carole refused to go, and why she didn't want me to go, because of all the questions people were bound to ask. I'd have to talk about Mitch and about Luke. Obvious, right, but I didn't see it coming. I never anticipated it myself, and whatever Carole said, I didn't hear. In fact I was so deliberately unprepared for what happened that I find myself wondering if my being interrogated wasn't the point. Wasn't what I wanted, deep down.

"Of course, once I'd seen Elizabeth's page and read her bio, I did want to ask her about her daughter. And I certainly seem to have been talking from the depths of some unconscious sinkhole when I embarked on that unfortunate line of inquiry. But way before that, as far back as last winter, when the reunion was just an idea rather than a collection of particular individuals, I wonder if I wasn't planning to use it as a . . . a . . . I was going to say crowbar, but a better metaphor would be solvent. If I hadn't wanted, unconsciously, to immerse myself in an environment that would have a caustic effect on whatever defenses I'd built around my psyche, a solvent that would eat away at them and force me to deal with what I've hidden from myself. Issues that need to be examined—or maybe just acknowledged—but that I wasn't ready to approach before now.

"And then in reaction to this—this interrogation or crowbar or solvent or whatever I'm calling what I'm applying to my defenses—I take on too many patients, I run myself ragged chasing down other people's problems, because I'm fearful of my own. Part of me prefers being defended. So I'm conflicted, I'm ambivalent, unresolved conflicts are filling me with anxiety. Anxiety I try to keep at bay with obsessive sex fantasies. Does that make sense?" Will sees Daniel's expression and answers his own question. "Yes," he says, "it does. It does make sense to me."

Daniel smiles. "Well, your interpretation would satisfy my favorite analytic axiom, one I know you must be sick of hearing, that the unconscious . . ." He leaves it to Will to finish the thought.

"Is always on your side," Will says. "My side, in this case."

"Exactly," Daniel says. "I'm afraid you don't really need me, Will. I'm just an old dog whose tricks you already know."

"No, no. I do need you. I need you because it isn't until I'm sitting before you, determined not to disappoint whatever faith you may have in me, that I see myself at all."

The two men are silent until Daniel speaks. "What are you feeling, Will?" he says.

"Not much."

"Care to guess why that might be?"

Will, who is leaning forward with his elbows on his knees, drops his face in his hands. "I imagine," he says without looking up, "that I've successfully protected myself—defended myself—from my feelings by being so hyperanalytical, so . . . so cerebral, in reference to my defenses."

Daniel nods. "You're a good psychoanalyst," he says.

"And a crummy patient." Will looks up. "But I still don't think I'm wrong."

W ill and his father are at La Luncheonette, a little bistro all the way over on the West Side.
From where he's sitting, Will can see the red stack of a barge moving
slowly up the Hudson through a gray-green slice of the river. "So,
how's your love life?" Will asks his dad.

"Not bad. Yours?"

"Never mind. You're the art-world ingénue having an affair with
his wealthy patroness." His father smiles, a little wearily, Will thinks.

"Considering my advanced age and modest circumstances, I
think it's going well enough. At least my wealthy patroness hasn't
voiced any complaints." He holds up one hand to flag down the waitress, a Vietnamese no older than eighteen and very beautiful, her
shining hair gathered into a chignon. It's the sort of seemingly artless
arrangement of hair that might take a woman hours to pull off; in the
case of this girl, Will would bet she really has just slipped down the
wine-cellar stairs for a moment, twisted it into a coil, and skewered it
with a pencil so that it remains there, at the nape of her neck. The
few strands that have escaped look like a painter's finishing touch,
highlighting her cheekbones and calling attention to the line of her
jaw.

"Not ready to order," his father says, "just wanted to see you
close up."

Will braces himself for a tart response, almost closing his eyes so he doesn't have to see his father being rebuffed, but instead, the girl beams at him. She ducks her head so close to his that for a second Will thinks she's going to kiss him.

"*Bonjour, mon ami intéressant,*" she says.

"What did she call you?" Will watches the girl go to the bar for the glass of water his father asked for.

"Nothing scandalous. Her interesting friend, that's all. I eat here every so often."

Will raises his eyebrows; his father shrugs.

"Apparently you've reached the age where you can get away with anything," Will says.

"We'll see." His father picks up his knife and slips its blade between the uneven tines of his fork, straightening them by leveraging one against another. When he's satisfied that the job is done, he polishes the fork on his napkin and replaces it on the table. "We'll see what I can get away with," he says.

"You make it sound as if you're about to be subjected to a test of your not inconsiderable charm."

His father smiles and takes a sip from the water the waitress has put before him. "Charlotte's husband showed up last week."

"I didn't even know she was married."

"I did. But the way she told it, she made it sound like a nonissue. Said they hadn't lived together as man and wife for more than ten years."

"So why's he dropping by?"

"It's all on account of a cockroach. Two cockroaches, in fact."

"What's that supposed to mean?"

"He's having his apartment fumigated. Girlfriend found a roach in her shoe."

"And?"

"And?"

"You said two. Two cockroaches."

"Oh, right. Another bug set up shop in the cheese drawer of the fridge."

"So he just comes back any time he wants?"

"Guess so. Has a key. And a room."

"You never noticed the room?"

"I thought it was a guest room. No personal effects on view, and it's not as if I go around checking closets and drawers."

Will takes off his tie, folds it, and puts it in his jacket pocket. "Was he civil?" he asks his father.

"Very civil. Friendly. Put his hand out to shake mine—this was at breakfast the next morning. All of us sitting down together eating muffins and reading the *Times*. Fancy muffins, size of footballs. He went out for them. And for juice. Strawberries." Will's father shakes his head. "He told me the mayor wasn't even five feet tall."

"What does that have to do with anything?"

"I don't know. Must've been something in the paper, but it stuck in my head. All week I've been thinking, apropos of nothing, 'The mayor's not even five feet tall.' Guess I'm a little discombobulated by the whole setup."

"He'd come in the previous night?"

"Middle of the night. 'Who's that?' I ask Lottie when I hear the door, someone rummaging around in the kitchen. 'Must be David,' she says.

"'David who?' I ask.

"'No one,' she says.

"'No one?' I ask.

"'My husband.'

"'I thought he was an ex-husband.'

"'He is,' she says, 'he is for all practical purposes.'" Will's father takes another swallow of water. "At the word *practical*, she gives me a little goose down belowdecks, sort of pats me there. Then she goes back to sleep. Next morning she wants to, you know, but I can't, uh, can't . . ." Will raises his eyebrows. "Can't muster myself for the job at hand," his father clarifies. "I mean there's the guy sleeping on the other side of the wall."

"I'm sorry, Dad. That must have been weird."

"Guess so. Kind of disorienting, anyway. Can't concentrate. Went to the movies three times in two days." Will purses his lips, shakes his head. Going to the movies has always been his father's response to stress. When Will and Mitch were growing up, if his father had had what he called a "five-flick week" that was reason enough for them to behave very well.

"Also, and here's the worst of it, well, not the worst, maybe. Trying to be polite, I guess, the guy keeps dragging me over to where Lottie's hung my prints. Wants to talk about them. Wants me to talk about them. Asks questions. Not the stupid kind, but still."

"Oh boy."

"You remember which ones she bought."

"Of course. How could I not?" Will thinks of his first look at one of those photographs. Uncharacteristically, his father had mailed him a print, sandwiched between two pieces of cardboard joined with duct tape. "Look," Will had said to Carole, who didn't glance up from the pile of mail she was sorting, pulling out the catalogs to add to the recycling bin. He laid the photograph on the dining table, and she walked around and stood beside him so she could see the image right side up. Briefly, he'd considered keeping it from her; he couldn't say whether this was selfishness or kindness or a murky tangle of both.

"It's sort of . . ." She stopped, her lips together, and sucked inside her teeth, leaving just a line where they'd been, one of her many strategies for suppressing tears. "Beautiful," she managed, nodding.

She had her hands on her hips and her feet were planted a little apart, as if she were about to begin a set of calisthenics. Will remembers this, because it looked so odd, intentional, as if it might be another grief suppressant, equally ineffective, because her cheeks were wet; tears were running down her neck.

"It is, isn't it?" He picked up the photograph, careful to hold it by the edges, to keep the oil from his fingers from marring the image.

How had this happened? Was it Luke who'd given his grandfather this new vision, one both tender and exalted? Could he have shown him the view from on high, shown him what God or a god might see were he to look at humankind, creatures who greeted death with starched curtains and polished door knockers? McCaddam's Funeral Home, with its swept steps and braided mat, plumped cushions on the porch swing, a sign whose letters were painted with care. Will had paused on those steps the first time he entered, noting where faint ruled lines had ensured that whoever made the letters would keep them absolutely straight. Here was a house where Death, no matter how punctilious, wouldn't hesitate to spend a night, confident that pots were scoured and toilets scrubbed. Perhaps wearing white gloves so as to check along the picture moldings and the tops of door and window frames, just to see, as in the old TV commercial: Had everything been dusted?

Inside, across the silent room with the too-short casket, that much more obscene for being child-sized, Carol was sitting next to his mother, her head in his mother's lap, her eyes open, her face expressionless. His mother's hand moved over his wife's head, smoothly and steadily, like the pendulum of a big clock, a nearly frictionless arc marking the passage of time. His mother wasn't brisk with Carole as she was with him. It was easier to love his wife, perhaps. After all, Carole never baited her like he did.

Will has always found his mother reliable, industrious, and reticent, if not actually guarded. She doesn't seem to have much of a sense of humor, and her feelings, though spontaneous, are controlled; they never carry her away. He wonders sometimes if the mother he knows might not be a deliberate construction, a false front assembled to disguise the more unusual and complicated structure behind it, but then he has to ask himself if this idea might not issue from his desire for a less emotionally circumspect mother. A mother who is . . . who is what? Indulgent, he guesses.

At some point during that long afternoon, that endless day, Carole sat up and his mother stood to retrieve his father, who was, they all assumed, still in the old station wagon with the fake-wood side panels, the dog fence in place behind the front seat, even though it had been years since he'd had any occasion to pick up or deliver an animal. Will's father understood the pain of animals. The suffering of a dog was suffering for which he had an arsenal of responses. But what was it that could cure, or even assuage, human misery? Will imagined his father with one hand on the steering wheel, the other on the key, which he hadn't removed from the ignition. Possibly he hadn't moved since turning off the engine and was frozen to the car's vinyl seat, hidden by the reflection on the windshield, as motionless as one of his own perplexing still lives. But when Will looked out the window, he saw his father kneeling on the sidewalk with his head under the black cloth, peering through his big box camera at the funeral home.

"Hank!" his mother said, and she said the name again, more loudly, but Will's father didn't answer, and she left him there.

The funeral home was in fact a *home*, a white clapboard house built in the thirties, with round wood columns, copper rain gutters oxidized green, meticulously painted black trim and window frames, dormers on the roof, a stone chimney, a brass door knocker cast in the shape of a hand, fingers curled to rap the polished plate beneath them, starched white curtains hanging in freshly washed windows that reflected the nearby lake, itself lit by the bright sun, each pane shining silver—it almost hurt to look at them.

Will's father took his time under the black cloth, exposing one negative after another while, inside, Will completed arrangements for having Luke's body cremated.

"Didn't you want to come in, say good-bye?" Will asked before his parents drove away.

He leaned into the driver's-side window, and his father looked at him. He shook his head. "I'm sorry, Will," he said. "I thought I could, but I can't." His father got out of the car and hugged him, a long hug, longer than any in memory, Will keenly conscious of his father's body and the comfort it offered him. Flesh of his flesh. He remembers, after the accident, thinking the words over and over, applying them to his son and not, until that moment, to his father. After, when they'd released each other, they stood in the bright sun, silent and even shy, each man, Will is sure, unable to dismiss the feeling of the other's silent crying, how fearsome it was, to feel a man's back shake under your touch.

"This David character," Will's father is saying to him now, "he has a lot to say about each photograph, some of it the expectable claptrap, negative space and kinetic something or other, plus a few genuine comments here and there. Bends my ear for an hour. Very complimentary, but I found myself wanting to punch him."

"Yeah," Will says. "I kind of feel like I want to, too."

But what Will really feels is a grudging bond with the man, whoever he is. He expects people to be impressed by his father's work. Especially by the prints Charlotte bought, six among a series of thirty that will be published as a monograph in the coming year.

His father's camera had looked at McCaddam's straight on from the sidewalk, so the photograph presented only the front of the building with its painted door and clean windows, but, curiously, the effect was of seeing it from a distance, or a great height; it implied perspective. To look at the image was to understand that we are mortal, all of us, and that in the moments we know this, we're afraid, and that when it comes down to brass tacks, this fear doesn't inspire sonnets or arias or Impressionism so much as it does the determination to do very well the small habitual thing we do every day: keep house.

Brass tacks. If those weren't the weapons of a housewife, what were?

In the year after Luke's death, Will's father made a pilgrimage up and down and all over New York, Vermont, Connecticut, New Hampshire, even up as far as Augusta, Maine, taking photographs of funeral homes, small mom-and-pop places, each image composed so that the viewer saw the business as if he had hesitated on the sidewalk, paused to take a breath, gather resolve, say a prayer: whatever was required to prepare himself to walk the path and ring the bell. This was as far as Will's father ever got—*I thought I could but I can't*—and over and over, in one city after another, he recorded the same moment, a failure for which Will can't fault his father because he finds it quintessentially human: brave, but not enough to go inside; intelligent, but not enough to understand; awake, but not enough to be entirely conscious. Filled with love, but not enough to overcome fear. Made in the image of God, perhaps, but, if so, like a fifth-generation photocopy, or the fax of a fax of a fax, so that even the outline is approximate.

Daniel has asked Will if he is angry at his father for not going inside McCaddam's, and he's told him no. In fact, while looking at the photographs his father has made of funeral homes, Will has been overwhelmed not by anger but by love for him, and the feeling has arrived physically. Deep under his ribs, he's felt something he imagines like the crease made by folding a sheet of paper: a sensation, al-most pain, that's shown him a place he might tear more easily.

Across the table, his father is buttering a slice of bread. "I'm standing there, my hands in my pockets, thinking I don't know what, probably that the mayor's not even five feet tall, and the guy says to me, 'Did you intend for them to be religious images?' He stands there, looking at me with his arms crossed, waiting for me to ex-pound."

"What'd you say?" Will asks.

"Nothing. Smiled like an idiot." He shakes his head, opens the wine list.

"Did you?"

His father looks up. "Did I what?"

"Did you make them out of some religious impulse?"

He shakes his head. "That's not the way I think of them."

"Then how? How do you think of them?"

"I don't." His father shrugs. "I see them, that's all."

Will nods. "He still there?" he asks after a minute.

"Off and on. Went back to his place but seems to have left things behind, has to keep coming around to look for them."

"Does he work?"

"Dermatologist."

"Geez," Will says. "Everyone's a dermatologist."

"No, they aren't. What's that mean?"

"Nothing. I guess I was thinking of someone I ran into last sum-mer, a woman who's become a prominent dermatologist."

"Who's that?"

"No one. A girl I was boffing twenty-five years ago."

"You know what you want?" his father asks him.

Will looks over the menu. "Free-range chicken."

"Glass of wine?"

He shakes his head. "Takes the edge off."

"Isn't that the point?" his father says.

"Yes, but I have a session at three, and even one glass makes me that much less, what, present, I guess." Will takes his glasses off and lays them on the table, rubs his eyes. "Even were I inclined to dull my edge, this wouldn't be the day to do it. I've got a couple of patients right now for whom I really have to be at the top of my game. Consistently at the top." He puts his glasses back on. "Well, one of them I just have to get rid of."

"What do you mean, 'get rid of'?"

"Refer to another therapist."

"Personality conflict?"

"No. She's out of control. I'm going to send her to a woman."

"How come?"

"Long story. Well, not that long. Begins treatment because she has a history of compulsive promiscuity. That's what she says, anyway. *Promiscuity* is my word, not hers. 'Collecting' is what she calls her pattern of staking out older men and enticing them into sex. It's about power more than sex, her ability to seduce."

Will's father frowns in concentration. "Hookups," he says. "Sex for sex's sake. No emotional entanglement."

"Right," Will says, "exactly." Every once in a while his father makes an observation meant to prove he's not out of touch, leaving Will feeling less impressed than protective of whatever inspires this earnestness, because this is the quality that's most palpable when his father produces what he believes to be evidence of his being hip, or, as he'd say, "in the know," and it's the same quality that insures he'll never be hip.

"She's very flirtatious," Will says of the girl. "Which, ordinarily, isn't an issue. A lot of patients flirt. Some can't convey affection or even respect without using a vocabulary of implicitly sexual words and gestures. But this is different. Deliberate. Conscious rather than unconscious. She spent an entire session giving me an unnecessarily and provocatively detailed account of how she came on to a professor she picked up at the place she waitresses. I'm talking explicit. There's nothing this girl doesn't say. No physical transaction she won't fully describe. Then, at the end of the session she, uh—well, she kissed me."

"Kissed?"

"Kissed."

"How'd she do that?"

"Smoothly. Very, very smoothly. When I thought about it later, it reminded me of the time I got mugged by that kid on the bike. Remember my telling you about that? Came up from behind on the sidewalk? Just glided in front of me, cut me off, and caught me in the angle he made with his bike and the wall. Expert, almost choreographed. Same thing with this girl. As she's leaving, she pretends to have trouble with the doorknob. Says she needs my help. I come over to where she's waiting, and before I even get to the allegedly problematic knob, she's doing it."

"Wow." His father whistles. "Doing it how?"

"Not chastely."

Will's father raises his eyebrows. "Sexual?" he asks.

"Definitely sexual."

"Mouth open?"

"And a lot of tongue."

His father smiles. "So what'd the doctor do?"

"Nothing. I didn't do a thing. She slipped out the door and left me standing there like some hormone-addled teenager." Will leans forward over the table, lowers his voice. "She put her hand on my fly, too, Dad, and I was clearly not, uh, unaffected."

To this, Will's father says nothing, and he doesn't smile. His expression, if he has one, is of judgment withheld.

"I see her Thursday," Will says. "I've called her already, left a message. Told her I was referring her to a couple of other therapists. Both women."

His father puts his knife and newly straightened fork to one side of his plate. Having been a veterinary surgeon, his handling of any small implement is dexterous, unusually graceful. "I guess you had better," his father says, and he says it again. "I guess you had."

Y ou know what's weird?"

"What?" Daniel asks.

"I'm dogged by the sense that I'm lying even when I'm telling the truth. Or especially when I'm telling the truth." Will shakes his head. "Not that I'm ever dishonest with you—I'm not. What I mean is, it's when I'm especially conscious of trying to tell the absolute truth that I feel most strongly that I'm lying."

Daniel frowns and shakes his head slowly, communicating Will's failure to make him understand.

"In here, I mean," Will says, "with you."

"Are you talking about omissions?"

"Omissions? Omissions of what?"

"I thought you were telling me—for a moment I thought you might be saying that there was more to the story of what happened between you and that patient. More than you'd reported."

"God no! Don't you think a French kiss and her goosing me is enough?"

"I'm sorry, Will. Please, go on."

Will stands. He paces in front of Daniel's desk, his hands in his pockets, agitating the coins and keys within. He stops in front of his chair and faces Daniel, but he doesn't sit. "In this room, talking to you, I am scrupulously honest. I know that. I'm as honest as I know how to be. But as soon as I've said something, or even sooner, while I'm still speaking, I'm flooded with the sense that I'm lying. I feel guilty. I reexamine what I've said. Succumb to doubts. It's as if everything I say breaks down under the pressure of my scrutiny. The whole idea of anything being completely true seems ridiculous."

"It is," Daniel says.

"I know. I know. Truth's a direction, not a destination. No capital *T*." Will makes a chopping gesture with one hand, lets it fall to his side. "That's not what I'm talking about. I'm not speaking philosophically or even analytically. I mean that I, literally, in the most pedestrian sense, feel as if I'm telling lies. Whoppers. And I'm not." He drops back into his chair. "Why?"

Daniel silently turns his unlit pipe in his hand. It's at least a minute before he speaks, and it feels to Will like ten. "I had a patient," he says, "who told me that each time as she prepared to come here, as she rode the train and walked from the subway stop to my office, she invented falsehoods she intended to tell me. Right up until the moment she was on the couch, silently she'd be embellishing intricate tales of abuse and perversion, of adulterous relationships with colleagues, of eating disorders she didn't have. Shoplifting. Setting fires. Pedophilia. You name it."

"And?" Will says when he doesn't continue.

"I wondered what you made of it."

"A defense. She overcame her reluctance to make herself vulnerable by imagining that she wouldn't reveal herself to you. Instead, she'd disguise her true neuroses with decoys, those she made up."

Daniel nods slowly, still frowning at the pipe in his hands. "That was my conclusion."

"But what does it have to do with me? With what I've told you?"

"Maybe nothing. But it seemed to me that her case offered us a hint."

"What is it?"

"There's no direct parallel. She rehearsed lies and told the truth. You intend to be truthful, and in fact you are truthful, but you feel that you're lying."

"So she fears being revealed, and I fear that no matter how hard I try, I'm not revealing myself?"

Daniel shrugs. He smiles at Will and lifts his hands over his desk, palms up, empty, holding no answers.

On Little Squam Lake, in New Hampshire: a shingled summer cottage at the bottom of a track through the woods, a steep incline that made it impossible to walk toward the front door, especially if you were carrying something heavy, a suitcase or a bag of groceries. Gravity pulled you into a run, flung you at the house, which was long and low and filled with liquid, green light, sun reflected off water and filtered through trees in lush, midsummer leaf. They'd rented it for a month, sight unseen, through one of those minuscule ads in the back pages of *The New Yorker*.

A lake chart was tacked to the kitchen wall, where renters would be sure to see it. Originally, the chart had been black-and-white, but someone had amplified it with a red marker, highlighting certain rocks and shallows. With time, one wet season following on another, the ink had spread into pink aureoles, as if those places were charged with magic rather than danger. During the day, you didn't hear the lake tonguing the foundation. You heard outboard motors and the cries of swimmers; you heard neighbors laughing or arguing, the sounds of a distant tennis game, the percussive return of the ball broken by an occasional long pause when one of the players went off into the woods to retrieve it.

Will can picture the four of them eating dinner in that house, laughing, talking, helping themselves to more food, their faces flushed and shining, and he aches with sympathy for the family he sees, innocent of what's to come. The people at the table are like the cast of an expertly made movie—Will doesn't know them, not personally, not anymore; and it seems impossible to him that they are so carefree, that they don't feel something—anything—for how can destruction not announce itself, the way earthquakes and tornadoes are said to do with a peculiar, heavy stillness, a greening of the light?

But in that house the light was green already, and the family around the table saw nothing, not so much as a ripple on the surface of the lake. Did they miss it, a warning that only a more evolved species might perceive? A single high note, perhaps, out of the range of the human ear?

Outside, tied to the dock they shared with the neighboring cottage, was the Sunfish Will had rented in town. When the wind rose, the lake nudged it into one of the pilings. "Can't you stop that?" Carole said when he came to bed that night, the last night. Luke's last.

"Stop what?"

"The boat. Every time I fall asleep, it wakes me up." She spoke from under the pillow, where she'd hidden her head to muffle the keening of loons, the trickle and slap of the lake, the knocking of the boat. "Can't you tie it so it doesn't do that? I keep dreaming someone's come to the door. That I have to get up and answer the door."

"Maybe. I'll go out and see."

He stumbled on the steps leading down to the dock, mesmerized by moonlight on the lake, like countless sequins on the water's heaving black bosom. He retied the boat, pulled it snug so it wouldn't knock, and sat dangling his feet from the dock, listening for another of the loons' weird calls.

———

He was never a careless person. Particularly, he was never careless with the children, who always wore seat belts in the car, helmets when riding bikes, and life preservers on a boat. When he played baseball, Luke wore the chest guard he hated, but, as had been established by the misfortune of other families, a perfectly placed blow to the sternum could stop a child's heart. Luke was two when Will enrolled himself and Carole in a course called "Baby Life." Taught at a local hospital, it focused on infants and young children: what to do in case of a head injury, when to call Poison Control, how to recognize the onset of anaphylactic shock, and how to perform the Heimlich maneuver and CPR on small bodies. Health insurance; home insurance; trip insurance: maximum coverage never struck Will as too expensive. He paid to have his children's teeth sealed against cavities, checked their bodies for deer ticks every night after a day spent in the woods. Flu shots. Multivitamins. Antimicrobial soap. A water filter installed on the kitchen tap; fire alarms hardwired throughout the house; window guards on every window above the first floor. Regular maintenance on the car and the furnace.

A friend of Carole's had given her a joint as a little going-away present, and Will wasn't as enthusiastic about the gift as she'd expected. "Maybe we should just leave it at home," he said while they were packing.

"No," Carole said. "Come on."

"I don't know. Lake sports and dope—it seems like a bad combination."

"Will, it's not as if we're going to get stoned and go water-skiing."

To counteract any perception of himself as an uptight killjoy, Will was the one who suggested they smoke the joint. They'd been at the lake for a couple of weeks. The kids were in bed, and he and Carole were sitting outside on the dock. It was true what they said: marijuana was a lot stronger than it had been when he was in college.

Before they'd smoked even half the joint, they were lying on their backs reduced to monosyllables, holding hands and watching a sky spattered with stars they never saw in the city.

"It's . . ." one of them would say. Or, "I wonder . . ." But neither of them finished a thought, and the two of them laughed at each other, and themselves.

"Let's swim," Carole said after a silence so long that Will was lost in some genius theory that interpreted constellations as if they were messages rendered in a Braille-like language of luminous dots, sentences that shifted with the reader's vantage so that inhabitants of one galaxy received one message while other beings on other planets read something entirely different, allowing God an infinite combination of signifiers to manipulate, tailoring revelation to the particular needs of—

"Will? Let's go swimming."

"No."

"Please. Why not?"

He laughed. "Way, way too fucked up." A long pause.

"We could stand," she said.

"Stand?"

"Stand in the water. Instead of swim. We're not too fucked up to stand."

"Okay. But first can I tell you what I was thinking?"

"What?"

Will tried to articulate his theory of celestial communication but got no farther than drawing an analogy between stars and Braille dots before understanding that the revelation he'd experienced was itself a pattern of dots and therefore untranslatable into English. He stopped speaking.

"We could get naked," Carole said, enough time having passed that she'd forgotten whatever weird point Will had started to make.

"Yes. Let's."

So they stripped and dropped their clothes where they'd forget to collect them, and stood together in the shallows, bodies pressed tight, feet sinking into the cool, velvety ooze of the lake's bottom.

"We don't kiss enough," Will said when they pulled apart.

"Because we're in a hurry," Carole said. "We're always in a hurry."

"I'm not always in a hurry."

Carole laughed. "I am," she said.

"How come?"

"Greedy. I'm a glutton. An orgasm pig."

Will slipped a finger between her legs. "Because you can be. If men could have multiple orgasms . . ." He didn't finish the sentence.

"Then?"

"Death of civilization."

"Beginning, more like."

"Yeah?"

"Uh-huh. Because men would fornicate without stopping, and women would run things. We'd use you for stud, that's all."

"In that case," Will said, "let's go inside. I have to practice for the regime shift."

In the morning, Luke and Samantha brought their parents' clothes to the breakfast table. "Did you guys take your pants off outside?" Luke asked, frowning.

"Mom washed them in the lake," Will answered. "Like an Indian."

"Native American," Luke corrected.

"Right. Native American. Although I believe Native Americans refer to themselves as Indians."

"But so do black people sometimes call each other niggers."

"Excellent point." Will shook the arts section out of the paper and handed it to Carole.

"Anyway," Luke went on, "it's not true what you said about Mom washing clothes in the lake, because they're not wet, they're only damp from lying out in the dew." Will looked at him.

"Can't you stop being so smart for a minute? Eat some toast or something?"

It was later that day, about four o'clock, that Will woke from one of those disorienting daytime naps he never knows whether to consider a luxury or a mistake. "How about a sail?" he asked Luke when he came outside, figuring it might dispel the dull, hungover feeling that always overcame him after sleeping during daylight hours. Off the dock was a shed, and inside it old fishing rods, a tangle of mildewed tarps, a rusted shovel and rake, and a few life jackets, also mildewed. He chose the smallest for Luke; once he'd tightened the webbing belts it didn't seem overly large. His own was missing its plastic clasps, and so he tied the belts, using not one but two knots and making a show of the procedure as an example to Luke, a claustrophobic child who tended, surreptitiously, to squirm out of whatever he found confining. Luke rode miserably in a car, holding the seat belt's diagonal strap off his chest and away from his neck because if it touched him, it made him "sweaty," it made him "carsick," it made him "suffocate."

"Isn't it a little late for sailing?" Carole asked as they walked past her chaise on the way to the dock, and Will saw himself reflected in the mirrored lenses of her sunglasses. He didn't answer what was more comment than question, and she unscrewed the lid from the Coppertone bottle, reapplied it to her shins, and went back to what she was reading. When Will thinks of that scene, Carole in the chaise on the dock, he sees her with one of her lust murders. But this is wrong, anachronistic. They are a habit she acquired after Luke's death.

The Sunfish was not even fourteen feet long, white fiberglass with a wood daggerboard, a mainsail—no stay—striped red and yellow and blue. On the weekends the lake was crowded with others like it, a popularity granted by the boat's size and lightness, the simplicity of only one sail, and a kick-up rudder that made for easy landings on a beach. It seemed more toy than real boat, an invitation to the inexperienced, and the people who sailed Sunfish often had mishaps. They collided and capsized and lay their bright sails down on the dark water surrounded by woods, water that looked black no matter what the hour. From the dock Will had watched a number of accidents, all greeted with hilarity. Often the sailors were laughing so hard, hanging on to the hull, that it took them some time to right their boats.

It was one of those perfectly clear midsummer afternoons, the kind that require people without sunglasses to duck their heads—squinting wasn't enough. Even late in the afternoon the silver face of his watch was invisible under the crystal's hot stare. What—who—could stand up to the sun's relentless scrutiny? Only the water; the rocks and the hammock-sized spiderwebs; the trees on the shore, each leaf shining dark and impenetrable, mysterious; mushrooms glowing orange in the shadows; the heads of mallard ducks that glinted from the lake like giant cabochons. As for himself: soft, smudged, and apologetic, excluded from the light's benediction.

Why does he describe it like that? Was that how it was? He's been reading a book that attempts to explain the process of memory. Written by an expert on the nature of consciousness and the neurochemical impact of torment versus pleasure, the text summarizes the results of clinical trials suggesting that each time the mind revisits an experience, retrieving a scene from where it's stored, that scene is contaminated by the new context. For example, if, having attended a party that Carole missed, Will subsequently told her all that had transpired, who had said what and to whom, the next time he remembered the party it might seem to him that his wife had been there. He might be so sure that Carole had joined in conversations he'd shared with her only after the fact that he'd argue the point, willing to bet on his word over hers.

This adhesive property, the tendency of memory to incorporate what it encounters—like a stream of water carrying along silt, pebbles, lost lures, a message in a bottle, all that it passes over and through—applies to emotion, as well. A happy, sunny moment can darken if exposed to grief. A smell, like that of Coppertone, generally evoking languid contentment, can become its own opposite, summoning anxiety and dread with notes as clear and loud as Pavlov's bell.

They got in the boat, and once more Will checked Luke's jacket. They waved and called good-bye to Carole, who was still trying to read, and to Samantha, standing by her mother's chair with a mud patty in her hands. "No, honey," he heard Carole say, "not on the chair. Put it in your bucket." Trying to come up with something, anything, that might occupy a five-year-old while she skimmed another paragraph, she asked Sam to fetch a plastic cup of water and pour it on her feet. "Mom's toes are so hot and thirsty. She needs you to water them."

They crossed the lake, laughing because it was so much fun and so effortless. Will had the tiller and Luke sat, leaning when his father told him to lean, closing his eyes to give himself more completely to the acceleration. It felt as if they were riding a few inches above the water, on air, and trusting his ability to recall the lake chart, the position of those pink-ringed rocks, Will continued on around the little island in the middle of Squam, beyond the part of the lake he'd sailed before. Despite the sun, it was cold on the water, and Will was glad he'd nagged Luke until he put on a sweater. Even so, the boy's lips were blue. It was time to go back. Will said, "Come about," and reminded him to get out of the way of the boom. Luke had had three sailing lessons—Carole enrolled both children in a beginner's class when they arrived in town, and he knew the basics—

but before they could change direction the prow struck one of those submarine rocks outlined in red on the lake chart in the kitchen. Scale, scale, Will thought. Had he never checked the scale? The lake must be larger than he'd known, much larger, the rocks farther from the shoreline.

As they capsized, there was a moment when Will and Luke touched. A part of his son glanced across Will's face, his thigh, perhaps, because his torso and arms were covered, and Will has the distinct memory of bare skin warm and smooth against his mouth, like a violent kiss, an indelible instant to which Will has returned again and again—how many times, he wonders, were he to add up all the waking and dreaming moments in a year? Say an average of ten per day, times 365 days, times three. 10,950. And yet ten seems to him a fair, even conservative, estimate. The rate having decreased from fifty or maybe even a hundred times a day in the first weeks and months to now, when occasionally a day passes without his revisiting the accident. Progress, he thinks, when he notes such a day, the note being itself a reference, but secondary.

"Not direct," he reports to Daniel. "And this is good. I know it's good, it's right, it's what Luke would want. But"—he stops until he's able to speak again. "It's . . . it's as though I've abandoned him."

"Will," Daniel says. "Will. Can you not counsel your own best self as you would a patient? Can you not be grateful for whatever resilience you possess?"

They surfaced on opposite sides of the Sunfish—at least Will thought they did. Even without his glasses—he'd lost them when they capsized; he wasn't wearing the Croakies Carole had bought him, the elastic strap that might have kept them on—he could see

Luke's orange life jacket in the water just beyond the boat, and he swam for it, afraid Luke had been knocked out, because he couldn't see him kicking and he didn't answer when Will shouted his name.

As he swam he reviewed the basics of CPR for children. Check for breathing, check for pulse—it could take him as long as five minutes to get him to the shore, then, if—God forbid—if there wasn't a pulse, if he didn't breathe, please God don't let that happen. But if, oh God, if it did, then onto his back on a flat surface, lift his chin, tilt his head, open his mouth. Check for an obstruction in the airway— no more than a minute's grace by then; he would make it enough, there wasn't a choice. Pinch the nose closed and breathe into the mouth, lips sealed around lips, and look to see that the chest rises with each breath. Then find the right spot: two fingers' width above the xiphoid process, and with the heel of his hand on that part of the sternum—never press on the xiphoid process itself, a rib could tear away from the notch of cartilage, it could puncture a lung—he'd push down, gently and firmly, straight down, no more than an inch. Then release. Press and release. Press and release. Five compressions, five seconds apart, and another breath, a slow breath, just enough to see the chest rise.

But when he got to the life jacket, it was empty. Unbuckled. As was his habit, Luke must have undone it while his father was occupied with sailing the boat. Too clearly, Will could see his son, unconscious, sliding from the jacket's embrace, down below the surface, dragged by sweater and shoes.

"Luke!" He called the name over and over, and when he paused to breathe, he heard children, the antiphon of a distant game of Marco Polo. Marco? Marco? Then someone, far away, answering Polo.

It used to be, when Will thought about the accident, that he brought his hand to his mouth, not a gesture of shock or even grief but an attempt to conjure the sensation of flesh glancing off his lips. At times he did this over and over, not purposefully—he was never really conscious of the act and, on occasion, performed it in public— on the subway, sometimes, or while listening to someone on the other end of the phone. Once, at a dinner party, Carole pulled him aside to tell him to stop. It disturbed people, she said, and not without reason. "I know what you're doing, but they don't," she whispered.

There was a dog on the shore, and the dog was barking. A man came out of a house and called to the dog, but the dog wouldn't come. The man yelled, *Nine-one-one, nine-one-one*, a message for him, Will assumed, a question. *Yes! yes!* he yelled back, and the man disappeared; presumably, he'd gone inside to dial.

It was more than an hour before anyone called Carole. Later, she told him she'd seen the rescue boat cross from one side of the lake to the other, and when the phone rang she was watching from the dock. She was wondering what had happened, and to whom.

W ill buzzes in his three o'clock—that is, he buzzes in someone he thinks is his three o'clock but, as announced by her distinctive, staccato ascension of the uncarpeted stairs, it's the girl. It's been three weeks since he terminated treatment with her—since he told her what she has not accepted. Instead she's hounded him with messages and voice mails, some polite and beseeching, a few bordering on abusive. She's even called his home number, spoken with Carole.

"You have to leave," he tells her now. "I'm expecting a patient."

"I have to talk to you."

Will inhales deeply, lets the breath out through his nose. "My— we don't have anything to talk about. We are no longer engaged in—"

"No," she says. "You don't understand. I need to talk to you. Please." The look on her face is one of what appears to be genuine desperation.

"Have you contacted either of the people to whom I referred you?" he asks her.

"No. No, I—"

The buzzer buzzes, and Will pushes a button by the light switch to release the lock downstairs. "My three o'clock," he says. "You have to leave now."

"I'll wait," she says.

His patient starts up the stairs; the girl starts down; as they pass each other, the patient averts her face in the usual manner of an encounter at the analyst's office: deferential, blind. As Will closes the door behind her, he sees that the girl is sitting on the landing downstairs, rummaging in her backpack.

When he looks out his door at 3:50, she's reading.

"What can I say to help you understand that we cannot continue to work together?" he says as soon as his patient has left the building.

"Please," she says, coming up the stairs. "Give me another chance. I don't know why I pulled that shit. I know I behaved badly, but I promise nothing like that will ever happen again." Will watches her face as she speaks. Either she's sincere, or she's an actress with genuine talent.

"It's best—best for you—to begin over again, with someone else."

"I don't want to! I can't. I swear I can't. Please!" Will doesn't answer. If only she'd stop saying "please" like that. Mitch could always get him to do anything if he just said "please" enough times. Will's impulse—his determination—was always to even things up between the two of them.

"Please forgive me," the girl says, striking at this vulnerability with the accuracy of a mind reader. "We can start over."

"Our professional relationship has been compromised. Compromised in a way that would lessen my effectiveness in treating you."

"But why can't what happened be part of what we talk about? Wouldn't that be, like, useful? Useful in figuring out what makes me do these things?" Will doesn't answer her, and she throws herself onto the couch. She's wearing a pair of trousers that are, he guesses, a kind of commentary, or protest. Made of camouflage material in which the army greens and browns have been replaced with bright pinks and purples, their legs are absurdly wide, each one sewn from enough fabric to upholster a chair. "I don't get why you're making such a big deal about this," she says. "You act like I stabbed you or something."

Sitting cross-legged, the girl takes off her pullover the way a little boy might, by grabbing the scruff of its neck and dragging it over her head, making her hair crackle with static. Underneath is one of those sleeveless undershirts commonly known as wife-beaters. Her bra, visible through the sheer fabric, looks like the top of a bikini; it's striped blue and white. She reclines, arms behind her head.

"Please do not lie on my couch."

"Because I'm not your patient?"

"Yes." Will turns his back on her, and on the little surge of panic he feels, dismissing it as claustrophobia. Across from his office, someone turns on the light in the dance studio. A few students enter and begin stretching. Will twists the Lucite wand that adjusts the blind; he turns around to tell her once and for all to go, good-bye, good luck, but what he sees stuns him into silence.

"Put on your clothes," he says as soon as he's recovered his voice. "Put them on now."

"No."

"Yes," he says. "Or you'll have to leave without them."

"What are you going to do? Drag me out into the street? That doesn't seem like such a great idea, actually. I mean, all I have to do is start kicking and screaming, right?"

Will opens his mouth, then closes it. If she screams, if she accuses him of assaulting her, then what? He has no witness to prove otherwise. She takes a compact from her backpack and consults the mirror within, considering her reflection. Paralyzed, he watches her. She's still young enough to be caught instantly by her own reflection, caught and consumed. She stares into her own face, licking her finger and rubbing at the makeup smudged under one eye, and Will—as is his tendency when threatened—responds by hyperanalyzing the situation, sure that in the moment she's forgotten him.

Wouldn't that be the appeal of an affair with a much younger woman? All those times she didn't understand or even notice you, and the attendant freedom from having to work constantly at interpreting pregnant silences and meaningful glances, all the weary, oft-traversed terrain of marital responsibility. And it's not just Will. It's the same with every patient, every marriage: an unlimited number of dialectics leading to the same disagreement. To each couple its own insoluble, often inarticulable conflict. If you discounted lust—which would, of course, be a mistake—the key motivation for infidelity might be the chance to bed a woman who didn't engage reflexively in the fight you'd fought so often before, the Rome of every conjugal union, the one to which all quarrels lead.

And what's his own? The psychic equivalent of an earthquake or tidal wave, Luke's death revised the landscape of his marriage, shoved aside the mountains he and Carole had made of molehills, filled in the old quicksands and quagmires and rabbit holes. And, yet, how long did it take, really, before he and Carole began to redraw their respective maps, excavating paths they used to travel? No matter how a fight begins, still it always arrives at a point that reminds Will of one of those Starship *Enterprise* doors that slide quickly and silently shut, separating one of the *Star Trek* crew from whoever is on the other side.

What is it with him? Why is he subject to these damningly juvenile references, consistently failing to produce the Proustian allusions such situations demand? Or forget Proust, he'd take Updike, Chandler, Norman Mailer. He would, except that his wife does happen to remind him of Dr. Spock: evolved, intelligent, a being of one mind, never two (let alone more), not quite, it would appear sometimes, human. And yet, those redemptive glimpses of emotion, of her poise breaking down every once in a while into irrationality. As for Will, prey as he is to lust, he's stuck being Captain Kirk, whose gold uniform always made him look that much more like a man losing a battle with his appetites. That insatiable, wolfish squint. With Carole it's only so far and no farther. Will is scripted as the one who knocks; she as the one who may not answer. He leans forward, she leans back.

"What is it with you?" Carole says if he tries to articulate this dynamic. "You invent problems that don't exist. You're a conflict junkie."

"No, I'm not."

"Yes, you are. You absolutely are. It must be recreational for you. Or you can't stop working—you come home but you're still at work. Your head's still at work. Righting wrongs. Except in our case there isn't one. There's only what you imagine as a problem."

On and on they go. They might never stop but for exhaustion, and sometimes it strikes Will that this might be the glue of marriage, not just his but everyone's: both partners continue to show up for battle, helpless to resist it. Perhaps even eager for the comfort of it, the familiarity: this is our fight we're fighting; this is who we are; this conflict defines us; it makes us different from the rest.

If self-knowledge is the goal of psychotherapy, identity must be its most intractable enemy. When Will fails a patient, when he can't move a person toward a more livable life, it's often because that patient refuses to relinquish his or her neuroses, even costly and dangerous ones. How can she, if whatever it is—anorexia, OCD, agoraphobia, pyromania—is part of what that patient relies on to recognize herself; if the illness is what gives the individual a means of picking her small self out of the terrifying, endless mass of indiscriminate humanity?

Will looks at the girl looking at herself. She may not be drop-dead beautiful, but her body comes close, very close. She snaps her compact closed and tosses it onto the pile of her discarded clothes. "What's the matter, Dr. Moreland?" she says, taking a step toward him. "Pussy got your tongue?" She's close enough now to put her hand on his crotch. "See?" she says. "I told you you liked me." Deftly, she unbuckles his belt, unbuttons and unzips his fly, and puts her hand against his cock, feeling how hard he is through his shorts before pushing and pulling his trousers down, underwear along with them.

Will stares at her breasts, at what strikes him as their almost impertinent defiance of gravity, the delicate color of her small, flattish nipples. Carole, by contrast, has big, ruddy nipples, sexy but in a very different way. She's nursed two children for a total of more than four years and in doing so reformed her breasts into flesh that is deferential, not pert but self-sacrificing, at once modest and unselfconscious. They're mammalian, he supposes; their attraction rests in the fulfillment of nature rather than in the conceit of beauty for a beholder. Although, in the end, isn't it just that the girl is young, Carole not so young, a simple animal fact that he has convoluted into a thesis?

Her legs look even longer unclothed, and her pubic hair has been barbered into a narrow strip. "Brazilian," she says, seeing him look there.

"Brazilian?" he repeats. He hears his own voice as if it's been brought to him long-distance, in the days before fiber-optic cable, delayed as if it were an echo.

"Yeah. A Brazilian wax. You know? As in J sisters?"

"Jay sisters?" Maybe he really can't talk anymore, only parrot one or two words.

"Yeah. J as in the letter *J*. I thought everyone in this city knew about the J sisters. Where the bikini wax was, like, invented? At least for Norteamericanas." She lifts an eyebrow at him.

"Skip Brazil," she says when he still hasn't replied or moved so much as an inch from where he's standing. "Think of it as your landing strip." She sits and pats the couch next to her. "Why don't you take a step closer because . . . well, your cock's big, but no one's is that big." She takes him in her hand, guiding him forward. "Cold hands, warm mouth," she says, and then he's on his back on the narrow, black leather couch not even seeing the ceiling, not even seeing, eyes open and blind because of what she's doing. Between his legs, with her teeth, gently—gently enough—she's nibbling along the shaft of his cock, her tongue hot and slippery and all over the glans, the root of it in a tightening ring of thumb and forefinger and—"You just have to . . . you have to stop," he forces himself to say, "just—stop. Please. Don't move your mouth. I . . ." But instead, she picks up speed, tightens her grip, and he comes fast, feeling it up to his neck, those last strokes or licks or sucks or whatever it is that she did, every atom of him concentrated into one accelerating charge. "Oh God, oh Jesus, oh—" and Christ, she doesn't break stride, doesn't even flinch. She's a swallower, heaven help him. Different, not better, just different from Carole. His wife's less predatory, but that's just a—

"Okay, now we fuck." Will picks his head up to look at her, back at work lest he get soft. She's keeping the blood in his cock with some twenty-first-century tantric vacuum trick. Not a little-girl pout, after all, he—

"Check," he pants. "Check—"

"Check what?" She sounds irritated by the interruption.

"Door."

She stands to let him up from the couch. "I think we better get down on the rug, anyway," she says after he's ascertained that the door is, in fact, locked. She points at the couch. "Too narrow," she says.

As soon as he lowers himself to the floor she takes his cock in one hand and plants the other in the middle of his chest and pushes until he's flat on his back. Less than a minute in her feverish mouth and he's hard again, as hard as before. She straddles him and starts moving, back arched so that her pelvis is tilted into the shaft of his cock and going at it hard enough to make him ache. "Do I have the right tempo?" she asks, clearly uninterested in his response to a question that's just knee-jerk sexual etiquette, no more personal than saying bless you to a sneezing stranger. He watches her face, her eyes open and glassy, preoccupied by what she's doing to herself with her fingers.

She comes again and then once more, each time arching her back to pump him until it hurts. He searches her eyes, finds them empty. Not that he'd expected affection, or any other emotion, just some indication of pleasure. But she looks businesslike.

"Your turn on top," she says, "but only if you promise not to come. Not yet. I might want to go back to this. And I don't want to skip all fours." She lies on her back and slowly guides him into her. She's unbelievably wet and tight and impossibly, almost unnaturally, slippery.

"Astroglide," she says, reading his expression.

He stops moving. "What?"

"I used some—a lot, actually—while your attention was, let's say, elsewhere."

"A lot of what?"

"Astroglide?" She lifts the last syllable into a question: You're so last season / last year / last century that you've never heard of Astroglide?

"What's that?"

"Some super-poly something. Poly-propyl-glycerin-glyco-blah-blah-whatever. Lubricant, but different from that old K-Y junk. This stuff's for real. Better than spit. A triumph of science over nature."

What happens when she's through with him? Will she move on, according to habit? That's what he's counting on, he realizes, that's what he's decided will happen. Having collected him, she'll lose him, lose interest, refocus on the next in her series of old guys. Maybe she'll leave afterward, and tell no one, and he'll get away with it, this transgression that's been forced upon him. Hasn't it? Already he's trying to figure out just how culpable he is in this. Whether he communicated his lust to her unconsciously but still intentionally. Whether the fact that he's as turned on as he is makes him guilty, no matter who initiated the sex. Whether his fear of being exposed and accused of attempted rape makes him dishonorable. Well, of course it does. She reaches over her head to where a little bottle with a white cap is lying on her camouflage pants, almost invisible.

"Check this out," she says. Before he can protest she has a finger in his asshole, all the way in. "Hey, relax will you? This'll be good. I know how to make this feel good."

Will closes his eyes. The only other finger that's ever been up there is the internist's, a quick rubber-glove (and, yes, K-Y) check of his prostate, neither man looking at each other and neither, he's quite sure, with an erection. But with her space-age product she's doing some kind of inside-out hand job—finger job, he guesses he'd have to call it—and it's . . . it is good. It's really, really good.

"Oh no," she says, "no no," just as he's wondering shamefully (meaning he's ashamed but he's still thinking what he's thinking) how suspicious Carole would be were he to introduce her to a little bottle of—

Out goes the finger, and she pulls away on the back stroke, rolls right out from under him. "Getting a little too close to the finale."

Will doesn't answer, jerked back from the precipice so suddenly that he's dizzy with teased lust; but it doesn't matter, she goes on talking regardless of his regression into a state of mute passivity.

"Here's the deal," she says. "First you go down on me. I want to get off at least three times. Then I'm still bottom, you're top, but this time it's from the back, hands and knees, and I want it in the ass with plenty of this." She holds up the bottle. "Don't worry. I'm clean. I always make sure. After that, when I tell you, we do vaginal but still on all fours and you fuck me, and you go deep—you're in as far as you can possibly get, until I come, which might take a little while, or it could be fast. We'll just have to see. The good news is then you're rewarded for all your hard work. You don't have to hold back any longer."

It's accurate to say that a lot of him feels good while somewhere on the periphery of himself he's aware of a slight, shivery sort of nausea, like the distant approach of a migraine or fever, that first warning of infection. "My God," he hears himself say to Daniel, "do you know what I've done?"

She tastes like no other woman he's encountered. Of course, he hasn't had his tongue between anyone's legs besides Carole's for seventeen years, and it's not as if he was some junior Casanova before, but something about this girl, maybe it's the Astroglide, reminds him of a low-calorie sweetener, sucralose or aspartame, a slightly puckery, syrupy savor like those old fluoride treatments he'd get at the dentist's office when he was a kid, anticavity gel leaking from the mold into his mouth, a gaggy trickle going down the back of his throat.

Her first orgasm is demure compared with the bucking and howling he expected; the second, after an intermission of less than a minute, a carbon copy of the first. The third he has to work for, resorting to a fail-safe, tongue-punishing technique that leaves his mouth ringing with exertion. She curls up so abruptly that it's a challenge to hang on to her, to keep his tongue in the spot he's found, the right spot, the one that makes her writhe and howl, a freaky, unfeminine noise, the kind of noise, frankly, he would have thought a woman couldn't make, but so sexy: throaty and wet, a low growl that rises octave by octave into a wail. As long as it takes for her to arrive at this climax, and as long as it is that she manages to ride it, there's no denouement: one minute she's curled up, spine lifted from the floor and her face twisted in a knot of concentration; the next she pops up and flips right over, pushing the Astro stuff into his hand before she settles into position on her hands and knees.

"Slather it all over," she says. "Enough so you're, you know, really slick, and put some on me, too. You don't have to put your finger in or anything. I mean you don't if you're squeamish. If you're not, it's okay by me."

Will squirts the clear, colorless stuff on himself, a line of mustard on a hot dog, more than enough, it turns out. He uses his shirttail to wipe some away, otherwise he'll never achieve any friction at all. He holds his breath and pushes in. The girl gasps, very softly, a whispered gasp, if there is such a thing, and he pauses, a bit too long, evidently, because she twitches in obvious irritation.

"Hey," she says. "How about, you know? Moving? It is supposed to be a form of, like, sex."

Will pulls back and pushes in, feeling the rush of blood summoned by the heat of her. She's tight, tighter than anything he's ever felt before, and beyond that close grip, the rest of him is in a hot, soft place, encountering no resistance, none at all. Hands on her hips, he's got the two of them in a slow back-and-forth, guiding her along the shaft of his cock as much as thrusting himself in, afraid to hurt her.

She's sweating; tiny glittery beads form on her shoulders and spine, and she shivers; he feels the tremor under his hands. "Am I—I'm not hurting you, am I?" he asks, but all the response he gets is a huffing uh-uh. Or is it *uh-huh*?

"Keep moving," she says, and they go on until, as before, she takes the opportunity to pull away on his back stroke, sliding off him and onto her stomach.

"Are you clean?" she asks after a minute, sitting on her heels, her back to him, breathing hard enough that he sees her ribs rise and fall. "Just look all over yourself, will you? On the underside, too. Because you have to be, like, totally clean." She walks forward on her hands, back in position.

"All right," he says. "I'm . . . I am."

"Go on, then. Use more glide if you want."

After so many and so deliberate a sequence of preludes, intercourse itself seems an afterthought if not, by definition, an anticlimax. As with all that preceded it, Will has no sense of any choice, and when she says "Deeper!" he thrusts deeper. Ditto faster, ditto slower.

He's stupid with sex, or maybe the right word is *stuporous*. When she comes, moaning, the noise startles him, as if he's forgotten what they've been doing. His own orgasm, produced dutifully, is silent, second-class, undeserving of sound effects.

They both lie on the carpeted floor, saying nothing, she on her stomach, he on his back. He closes his eyes and is instantly asleep.

7:07 by the digital clock on the desk. Will sits up. "I'm leaving," he says. He stands to gather his clothes, and the abrupt ascension makes his head reel so that he has to sit back down on the couch. When he looks at her, she's sitting up, her left cheek bearing the impress of the ringed fingers she laid it on. She tilts her head to one side, scrubs at her eyes with her knuckles.

"I keep expecting you to guess who I am," she says. "I don't know why. For some reason it seems so obvious. Like it should be obvious to you."

Will is bending to retrieve a sock from under the couch. Something is about to happen, he thinks to himself, remembering that before they began, he'd had the sense, for a second he did, that he was failing to save himself, protect himself, to say nothing of his wife, his family, from getting shanghaied into a fateful—perhaps he means *fated*—voyage.

Something that will change everything is about to happen, Will realizes. But no thought follows this one, which disappears, sinks without leaving even a ripple on the smooth, reflective surface of his consciousness. He pulls on the left sock, then the right, and sits up, a hand on either knee. He makes a dizzy survey of the content of his own head, everything bent and inverted like the picture in one of those convex mirrors placed in a hairpin turn. But that kind of warning works only reflexively; allow yourself to engage with what's in the shining orb, try to think your way toward correcting the reflection's backwardness and distortion, and it's too late: you've already crashed.

The girl stares back at Will, whose thoughts tumble forward, pulled by their own momentum and the logic, or illogic, of undirected association. *Free* he'd call it, talking to a patient, as in free association, an exercise at which he's always been particularly bad because of his hyperactive intellectualizing. But for the moment something—adultery?—has incapacitated the rational part of his brain and, as if he's lost his footing on a hill, he slides from one image to another, from the round mirror in the road to the one his mother used to set on the holiday table. Meant to represent a frozen pond, on its shiny surface she arranged a set of lead figurines, tiny people dressed in furs who skated, danced, and trimmed a tiny tree. One rode behind another on a bobsled no longer than a matchstick. Each year their father made a wreath of holly to disguise the mirror's edge. "Poisonous," he'd say. "Remember the berries are poisonous." Invariably, their mother would add, then, that lead was poisonous, also.

"Who are you?" Will says at last. Again that distance and delay in his voice, as if he'd taken an international trunk call from himself. His head feels like a filled balloon, at once empty and under pressure.

"Jennifer."

"Jennifer?"

The girls nods and gives him a mild, almost social smile, as if they've only just been introduced. "You know. Elizabeth's daughter?" She reaches up and pulls a strand of hair from her head, holds it out to him. "You wanted one of these?" She gets up from the floor, still naked, and takes a step toward where he sits on the couch, the single strand pinched between her thumb and forefinger. "Here," she says. "A little present from me to you." Will doesn't move. The single hair hangs in space, glinting, a tiny filament blowing to one side, pushed by an air current too small to feel.

"Don't you want it?" After a minute she drops her hand to her side. "The thing is," she says, "even if you do have the DNA analyzed to compare mine with your own, and even if it does match, you still won't know."

"I won't know." His words are neither question nor assent, just an echo of hers.

She shakes her head, continues as if this were ordinary small talk, words exchanged in a waiting room or between bites of a sandwich. "No. Because twenty-four years ago—twenty-five, I mean—my mother was sleeping around. But that's not the point. I mean, she's not the point, her sexual mores aren't. The point is that when you were having sex with her, she was having sex with four men. You. Paul—that's my dad. A guy called Tim DeAngelo." She counts them off on her fingers, leaving the last one up. "And Mitchell Moreland."

"Mitchell? My . . . my brother Mitch?"

She nods, expressionless. "Your twin brother." Her voice, too, is without affect, flat. As if what she says is so unremarkable that it summons no inflection. "Whose genetic material is the same as yours."

She stands and rummages through her pile of clothing until she finds her underpants. Styled like boys' briefs, they're red with a fly piped in bright blue. On the butt is a silk-screened picture of a waitress with a tray. Underneath, a caption reads "Patsy's Oyster Bar." She pulls on her socks, then her black sweater and voluminous pants, leaves her bra lying next to her boots. Will watches her dress, saying nothing. He has a hot feeling in his head, behind his eyes. Not a headache but a . . . a what? He doesn't know.

"The way I figure it, if you don't have the hair tested, the odds of my being your daughter, biologically, are one in four. If you do have it tested, you either find out, first, that we're not related at all or, second, that I'm maybe your daughter, maybe your niece. And if it's the second, since both the potential fathers have the same DNA, nobody will ever know whose I really am." She sits on the floor to pull on her boots, crams her bra into her backpack. From the outer pocket she takes an envelope and hands it to him. "Just the way you wanted it. A hair taped to an index card." She swings the backpack over her right shoulder. "Bye," she says.

He's still staring at the envelope, sealed and addressed in green ink to #39, when a pair of feet come drumming up the stairs and someone knocks at the door.

"Who is it!" He stands at the door listening carefully. What else could she possibly want?

"Hey!" she says, loudly, almost yelling. "I forgot my coat." She pushes past him to the closet, jerks the sleeve of her long suede coat so that it comes off the hanger into her hands. She drops her backpack to put the thing on, and again he finds himself staring at the grease stains around its pockets, remembers—it seems a year ago—having interpreted her slovenliness in a sexual light. She fastens a button as she walks out. The metal hangers are still chiming together as the door sighs shut behind her.

An hour later, Will is lying, fully dressed, on his couch, rubbing one thumb on the smooth black leather that matches that of his emblematic Eames chair. He's in shock, or something like it, a feeling that reminds him of coming home from the dentist's and touching the part of his face that hasn't awakened from the Novocain. The way the information from his fingertips argues against that from his brain, insisting that the warm skin and stubble of beard belong to someone else. He tries to scroll through all the surprising revelations that have been uttered in this room, crises created and/or endured by the people who have lain on this same couch. Surely some must have been as bad as this. But he can't remember them. He can't think of anything, can't address one issue—the possibility of incest—because others keep interrupting. The betrayal by his brother, by Elizabeth. His own betrayal of Carole, of himself. Even of the girl, a girl who was a patient and whom he failed to protect from herself. Elizabeth, too, in a way. He should have suspected. Known. Why didn't he?

He sits up, elbows on knees, head in hands. Carole must be tucking Sam into bed about now. He called her and said he had a patient emergency and would be home late. He's given himself until midnight to pull himself together. Looking forward to that hour when one day turns into the next, when today will be yesterday. So unlike himself, the time miser—to want to hasten the clock.

What has he allowed to happen? It's—if it's true—it's the kind of scene familiar to audiences of Greek tragedies, a transgression both fated and unintended, proceeding from the hero's tragic flaw. But what is Will's? Aren't tragic flaws supposed to be a bit more grand than lust? After all, lust belongs to man's baser, more animal nature, it doesn't grasp for what can belong only to the gods. And was it lust that got him into this mess? Maybe it's whatever Elizabeth identified as his attempt to stanch grief with the fantasy of having fathered another child. What did she call that? Aside from a pathetic illusion? If only, please God, it could be. How he wants Elizabeth to be right.

He's just had sex with a girl who may be his daughter. She may not be, but if she is, according to the ancients, he's knocked the cosmos out of kilter. A blight on harvests. A blight on herds. A blight on women in childbirth. Plague and bloodshed. Athens wrecked. Jocasta in her blood-soaked bed. Right about now, in the wake of discovery, Will is supposed to be gouging his eyes out, or falling on his sword. What he's done—what he may have done—reduces adultery, only this morning a significant sin, almost to marital misdemeanor.

Unless Jennifer is lying, unless Elizabeth has lied to Jennifer, there's another betrayal: Mitch's betrayal of him, with Elizabeth. A hateful, perverse theft, to cuckold your own brother. Of course, if it's true, then Will has been cuckolded by Elizabeth, as well, but that seems a lesser insult. What Mitch has done is . . . It's just . . . it's . . . What is it? Will doesn't have a word for what he feels.

That it happened twenty-five years ago seems to make no difference. He's only just found out about it, so for him it's happening now, inspiring brutal fantasies of smashing in his brother's head, cutting off his perfidious balls. Anger so intense it summons the restless, coiled energy that demands violence, the feel of something— anything—yielding under his hands, even as it's short-circuited by something else: shame. Mitch, the brother he fought to protect, the person whose anguish he felt more keenly than his own—how can he think of hurting Mitch, killing him?

As if trapped in some awful carnival contraption, a Tilt-A-Whirl or whatever it is that jolts back and forth and up and down, Will lurches from horror to anger to shame and then back, whipped along a sickening emotional arc, unsustainable. In between scenes of violent dismemberment, his own and his brother's, his eyes for Mitch's balls, he keeps returning to the toast Mitch made at his wedding, the reference—suddenly less cryptic—to first girlfriends, and the bitterness in his brother's voice.

But that's nothing. Mitch's hostility that once seemed so intense, even threatening, it feels like nothing compared with Will's anger. Especially at the person who got him into this mess: himself. Why does he feel, though, that he doesn't know what's going on, exactly? Can it be paranoia that insists there's some worse something lurking beneath what's already a disaster?

Immediately, his own house is made strange to him. At the insertion of his key a new music tumbles from the front-door lock. Hinges keen, floorboards sigh under the weight of his feet. As he walks in, hours after midnight, Will is reminded of house hunting with Carole, afternoons long past, the two of them following real estate agents through one house after another, rooms that seemed as if they'd been evacuated by the arrival of catastrophe rather than for a prospective buyer. And, who knew, perhaps they had—not an earthquake, war, or epidemic, but the smaller, private cataclysm of financial ruin, divorce, a death in the family.

Lingering behind his wife and the agent, Will was so distracted by the evidence of other lives—titles of books on shelves, photographs hanging on walls, a series of framed paintings made by a child, Joshua, age eight, eleven, twelve—that he had trouble concentrating on the relevant features of whatever house they were considering. Kitchens, bathrooms, bay windows, walk-in closets, laundry rooms, skylights, coffin turns, pocket doors: he missed all of these as he hung behind to look at what had been pinned to the bulletin board by the door: memos, receipts, invitations, a snapshot of a child—Joshua?—wearing a fireman's hat, a list of names under the heading Thank You Notes, the first few crossed off.

Now, coming home—God, how did it get to be 3:47?—it's the same with his own house. *Who are the people who live here?* Will finds himself wondering as he walks through the living room. *Whose chair? Whose collection of inkwells gathering dust? Whose subscription to* The Atlantic?

A single plate rests in the drainer by the sink, and he picks it up, thinking of the long-ago couple who bought the set of blue and white china from Macy's Cellar, spending whole hours on a choice that made so little difference: What color? What pattern? The owners of the dish in his hands are people he no longer knows. In fact, it's hard to picture them.

I should eat something, he thinks, not at all hungry, but his head aches and he's dizzy; it's been fourteen hours since he had lunch. He gets out a loaf of bread and tries to find the jar of peanut butter, stands staring into the open pantry door, his hand on the knob, asking himself questions the real owner wouldn't ask.

Where would they keep the peanut butter? he wonders. Not we. They.

ronic," Will says to Daniel. "Don't you think? Carole grows up in a house where all these languages are spoken, inspiring her to devote most of her waking life to helping children learn to communicate effectively, and yet she herself turns out to be so cryptic and unforthcoming. I find her very resistant to revealing her inner life. There's a secretive aspect to her silences—whenever I ask her what she's thinking, she says, 'Nothing.'

"And then there's yoga, her downed dogs and one-legged roosters or whatever she calls them—I just can't help feeling suspicious of yoga. There's something so smug and self-satisfied about it. All these punitive-looking postures maintained for unnaturally long periods of time. Doesn't that imply—or require—a dedication to restraint, to being self-contained to a fault? The whole point of yoga, for Carole anyway, is to practice a kind of refusal to let down her guard. At least that's what I think it is."

Daniel, who is examining the end of his tie—a lustrous, pearly gray silk with small polka dots in different jewel-like colors—looks up at Will. "Have you always found her so opaque?"

Will takes off his glasses, replaces them on his nose, takes them off again. He's caught himself doing this lately, when he's with Daniel. Why? he wonders. Is he acting out some ambivalence about seeing clearly? "I don't know," he says. "I've asked myself if Carole seems more intent on maintaining—what?—not silence, exactly. I've wondered if she's more reserved since Luke's death, but it's impossible to say, for the standard reason—projection. Any answer I give is my answer. Reflects my loneliness rather than her intent to evade me. I know that."

Daniel nods, says nothing, folds his hands on his desk, looks at him expectantly. "What are we talking about, Will?"

"That patient?" Will says, surprised to hear the words. "The one who kissed me?"

"What about her?"

"I had sex with her."

Daniel's expression remains as it was: attentive, calm. "Before or after you terminated treatment?" he asks.

"After."

"Tell me what happened." Daniel betrays no more interest in Will's revelation than he would if Will were telling him what he'd had for lunch the previous day. "Huh," is all he says when Will has disclosed the whole mess, including Jennifer's announcement of his possible paternity. And then he says it again, "Huh." After a silence, he asks, "Have you told Carole?"

"No."

"Why not?"

"Well, for the obvious reasons. Cowardice. Avoidance of conflict. And I wanted to talk to you first. But also because, I don't know, I keep going over all the pieces, trying to figure out, I don't know what. It's all so weird. It feels . . . old."

"Old?"

"Old like it happened before. Like déjà vu. Arriving in a city where I know I've never been, and yet I could swear I had. Also, I don't know how to predict how Carole will react. If I knew what to expect, it might seem less impossible to tell her. But the more I think about it, the less sure I am where Carole is these days. I mean, she could flip, of course, and how would I know what that would be like? We've never had any real knock-down-drag-outs. Maybe we should have. What if she's weirdly understanding? That could happen. I mean, it's not as if I knew this girl was . . . well. And I've waited years now for Carole to lose it over Luke, and she never has. Shouldn't she scream at me or, or keen or . . . shouldn't she do something? It seems like it can't be over, Luke's death won't ever be over, until Carole reacts, really reacts. But she hasn't. So maybe she wouldn't react to something like this, either."

"What has your response been to her grieving so quietly about Luke?"

"My reaction to her nonreaction?"

"To her apparent nonreaction. You told me she cried a lot in the early months."

"Yes. Silently."

"Does that make the tears invalid?"

"It stresses me out! As if my head were this emotional seismograph—an affect-o-graph. Turned up way too high, sensitive to every minuscule mood vibration, pens scribbling all the time, reams and reams of fluctuations to interpret and parse and, and—I don't know what. All in the service of predicting when it's going to happen. When the fault lines split open and swallow up everything— marriage, child, careers, house, car. Annihilate us."

"Annihilate."

"Yes. Because I have to assume it's coming, the big one. It's delayed, that's all. It's only a matter of time before she blows. Because the longer it takes to arrive, the more forcefully she's repressed it, the more she's felt she had to repress. Thus the more intense and destructive it's going to be."

"Maybe you're wrong. Maybe she isn't going to 'blow.'"

"Maybe."

Daniel sticks his index finger into the bowl of his pipe, twists it around with a thoughtful look on his face. "Is it possible you let this happen to provoke Carole to anger? To get the dramatic response you crave? Like lancing an abscess?"

"But I didn't *do* anything. I mean, I told you. She took her clothes off, said she'd scream rape if I . . . maybe I should have . . ."

"Should have what?"

"I don't know. If I'd called the police or even just charged past her, out the door, she'd have framed me."

"All right. Say you were passive and compliant to avoid further persecution. Then why use words like *hidden* and *sinister*?"

"I wasn't . . . it wasn't a reference to myself so much as to . . . to this sense I have that I'm missing what's going on. Really going on."

"What do you mean?"

"I don't know what I mean." Will puts his face in his hands. "Lately I feel like I'm thinking so hard I'm doing damage to my brain. The actual gray matter. Like redlining a car engine. And to no purpose. Getting nowhere. Spinning wheels."

"All right, Will. As far as I understand it, what's happened is that you didn't effectively prevent a young woman, recently your patient, from manipulating you into sexual intercourse. You were not the aggressor, but you didn't stop it, either. And while you're anxious in the wake of betraying Carole—anxious about the possibility of incest and about sexual contact with a woman so recently in your professional care, angry with your brother, angry with your wife, you're also troubled by your own behavior. Worried that there are motives you don't perceive." He stops, looks at Will, who says nothing. "Is that a fair statement?" he asks. Will nods. "And yet today you began by talking about what you find is Carole's tendency to be withholding. But, in fact, it's you who are keeping a secret from her."

"I know. I know." Will shakes his head. "Embarrassing to be so obvious a case."

"Will?" Daniel interrupts a lengthening silence. "Where are you?"

"I was thinking about our different—I won't say conflicting—orientations. My insistence on parsing and interpreting and assigning meaning to everything, and Carole's tendency to just, I don't know. Live instead of think, maybe. Like she's discovered the trick of being rather than becoming."

"Becoming?" Daniel says.

"Yes. My whole life, my work life and my personal life, is devoted to this . . . this conceit of becoming. To helping people become better adjusted, free of neuroses and compulsions on which they squander their time and energy. Conscious, if they can't be happy.

"And consciousness—becoming more and more fully conscious—is what I want for myself. I accuse Carole of campaigning to evolve, but that's unfair. I'm just seeing myself. Just because she corrects impaired children's development doesn't mean she's bent on her own evolution. In fact, she never seems to struggle to attain her calm collectedness. She's not really any different from the young woman she was when we met."

"Why do you call it a conceit?"

"Call what a conceit?"

"Becoming. The idea of becoming."

"I don't know. I mean, obviously, I believe in becoming. But maybe the god I serve is false. Maybe I'm deluded."

"Maybe we all make our own gods, each as valid as the next person's."

"Uh-uh," Will says, "I'm not going there with you."

Daniel smiles at him. "Just because I'm an atheist?" he says.

He nods. "Did I ever tell you about our first date?"

"So that's why you're a speech pathologist," Will said to Carole. She'd just finished telling him about her father's death. She stared at him.

"Why?" she said, gray eyes wide in anticipation.

"Because." Will frowned. "Well, here you were in college, studying communications, and you had this, this articulate and gifted father, who has a stroke, a series of strokes and, having been a polyglot, a man who commanded ten, eleven languages, he loses his ability to speak. Loses it one language at a time, and dies unable to say a thing. Unable to say two words to his daughter—Happy birthday. Happy birthday, Carole. This accomplished and generous man, a translator and a scholar who helped so many other people understand one another, this father you adored, he died. And immediately you change your major, you go from communications—media—to speech therapy, so you can become someone, ultimately, who helps children who can't speak, who guides them at the very important beginning of their lives. These people, very young people, who can't make themselves understood, who come to you and falter in the same way your father did at the end of his life. They open their mouths and nothing comes out. Or the wrong thing comes out, a sound they didn't mean to make. And you've made it your purpose to change that, to help them—and thus yourself—toward a different outcome." Will stopped here, feeling quite satisfied with this interpretation, reductive though it might have been. The pretty woman across the table would understand him to be a sensitive and aware sort of male, the very kind, he hoped, who would appeal to her. Convince her, just possibly, to sleep with him. Maybe even that night, after dinner, dessert, another glass of wine.

Carole tilted her head to one side. "I never thought of it that way," she said.

"You didn't?"

She shook her head.

"But what other way is there to think of it?" Will regarded her with puzzlement. Here was a woman who worked side by side with social workers and school psychologists and family therapists and all the other energetic zealots who populated the landscape of secular optimism—and she made no connection between her father's being silenced and her own missionary pursuit of fluency? How was that possible?

"I don't know." Carole made a face, eyebrows drawn together, as if straining to understand what Will thought was so obvious. "I took this phonetics class, and I learned this system of . . . well, what phonetics is, is the discipline that breaks language down into phonemes, which are the smallest units of sound. Each has its own symbol, so a phonetic spelling of a word doesn't look like English. Anyway, I found it very clean and straightforward. It's transcribed in what's called IPA, for international phonetic alphabet, and I learned it easily, almost without effort. It was fun, that's all." She shrugged self-consciously at this admission. Worrying, perhaps, that he might judge her as shallow.

"So," she continued, "I began transcribing everything, all the notes for my other classes, in IPA. No one could borrow them—they didn't understand them. It was a foreign language, after all, a code, a set of signifiers. But it was easy, nothing like learning German, which I'd found so impossible. IPA was, I don't know, irresistible I guess. And I didn't resist it. I'd almost completed the requirements for a communications major when I switched to speech pathology, so I had to stay another year. Well, a year plus one semester." Carole put down her fork and picked up her napkin. She held it in front of her mouth, not dabbing but covering her lips, as if she were hiding them from him.

"Dessert?" he asked. "Another glass of wine?" Or maybe he offered her—he hopes he didn't, but maybe he asked did she want Armagnac or Remy or something he thought might imply sophistication.

She shook her head, still holding the napkin. He picked up the check and they walked together to her apartment, where he stood with her on the street for what seemed a long time, waiting for her to ask him upstairs. He doesn't know why, but it wasn't uncomfortable. He remembers that when he looked down, so as to take a break from looking at her face, he saw that her feet were aligned, precisely together, and her knees were, too. She held the strap of her handbag with both hands, one fist next to the other, both right in front of her crotch. And she looked right at him, smiling slightly, a friendly look that didn't seem expectant. Self-contained, Will guesses it was.

"Are you thinking about what I said at dinner?" he asked her.

"Said about what?"

"I don't know. Your father. The speech thing."

"No." She shook her head.

"What then?"

"Nothing."

He took a deep breath and held it, puffed out his cheeks, let it go in a gust. "So, uh—"

"Do you want to come up?" she asked.

"Of course."

She nodded, still staring at him in that disconcerting, almost detached way she had. "Are you prepared?"

"Prepared?" he said, confused.

She looked away and then back, conveying exasperation, but not in a hostile way. "Did you bring a condom with you?" Will flushed, not something he did often, but he felt as he had when he was chosen to act out an exemplary scenario for his junior-high health class. He'd never slept with a girl who wasn't on the pill or didn't have an IUD or a diaphragm. This was before safe sex, after all. What could it mean, her not routinely using contraceptives? Impossible that she was still a virgin.

"Do you want me to go with you to buy them?" Carole asked. She took his hand and walked him west along the block. "I'll stay here," she said when they went into the drugstore, and she began to look through a display of greeting cards. She pulled one out to read the message inside. He still remembers the picture on the front. It was Linus, drawn by Charles Schulz, and he was in midair, upside down, Lucy having pulled his blanket out from under him.

As a child, Will used to follow *Peanuts* with attention rather than pleasure, as if it might tell him something he needed to know. He cut out the little black-and-white daily strips, which always seemed more serious and instructive than the colored Sunday ones, and saved them in a binder, organizing them by topic and (as if unconsciously anticipating the reference manual of his as yet unknown career, the *DSM*) cataloging emotion as if it were disease. He called one section "The Effect of Unrequited Love," and there were also "Anger and Betrayal" and the thickest section of all, "Angst." He was twelve, a seventh-grader whose reading comprehension tested at college level.

"I wish I still had that binder," Will says to Daniel. "I'd like to look through it, assess its assessments. Even then I was trying to figure out what the fuck was going on. Figure out my brother. *Peanuts* isn't a very funny strip when you think about it."

And they were never really children, those awkward, tormented characters, hunched over Bible verses or Beethoven scores, as alienated by talent as by failure, pining for unavailable valentines, losing their kites, losing their softball games, quoting the Book of Luke on the birth of Christ, suffering gender dysmorphia and slavish devotion (Peppermint Patty and her weird little sidekick who called her Sir), dragging along their tattered transitional objects, waiting with Beckett for the Great and Nonexistent Pumpkin-Godot, and, in the end, seeking dismissive counsel at Lucy's five-cent psychiatry booth.

"So," Daniel says to Will, glancing at his watch—an abbreviated gesture, not to see the time but as a cue: ten minutes before the hour.

"So," Will repeats.

"Now what?"

"I guess I contact Elizabeth. Check the story out. Be sure it's all true." Will stands, hands in his pockets. "Then I'll talk to Carole. I'll call you. I'll keep you posted."

"Please." Daniel walks him to the door. "Next week?"

"Unless you think I've got my multifaceted crisis all wrapped up."

Daniel puts his hand on Will's shoulder, a gesture Will notes for its infrequency. Rarity. In this room, they do not touch beyond the occasional handshake. "Take care," Daniel says, squeezing the shoulder.

B ut she was. In New York City, in 1987, Carole was a twenty-four-year-old, post-sexual-revolution virgin.

"Really?" Will said, and then he said something ridiculous. "Are you sure?"

"Am I sure?" Carole laughed. "Yes."

Why? he wanted to ask, but he couldn't think of a polite way to put the question. In any case, what he meant was, *Why me?* What about him invited or allowed this . . . this what? Awakening? Rite of passage? But he wasn't going to ask that question either, lest her answer was to change her mind.

"I mean, I'm not completely without experience. I've . . . well, I've . . . I just haven't done that."

Will nodded. "The first time for me," he said, "I was fifteen."

"Okay."

"Okay?"

Carole looked away and then back. "I mean, I don't mind, if that's what you're asking. Does it matter?"

"No. No, it doesn't matter. And you, your . . . it's nice. For me, I mean. But . . ."

"But what?"

Will shook his head. "Nothing." He'd been going to say that he felt a burden of responsibility, but that wasn't the right thing to say either. "I just want to know if you're sure, that's all. Sure you want to do this."

"Yes, I am." Carole unbuttoned her shirt and shrugged out of its sleeves, stepped out of her shoes and skirt. She reached around her back with both hands to unclasp her bra. It was black; he remembers this because he'd expected it to be white, because of stereotype: didn't virgins wear white underclothes? But her panties were black, too, sexy against her white skin. Not only does he remember being aroused, he can almost feel the barely contained, wet-dreamy quality of that erection, intensified by the slightest stimulus, physical or imagined. She pushed the black panties down and sat on the end of her bed, knees together, and watched as Will untied his shoelaces, leaning over in her rocking chair so that it tipped all the way forward.

"Maybe you don't want the overhead light?" he suggested when he looked up. "Maybe a candle or something?"

"Okay." Carole stood. "I don't have candles. But I could turn off the overhead and leave the bathroom one on with the door ajar. That way, only a little would come in."

"All right." Will left his clothes on the chair and lay on her bed. Feeling self-conscious, he put the condom on her bedside table. Carole stood at the end of the bed for a moment, then she lay down next to him.

"Can we kiss for a while first?" she asked, breaking the silence. He nodded and pulled her on top of him, and then one smooth thigh was on either side of his cock.

"I'm going to be . . . I'm going to do the best I can," he said, pulling back from her mouth, and again she laughed. "I don't mean to be funny. I . . . I know this is the second time I've made you laugh. But, well, I was being sincere."

"It just sounded funny, that's all. Like taking the GRE or M-CAT's or something."

"I'd like . . . If it's all right with you, I'd like to touch you first."

"Touch me?"

"With my mouth." He put his hand between her legs. "Touch you here." She nodded and reached for the condom where he'd left it on the table by the bed. "What are you doing?" he asked her.

Carole sat up. "The books, um. I read a book that said I should . . . I mean that the girl, the woman, she should make putting the condom on part of foreplay. You know, so it's, uh, erotic."

"*The Joy of Sex*?" Will asked. "Was that the one?" Now it was she who flushed. "That's all right," he said. "I don't . . . I'll do it after, when I'm ready."

"I don't mind doing it."

"No, I . . . It's just that they're not sexy. Condoms aren't. So I'd rather do it. But not until after I do this." Carole lay back down, and he settled himself between her legs, nudging them farther apart with his shoulders. "Bend your knees," he said, and when she didn't move he took her, one ankle at a time, and arranged her on the mattress.

"Sorry," he said, after they'd made love and had rolled apart. "I didn't last as long as I wanted to." Carole pulled the blanket up, covering both of them. "I was, uh, I guess I was excited."

"More than usual?"

"Well, your being a virgin. I . . . I guess the idea of it, of your having never been with anyone before, it . . . I lost my, my restraint."

"That's okay."

"Was it—did it feel all right?"

"Yes." She rolled up against him, her cheek on his chest. "The thing is," she said, "what you did with your tongue felt so good that the rest was a little anticlimactic."

"No pun intended?"

"Pun very much intended."

"Why me?" Will asked after a silence, but the question came out wrong. He'd meant to sound grateful, not perplexed, and he worried that to her ears the question might have sounded worse than perplexed, even petulant.

"Why you what?" she asked.

"Why am I the first?"

"Oh," Carole said. "Because."

"Because why?"

"Because I'm going to marry you."

Will didn't reply. He was still trying to figure out her meaning—irony? romantic fantasy?—when she kissed his cheek. "You'll see," she said, and she turned over and went to sleep.

E lizabeth has agreed to meet him at Philadelphia's Thirtieth Street Station, a point midway between his home in New York and Baltimore, where she lives. They are to meet at 11:30, but Will's train arrives at 11:12, so he waits for her in one of the station's big pewlike benches, watching as clots of passengers emerge from the platform stairways. A few people move briskly toward one or another exit; others set down luggage and packages to consult the readouts on their cell phones, make calls, locate connecting trains on the departure board. Or they just stand, passive and expectant as children, awaiting the arrival of friend or kin, someone to collect and bear them away.

He hasn't told Carole where he was going and doesn't expect to be caught in his subterfuge. It's Thursday, so Samantha stays after school for a swim class that isn't over until 4:45. He plans to return on the 1:40, arriving at Penn Station by 3:00, so even a major subway snafu, like a stalled train or a sick passenger or a police chase, any of the menu of expectable daily disasters (assuming terrorists are lying low, plotting rather than acting) that could slow him down won't stop him from getting back home to pick Samantha up in time.

So far, Will isn't enjoying the discovery of how easy it is to exit his life without explanation, like slipping unnoticed through a secret portal, leaving one world, waiting to arrive in another. The ridiculous transporter from *Star Trek* pops into his mind, that shimmering column of a crew member in the moment when he's neither aboard the *Enterprise* nor reassembled on an unexplored planet but in the limbo of molecular disarray, a trembling, staticky silhouette. He tries to shove aside the thought of himself back home that evening, glancing across the room at his wife, trying to decide what to say as he searches Carole's face unobtrusively. On top of feeling sick about what happened with the girl, Jennifer, although he hasn't quite gotten to the point at which he can think of her by that name—a guilty, nervous nausea that intensifies when he's near his wife—he'll be that much more disturbed having disappeared successfully for these few hours. Assuming he is successful in his deceit.

11:35. Maybe her train has been delayed—a mechanical failure, or a human one. The word *stickup* pops into Will's head animated by Daffy Duck sputtering in cartoon fear, flecks of spittle flying everywhere. Why is it that the more agitated he gets, the more childish are the images that assault him, all of them dating back to afternoons spent with his brother, the two of them on the living room floor under the television's blue gaze?

Maybe she isn't going to show. But how could she not? Will's e-mail described a young woman with a pair of stainless steel studs on either side of the bridge of her nose, fingernails bitten to the quick, and a citation from Cicero's "First Oration Against Catiline" tattooed on her chest. Not even New York City could contain two such young women.

Almost six months have elapsed since the college reunion, months during which Will has changed from the man he used to recognize as himself. After fifteen years of negligible marital sins, those of omission, mostly—instances of laziness or lack of consideration inspiring the familiar wifely complaints—he's become not only an adulterer but possibly an incestuous father, a man whom almost every culture throughout all time would recognize as a criminal breaker of taboo. His chronic fear of seducing a patient has been obliterated by a set of new terrors resulting from having been seduced by a patient. For the first time in memory, Will can't get it up. The previous evening, after lying next to him in the dark for a few minutes, Carole sat up in bed and switched the light back on.

"So, uh, Will?" she said.

"Yes?" He was lying on his back, one arm across his face to keep the light out of his eyes.

"What's up?"

"I don't know," he lied. "I'm not feeling great, I guess."

"You mean you're sick?"

"No, not sick exactly. Sort of."

"Because—tell me if I'm wrong—but I think we've made out when you had the flu, I mean the real flu, that Coxsackie thing you caught from Sam, several sinus infections, strep throat, the back thing after the cab accident, innumerable colds, fevers, upset stomachs, et cetera. I can't remember your ever being sick enough to forgo sex." Will didn't answer. "Is there anything going on?" she asked. "Anything we should maybe talk about?"

"No," Will said, "not now. I'm just . . . I don't feel well. Can we turn off the light?" She did, and they lay there, awake but not talking for what seemed a long time. Both of them must have noted that it was Carole who pressed for dialogue while Will resisted—not a first, but very unusual.

And here's another distressing development: lately Will has caught himself immersed in sadistic fantasies of fratricide in which he goes after his brother with a blowtorch, or, in the more elaborately plotted scenario, drives a Humvee, one of those automotive paeans to testosterone, through the desert with Mitch chained to its massive bumper. Will forces his brother to walk barefoot as fast as Will chooses through a desert terrain, over blistering sand and rocks and cactus spines—the inverse of the environment of his expertise, cold water. Soon lamed, Mitch falters and begs, completely at his mercy.

Will slumps on the bench, rests his head on the wood back, exhausted by himself. Looking up, he sees that birds are flying inside the station. Its central hall is so large, the ceiling so high, that they appear content to swoop back and forth, gliding by the vast windows without succumbing to panic and diving against the glass panes. Directly over his head a shiny silver Mylar balloon is trapped in a ceiling coffer. Will dislikes these balloons and their forced, tinselly enthusiasm, the way they imply the inadequacy of regular balloons. And they never burst. Samantha got one on her last birthday, and the thing has remained in the house for months, floating at eye level, wrinkled and flaccid but still ascendant, somehow needling in its longevity, the way it persists in celebrating an occasion that even Sam has forgotten.

11:41, according to the oppressively large clock on the station wall, the slack middle of a weekday, without the bustle and press of commuters, and yet Will would have picked her out just as quickly from a crowd. She rises from platform 3 into the waiting area, her bright head gliding upward, carried along the unnaturally smooth trajectory of the escalator. When she steps off, she's standing in a long pale bar of sunlight that falls from one of the monumental windows. Without looking around, she turns herself in his direction, as if she knew by instinct which bench he would choose, and approaches with her characteristic walk, efficient and unhurried, her feet, in their low heels, striking the floor soundlessly. Her hands are shoved in the pockets of her belted black trench coat, which makes the color of her hair appear even more flamelike.

He stands, and she stops walking. Obviously she's decided against contact even as minimal as a handshake. Two yards—the length of a body—remain between them. "Elizabeth," he says.

"William."

"Why don't we sit over there?" He gestures toward the food court.

"Fine," she says, and she sets off in that direction.

He follows her through the concessions. "Do you want anything?" she asks. "Because I never had breakfast," she goes on, as if to justify the distasteful necessity of sharing a meal with him, "and by the time I get back to the unit I won't have had a chance to eat." Without waiting for him to answer, she takes two croissant sandwiches squashed under Saran Wrap and slaps them on a tray.

"What was it you said you practiced?" he asks, straining for a neutral prelude to what will be a necessarily unpleasant dialogue. "What kind of dermatology?"

"Burns."

"Burns. As in fires?"

"Or chemical. There's also the occasional idiot who pulls off the trick of a third-degree sunburn. I direct the acute-care facility at Johns Hopkins." Her voice conveys either surprise that Will can have forgotten an appointment of this stature, or her more general—and justifiable—irritation with him for having created a crisis that has interrupted both their lives and demanded the inconvenience of this meeting.

"Sorry," he says, "of course. I'm preoccupied. Lately, I mean." How clearly he can picture Elizabeth presiding over a room filled with those state-of-the-art tank beds, each holding a body suspended in some advanced regeneration gel. Suddenly, he remembers that the previous night (in anticipation of this meeting, no doubt) he dreamed of austere white-coated Elizabeth as she ministered to a body on a bed of unguent, a body so burned that it had no skin. And yet there was no blood, either, no unsightly, blistered bits or charred wounds. It was flesh as decorative as that of a transparent man in an encyclopedia.

"Well?" Elizabeth says. She shoves a waxed paper cup under a nozzle that pours Diet Dr Pepper over a few lumps of ice. This is his, evidently, because she moves on to a selection of tea bags, picking through them until she finds one she deems acceptable. She unwraps it with care, leaving the fragile paper envelope intact, drops it into a Styrofoam cup, and pushes a red button to discharge a stream of hot water onto the bag. Then she marches, with him in tow, to the cashier. "Your treat." She enunciates the word *treat* so sharply that it sounds as unpleasant and cold as, say, sleet.

The only unoccupied table is a large one with a big, striped umbrella planted in its center. "God, I hate that," Elizabeth says. "It's just too stupid. As if to fool you into thinking you're dining on some patio on the Riviera." She points at the chair opposite hers, an imperious gesture, employer to underling or professor to failing student. Three plastic saltshakers are lying on the table among a scattering of crystals, and she rights them in the center, brushes the spilled salt off with a paper napkin. Having spent only ten minutes in her caustic company, Will is already debilitated.

"So," he says, "I'd just like . . . I know time is short, but I'd like to quickly sum up my encounters with your daughter."

"Jennifer."

"Jennifer."

After saying the name they both look at each other in silence. "So," he begins after a swallow of Diet Dr Pepper. "Last month a young woman who calls herself Andrea, and who claims she's been referred to me by another of my patients, begins treatment for a specific problem. She describes a compulsion to seduce older men and characterizes her pursuit of these objects as driven by a rigid set of criteria. They must be no younger than forty-five. They have to be professionals, gainfully employed. Glasses are a plus; baldness, obesity, and hearing aids unacceptable. There's more, but you get the picture.

"As she tells it, it's clear that her physical satisfaction is secondary to the brief reassurance, or abatement of anxiety, that sex with these partners affords her. She draws an analogy between her sexual trophies and a collection of paperweights to which she was attached as an adolescent." Will pauses to underscore the paperweight allusion; Elizabeth regards him without affect, as if his face belongs not to a human being but to a clock or a speedometer, a tin plate under a veneer of paint. As they watch each other, Will feels a profound weariness, so leaden it's as if his substance, the stuff of which he's made, has changed without warning, his molecular weight doubled or squared so that gravity now presses him that much harder into his plastic chair. It's the moment when the twinkling silhouette disappears from the *Enterprise*, the transported body of whoever it was reassembled on a planet with an alien, possibly injurious atmosphere.

Elizabeth is still tilted forward in her seat. What's he doing here anyway? It's not too late, he can stand, apologize for inconveniencing this woman who has become, after all these years, a stranger. He can go home. He can, except that somehow he can't.

"Well," she says, "we don't have all day, William. I don't, anyway."

"So far there have been, the young woman estimates, thirty-eight of these seductions. A better word would be *transactions*, because the intercourse she describes is without emotional content. She has no interest in her partner's feelings; the sex is dispassionate; the partner fits a profile, no more, no less; this is the extent of his worth." Will watches Elizabeth sip her tea.

"I'm listening," she says, looking down at the unfinished sandwich on her plate. The part in her hair is very straight and pale, and Will thinks of the girl's bitten fingernails, the shiny pink flesh that rises around them, hot and swollen. "Angry," his mother would say of the bitten nails, as in "an angry cut."

In spite of his intent to banish them from his consciousness, the unfortunate tips of Jennifer's fingers have become an erotic snag, a penetrating detail that insinuates itself into his thoughts, pulling the girl's whole body along after them. Even so tangential a catalyst as the controlled part in her mother's hair is enough to summon them, the clean line of the part demanding the answer of their raw vehemence. Under the table, the red-tipped fingers find his fly; they close around his cock, even as his awareness of having potentially bedded a girl who might be his own child makes him feel literally sick. Will stops unwrapping his sandwich, unbuttons the collar of his shirt.

"So," Will goes on, "the young woman tells me she's tried approaches other than psychoanalysis to cure this problem. She's seen counselors at school, dismisses them as incompetent; ditto for cognitive therapy, the Skinnerite behavior-mod specialist, the Menninger disciple, the yoga instructor, the acupuncturist, and the chiropractor, who tried to remove whatever obstruction had diverted the flow of her sexual energy, making her desire old men.

"Anyway, as I said in the e-mail, the young woman, 'Andrea,' knows details of your past that only you can have provided, and she has *'Quo usque tandem'* et cetera tattooed on her chest. Clearly she is, unbeknownst to me, your child, with whom you've shared my impulsive suggestion of DNA testing." Will, whose mouth is dry, takes another swallow of the Diet Dr Pepper, which tastes more vile than he could have imagined, like watered-down, carbonated prune juice. Elizabeth continues to regard him without expression.

"Well?" she says, when he doesn't say anything. "Will you please get to the point? We do know all this. We have established this much."

"Here's the point. While I assume that she bears no relationship to me—why would I think otherwise?—she's checking me out. She has a definite agenda. She arrives on time for her second session, and we address the problem she described the previous week. This entails a detailed account of her most recent 'date' with an older man, a narrative that strikes every possible erotic note and one that's obviously an attempt to put the moves on me."

"On you!" Elizabeth slaps the table with her open hand. "My God, William, have you completely lost it?"

"Let me finish. So after a 'blow-by-blow'—her words, not mine—description of how she seduced a professor at the place where she waits tables, she gets up to leave and hesitates at the door to my office. Asks me for help with the knob because, she claims, she has carpal tunnel syndrome and can't turn it. This being the very same knob she turned the previous week, but what she really wants has nothing to do with the knob; she—"

Elizabeth surges up from her green metal chair, her thigh hitting the tabletop so that the umbrella sways, tea and Dr Pepper slosh over the lips of their respective cups. "She does! Jennifer does have CTS, and as you'd know if you were a real doctor, it is not a constant thing, it goes into remission for a time and then it's—"

"Fine," Will says. "Fine. Jennifer has carpal tunnel. But it didn't prevent her from accompanying her open-mouth, big-tongued kiss with some very dexterous, very nimble manipulation of my genitals. Despite her crippled hands."

"She did not!" Elizabeth cries. "That did not happen!"

"Yes," Will says. "It did. But that's not all, Elizabeth."

"You're telling me that my daughter put her hand down your pants?"

"Not exactly. She fondled me through the fabric of my trousers while she French-kissed me. And that's still not the end."

Elizabeth sets her lips in a tight line.

"I discontinue treatment and refer her to a colleague. I assure her that I will not share any of our conversations or her unusual behavior with that colleague. She'll have a fresh start, a clean slate, whatever she wants to call it. But that's not what she wants. She has no interest in starting over, no interest in analysis or any other kind of psychotherapy. Her agenda is decidedly outside of the therapeutic envelope. She calls me; she leaves messages with my service. When I don't return her calls, she tracks me down at my home number. I hang up, or, when Carole answers, I refuse to take the call, explaining—honestly, or so I think—that I'm under siege from a patient with whom I've discontinued treatment. I even tell Carole why it was I discontinued treatment, and we talk about the occupational hazards of working with unbalanced individuals.

"Anyway, when she can't reach me by phone, she comes to my office one afternoon and, thinking she's my three o'clock, who happens to be late, I buzz her in. I manage to get her out of my office when the patient does arrive, but she doesn't leave the building. Instead, she sits on the stairs, she comes back up when the session is over. She has to see me, she's sorry, needs my help, doesn't want to start over with a different therapist. Please, please. And why am I making such a big deal out of a kiss if, as I've told her, she's no longer my patient? After all, outside the context of any professional involvement, a kiss is no big deal. By now, I've turned my back on her for a minute so I can collect my thoughts, figure out how to get rid of this person without physically throwing her out of the building. But whatever I've planned to say goes right out of my head. That's how shocked I am to find that while I wasn't watching her she's taken her clothes off. All of them. She refuses to dress or to leave. She threatens to cause a scene—'kick and scream' is how she put it—if I don't play the game her way."

Elizabeth's mouth, which has been open for some time, begins to speak in an unnaturally calm and measured tone, the voice of someone who works a 911 line, who gives the same directions countless times each day, who is prepared to listen and respond to heart attacks and drug overdoses, babies who can't be woken, criminals with guns, fires in the attic, and more. "There's a phenomenon," she says, "I'd think you'd be familiar with it, William. It's called erotomania. Erotomaniacs suffer the delusion that other people are sexually fixated on them. Maybe after the accident, after your son drowned, maybe you got a little unglued and—"

"Of course I came unglued! Not a little, a lot! And, yes, Elizabeth, I do know what erotomania is. How is it that all these years later, as other people our age arrive at a more nuanced and humane maturity, you remain so condescending? Do you actually believe you've got it all figured out? That the rest of us are just struggling to catch up? I'm not talking about erotomania, and I'm not talking about me. I'm talking about a young woman who is endangering herself and others with her amoral and pathologically narciss—"

"Oh, spare me! I'm not one of the suckers you can fool with your psychojargon. As you've said, Jennifer is not your patient. You have no idea who she is."

"Do you? Do you have any idea who she is? Maybe the rest of this story will be illuminating. Maybe not. Maybe it will come as no surprise." He folds his arms, waiting for her to ask him to continue.

"Well," Elizabeth says. "Don't stop at the cliff-hanger. What happened?"

"She steps up, unbuckles my belt, unzips my fly, and we have sex."

"Oh fuck," Elizabeth says, and she closes her eyes. Her face, no longer animated by her eyes, looks exhausted. He sees lines he hadn't noticed before, around her mouth and on her forehead. "Why! Why didn't you stop her?"

"Well, first of all, don't forget, I think she's Andrea whoever, a young woman who is no longer my patient. Second, I'm . . . she . . . I was worried about protecting my career, my family. I didn't have any faith that I could resist her effectively. Without her framing me. I was—"

"You were a schmuck!"

"And you know what's the worst part of this mess? I don't know what I should be worrying about most. Potential incest? Adultery? An STD? Or the idea of you and my brother?"

"Your brother?" Elizabeth looks at him sharply. "What does your brother have to do with this?"

"Jennifer said you were sexually involved with both me and Mitch at the same time. And two other men. Four potential fathers." Elizabeth stares at Will, not saying anything. "After Jennifer offered me a strand of her hair," he goes on, "she explained that it might not be so bad. I hadn't necessarily done it with my daughter; she could just as easily be my niece. And that's because"—Will's voice gets louder—"you were fucking my brother!"

"Don't yell," Elizabeth says.

"Were you or were you not fucking Mitch?"

"Don't yell."

"Were you?"

"Yes."

"Yes!"

"I told you, yes."

"I cannot, I can not—well, I can—but no, I cannot believe that my brother, that, that you . . . why?"

"You know, William, I can't help but suspect that you're making a big deal out of this in order to draw attention away from the fact that you had sex with my daughter."

"She assaulted me."

"According to you."

"She was the aggressor, and I didn't know her real identity because she lied."

"Okay, so you were screwing a patient twenty-five years younger than you. Ex-patient. Let's not claim moral high ground. Anyway, we're talking twenty-five years ago. When we were kids. Is it such a big fucking deal if when we were kids I slept with your brother?"

"Why?" Will asks. "Tell me why. Why were you screwing Mitch and me at the same time?"

"Oh, Christ. Can we get back to the real topic? And it's not like it started out that way. For a long while it was just you."

"And then?"

"And then it wasn't. But we're not talking about the past. We're talking about—"

"It was and then it wasn't? What is that supposed to mean?"

She shrugs. "I don't know. I guess he came on to me."

"Mitch came on to you? When did he?"

"Actually, it was more complicated than that." Elizabeth frowns, pinches her lower lip. "He sort of led me to believe it was you, that he was you, and by the time I knew he wasn't, it was too late."

"How the hell did he do that?"

Elizabeth raises her hands, wiggles her fingers theatrically. "Under cover of darkness," she says. "You're twins, remember? Identical. Built the same, sound the same. You guys were so square you even had the same haircuts." She takes a sip of her tea, now cold, and makes a face.

"Go on," Will says.

"He came over, this was sometime senior year—I was living off-campus in that house on Maplewood—and he slipped in that back door—you know which one, you used it yourself. So he made his way to my room and got into bed with me. I thought that was pretty ballsy. I liked it—it was sexy. You seemed suddenly sexier, or you seemed sexy in a way you'd never been before. Of course at first that's who I thought it was—you. After, when he revealed himself, I was irked."

"*Irked?* You were *irked?*"

"Yes, pissed off. I guess because I was a little freaked out. But then, after a minute or two, it didn't seem so bad."

"A minute or two! That's how long it took you to adjust?"

Elizabeth leans forward. "About as long as it took for Jennifer to go from being a person to whom you owed professional respect to just another piece of ass."

Will ignores this. *Sexy in a way you'd never been before.* Mitch, who he thought was celibate. "So was that . . . was it . . . was that the only time?"

"No."

"No?"

"No."

"How many?"

"I don't know."

"You lost count?"

"I never tried to count. Jesus, why are men so petty and small-minded? Do you think I made hatch marks on my bedpost? I'm a woman, I don't have to do that. I'm not living in constant fear of sexual inadequacy. I don't worry that my penis isn't big enough or that I won't be able to get it up or—"

"Okay, okay. For how long?"

"I don't know. He came back. I didn't stop him. I don't remember for how long."

"Yes, you do."

"You're right, I do."

"Why?" Will says. "Why did you let it go on?"

"It was, I don't know, interesting."

"It was *interesting*?"

"Yes, interesting. Sophisticated. Cool. It seemed hip and liberated. Counterculture. All those things we wanted to be. It seemed free."

"Who? Who wanted to be cool and counterculture?"

"All of us." She raises her eyebrows at him. "I did. Didn't you?"

"What's free about deceiving someone? A person who loved you?"

"I don't know, William. You were always . . . you made everything so claustrophobic. You were always all over me, and I don't mean physically. I felt like I couldn't get any air when I was with you." She stops, frowning in concentration, and he sees the same frown as her daughter's. Why, why hadn't he put things together? "In retrospect," she says, "I think it must have seemed like a way to escape you without doing anything terribly wrong. You and Mitch being twins made it seem like it wasn't cheating, exactly, or it wasn't such serious cheat—"

"Are you kidding! It's worse that he's my brother!"

"Now, maybe. To you, maybe. But to me, back then, the fact that he was so nearly you mitigated that aspect of it. I know that sounds like a rationalization, but it is how it felt. And it's not as if you and I were engaged or something. I never said I wasn't sleeping with anyone else. Besides, I didn't think you'd get hurt. I didn't think anyone would find out. And no one did, William. This all started because you were so weird and fixated at the reunion. I mean, it's been twenty-five years. Have you forgotten that we were young? We were, you know, kids. Careless."

"I wasn't. I was never careless with you."

"Well, I guess I just must have been less *evolved*."

"Less evolved! The person you're describing is someone with the moral intelligence of a bait worm!"

"Jesus, William. Will you just lighten up?"

"Who was better?" he asks.

"Better?"

"Who was better in bed?"

"You must be joking."

"Not at all. Who was the better lover?"

"Both of you were what, twenty? No one is a *lover* at twenty." Elizabeth uses the index and middle finger of each hand to make quotation marks in the air when she says the word *lover*.

"Fine. Who lasted longer? Who was more considerate, more deft, more creative? Who made you feel good? Who went down on you? Who made you come?"

"I'm not going to answer any of this."

Will reaches across the table and grabs Elizabeth's wrist, aware that he's out of control, but it's like noticing your car's brakes have failed when you're already going down a hill: he can't stop. "Yes, you are," he says. "You are."

She twists out of his grasp, stands up. "I'm leaving. I've had enough."

"So have I. But it's not over yet."

"Yes it is." She ties the belt of her trench coat and shoves her hands in her pockets. "If you contact me—if you e-mail me again, or call me, or Jennifer—I'll report you to the police. I'll tell them you sexually assaulted my daughter. If Jennifer is half as calculating as the person you've described, then maybe she didn't use a condom because she wanted her underpants to collect some, what shall we call it? Proof of your trespass?" Elizabeth looks at Will and, when he doesn't answer, continues. "Any number of strategies might present themselves to an amoral, ambitious, sexually experienced girl like Jennifer. I hope she didn't perform fellatio on you. Only too easy to have hidden a Ziploc bag somewhere. A quick spit and, zip, she'd—"

"There was nothing like that," Will says.

"Oh, I don't know, William. And neither do you. Under such circumstances you must have been distracted. 'Thinking with the little head' would, I believe, be the appropriate expression. Consider this. You're a forty-seven-year-old man. She's a girl of twenty-four. Who do you think anyone would believe?" Without waiting for an answer, Elizabeth turns and starts walking away, toward the platforms.

How long before it occurs to Will that if Mitch slept with Elizabeth, he might have slept with other girls—other of his girlfriends?

On the crowded train home from Philadelphia, Will has a backward-facing seat and blames this for contributing to his sense of disorientation. He stares silently out the window, watching the string of fenced yards unspool backward into the distance, as if they were moving and he sitting still. Squalid little houses, some of them, sagging laundry lines and broken toys spread across the withered grass. Something that looks like half a house slides past, rooms missing walls, naked and flimsy under the pale afternoon sun. As for Will, a big chunk of his own foundation, the block of certainties upon which he'd piled all sorts of other assumptions he'd made about his life, has officially been removed. Is this melodramatic? Yes. Still, he wonders if the chunk was a keystone, and how much of the rest of him will go down with it. Isn't this how patients describe breakdowns? First that vertiginous sense of losing one's footing, then the teetering, finally the plummet. How bad would it be? How far?

Will reviews his list of worries, something he pictures like a pull-down menu on a computer screen, growing ever longer. Now it includes the possibility that Jennifer has saved his semen, that his brother betrayed him with other people, that even as he struggles to direct his patients to deeper levels of self-awareness, he doesn't know essential aspects of his own life.

Incest. He has a patient whose background includes her father's molesting her; having seen her for fifteen years, he's still surprised by the malarial quality of the damage, the way it won't fade, arrives without warning and dismantles her. "I'm no better than a dog on a chain," she said. "I can only get so far before it yanks me back. I'm forty fucking years old, and it is never ever going to go away." But Jennifer isn't a child; he didn't force himself on her; he didn't know. And it might not be true. Please, let it not be true.

And now what? What's he supposed to do now? He doesn't understand Elizabeth's casual attitude toward sleeping with twin brothers, her lying to him and, presumably, to the man she married. And what to make of her suggestion that he and Mitch were not entirely distinct from each other, not enough anyway to be considered separate individuals? Didn't that have to be bullshit, a tidy lie to ease her conscience? And yet, hasn't Will himself feared their over-identification? Still, his deepest sexual transgression—with the girl, possibly breaking taboo—was unknowing. While Mitch's, also in defiance of taboo, was conscious, deliberate.

Will remembers his own lust at twenty, twenty-one. His brother's would have to have been the same, wouldn't it? Same biology, same wiring. And Mitch had always been too self-conscious about his disfigurement to even talk to a girl. Too proud to allow anyone the tiniest sliver of compassion for him, because he could never feel sympathy as distinct from pity.

He should just let the whole thing go, shouldn't he? If he can't do this out of generosity toward Mitch, if he can't summon forgiveness, then perhaps he can out of a sense of self-preservation. Let go before it develops into exactly the kind of obsessive pursuit he's heard patients describe as the prelude to a crisis. Because Will has enough crises. Infidelity. Impotence. Incest!

Every time he approaches the idea of Jennifer, whatever analytical ability he possesses disappears. Thoughts don't proceed in logical argument; they ricochet around inside his skull, cracking into one another like pinballs and destroying every coherent mental construction in their path. Images of Carole and Samantha jumble with parts of Jennifer he wishes he'd never seen, paranoid scenarios of sex police knocking at his door, incarceration in dank jails filled with rapists and pederasts, his old, respectable colleagues replaced by new ones: criminals, perverts. Perps.

He takes out his cell phone and dials Daniel's number, gets his voice mail, and leaves a message.

What does it mean to be caught in two simultaneous snares of obsessive thought, both concerning sexual transgression? Thoughts of Mitch with one woman competing with thoughts of himself with that same woman's daughter, a daughter who isn't much older than her mother had been when her mother was involved with Mitch and Will. Were these a patient's parallel obsessions, Will would have to agree with Elizabeth's initial, knee-jerk diagnosis: the whole construct must represent an unconscious strategy for avoiding an even more unacceptable and unbelievable something. But what? Luke's death? It's been three years.

Of course, that argument does tend to collapse in the face of his fury over Mitch and Elizabeth having been involved twenty-five years ago. And, if his patients are at all representative of the human condition, the past isn't past until it's lived. Not lived through, *lived*. Felt.

Fuck it, Will thinks. Fuck me. Fuck you, William Moreland. And fuck you, too, Mitchell Moreland. You have made a big fat fucking mess, so fuck you. He hits redial, gets Daniel's voice mail again, and hangs up. Then he reconsiders and hits redial to leave a second message. "I have to talk to you," he says. "I have to talk to you tonight."

How is a person to ignore information that changes everything? It's not as if he's made any of this up. And it's no small deceit that Elizabeth described—Mitch's entering her house after dark, pretending to be Will, and penetrating Elizabeth's room, her bed, her body, a trespass followed by the confession that he wasn't who she assumed—no, not a confession. Confession implies shame, and the scene Will imagines doesn't include his brother's feeling ashamed. When had Mitch ever betrayed any form of regret? Mitch was angry, angry enough to have always spoken in a soft voice and moved with silent grace. If he hadn't been conscious of his rage, some part of him knew he was carrying explosive cargo and carried it very carefully. So carefully that even his twin—or especially his twin: his obligingly, willfully blind twin—hadn't felt it.

Will had been nearing the midpoint of his training analysis before he could attempt to address his brother's peculiarly thoughtful and deliberate passage through the years, leading up to college, acts of what seemed to be impulsive, helpless generosity accomplished with a nearly visible tremor of determination. Mitch hadn't lied when he said he couldn't resist carrying an old woman's groceries to her car or mowing the neighbor's lawn while that neighbor recuperated from surgery. When he first began to question his brother's motives, Will misunderstood these as acts of hypocrisy, but in truth they'd been far more insidious. They were opportunities for Mitch to cloak his misanthropy, to disguise his hatred for the unmarked faces all around him. Hide it from himself before anyone else. Because, like anyone dedicated to a performance, Mitch was his own first audience, the one person above all others whom he had to convince.

In the dark, in Elizabeth's bedroom, having just fucked her, Will's brother wouldn't have confessed his identity; he'd have announced it—crowed, in effect. He would have loved how it felt to steal Elizabeth. Loved the discovery enough to do it again, and again.

If in fact this was a discovery.

If Elizabeth was the first of Will's girlfriends that Mitch seduced.

Will closes his eyes. His head aches and he succumbs to a flight of hypochondria, hurrying through the relatively benign and less interesting causes of cranial miseries—eye strain, sinus infection, food allergy—to arrive at potentially fatal diagnoses, like critically high blood pressure, which would explain why he always feels his collar tightening during the course of a day. Then there's the even more affecting brain tumor, which he accessorizes with tableaux of his confinement in a hospital bed, Samantha playing with the buttons and making his pitifully bandaged head and wasted legs go up and then down. Stoic and pale, Carole resists going over all the papers and insurance documents he wants her to review before his death, insisting that he can make himself better, if only he will try to believe in the possibility of recovery, and swallow ayurvedic potions.

Will gets out a pad of paper and begins a list of some of the girls he's dated. The ones Mitch could maybe have crossed paths with.

April Pedly

Marna Yardham

Esther (Newton?)

Christine Johnson

Elizabeth Fuller

Julie Applegate

Lisa Christianson

Jean McMinnamin (sp.?)

So, start with April, the girl with whom he lost his virginity. April had been at camp with them, not the camp from which Will had been expelled, but the one he and Mitch attended the following summer, when they were fifteen. Pale and lanky—languid—her limbs a little too pliable, she'd seemed lacking in vitality, a doll whose batteries were drained. But Will had found her blue eyes extraordinary. Blood-shot and red-rimmed from allergies, they suggested not hay fever so much as a consuming, destructive passion. In the context of her ener-vation, they seemed to indicate a secret love marked by epic, unre-quited weeping in her bunk on the girls' side of the camp.

Penetrating the divide between the boys' and girls' sides hadn't presented a problem. The junior counselors, who lived in the cabins with the campers, never even tried to prevent the consummation of nighttime pilgrimages through the little copse of struggling maples and birch trees that separated the two clusters of cabins—too much of a hassle, not to mention a loss of sleep, and for what? Under the trees the ground was lush with poison ivy, and if that didn't dampen lust, what could? Of course, any kid who wanted to advertise himself as an initiate into the mysteries of sex didn't wear socks or long pants because he considered a poison ivy rash to be a badge of honor. Any-one with raw and oozing shins claimed, in effect, to have gotten his rocks off. Now that Will thinks about it, there must have been more than a few boys who went only as far as the copse, exposed their un-protected legs to the oily green leaves, and then headed back, seeking to enlarge their reputations rather than their experience.

Will made at least five nocturnal visits to the girls' side, summon-ing the wan and ectomorphic April from her cabin. She slept lightly, wheezing by a window whose flimsy screen could be removed with little effort. After they'd done it—not so much a memorable initia-tion as his confused fumbling toward what must have been a painful disappointment for April, a few stabbing thrusts and then he pulled back enough to come on rather than in her—Will hurried back to his bunk. The next morning he showed off the broken skin above his sock lines, barely waiting past breakfast to prop his red legs up on benches and fence rails, scratching exhibitionistically, silently bragging that he was no longer a virgin.

Will never told Mitch about visiting April—he never spoke with his brother about any of his romantic quests, even the failed ones, because he didn't want to hurt him or underscore his isolation, his imprisonment behind his face. But Mitch knew—of course he did, because everyone knew who was getting any and how often. It would have been a simple thing for Mitch to lie awake until he was sure that Will was asleep in the bed above his, that Will wasn't going through the copse that night. Then, in the shadows, only too easy to slip out and over to the girls' side, legs well protected, pants tucked into socks. Who slept in which cabin was practically announced by the camp post office, where mail was sorted into boxes labeled with the names of the cabins. Perhaps April, Will's first, was also Mitch's first, and camp the setting in which he acquired the cover of night as his M.O.

Given the pressure of the moment—the hurrying, the excitement, the lust—it would have been easy to mistake Mitch for Will. As long as Mitch chose a night when the moon was new or the sky overcast, as long as he kept within the shadows, April, like Elizabeth, would have had no reason to suspect the boy who came to her might be anyone other than Will. In retrospect, she didn't seem a very perceptive girl, not the sharpest blade in the drawer. But that's not fair. Probably it was just that April, like the rest of them, was self-involved to the point that she paid little attention to anyone but herself. At fifteen, the prospect of getting laid was more than enough to eclipse every competing thought, and even older lovers are blind to a lover's true identity. The bed trick was one of the oldest in the book—all the way back to Genesis. Abraham, Leah, Rachel.

So, April, then. Will uncaps his pen, staring at the little houses that flash by his window, each a white square, identical except for the odd detail, racing past like single frames of a film. Will and Mitch sharing the same girl. Almost like fucking each other, Will thinks, allowing the thought for only a second. Funny how you could hold one of the houses in your vision, follow it for a beat or two, so long as you picked only one from out of the stream. One second was enough to note two or three details: the empty plastic pool, the red tricycle next to the round, red barbecue. For an instant he could see all this, and then it was gone. And, for a finger snap of consciousness, Will understands that, driving into the red-eyed, pale-lipped April, Mitch had chosen the wet center of a girl as the place for the brothers' brief reunion. What better than this primal consummation for two who were once one, two who would always remain a single idea for a person?

The epiphany—if that's what it is—lasts no longer than the image of the one little house among many; it arrives, departs, and is replaced by another. And maybe it's more a conceit than a truth, a projection of Will's, not Mitch's but Will's, desire for the return of his absent twin, the version of himself defaced. The birthmark had robbed Will's brother of a face, left him faceless, humiliated, having suffered a literal loss of face. Well, whatever the thought is, Will has no time to explore it before it's gone, returned to his unconscious, out of reach, but not before a few synapses have fired in its wake, a sequence that summons a wave of tiny contractions, minute *erector pili* muscles, one per follicle, each lifting a single hair on the back of his neck, together raising his hackles; Will shudders. It's the deep sort of shudder imaginatively linked to a stranger walking over one's future grave. He shifts in his seat, makes a check mark next to the name April Pedly, indicating that he's thought through a scenario and concluded that betrayal was plausible, if not proven.

Marna Yardham he can't quite remember, or, to be more truthful, he remembers a few parts of her so well, so pungently, that they obliterate others. Marna was his tenth-grade girlfriend; she lived off Majors Road, one of those girls who kept a horse, sexually precocious with her own species while romantically fixated on another. Will used to visit her at the stables and watch as she braided Pilot's mane with ribbons, clamped a big foot between her thighs to pick the bottom of its hoof clean. She washed, curried, and kissed Pilot, fed him a carrot with her own mouth, lips puckered around the wider end of the root, waiting for his big teeth to eat their way nearly to her face before she let the last bite go.

Esther—forget Esther, he can't even be sure he's remembered her last name correctly. He can't remember the color of her hair. All he knows is she had a car too small for sex, a blue Toyota Corolla, and that that hadn't stopped them.

Christine Johnson: dark hair, round face, long legs. Earnest to a fault, no sense of humor, especially with regard to herself. Christine had intended to Make a Difference. She was going to be the next Madame Curie or Mary Wollstonecraft, transcend injustices imposed by the patriarchy, redeem womankind. They dated Will's freshman year of college, which would have been Mitch's freshman year as well. Poor Christine. At the reunion he'd heard she married a religious fanatic and was living in a commune, raising six children, each named for a Hindu deity—Parvati, Rudra, Siva—he can't remember the other three.

At home Will's parents had debated the advantages and disadvantages of Will and Mitch attending the same university. Mitch, present for these after-dinner talks—he wasn't given a choice—said nothing, and neither did their mother, while Will and their father crept toward the conclusion that perhaps the right institution could provide an interim period of adjustment for the two brothers. Cornell was a big school, large enough that each twin could find his own separate path, and yet students lived within walking distance of one another. Mitch could draw comfort from Will's relative proximity.

Or, were this his brother's purpose, figure out a way to secretly share Will's sexual partners.

Will looks at the little paper with the list of girls, then folds and shoves it into his breast pocket. He'll Google all the names at home, later. Or he can use Cornell's online alumni directory. As a graduate of the university, he'd been given a code that allowed him to access its database. A resource he discovered at the reunion, the fateful reunion.

W ell?" Daniel says as Will sits down.
"I haven't told her."

"No?"

"I feel like I'm . . . I just have to get a few things straight before I talk to Carole. Straight in my head."

"How will you do that?"

"I've contacted one of them, a woman named Lisa Christianson. E-mailed her. She said she'd see me."

"See you."

"Yes. Talk to me. I mean, I didn't tell her what it was I wanted to talk about. I . . . well, I led her to believe that I was going to be in the area. In Albany. Said I'd like to stop in."

"What will you do?" Daniel says.

"Ask her, I guess. I'll ask her."

"Then what?"

"I don't know. I'm not sure. If she says no, that it never happened, then I guess I might try someone else. And if that woman says no, I'll drop it. I'll tell Carole what happened with the girl. Ask her forgiveness. I mean, what are the choices?"

"And if she says yes?"

"Lisa Christianson?"

Daniel nods. "What if she confirms your suspicions?" he asks.

"I don't know. I have no idea. I mean, I already feel like I don't know anything anymore. Or anyone. Or myself. I ran into a friend yesterday, John York. We talked for a while; then he asked me to return his boxed set of Charles Mingus. Said he wouldn't ask if it weren't a rare recording that's no longer available. But I never borrowed any CD's from him. The only time I see the guy is on the racquetball court." Will shakes his head. "It wasn't that he accused me, but I could tell he didn't believe me when I said I didn't have it. That he thought I'd borrowed the recording and forgotten about it. Or that I was lying intentionally. And even though I was sure I didn't have his CD's, that he hadn't ever loaned me any recordings at all, when I got home I went through all our music, twice, looking for something I've never seen before."

Daniel is silent. Then, "Another instance of confusion or ambiguity over what's true, what's a lie," he says.

"I know. I know. But I don't get the significance. I mean, was I being paranoid? Maybe I was. Maybe he didn't think I was lying. Maybe my feelings about that transaction have nothing to do with John at all, but with something else, something present under or behind every essentially meaningless event, with the power to show through what's happening on the surface. Like, like a black bra showing through a white blouse." Will shakes his head. "I'll have to . . . if Lisa says yes, I'll have to go through the past. Factor in this, this . . . factor in whatever she tells me. Correct my misapprehension of everything."

"That's a striking image you used."

"What? The black bra?"

"Yes."

"Sexual," Will says, nodding. "It just popped out."

"So I assumed."

"You know, I can't . . . ever since Jennifer, I can't get it up. I don't know if it's the possibility of her being related to me, or if it's that . . . well, it wasn't my plan, but I did cheat on my wife." Will slumps down in the seat, pinches the skin over his Adam's apple. "Or if it's because of Mitch." He closes his eyes, stops speaking.

"If your ability to perform sexually has been dismantled by what you've learned about your brother?"

Will nods. "You know," he says after a silence, "I'm not going to get anywhere in here, with you, until I've straightened out this, this thing about Mitch. Until I know if it was just Elizabeth or . . ." He stands up. "I'm sorry. I think I'd like to leave, come back to talk after I've seen Lisa."

Daniel pushes his chair back from his desk and stands. "You know, Will, I think it's been a mistake not to use the couch over the last few months."

"A mistake?" Will looks at him. "Don't you mean a dodge?"

Daniel nods. "Yes," he says, "that is what I mean."

He drives their blue minivan north without stopping for anything but gas, coffee, and a Little Debbie cinnamon roll, the pastry stuck to the clear wrapper with white sugar glaze. After a couple of bites, he drops the rest into the garbage can next to the pumps. The bonsai nursery Lisa Christianson runs with her husband is a little less than 200 miles northwest of New York City. To get there, Will follows the MapQuest directions he got off the Internet, pulling off I-87 onto a poorly paved road through short, forested hills, where evergreens give way to pockets of deciduous trees, naked now, their branches bare. A light snow is falling.

The greenhouses, eight of them, are in a small valley, each one vast and filled with steaming life. So much condensation runs down the inside surface of the glass panes that the plants within look blurred, like an Impressionist painting.

Will pulls the minivan off the narrow access road and parks where he won't block anyone's way. When he gets out, a small pack of lap dogs comes tearing out from behind one of the glass structures, barking and jumping at him. The most aggressive is a Yorkshire terrier that seems as if it may actually bite him or at least take hold of his pant leg, and despite the foolish aspect of retreating from so small a foe, he's just getting back into his car when a woman in a khaki barn coat emerges from one of the far greenhouses. She calls the dogs off with a whistle, the kind requiring two fingers under the tongue, a trick that many times he'd tried and failed to teach Luke. The woman in the khaki coat approaches.

"Hello," Will says. She looks different than he expected.

"Hello," the woman says. She stands with her hands shoved in her coat pockets. Either she's changed in some way he can't identify, or he can't remember her twenty-one-year-old self well enough to make a match with the woman standing before him, and this disturbs Will; it makes him feel as if he can't be sure he's arrived at the right place after all. He has to fight his desire to ask all the questions that were already answered during their e-mail correspondence. Is she the Lisa Christianson who double-majored in economics and art history? Whose sister had lupus? Who slept with him for a couple of months the summer between junior and senior year?

"I have some work I have to finish," she says. "Maybe we could visit while I . . . I guess what I'm saying is I'd be more relaxed if we could talk while I work."

"Of course," Will says, and he follows her back to the greenhouse.

"I have a couple gross of trees to prune and train, and others to pack for trucking. Sean's over at his brother's, and both our workers are out with some flu thing."

The little trees, each planted in a glazed, black ceramic dish, are grouped along a huge trestle table, its surface pitted and stained. To one side are shelves filled with unassembled cartons and stacks of Styrofoam inserts sized to fit inside the cartons.

"We move a lot of plants during the holidays," she says, and Will reaches out to touch the dark, shiny green leaves on a tiny, gnarled tree. "That's a Fukien tea tree. Subtropical. All the ones inside are subtropical. The evergreens and deciduous—maples mostly, but we do some birch and crab apple—they stay outside through the winter."

"Do you sell them to florists?" Will asks. "Or to, I don't know, garden centers?"

"More and more, we sell them online and ship them via UPS. The rest go to retailers closer to the city."

"It must be—I imagine you have to harden yourself to the idea that a lot of the trees that thrived under your care die after you sell them," he says. Lisa looks at Will as if he's said something strange.

"So," she says, turning toward a table whose surface holds an array of small clippers and spools of wire. "You didn't come here to talk about horticulture, did you?"

"No. I came because"—*I'm going through a midlife crisis*, he almost says, a tempting if radical abridgment of the truth. But if he wants her to be forthcoming with him, then he has to be honest himself. "I need to talk to you about something. For the past fifteen years or so I've been estranged from my brother. I think you may have known that I had—have—a—"

"Mitch," she says, nodding. "Except that now he's the renowned Mitchell Moreland."

"Right."

"Estranged?" She tilts her head to one side in a questioning gesture. "How come?"

"I'm not sure," he says. "I don't have . . . what I'm going to ask you—your answer, I mean—I hope it may illuminate something." As if he were a teenager again and trying to get up the nerve to ask a girl on a date, Will feels his heart accelerate, that funny, dizzy headache he associates with standing up too quickly.

Lisa Christianson shifts her attention away from him to the tiny spruce in front of her. She turns it around and around on the table, considering its shape before taking off one branch, and then, after another revolution, a second. She bends one of the remaining limbs, wires it, and bends it further, until it assumes the asymmetry she wants. She looks up at Will. "What do you want to know?" she asks. The tone of her voice strikes him as wary, or is this his imagination?

"This is awkward, but I'm wondering . . . did Mitch . . ." Will stops, silently rehearses his question and then blurts it out. "Were you ever sexually involved with my brother?"

Lisa sets the little clippers on the plank table. Rather than looking at him, she addresses a spot over his left shoulder. "I guess I thought you knew that," she says.

Will closes his eyes briefly, feeling the adrenaline wash through his body from somewhere in his chest, all the purely physical responses it provokes, pulse climbing, arms tingling.

"Do you . . . I drank a lot of coffee on the road," he says. "I should have asked to use the men's room before we began talking."

"There's a, well, it's not a men's room. More like a porta-potty." She points through the wet glass to a green blot. "Back over by that last greenhouse." She looks at him again, as if she's trying to figure something out.

The porta-potty must be for the hired hands, he guesses, breathing through his mouth to avoid the smell of disinfectant with its undertow of human waste. He stands for a moment before going out the green plastic door, trying to collect his thoughts.

"Are you all right?" Lisa says when he returns, not very promptly. "I, um, I do have enough time for us to go inside for a bit. Have a cup of tea or something."

"I'm fine," Will says, manufacturing an expression to go with the words.

"Well." She stands up. "I think I'd like to go in."

He follows her into the house, which conforms to his idea of a dwelling occupied by a pair of bonsai experts. Sleek, modern furniture, blank white walls—not one picture—a long, narrow table holding six bonsai in red dishes.

"No kids?" he says, not so much a question as an observation prompted by the absence of stains and clutter, the temerity of owning a pair of white sofas.

"Nope." She slips out of her yellow rubber work clogs. "Tea?"

"Water's fine."

"So I take it you didn't have any arrangement with your brother, any of those weird twin things, where you conspire to have some fun with a girl who's good-natured enough not to take it too hard when she discovers herself in flagrante with the other brother, rather than the one she thought she was with?"

Will shakes his head slowly. "No," he says. She sits on the sofa across from the one he's chosen, puts her hands together and clamps them between her knees, studies his face.

"Do you not feel well?" she asks him.

"I've felt better."

"Yeah, I guess you would have." She bites her lower lip. "I'm . . . I'm sorry. But—"

"You're not at fault."

"Couldn't I get you something? Seltzer maybe? I think we have ginger ale."

"All right. Yes." Will closes his eyes, unable to determine if he feels suddenly sick, really sick, or if he's felt this way for weeks now and his ability to deny it has been disabled without warning. When he opens them, she's standing in front of him, glass in one hand, coaster in the other. "Thank you," he says. "Perhaps I'll just wash my hands?"

She points at a hallway. "Second door," she says.

At least it's just bile, he thinks. And no carpet. Thank God, no carpet. He's turned the bathtub taps on in an attempt to mask the sounds of his vomiting, doesn't even know if the tears coming out of his eyes are a response to all the stomach acid he's forced up into his sinuses or if he's really crying. It requires a focused, almost impossible act of will to stop retching, and then, sitting back on his heels, he's subject to convulsive aftershocks, like the residual heaves of sobbing.

He leans on the side of the tub and turns off both taps, looks around himself.

He's on hands and knees, hunting for splatters and wiping them up with toilet paper, when he hears just what he's been praying he wouldn't hear, a hesitant knock on the door.

"Yes?" he says, surprised by the normal tone of his voice.

"I just . . . nothing."

"I'll be out in a moment."

He washes his hands, his face, rinses his mouth, checks his shirt, his trousers. He feels awful but he looks all right. Back in the living room he sits carefully in the spot he'd chosen before. The couch is upholstered in a suedelike fabric, very soft.

"Look," Lisa says after a silence. "Am I supposed to, what, pretend that you weren't just violently ill?" Will returns her stare.

"If you wouldn't mind," he says.

She tilts her head up, her face toward the ceiling. Hands folded in her lap, she remains in this posture for what seems to Will a long time. Her shoulders rise and fall with a deep breath she takes through her nose, a relaxation technique maybe. He wonders if this might be a gesture of dismissal, if she's going to remain like that, her face averted until he gets up to leave, when she looks back at him. "Okay," she says, "so." She claps her hands together, and the sound they make is a crisp snap, like that of a wet towel. "Do you want to know anything more?"

"More?" he says stupidly.

"Yes. I assume that after driving all this way you might want more than . . . than, well, just more, that's all."

He nods. "How many times?" he asks.

"How many times did he . . . did we—"

"Yes."

"I don't know." She lifts and drops one hand. "How long were you and I involved? July, then August? So, two months times a couple, maybe three, times a week. What does that come out to? Twenty? Twenty-five?"

"And after the first time, after that you knew? He revealed himself the first time?"

"Yes. You—no, not you, it was his idea, but I thought it was yours, or what I mean is, I thought he was you. He said for us to meet in my dad's milking parlor at one. One in the morning. So I go there to wait, and he—but I think it's you, right? I don't know it's your brother—he sneaks up behind me and says, 'Close your eyes.' Then he blindfolds me and says he's going to take me to a special place. Have I ever been skinny dipping? he wants to know. We end up at the quarry, where he asks, have I ever done it in the water? Have I ever had sex in the water? 'Making love' was probably how he put it. And of course I hadn't. I was, what? A kid. A girl with an overbite from upstate New York."

"I knew there was something," Will says. "I was trying to figure out what was different about you."

"Yeah." She touches her mouth, a reflexive gesture. In it, all the polish she's acquired evaporates. "I got them fixed when I could afford it. My folks never did have that kind of money. They just, you know, we were dairy farmers. They didn't have money to spend on stuff like braces. But as soon as Sean and I were in the black, I got them. Anyway." She sits up straight, once again someone other than a dairy farmer's daughter.

"So Mitch took you blindfolded to the quarry for submarine sex?"

She smiles, self-conscious. "I know it's silly. When I think back, I do see that it was dumb. But then I *was* dumb. What did I know? I was a kid. Undiscerning. Nervous. Easily impressed. I'm sure I must have thought it was going to be romantic. When we got there, it was so dark, pitch-black, that even without the blindfold I couldn't see a thing, practically. I still didn't know it wasn't you.

"Anyway, well, I don't know if you've ever tried, but it's not that easy having . . . doing it in water, even under the best of circumstances. And do you remember the quarry? All that slime underfoot? It was hard to keep your footing. As for the sex itself, it's not like everything glides into place. The water, somehow water just does not help. It wasn't how I imagined it would be. We couldn't even . . . in the end, we had to get out before he could even, you know, get inside me.

"He had this blanket thing spread on the ground and, this is going to make me sound, I don't know, dumb or superficial or something, but I was getting eaten alive by bugs. I counted, honestly, over a hundred mosquito bites the next day. So by the time I figured out it was him instead of you, I think I barely reacted. I was just begging him to hurry up so we could put on our clothes and get out of there.

"And it wasn't until I was back home that I thought about how strange it was, the whole night. On the drive back I just sat there like a lump. I don't remember thinking a single thing. I wanted to go home, that's all. And the next morning, gosh, my parents and my sister were mystified by the welts all over my arms and my back, everywhere. They asked all these questions. Did I take the screen off my bedroom window? Did I sleep without pajamas?" She pauses. "I didn't say anything in the e-mails, but Margie died."

"She did? I'm so sorry. When did she?" Will tries to picture Lisa's pale sister, who stayed inside all the time because the sun aggravated her lupus and gave her rashes.

"The fall of 'ninety-nine. Just before Thanksgiving."

"I'm, I'm very sorry. How old was she?"

"Thirty-eight. It pretty much destroyed my folks."

"I'm so sorry," Will says again.

"Yeah. Thanks. Me, too. Anyway"—she shakes her head as if to clear it—"later, after the bites stopped itching so much, I told myself I had to talk to you, or to Mitch. Sort of sort it all out. I mean, I just didn't know what to think. Or even how to feel."

Will slouches down in order to rest his head on the low sofa back. Without raising his head he asks her what she thinks about it now.

She snorts. "Well, obviously, it didn't have much to do with me. Whatever it was, was between you two. I was just the chump."

"By why didn't you ever talk to me?" He tilts his head to see her face. "How could it have gone on for six or eight or however many weeks without my knowing about it?"

"Because when I went to your house to talk to you, your brother was there, and he made me promise never to bring it up. He told me it was this thing the two of you had, you and him, and the deal was that talking about it, even mentioning it, wasn't allowed. He said that if it ever came up, everything would be over between us—all three of us. Not a bad idea, right? But the thing is, I was scared. Scared of Mitch. He seemed—not that he was ever violent or abusive, he wasn't—but I could tell he had that capacity. He never yelled at me or punched walls or anything direct like that. He just had this . . . this . . . I don't know. This concealed rage. Except every once in a while I'd catch a glimpse of it. He'd overreact or something, you know?"

"Yes," Will says. "I do. I do know."

"Over and over, I almost said something to you, but then . . . I just couldn't. I thought maybe you knew. And I was afraid you might be angry, too. And remember how I had plans for that August? I was going to go down to Virginia, where my mom's sister lived. But then Uncle Rob had a fall, broke his leg, and I ended up staying home. So it wasn't over when I told myself it would be, but then there was only a few weeks left before school, and I, I just went through the motions, you know?"

"Did you go on dates together? Movies? Out to dinner?"

"No, that was only with you. With Mitch it was always just sex. Sex at night. Late." She shakes her head, frowning. "Weird, I know. Like I had this boyfriend who was split into two halves, one who took me out for ice cream or whatever and one I had sex with."

"But," Will can't help saying, "but we had sex, too."

"Of course, of course. I didn't mean we didn't. Just that—"

"Just that it wasn't sexy sex. Sort of comfortable and safe, like a back rub or an old armchair."

"No. That's not what I meant."

"My brother, the demon lover."

"Will." She says it with two syllables. Wi-ill. "Come on, you can't not know it was all about his face. Anyway, I wouldn't have been so passive if I'd been older. But it's hard for girls—you can't know. As a man, you don't realize that there are a lot of things girls feel they have no choice about."

"No," says Will. "I do get that." He closes his eyes, and for a while neither of them speaks. It's so quiet in her house that he can hear the faint buzz of an appliance in another room, a clothes dryer, maybe.

"Hey," she says. "I'm alone here today. Like I said, Sean's gone to pick up some stuff, and I have no help." She brings her hands together in another little clap, an awkward, hearty gesture. "So I have to get back to work. But you can . . . I think it would be a good idea for you to take a nap or even just a rest before you get back on the road."

"Yes," Will says. "I should do that."

"You stay there." Lisa stands up. "I'll get you a blanket."

After parking the van, its sides streaked with mud, Will sits for a few minutes in the driver's seat.

Inside the empty house, he stops to use the bathroom and then heads upstairs to Luke's room, undisturbed for more than three years now. Not untouched, because once a month or so, Elena, who cleans the rest of the house, comes in to dust and vacuum. Hired after Luke died, she's never asked about the child who does and does not occupy the room. Either she refuses to trespass where she might cause pain, or her nascent English cannot accommodate the questions she would ask in her own language.

Will sits on his son's narrow bed. Characters from *The Adventures of Tintin*—Snowy, Captain Haddock, and Tintin himself—pursue one another across the bedding that Carole discovered by chance in a SoHo boutique. Will found he couldn't object to the price tag, not really; he loved Luke's discovery of the 1930s comic by Hergé, his reading and rereading and then reading once again English translations of all the old adventures, sitting up in bed, literally bundled within the romp of imagined intrigue, asking endless questions about Soviet spies and Shanghai gangsters.

In the bookcase are other favorites of Luke's, *A Wrinkle in Time* by Madeleine L'Engle, *The Chronicles of Narnia*, and *The Lord of the*

Rings. Religious stories, all of them, David and Goliath tales of good battling a vast and seemingly uncontrollable evil, of love prevailing only at the eleventh hour (the fifty-ninth minute, fifty-ninth second), the moment of absurd, laughable—necessary—hope.

Tintin sheets, fantasy novels, and the mythic athlete-hero: Luke's bedroom is papered with posters of Derek Jeter, Jason Giambi, Alfonso Soriano, Yankees mostly, out of geographic loyalty, but there are stars from other teams as well. Suzuki, A-Rod, Bonds, Sosa. Of course, now A-Rod was a Yankee, Soriano gone, Will can't remember where, because he can't watch baseball, can't listen to it on the radio or follow the box scores, not anymore. Not yet. Luke had been so earnest and credulous in his love; his adulation of Sammy Sosa, for example, blinded him to the man's obvious deceit.

"Lukey," Will remembers saying, gently, "there were maybe thirty or forty bats to choose from, and Sosa took the one corked bat. It's just not likely for that to have been an accident."

"It was just a mistake," Luke said, not even defensive.

Over the desk was a huge black-and-white poster of Muhammad Ali, with the caption "Impossible is nothing," the fighter in his beautiful prime, white satin trunks luminous against his velvet skin. "That's how Jesus looks," Luke had told Will, prompting a spasm of guilt that he and Carole had never managed to get it together to send their kids to Sunday school or provide them any religious instruction whatsoever.

One entire wall of Luke's bedroom is consecrated to Mitch, the uncle he never met, the one he discovered in a magazine article, a man with the same last name as himself and his father, a man bearing his father's familiar face, except for the livid splash of purple, which, in two dimensions at least, presented itself as the distinctive feature of a superhero, a demiurge endowed with powers that, like any other immortal's, marked his face and body. Spiderman was masked by webbing, the Hulk prone to shirt-tearing episodes of swelling green muscles, and Mitchell Moreland had an arresting yin-yang face.

"I don't get why you guys don't even talk to each other," Luke complained to Will, unable to reconcile himself to the injustice of having an uncle who was a bona fide sports star and never getting to see him, not even on a holiday, not even once a year. The more Luke pressed for rapprochement, the more terse and defensive Will had become, unable to manufacture a seemingly casual that's-just-the-way-it-worked-out response.

With a child's unerring ability to identify, aim for, and repeatedly strike his parents' weak spots, Luke became a clamorous Mitchell Moreland fan, loudly celebrating Mitch's exploits and media conquests, making a show of tearing pages from magazines, sending away for not one but three pairs of swim goggles endorsed by Mitch's signature and acquired with proofs of purchase torn from boxes of a cereal no one could stomach but which Carole bought under the duress of an aisle 5 (breakfast foods) tantrum. Carole sidestepped public conflict even more determinedly than the domestic variety, and having threatened a supermarket tantrum, Luke hadn't even had to work all that hard for the five or ten or however many box tops torn from the inedible vitamin-rich whatevers.

In the year before he drowned—irony, irony, yes, Will does recognize irony—Luke discovered that he could use the cable guide to hunt for mentions of Mitch on ESPN or ESPN2 and he found the rerun of an interview that included tape of swims Mitch made between 1990 and 2000, a sports documentary that aired once during school hours and again at 2 A.M., necessitating a video recording, which, as they didn't get ESPN, Will had dutifully petitioned a friend to make, resisting the temptation to say the show had been canceled. For faithfully fulfilling this promise, he was repaid by Luke's replaying it over and over and over, not so much for its entertainment value (there was so little), Will suspects, as for its ability to dissolve his parents' composure.

Every so often Will visits Luke's room and lies on the Tintin quilt, staring at the Wall of Mitch, as he's come to think of it, a sort of private Wailing Wall whose cracks he wants to find, chinks into which he can thrust little folded prayers, or, more likely, questions. Questions like, *What the fuck happened? Tell me why. Tell me how.*

Or: What's the meaning of having a brother who swims with the unnatural ease and grace of a fish and a son who in an instant slipped from the safety of a little boat—a boat his father failed to balance— and drowned? How can Will accommodate the coincidence of his identical twin, a disfigured copy of himself, vanishing onto the page and into the broadcast, multiplied into a legion of virtual incarnations who swim into the death of human, familial attachment, and a son who failed to swim and sank to a terribly nonmetaphoric death?

Is irony the only vantage from which to observe these irreconcilable facts? Irony isn't what Will wants, nor what he's come to understand he needs. It isn't transition. It isn't a way from here to there. It grants no solace, no transcendence. It's cheap. It's a last resort. It's a word to apply to the limits of human comprehension, a word that makes the inadequacy sound like sophistication.

"He's so cool. It's just not fair that I never get to meet him or anything." That Will couldn't explain his estrangement from Mitch made Luke regard his father with suspicion. It must be that Will had blundered somehow, insulted and alienated Mitch. Or maybe, Luke never said but implied, it was because a star like Mitch might not have had time for a brother who was a shrink. Some of Luke's friends—"Who?" Will demanded. "Who?" "Parker, that's who."— said that psychoanalysts were just plain psycho and that they were also homo and freakazoid. And if Will was a psycho-homo-freakazoid, then why would his cool brother want anything to do with him?

"Look," Will said to Luke, "you're right. Mitch is cool. He's famous and cool, and a lot of people admire him. But that wasn't always true. Because of the way he looked, the way his face was marked, he had a hard time as a kid. He was shy. He didn't have friends. He spent a lot of time alone. And when he was older, when he was a teenager and then a young man, he spent all his time swimming, hours and hours of swimming by himself, which was not only a way for him to stop feeling bad about his face but helped him make himself into a great athlete. And now that so many people admire and respect him and don't care about how he looks, or maybe they even think his face is cool because it's his—now that all those things are true, maybe Mitch just doesn't want to be with the people he was with when his life was hard and he was unhappy. Maybe Mom-Mom and Granddad and I remind him of a painful time, when he was young and living at home, and when kids at school either didn't talk to him or they teased him, and when he was so self-conscious that he was afraid of girls, afraid they'd never see him behind the birthmark on his face. It could be that now he's started over, now that he has a new life, he prefers not to be with us because that would force him to remember the old one." Will stopped, realizing that, faced with Luke's grave, assessing stare, he'd begun to repeat himself. "Do you understand what I'm saying?" he asked.

"Yes," Luke said. "But I don't think you're right."

"Why?"

"Because."

"Because why?"

"Because that kind of person who would just go away and never talk to his mother or father or brother—that would be a coward."

"He would be a coward."

"That's what I said."

"No, you said *that* instead of *he*."

"Okay, okay, so *he* would be a coward, and a person who goes to the Bermuda Triangle and swims in water with sharks where whole airplanes have disappeared can't be a coward because, you know, a great white shark could easily kill him. It would take—it would be like you killing a little bug or something."

"But, Lukey, there are different kinds of bravery. I agree absolutely that Mitch is brave—very brave—but I think it's a kind of bravery that he had to invent to help himself feel better about the early part of his life. Did you know, a lot of people who were unhappy as children turn into adults who achieve great things? Like Abraham Lincoln. Or President Clinton. Mike Tyson. Well, maybe Mike Tyson's not such a good example. No, actually, I take that back. He is. Because Tyson's way out of the misfortunes of his youth was his talent as a boxer, but even though he developed that ability, made it bigger and more powerful, he remained a complicated man; he couldn't really do what he wanted to do, which was escape his past. That's what all these people wanted to do—to get away from the unhappiness they'd lived through as children. And what they accomplished helped, it made them feel better, but it didn't erase what came before. And if that's true about Mitch, then his not talking to me or your grandparents wouldn't be cowardly, it would just be choosing to leave us behind."

Luke shook his head. "But it would still make him a jerk. And I know he's not a jerk."

"Why?"

"Because only jerks run away and hurt people's feelings like that. Like the way Mom says me and Sam have to not chase balls into the street or stick paper clips in electric sockets or get into a stranger's car, because if anything happened—"

"Well, yes, but Mitch is a man, not a little boy, and he hasn't run away or been kidnapped. He's just stopped calling or visiting."

"But why? Why did he?"

"I don't know for sure. I told you what my guess is."

"I think you're wrong. I think it's something else."

"Don't you imagine that as I grew up with Mitch, who is my own twin brother, I might know him better than you? That I might be able to guess his reasons a little more closely? Because actually you've never met him. So probably I do know him better."

Luke shook his head. "No."

"Why?"

"I just don't think you do, that's all."

A month after Luke drowned, Will's mother came to stay with them, and—just to keep busy, she said, just to be useful—cleaned their house. She began with the ground floor and worked her way up, at last arriving at the top-floor bedroom where Luke had slept and where she stopped and stared, her momentum destroyed so that Will had his chance to save the room from being dismantled.

"William!" she called down the stairs. "Will-yam!" She was waiting on the landing. "Have you seen this!"

"Well, yeah, Mom, obviously."

"I must never have come up here. You and Carole and the kids were always with us on the holidays, and I can't remember the last time your dad and I visited you in the city. So I must never have seen all this. And I have to tell you, William, if I had seen it, I would not have approved."

"No," Will said. "I don't imagine you would."

"But apparently you didn't consider this"—she waved her hand at the wall—"a, a, an unhealthy fixation. At least not enough of a problem to make him take it down."

"Mom," Will said. "It has nothing to do with my approving or disapproving. Carole and I agreed not to interfere because we found that even the slightest suggestion that we weren't pleased by Luke's interest in Mitch only intensified it. You know how kids are, Mom, they have this radar for psychic wounds."

"Well," she said. And she walked quickly across the room and had already torn down two posters by the time Will caught up with her.

"Hey!" he said. "You can't do that!"

Will's mother tried to pull her wrist out of his grasp. "Let go!" she said.

"No! Don't touch it! Don't touch any of it. And give me those." Will took the posters from her hand and smoothed out the creases. "Christ, Mom, it's been, what, a month? Leave it. Leave it."

"William. You of all people, with your jealous private parts and unconscious hostilities and whatnot. You should have been the first to put a stop to it."

"Well, it's a little late, Mom, wouldn't you say?"

"For Luke, yes. But there's Samantha to consider. You can't leave the room as it is, with all this, this . . ." She closed her eyes, waiting for the right word. "Memorabilia," she said.

"I am, actually. I'm leaving it just as it is."

"Why!"

"Because."

"Because why!"

"Because I haven't finished looking at it." Will leaned against the doorjamb, his arms crossed.

"Well, I'm talking to Carole about this. I think it's plain wrong. There's no point in morbid staring. You select a few special things and put them away, along with his schoolwork and report cards and all those condolence cards you got. You can take everything out and look over it when you're ready. The rest you take down and give away. Or, if it's not something another child can use, you throw it away. And you have this room repainted. You change the furniture around, maybe get a nice little table or a reading chair, and then you have a guest room."

"We already have a place for guests."

"So then you have a study."

"Each of us has an office."

"Well, get a billiards table or a, a, a big fish tank or something, for heaven's sake, but don't leave it like this because it's not good for anyone."

At dinner she enlisted Carole's support, and both women argued for not only stripping but renovating Luke's bedroom and then giving it to Will. "Look at all the options!" his mother said in her most chipper "Heaven Help You" voice. A mini-gymnasium with a treadmill and a set of free weights. A library for all those psychoanalytical texts he had moldering in the basement. A music room with a piano. A video and DVD haven with a gazillion-dollar, high-resolution, holographic, plasma screen monstrosity.

"I just cannot sanction your sitting up there in the shadows and dwelling on all that, that tragedy, or taking naps on that sad little bed." Will's mother began crying. Carole picked up her glass and let it hang in the air, neither taking a drink nor putting it back down on the table.

"Lukey's bed isn't sad," Samantha said to her grandmother. "It's nice and it's funny and it has pictures of Snowy, and Snowy is cuter even than a bug dog."

"Pug," Will said. "Pug dog. And you're right, sweetie, it isn't sad."

"Well." His mother wiped her eyes and polished the lenses of her glasses. "Well, hell's bells," she said.

Elena came in, she dusted, and every so often she ran the sheets through the wash, but Will would not let the room be changed. He took the occasional nap on the bed, not getting in but lying on top of the comforter. He noticed Sam was coming in, too, gradually removing all the Legos and the board games and those few construction sets she found worth carrying back to her room. Will found a note she'd left on her brother's desk: *Dear Lueky, if you want yore legos thier in my room. Love, Sam. P.S. monoply is ther too.* When he tried to pick it up he found that she'd taped it to the desk's surface.

Upstate, his mother ran out of improvements to impose on her own house (those she did make barely noticed by his father) and, after forcefully reorganizing her friends' pantries, reimmersed herself in her cleaning business. Since then, she's never referred to Luke's room, she rarely speaks of Luke himself, and she's developed a tic that attends anyone else's mentioning her grandson, a sort of helpless salute: her right arm flies up as if to block her eyes from an intense, sudden glare and then falls back to her side.

Will picks at the corner of a glossy fold-out from *Swim* magazine and peels it carefully away from the wall until the last corner lifts off. Where the photograph covered the blue paint is a clean rectangle, unmarked by the little-boy grime of the life that had unfolded in Luke's room. He steps back, all the way to the door, and considers the one blank spot. Then he folds the poster along the creases of the two original folds that allowed it to fit within the borders of a magazine.

The metal trash can in the corner, the one decorated with Yankee insignia, is empty, clean, and after a moment he balls up the poster and drops it in and listens to the sound it makes when it strikes the can's metal bottom, a low note that lingers in the silence.

The waiter is on his hands and knees, using a napkin to gather shards of the broken glass. "I am so sorry," he says.

"It's all right. Really." Will stands from the table. "It's only water."

"I hope it's not a bad omen," Will's father says wryly, a joke, although not the kind he makes ordinarily.

"Oh no," the maître d' says, having rushed over. "No no no. We will make it into a good one." He sends the waiter away, returns with two glasses on a tray. "An auspicious Pinot Noir," he says, his expression indicating that the wine is at least expensive, if not lucky. "*Very* auspicious. With our apologies."

Will sits back down. "Nice restaurant," he says. "Too nice." He gestures at the extravagantly appointed room beyond the table. "Is this an occasion of some sort?"

"No occasion. Figured it might be fun." Will's father takes a sip and puts his glass down. "Truth is, I'm going back upstate. Wanted us to go out on a bang." He fiddles with the knot in his tie, adjusting it around the unfamiliar confines of a snugly buttoned collar. "An occasion for expensive indigestion."

"Upstate? As in back upstate to Mom?"

"Yup."

"Wow," Will says. "Why? I mean, don't get me wrong, when it comes to my parents I'm just as conventional as the next guy. I want you and Mom together, in the same old town, same old house, et cetera. Did something happen with Lottie?"

"No." His father smiles, and the smile looks genuine, if a little foolish. "Nothing like a disagreement, if that's what you mean. Turns out this is a thing she does."

"What is?"

"Acquires works by some new face, then acquires the face. Moves on."

"You were just one in a series?"

"Something like."

"Was that . . . are you—"

"I'm fine." Will's father swats the air in a dismissive gesture.

"Yeah?"

"Yup." He nods. "I want to get back to work full-time. I get antsy when I'm down here. City's crammed with stuff I don't want to take pictures of."

"Huh." Will looks at his father. "So that's it? Back to Mom? Return to status quo? No questions asked?"

"Unless you know something I don't know."

"What could I know? It's not like I discuss you or any of this with her. I just thought, well, that she might be a little ticked off or something."

"Why? She wasn't before."

"You keep saying that. I keep finding it hard to believe."

"Well, Will." His father turns his palms up. "It's true." He picks up the menu in its black leather folder. "Know what you're having?" he asks.

"Hanger steak."

"I'll do the same." His father closes the folder, places it on the edge of the table.

"I thought you were trying to get off red meat."

"Gave up. I was sick of arguing with the doctor. Went on Tricor. Lipitor? I can't remember which. The thing is, once you're taking one of these damn cholesterol pills, then you feel like it's home free, anything goes." He smiles. "I had eggs for breakfast," he says. "Eggs Benedict."

"Does it work that way, really?"

"No, of course it doesn't. Anyhow, your mother will put the kibosh on all that. So, what's eating you?"

"What's what?"

"I said, what's eating you." Will's father leans forward over the table. "Something's on your mind. What is it?"

"That obvious, huh?"

His father shrugs. "You're doing that thing you do." He points at Will's left hand, thumb and finger pinching the skin over his Adam's apple. Will gives his hand a shake as if it might dislodge the habit. He takes a deep breath.

"Well, Dad, here it is." He stops, takes a swallow of water. "I got in touch with a couple of women who I used to know. Date, I mean. And I found out that they . . . they were with Mitch at the same time as they were with me."

His father doesn't say anything. Then he says, "What's brought this up? And why would you do that? Look people up?"

"Why?"

"No, not why. How? What I mean is, how'd all this get started?"

"The reunion. The Cornell thing I went to last summer."

His father takes a sip of wine, puts the glass back down on the table, turns it slowly as if considering some aspect of its manufacture. "So," he says, "these girls, these women, they were dating you and your brother at the same time?"

"Not dating, Dad. Fucking." He says the word again, one he's never heard his father use. "Fucking. Mitch and Elizabeth—that's who I saw at the reunion—they were fucking at the same time that she and I were fucking."

"Now, why would she do that?"

"Well, obviously, that's a very compelling question to which I wanted the answer. Mitch tricked her at first, and then she said it felt liberated and counterculture."

"I don't mean the sex part. I mean, why's she bringing it up now? Why talk at all about this, this . . . why discuss what's twenty-five years in the past?"

"Why ask that?" Will says. "Why is that your first response?" He returns his father's mild expression with a frown. "I started it. I started the whole thing by asking her—Elizabeth—something I probably shouldn't have."

"What was that?"

The waiter comes to them and silently sets their plates before them. "*Très chaud*," he says. "Please to be careful. Hot hot hot." Will waits for him to leave and then turns back to his father.

"Remember last time we had lunch? When I told you about a patient whose treatment I was about to terminate? A young woman who made a pass at me? Kissed me?"

His father removes his knife from the meat in front of him and lays it on the side of his plate. "Yes," he says, and he doesn't lift the bite on the end of the fork but lays that implement down as well. He looks at Will. "What does that have to do with the, the Elizabeth woman?"

"They're connected."

"The girl and the woman?" Will nods. "Well, that qualifies as ominous," says his father. "As in a genuinely bad omen."

"Except she wasn't an omen, in that omens predict. She was more like a . . . a . . ." Will surprises himself by starting to cry, not audibly, but tears fall from his eyes; he can't speak.

"A what?" his father asks, after giving him time to stop.

"A wish," Will says. "Not an omen, a wish."

His father picks up his fork and turns it in his fingers, looking at the cold morsel of steak. He puts it in his mouth, chews slowly in the manner of a person savoring what he eats. "I don't understand," he says after swallowing.

"No." Will shakes his head. "I haven't said anything understandable." He draws a deep breath. "In June, at the reunion, I got a class book that included letters from anyone in the class of 'seventy-nine who bothered to send one in. I went through them all, reading the ones written by people I remembered, a few friends. I came across Elizabeth's and read it closely—normal, right? she'd been my girlfriend—and in it I find references to a child born seven or eight months after we split up." Will stops. He looks at his father, who has cut his steak into precise squares and is eating them, one after another, no potato, no sip of wine, no salad, nothing between bites of meat.

"I'm listening to you," he says. "I'm paying attention."

Will drinks from both his water and wineglass. "So, are you beginning to understand?"

"Keep talking."

"I make the obvious conclusion. And, while I didn't admit this to myself in the moment—I wasn't aware of it—when I don't see Elizabeth the first night of the reunion I'm surprised by how disappointed I am. But the next evening, during this big reception, I do see her. We catch up on twenty years or so—pleasant, chatty, a little flirtatious. That tipsy, floaty kind of banter that can slide into a situation where you find yourself saying these, these things, and then later you wonder how it could have happened, how you could have been so, so— well, so the way you were.

"It's only a matter of time before I've told her about Luke. You know what's coming next. I ask if she was pregnant when she left me. And I ask if she might be willing to give me a sample of her child's— it's a girl—her daughter's hair." Will sees his father's expression. "I know, I know," he says. "Stupid. I hear myself tell you the story, and I know I've opened up what should have remained closed. But, honestly, Dad, while I was talking to her, at the reunion, it seemed like a natural enough desire. To know. It even seemed rational. Not risky or out-there."

"You wanted the hair for DNA testing?" his father asks.

Will nods.

"She give it to you?"

"No. She was pissed off. I should have backed down then, but I didn't. For some reason I just couldn't let go of the idea, couldn't give it up, and we part. Not amicably. We—I—well, the conversation deteriorated into something of a scene, raised voices, et cetera."

"Christ, Will, do not tell me—do not"—Will's father puts his hand up in a *Halt!* gesture—"do not connect the two stories into one big mess." He flags down a busboy and points to his empty wineglass.

Will slides his glass across the table. "Here, finish mine."

"You haven't eaten your meal," his father says.

"I can't eat and talk at once. So, for a month, two months, nothing. I do end up apologizing, via e-mail—no reply, and I'm increasingly relieved. I'm even—I have that little burst of excited happiness, like when a car just misses running you over—I know I've narrowly escaped screwing up my life."

"Enter the French-kissing patient."

"Enter the French-kissing patient. With whom I terminate treatment, and who stalks me, calls my office, my home, until, one day, she buzzes and, thinking it's a different patient, I let her in. Then she . . . well, she manipulates me into a sexual encounter."

"How the goddamn hell does she do that!"

"Shhh! Stop yelling."

"Don't tell me to be quiet! In your office! Your office! You had sex with her in your office!"

"Dad—"

"I want to know how the goddamn hell a twenty-year-old child can manipulate a forty-seven-year-old goddamn psychoanalyst into having sex with her in his goddamn office!"

"Twenty-four. And you know why I didn't throw her out right away? I'll tell you. Because she started saying 'please,' and 'give me another chance,' and it never occurred to me that she wasn't being sincere. The only thing I thought of, actually, was how when we were kids Mitch could always wear me down if he begged me long enough.

"Right after this, after the sex, she tells me who she is—Elizabeth's daughter, Jennifer. But that's not all she says. She says Elizabeth wasn't involved with me alone. She was also having sex with my brother and with two other guys. And since Mitch and I are twins, we'll never know, because the DNA could only show that it's one of us, not which one.

"I meet with Elizabeth, who confirms what her daughter said and is irate. Basically accuses me of being a rapist, a liar, and a nutcase. After talking with Elizabeth, it occurs to me that Mitch, who, incidentally, slept with Elizabeth not once but many times—slept with Elizabeth almost the entire time she was sleeping with me, tricked her into it at first, pretending to be me—Mitch could have had sex with other girlfriends of mine." Will shakes his head. "I don't know why, but I always thought of him as a—well, almost as a eunuch or something. He never seemed like he had a sex drive at all. I mean, when we were kids, there was the usual stuff. I knew he whacked off. He knew I did. We shared a bedroom. But by the time he was fifteen, sixteen, somewhere in there, he—it just seemed like he turned it off. Or funneled it all into swimming—that's what I assumed. The way an athlete—a real athlete who works out all day—is said to dampen physical desire, expend that energy another way. For a while I even thought he might be gay—"

"He wasn't gay," his father says. "And he wasn't a eunuch, either."

"I guess not." Will leans back to look at his father. "What do you know about it?" he says, but his father doesn't answer.

"Go on," he prompts Will.

"The first time with Elizabeth, at first she didn't know it wasn't me, because it was dark and there was no way to tell the difference between us in the dark. After all, she expected it to be me—it's not like she's going to, say, quiz him for answers only I'd be able to give. So the first time he tricks her." Will watches his father drink the last of a third glass of wine. "Aren't you at all drunk?" he asks.

"I wish I were." He stands. "However, I'll take the opportunity to use the men's room."

Will watches his father make his way through the tables, trying to decide if he expects the man he sees—white-haired, favoring his left hip—to help him pull himself together. Yes, he decides, he does. There may be no reason beyond habit, ancient filial hope, but this is enough. His father returns, sits in the opposite chair, crosses his arms. "All right," he says. "Let's get to the end of this."

"Okay. So. I use the Internet to search for whoever I can find from a list of all the girlfriends I remember—camp, college." Will looks at his father, who nods, makes a rolling gesture with one hand that says, Go on.

"I find a woman, Lisa Christianson, who lived not too far from us. I saw her the summer between junior and senior years, when both Mitch and I were home. That was the summer he got permission to use the high school gym, the pool and everything, and I was working for that landscape guy."

"The dairy Christiansons?"

"The same. She's upstate now, running a bonsai nursery with her husband. I e-mail to tell her I'd like to drop by. I drive up, go to Lisa's place, we talk, and guess what? I'm right. I can't believe it—well, I can, it's the reason I went up there—but I'm right, Mitch did have sex with her. Same idea. Tricked her the first time. Sometimes they even had sex on the same night I'd taken her to a movie or dinner. I drop her off at home, at eleven, conscientious because her dad was old-fashioned about those things. Two hours later—two hours after I've played the role of gentleman and fool—Mitch's screwing her.

"Again, the first time is undercover, in the dark, he has some blindfold trick and reveals himself only after they've had sex. Lisa doesn't think it's cool or liberated or whatever, and she's scared of Mitch. I don't know what he did to frighten her, but she doesn't disobey his directive to keep quiet. She goes on meeting him at night and follows his order not to tell me."

Will's father nods. "Then what?"

"Then what!"

"I mean, where are you now? Have you contacted anyone else?"

"No. I don't need to." Will shakes his head. "I don't know, Dad. What am I supposed to do with this?"

His father puts his hand across the table, takes Will's, gives it a squeeze.

"You know," Will says, taking his hand back, "I knew Lisa would tell me that it had happened with her, too. I did. I knew it. And yet I was shocked. Shocked sick. Literally." Will looks at his father, and the two of them watch each other without speaking until Will can't stand it anymore.

"I have a question, Dad," he says. "I've been thinking about it, thinking about asking you this question ever since I got back from talking to Lisa. No, before that. It occurred to me on the way home from seeing Elizabeth in Philadelphia, but I managed to, I don't know, put it aside." His father raises his eyebrows.

"Why did Mitch disappear after the rehearsal dinner? Why was it then that he broke off contact with us?"

Will's father leans back in his chair. He tips his head up, toward the ceiling, which, Will sees as he follows his father's eyes, is painted to look like the urban sky—not a celestial vision of *putti* and clouds, but buildings reaching upward, a slice of atmosphere between the expertly foreshortened façades of skyscrapers. After a minute, his father looks back at him.

"I told him to," he says.

"Why, Dad? Why?" Will shakes his head, eyes closed. "Oh shit," he says.

"She didn't know what to do. She came to me, knocked on our door at the hotel."

"What am I supposed to do with this!" Will says, loudly enough that the few remaining diners turn toward him, then look away.

"Look, I did what seemed like a . . . a . . . what seemed proportionate. Is that a word? The only thing I could think of that had a severity in proportion to the, the . . ." He holds his hands up, empty, and they look at each other. "I'm sorry, Will. I did what seemed . . . I did what I did. I hoped we'd all move on."

"Well," Will says. "I guess I know the punch line. I want the whole story. I want what came before." He pushes his plate away. "So," he says, "go ahead."

Will's father laces his fingers together and looks down at his hands. He makes a noise like a whistle, but lower. "You remember your bachelor party?"

"Not especially well. I was, I believe, getting plastered in the time-honored way."

"You remember your brother leaving at some point?"

"Maybe. I think he said he was going back to the hotel, that he was still in training, had to get a decent night's sleep."

His father nods. "Right. That would have been around ten-thirty, eleven."

Will shrugs. "We're talking fifteen years ago. All I know is that the party went on for a while without him."

"Call it ten-thirty. Carole and her bridesmaids, all the women from the rehearsal dinner, women friends from out of town, they were at—what was the name of that place?"

"I don't remember."

"Well, whatever the name was."

"It was a male strip club. Not Chippendale's, but the same idea. Her sister set the whole thing up. Carole was anxious about it, embarrassed. Thought it was vulgar. And it was, objectively speaking. Guys, handsome young guys dancing in G-strings. She was worried you and Mom would think it was white trash or something."

Will's father waves his hand. "We had no idea what it was. Anyway, at eleven, there's a surprise guest at the girls' party. Looks familiar, height, hands, knees, his face is hidden. Now Mitch's always been in top physical condition, but he carries some fat for insulation, and in a smoky, dark nightclub . . . Also, it's just before your wedding, when you were, what, thirty-two? Still working out, running in the morning." Will nods. "So, Mitch, wearing a G-thing and a—I don't know—whatever getup those guys had instead of clothes. He's gotten himself dressed in the club outfit, what there was of it. A G-thing and a bow tie, and he's wearing one of those gorilla masks."

"A gorilla mask?"

"Yeah, like King Kong. Black rubber with hair—fur—stuck in, big ape face, the kind of mask that covers your whole head. The only significant aspect is that it disguises the one physical thing that would distinguish him from you."

"Yes, I get that. Go on."

"He comes up behind Carole, speaking with a voice that sounds just like yours, says something to the effect that her little bachelorette party is nearly over and he has a special treat for her. Lots of giggling and shenanigans. The women're all drunk, too, remember. Making off-color jokes about deflowering, which really is a joke since, as we all know, today everyone lives together before they marry—if they marry—and the white dress is only an old-fashioned reference. But, anyway, there's some kind of playacting or teasing—your wife—your fiancée at that moment—she was too hysterical to tell us the exact subterfuge, but whatever it was, she ends up leaving the party to be with you. To be with a man dressed as a stripper who she thinks is you.

"She does find it strange that you insist on wearing the mask while making love, but she's tired and overstimulated and, like I said, drunk, and she figures that you, too, are tired, overstimulated, and drunk, and if she doesn't think it's funny, maybe you do." He shakes his head.

"Where is this happening?"

"In your room, yours and Carole's, at the hotel—Carole has the key. You—I mean Mitch, but she thinks it's you—you say you've left yours behind, you're wearing someone else's clothes over the G-thing—"

"String! G-string!"

"Okay. String. String. Somehow you've gotten separated from your clothes and had to borrow another guy's to drive back to the hotel. She's changed out of her party dress into a—well, I don't know. Mitch's wearing the King Kong thing, has sex with Carole—consensual, because, remember, she thinks it's you—and, as with Elizabeth and the other one, I guess, doesn't reveal himself until after it's over. Carole has no idea—why would she? It's unthinkable, so she doesn't think it. Until—"

"Until he pulls off his mask."

"At which point she starts screaming. It's late enough and she screams loud enough and long enough that other hotel guests alert the management. Someone calls the front desk to say there's a robbery or a rape or God knows what in room whichever. The front desk calls the room. Mitch picks up and hangs up the receiver without answering the person on the other end. Pulls on his trousers, and by the time the hotel has someone knocking on the door, he's back in his own room, lights out, all quiet. After all, the story was he was tired or what have you, he came back to the hotel to go to bed.

"Carole answers the door, pulls herself together enough to tell security or whoever they sent up that everything is all right, she saw what she thought was a man in her room but it turned out to be nothing, a coat hanging in the shadows, you know how that can happen. Why didn't she answer the phone? security wants to know. She doesn't know. It's late, she's nervous. She's sorry she's disturbed the other guests, but she's getting married the next day, it's just nerves. Is she sure there wasn't any man? Yes. Does she want a new room? No, no, everything is fine, she's sorry for causing any trouble.

"Hotel whoever leaves. She takes a shower, tries to calm down in the shower. The only thing she can think to do is to tell us, your mother and me. Her mother's not there yet, remember, and if she tells you, if she tells her sister, if she calls the police—if she does any of these, it'll end up ruining the wedding and hurting you. So she gets dressed, and she comes to our room. Figures we know Mitch. Assumes we do, anyhow.

"It's past midnight, both the parties are still going—yours and hers—only old folks like us are in their rooms, them and Mitch. She knocks at the door, wakes us up. Your mother opens the door, sees Carole crying and thinks the two of you have had a spat, or that Carole has cold feet or you do, or she's sick or you're sick, or it's late and you haven't come back from the party or—she doesn't know what to think. Asks Carole in, sits her down. For a long time, seemed like an hour but it couldn't have been that long, your wife is crying. She's curled up in a chair, feet on the cushion, hugging her knees, and, well, we're mystified, we have no idea what the heck is going on.

"Finally, after coaxing and coaxing and frankly begging, finally she says, 'Mitchell.'

"'Mitchell what?' we ask. Something's happened to Mitch? Mitch's sick? Mitch has had an accident? A fight—a physical fight— with you? What is it? We don't understand. We want to help but we don't understand.

"Carole is still, at this point, hysterical. Not hysterics as in loud, but she's shaking her head, crying, and not telling us a thing. At which point your mother decides to give her a pill, one of those old Miltown things, probably too stale to have an effect—after all, they've been in her handbag since 1972 or whenever it was she had that Bell's palsy and the doctor thought it was nerves. Carole takes the pill, and your mother has her lie down, puts a cold washrag over her eyes, tells her if she doesn't stop crying, her face will be swollen, and she wants to look pretty on her wedding day, of course she does, she wants to be beautiful, and finally—never underestimate the placebo effect, or the power of female vanity. Pride's maybe a better word. Don't get me wrong, I'm not saying Carole's vain. Anyway, she stops crying, she's calm enough to speak.

"'Will's brother came to the club dressed as a . . . as an entertainer,' she says. 'He was wearing a mask that covered his face and he said he was Will.' She's calm now. Absolutely calm. Considering the Carole of five minutes before, her composure is almost as disturbing as her hysterics, but, well, at least we're making progress. Your mother asks questions, Carole answers them.

"'Mitch pretended he was Will?' your mother says.

"'Yes,' Carole says. 'He said he was coming to take me back to the hotel and that then we were going to make love.'

"Hearing this, your mother puts her hand over her mouth and that's the end for her, she doesn't say another thing. So I start asking the questions. Carole's lying on the bed, and the washrag is still over her eyes. She speaks very deliberately, calmly. Your mother's a zombie, and me, well, somehow I've fallen into some goddamn Ingmar Bergman movie, one of those subtitled things where you don't really want to figure out what's going on.

"'He didn't have a key to our room,' she tells me, 'because he wasn't Will. But I didn't know he wasn't Will.'

"Bit by bit she tells us the story I just told you, and then we all sit there. Not one of us says a thing.

"'It's one-thirty,' I say, when that's the time. 'Everyone's coming back to the hotel soon. Will's going to be back soon—maybe he's on his way now. I think you should go to your room. I'll deal with Mitch.'

"'How?' She wants to know, and your mother wants to hear the answer, too. And, put on the spot, without having had a plan the minute before, I say that—assuming Carole doesn't want to press charges—and I ask her again, this is the fourth time, at least the fourth time, 'Are you sure you don't want to press charges?' Because she would have been—the fact that Mitch was about to become her brother-in-law didn't alter the fact that he'd sexually, uh, what, assaulted her. Well, not assaulted exactly, but a woman can't consent to be with someone who she doesn't know who he is." Will's father frowns. "That might've come out wrong, but you know what I mean.

"Anyway, Carole's sure she doesn't want to press charges. She wants to get married in nine hours, ten hours, however long it is until eleven that morning. As if ever since your mother told her to lie down and not cry and spoil her looks, she's decided that the thing to do is to go on with the show. She's adamant that you don't find out what happened—not now, not that night. It's not her fault, clearly, but she acts as if it is. She seems ashamed and—"

"How could you have allowed this to happen! How could you—my own father—conspire to deceive me? It's, it's—you contributed to what he did! You added to his betrayal!"

"I don't know. I guess I made a mistake, that's how. You know I'm—for Chrissakes, Will, it's always been a joke in this family about how bad I am in these situations. You know—Hank Moreland became a veterinarian so he'd never have to make conversation with a patient. Would never have to answer a difficult question. Not exactly serendipitous then, that a mess of this proportion would fall into my hands, but it did. And I made a mistake. I see that, I saw it long ago. But I wanted to do anything that would get Carole calmed down and just, I don't know, patch it up, have the wedding go on as planned. It was her marriage, hers and yours. I figured she knew best."

"You betrayed me."

"I apologize." They stare at each other.

"All right," Will says. "I accept your apology. What choice do I have?"

"Well, there's two," Will's father says. "You can accept it. Or you can refuse it." He takes a mouthful of water and swishes it around in his mouth before swallowing it. "Dry tongue. That's the trouble with red wine."

Will drinks from his glass of water. "I accept," he says. "I'm just angry, that's all."

His father nods. "Well, all right. I accept that. Your anger. Do you want me to go on with—"

"Yeah, let's get to the end."

"I tell Carole if she can stand for your brother to be at the service and the reception, then what I propose is, I'll tell Mitch that I know what's happened, that Carole's told your mother and me, and that he'll have to leave directly after the wedding. He's—he has to leave. If he doesn't comply, then he'll face rape charges. I suggest that she, since she's not reporting the rape, not being examined by a doctor or giving a sample of—a swab to determine whose sperm—maybe she can keep, I don't know, underpants or a nightgown or whatever might have Mitch's, uh, seminal fluid on it.

"There's nothing like that, she says, and anyway, what good is it if he's your twin? Obvious, right, but I'm so rattled I'm not thinking straight. She agrees to the plan, and I escort her to her room, check to make sure it's empty, safe, and then leave her there. I tell her to keep the chain thing on until you get back—I'll be talking with Mitch.

"Mitch answers his door. Pretends to have been asleep. He must know why I'm there, but he pretends he's confused, doesn't understand what I'm talking about. He's innocent, Carole's crazy. She was probably having sex with you and the both of you were drunk or something. 'Search me,' he says. 'Search the room. There's no mask or anything here.' 'Of course there isn't,' I say. 'What does that prove? Besides, Will is still at the stag thing, there's a roomful of family and friends who've been with him all night, and they know he didn't leave to spirit Carole back to the hotel for a, a romantic interlude.'

"So then he admits what he's done. He's without remorse." Will's father shakes his head, turns up his empty palms. "Carole's ashamed. He's not. How to square that? My own son—he seemed like no one I knew. He wouldn't speak of the motivation—the hatefulness— behind the act. He seemed like a, a sociopath, a person you read about, not anyone you know, certainly not someone you're related to. A person without the ability to imagine, let alone care about, another human being's feelings. Or to . . . to realize that other people's feelings are as important as his. Not that he's showing any emotion, he's not. I'm confused by him, the whole thing. Way out of my depth, whatever's happening inside that head.

"I tell him the conditions under which he can avoid being apprehended for raping his brother's fiancée on the eve of their wedding, and he agrees to them. Except he's not going to go to the wedding, he says. He's going to leave right that minute. Because if he stays through the next day, if he goes to the wedding, if he has to dress himself up as your best man, he'll tell you himself. Which"—Will's father makes what his mother calls his Abe Lincoln face, pained by human failings and more or less resigned to everything turning out badly.

"Which is probably what should have happened. But, well, we . . . I . . . I thought I could just get rid of it. Him. That Carole could tell you when and if she wanted to. And I was disgusted. Didn't want to look at him, wanted him out of, out of the picture, so to speak. Out of the frame." He shakes his head. "I didn't have much of an idea what would happen down the line, but I didn't imagine he'd never contact any of us again. I thought he'd just go off for a while and by the time he came back we'd've had time to figure out a, a . . . well, we'd've figured something out.

"End of story," Will's father says. He covers his face with his hands. "Christ, I'm sorry. What a mess." He takes his hands away, looks around the restaurant. Ten or twelve of the waitstaff are gathered around a table in the back, talking quietly and eating. Otherwise the place is empty.

"But why?" Will says. "Why?"

"Why what?"

"Why did he? How?"

"For the obvious reason, I assume. I don't have any other explanation. What else is there besides your unmarked face? The ease with which you moved through life when he was unhappy, struggling. He hid his anger—hid it from all of us. I think he must have been about six when he became self-conscious, aware of it—the thing—like he hadn't been before.

"You protected him, tried to make friends for him. Any situation, you always went on ahead of him, told other kids about his face and not to tease him or you'd make them sorry. At school, you'd pick out a few, bring them home to play. Punched a couple, the ones that said anything. But I don't know that any of that mattered to Mitch. Or that he noticed how you worked to save him from being hurt. How you loved him. Maybe all he saw was that you had a face that was perfect and he was a monster."

Will shakes his head. "I never understood why you and Mom were so complacent about the whole thing. Why you never tried to get it fixed. Why you didn't take him to New York, or even Albany, to see if you could get something—anything—done about it."

"We did! For God's sake, Will, of course we did. Your mother took him to a plastic surgeon in Albany for a consultation. Took him down to New York as well."

"When? When did you?"

"Well, the first time you would've been two. But she kept trying, after that she kept trying. The time you and I went fishing—you must remember, I know you do, because it was such a bust, we didn't catch even one fish and you just about got sun poisoning—that was the time your mother and Mitch went to the doctor in Albany. Then, another time, you and me at Saranac, and your mother with Mitch in New York City seeing a different plastic surgeon, guy that specialized in scars, birthmarks—cosmetic stuff. The thing was so extensive, he said, the vascular involvement, and at the time lasers were so rudimentary, that if he'd undertaken to fix it, the result would likely have been just another kind of disfigurement. We got as far as considering replacing that whole area of skin with a graft from his buttock, but it was a whole series of operations, too expensive, frankly, for us to manage. Long, painful, and it's not as if the result would have been a normal face.

"If we could have bought him a face that looked the same as yours, well, then we'd have mortgaged the house, the practice, whatever it took, but while it might have been better, it wouldn't look like a face someone was born with. And because you're twins, the injustice was that Mitch would always see an ideal version of himself, across the playground, the classroom, the dinner table. He couldn't escape you. We thought about boarding school, separation, but . . . I don't know. You were so protective of Mitch that we were afraid to send him out into the world by himself. We made mistakes. Probably we made mistakes. Hell, of course we did. But they weren't from lack of trying. Or for lack of seeing and caring about what was happening."

Will shakes his head. "My brother fucked my girlfriends, and he fucked my wife on the night before we got married. And my father and mother and wife keep this secret from me. For fifteen years. I have . . . I don't even know what my response to this is. Right now, I don't feel a thing. I'm too . . . too . . . I don't know what I am."

On the subway, Will isn't thinking of Jennifer, or of Mitch and Elizabeth, or Mitch and Lisa, or even Mitch and Carole, but of the first Halloween that his brother refused to wear the mask he'd chosen for himself. Their mother had never dressed them in matching clothes or encouraged them to regard their being identical—nearly—twins as special or even interesting, and they'd never worn costumes that were even slightly similar. Typically, Will was the grotesque of the two—not the kind of monster whose external ugliness cloaked virtue but one whose face represented a malignant soul. That year he wasn't any recognizable miscreant, not Mr. Hyde or Count Dracula or Dr. Frankenstein's terrible mistake, but a freak of his own making. Hunchbacked under ragged clothes topped by a repellent werewolf mask guaranteed to frighten the smaller children, he had green rubber gloves covered with putrescent warts and lumps.

Mitch was to be Clark Kent, not yet Superman but the earnest reporter on the verge of becoming Superman: the phone booth moment of transformation. He had on a suit that was a little too small (it had been purchased for a cousin's wedding the previous year) and a white shirt torn open to the waist to reveal the superhero's big red-and-yellow *S* emblazoned on his true-blue chest. Over his own face, Mitch wore a mask with Superman's blandly handsome countenance, with its cleft chin and iconic squiggle of black hair, hair too filled with vigor to remain tamed by brilliantine or whatever it was that supposedly kept the rest of it in place.

"I want to trade," Mitch suddenly said.

"No way."

"Come on. Please."

"No," Will said. "I hate being the good guy."

"I'll rake tomorrow."

"Unh-uh. No deal."

"Come on, Will, please. Did you see how many leaves there are? It'll take all afternoon."

"No."

"I won't go unless you trade."

"Fine. Don't go. What do I care?" Will took off his gloves to tie a shoelace that had come undone.

"Come on, Will. Please."

"No."

"All the raking, then. Not just tomorrow, but after, when the rest of the leaves come down."

"No," Will said. "No, no, no." Stalwart until Mitch cried, something Will couldn't stand and on which he tried and failed to turn his back. The sight of his brother giving up against his grief, the suddenness of Mitch's losing the ability to hide it: this had always had the power to dismantle Will. When Mitch cried, Will felt guilty and cornered and like he had to do something—anything—to stop it.

"Okay," he said, "here." He handed Mitch the mask, the gloves, the hunchback from last year's Igor costume, a cushion to which their mother had sewn two loops of elastic, one to go around each arm and hold it in place, and the ragged, grave-moldered cloak inherited from another year's vampire.

Will put on the Superman shirt and over it the dark suit; he adjusted the plastic do-gooder face. Without talking, he and Mitch went downstairs, stood patiently and listened to the usual cautions, and received quick hugs, each getting the embrace meant for the other brother. Will felt something different in his mother's arms, a communication that wasn't meant for him: an extra little squeeze of protective love and what was almost a tremble of maternal hope, the bodily equivalent of a prayer—please, please don't let them tease him. That's okay, Will told himself under the mask as the two of them went out the door and down the walk. That's okay with me. I don't mind because he needs that. Mitch needs more—more love, an extra cookie, a longer good-night kiss—a little more of everything. Still, he was stung—jealous enough that he knew he wouldn't have been able to hide it, and grateful his face was hidden.

They joined the neighborhood boys on the corner. As if by agreement, neither of them told the other kids that they'd traded costumes but continued under their masks to pretend to be each other. For Will it was a night of silent watching; he learned how seldom other children interacted with his brother. And it must have been, he imagines, a night of discovery for Mitch as well, jostled amiably, joked with, spoken to.

Later, at home, they dumped out their pillowcases to compare hauls, made a few trades, and argued with their mother about exactly how much candy they were allowed to eat that night, only Mitch complying with the limit she set. Then Mitch went up to their room, probably to sort through his baseball cards, shuffle past one after another hearty, handsome face, while Will stayed up with his father, watching *Creature Features*'s Halloween Marathon, and making his way steadily through his candy, methodically unwrapping and chewing what seemed imperative to get rid of and yet was too valuable to just throw out. It took until midnight to make himself good and sick.

"Well, that's a first, just about," his father said, holding Will's head over the downstairs toilet. "I can't remember the last time you threw up."

Will wonders how old he was that fall. He remembers that he'd felt very sorry for himself, so much so that he cried before he got sick, cried because he knew he was going to be sick and that it was his own fault. He didn't understand what he'd done to himself, or why.

The following year Halloween fell on a Friday, and the school held a party in the gymnasium. Will went; he convinced Stacey Davis to come with him to the stairwell, where she poured the contents of a red PixieStix onto her tongue and then let him lick it off before it melted away. Mitch stayed home and handed out candy. He wore a rubber political mask—Richard Nixon, Will thinks it was.

Mitch, his twin, the solitary swimmer, champion of the rights of manatees and hair seals, a man who can withstand whole days in the ocean. Does he remain the boy who traded ten or fifteen hours of raking and bagging leaves for one night of wearing the ugly mask instead of the handsome one? Did he hate Will already by that Halloween, or did that come later, the next year, when he stopped going out in costume, seemingly content to stay home?

Will's parents had done what his father called "their level best" to offset Mitch's antisocial nature. They pushed him into chess club, debate, Young Scientists of America, anything the A- and B-list kids, who filled the yearbook staff, football team, pep squad, and band, left to the losers and dorks, unfortunates who Will and Mitch's parents assumed would be less likely to focus on Mitch's face. Neither of them anticipated that the pariahs might be crueler than their pretty, popular classmates. They didn't understand that one untouchable resented being forced to make do with the damning company of others, that they were all venomous in a way that the luckier, more likeable kids never were. Always, Mitch capitulated to their mother's relentless goading—she called it "enthusiasm." He'd go to these gatherings once, only once, and then refuse to return.

And now, a new picture to add to the others, the image of his brother masked and slipping through the night to steal not just another girlfriend but his wife. An act of hatred? Of desperation? Would it even be possible to parse out one from the other?

So we've both lost a son, Will thinks, referring to himself and to his father. Scenes flash through his head like snapshots—or maybe they are snapshots, images he remembers from the old family albums. The three of them, Will and Mitch and their father, playing touch football in the backyard. Sitting together on the beach, shading their eyes with their hands. Will mugging from behind the wheel of the old station wagon and Mitch sitting on the hood, his turtleneck sweater pulled up so that only his hair showed.

W ill drops his briefcase on the table by the front
door. "Hey," he says to Carole, who's sitting
on the couch, her arms folded, the current issue of *Yoga Journal* in her
lap. At the sound of his voice, she uncrosses her arms, picks up the
magazine, and starts flipping through it.

Will glances up the stairs toward their daughter's room. "Where's
Sam?" he asks. He doesn't know that he's ever seen Carole take the
time to sit and read a magazine before their daughter was in bed.

"Watching a movie."

"Upstairs?"

Carole nods, but she doesn't look up.

"She okay?"

"Why wouldn't she be?"

"I don't know. She doesn't usually watch TV on a weeknight. I
thought maybe she wasn't feeling well or something."

"She's fine." Carole comes to the end of the magazine and then
starts again at the beginning, licking her index finger and using it to
flick past the pages, not so fast that she doesn't quickly scan each one.

"What are you doing, Carole?" Will asks her.

"This is what I hate about *Yoga Journal*," she says. She sounds so
fed up, it's as if she's at last voicing a serious complaint of many years'
standing. "Every issue, every single issue, there's something on the

cover that you can't find inside. Look." She thrusts the magazine at Will, talking faster than usual. "Seven Steps for Turning Bad Habits into Good Ones." She opens the magazine to the table of contents. "Look. Just look. Do you see 'Seven Steps for Turning Bad Habits into Good Ones'? No. No you do not. That's because it's not there. Page by page, I've gone through the entire issue, trying to find anything that might fit the description—'seven steps for turning bad into good'—and there's nothing. Not one paragraph." She slaps the magazine down on the coffee table. Will sits carefully in the chair opposite the couch.

"You don't have any bad habits, Carole."

"That is not the point. The point is—"

"Carole?" he interrupts.

"What?"

"Is something going on?"

"You tell me," she says. He glances upstairs.

"How long's the DVD going to last?" he asks.

"What?"

"I need to talk to you."

"Yes, I guess you do."

"What's that supposed to mean?"

She closes her eyes as if there's no expression, no other gesture that could possibly convey her exasperation. "Will—"

"Wait. There's something I have to tell you, Carole. I had lunch with my father and—"

"Will, I don't want to talk about anything until you listen to—"

He holds up one hand, as if directing a driver to stop. It's the kind of communication—wordless, and, in her opinion, appropriate only for animal trainers or airport ground crews—that has in the past provoked her to walk out on an argument. She makes a little huff of protest.

"We have to talk now," he says. "If we don't . . . if I don't say this now . . ." He shakes his head.

"What is it?"

Will takes a deep breath. "How . . ." He takes another breath. "Carole?" he says, after allowing the silence to grow uncomfortable. "I've, uh . . . something bad's happened. My fault. I did something stupid, and then I made it even worse. Not on purpose. I had lunch with my father. I . . . God, I'm telling this all backwards. I'm trying to go in the right order, but it's not—it's hard to make sense of. I asked him why Mitch left when he did, why he skipped out before the wedding. I had . . . I'd always suspected there was something. Why didn't you tell me, Carole?"

She takes her hands from her face but she doesn't look at him. "I . . . I don't know," she says. "We . . . I . . . I didn't plan to keep it a secret."

"But you did. You kept it a secret for fifteen years. And now, now I've done something terrible. And it's all related, it's all tangled up in the same . . ." Will trails off, watching Carole shake her head, her eyes downcast.

"After he . . . after Mitch . . . there wasn't any way to get back to how it was before," she says. "How I was. Because it was one of those things that—it just divided everything. Me. It divided me into before and after. And how could I change that?" She looks up at him, speaking faster than usual, and more loudly; her voice has lost its characteristic calm. "I mean from the outside would anyone even think I was raped? It was all messed up. Everything was. The person who I, who . . . the, the person was someone I invited into our room. And now there was this ugly, this dirty thing that would play out in front of everyone we knew, everyone we cared about. Our families, people from work, guests from out of town, friends from college. It would . . . I was afraid it would always be, 'Oh, you remember them, don't you? She's the one who was raped, or, or tricked, or . . . or whatever it was, by the groom's twin brother.'" Suddenly Carole is on her feet, pacing and waving her arms as she speaks. Will didn't even see her get up from where she was sitting; she moved that fast.

"I wanted to save face. Or I guess what I mean is, I didn't want to lose face. I was *scared*, Will. And I tried to tell you. Later, I did. But whenever I mentioned Mitch, you changed the subject. You were . . . I felt like you were avoiding the topic. So, I quit. I quit trying so—"

"No!" Will says. "I have no memory, none, of your trying to tell me anything."

"But I did. And how it turned out—that wasn't calculated. I didn't intend for you to not ever know. Maybe . . . maybe that was what your father wanted. Or maybe it was what they both—your mom and your dad—wanted. Or what I thought they'd want. Or vice versa, what they thought I would. I mean, Jesus, Will, you don't know how many times I've gone over this. Anyway, they're all after the fact, these interpretations. I can't remember what I was thinking then, that night, and that's because I wasn't thinking anything. Except I wanted us to get married and everything to be okay." She looks at Will, waiting for him to speak, but he says nothing, and she goes on.

"I didn't have any idea of how . . . how emotionally costly it would become. That wasn't something I even considered in the moment— why would I?—I never planned to keep it a secret. Not indefinitely. But the longer I didn't tell you, the more difficult it got. Once I'd said nothing for a day, since it was our wedding day, and then for all of our honeymoon—because I didn't want to wreck that. It was, you know, our *honeymoon*, and I wanted to protect it, that little bubble of time. And after, when we were back home, it just got . . . it got harder and harder to imagine myself introducing the topic. We'd be apart from each other all day, both of us working, and I'd have scripted a dialogue in my head, rehearse how I was going to begin it, but whenever the chance presented itself, I . . . I didn't. It got to be as if it never happened. Sometimes it seemed so unreal, it was as if it had been a sort of, oh, I don't know, some overwrought fantasy about myself and a famous person, someone who doesn't even exist outside the media. The way a teenager might dream about having a date with Brad Pitt or someone. Since that's what Mitch had become, a person who isn't even real. Not anymore, not for us."

She looks at Will, who leans forward, his elbows on his knees, considering this idea: Mitch's transformation from flesh to fantasy. He tries to imagine the comforts, and the cost, of what would amount to a kind of amputation, the erasure of a distempered part of himself, a version of himself he'd be better off without. Wouldn't the loss leave him desolate, prey to the psychic equivalent of a ghost limb—pain where there is nothing? Pain generated by nothingness. Has this happened already? Has Mitch been removed? Excised?

As if the words *bubble of time* were a tranquilizing spell, Will finds that he has panned back from the argument. Sees himself and Carole grow smaller and smaller, watches their living room shrink to the size of a shoe box. As he ascends, he listens to something like a voice-over inside his own head. A voice too refined to ever—even in extremis—grow loud or shrill, a voice with Alistair Cooke's British accent, the measured tone of one of his PBS program introductions, it talks to Will, making reasonable suggestions like "Let's look at the big picture, Will. Take the long view."

His arrival on this Zen peak, a height to which he's aspired but never even come close to attaining, with its atmosphere too thin to allow the waste of oxygen on untamed emotion, leaves him not only detached but with a clear head. It's as if, after an eternity of fiddling, he's at last managed to tune in his own thoughts without the interference of static or the indistinct mumbling of other channels.

"The other thing is," he hears Carole say, "do you remember

how fast we got pregnant? How happy we were? I was happy and you were, too, and I . . . I asked myself, why tell you now? For what?" She frowns, shakes her head.

Will sees movement on the stairs. "Samantha!" he says to alert her mother. Carole turns around.

"Hello, sweetheart." There is nothing in her voice to suggest the two of them might be involved in a conversation of any importance. "You must be ready for dinner, no?"

Sam doesn't answer. She stands in the middle of the staircase, looking from her father to her mother and then back. "The movie's over," she says, finally.

"How about another?" Will offers, and she shakes her head.

"I'm not allowed."

"Oh, we can break the rules. Every once in a while we can."

"No," she says, "we can't."

"Aren't you hungry?" Carole asks.

"It could be anything," Will says, "anything you want. It could be ice cream." Sam looks at him, at first with suspicion and then with a peculiarly grown-up expression, a miniature rendition of her mother's men-just-don't-get-it look, one delicate eyebrow raised, her mouth puckered in a wry, little twist. She turns to her mother.

"The thing is," Carole says, "Daddy and I are talking. We have something we need to figure out and—"

"What? What do you?"

"It's not . . . it's something . . ."

"Is it money?"

No, Will is about to say, but then he reconsiders—if ever an occasion excused a white lie, this would be it. "It is, Sam," he tells her. "It is about money."

"Grilled cheese?" Carole asks. "Or how about an omelet? There are apples from the green market, and I'll slice them the way you like." Samantha nods and pushes her hair behind her ears as she follows her mother to the kitchen, showing Will the pale, almost transparent skin of her temple.

"How do you know?" he asks Carole as soon as Samantha has eaten and gone back upstairs. "How can you be sure Luke isn't—wasn't—Mitch's child instead of mine? Because I do remember, and it was fast. Barely nine months from the wedding."

Carole is shaking her head before he stops talking. "I know," she says, "I know because he . . . because I made him pull out before it got to that point."

"You—"

"You don't think he could have—you can't think I wouldn't have known. That I didn't guess who it was. I knew right away it wasn't you. It just . . . I just didn't believe it. Myself. It took me that minute to convince myself that I wasn't crazy, that it really was him instead of you."

Will nods slowly. "My dad had it wrong, then. He thought it was the same as with the others. That Mitch didn't pull off the mask until the end, after . . . that he didn't reveal himself until it was done."

"The same as with . . . what others? What are you talking about?"

"It wasn't the only time. He'd done it before, with other girls." Will watches Carole's expression.

"Before? He did it with other girls you . . . girls you knew before?" She's speaking with her face in her hands, the way someone might cradle an aching jaw.

"Yes. That's the part that's . . . that's how this is connected to the . . . to the mess I've made. I saw a woman, an old girlfriend, at the reunion and . . ." He trails off. The two of them watch each other from across the coffee table.

"Elizabeth?" Carole says, finally.

"How did you know?"

"There's a message. On the machine." Will raises his eyebrows. "You'd better just listen," she says, and he gets up, goes to the kitchen phone.

"Hey there, Dr. Moreland," drawls a familiar voice. "It's Jennifer. I'm, like, looking at a lab report. Because guess what? As it happened, I found this little hair of yours glued to my thigh with spooge. So I guess we, like, traded—a long one of mine for a short, curly one of yours. And, so, hey, I'm interested in sharing my news with you if you're, like, interested enough to call me back. Or even if you aren't." The machine announces the time and date of the call, then clicks off.

"Shit," Will says. That Jennifer has left such a message for his wife to hear is a surprisingly destructive act, even from her. He hits the play button and listens to the message once more.

"This isn't from today, Carole. It's from . . . it says it's from Tuesday. Last Tuesday, when I was out of town." He comes back to the living room. "Unless the date thing's screwed up?"

"No," Carole says, her face expressionless.

"So . . ." Will shakes his head. "You've . . . you heard this before? Before today?"

"No. You know I always fast-forward through the ones from your patients. But, the . . . the person who left that, that message, Jennifer, her mother called today, just before you got home. After I talked to her, I remembered that before I skipped past one message, I'd heard someone identify herself as Jennifer." It isn't only her face. Carole's voice, too, is without affect.

"Elizabeth?" he says. "Elizabeth called here?"

"She asked me to tell you something."

"What is it?" Will says when she doesn't continue.

"I . . . I want to make sure I get it right." Like a student trying to summon a lesson committed to memory, Carole closes her eyes while she speaks. "A DNA analysis that Elizabeth's husband, Paul some-body, insisted be made, confirmed that Jennifer is not your child. Apparently, Jennifer told him—Paul—about the . . . about whatever's going on among you three, and he was angry enough to force the issue. One that Elizabeth considers is now closed, never to be re-opened. Jennifer is Paul's biological and legal daughter. If you attempt to contact Elizabeth or any member of her family, any colleague or associate, any friend or acquaintance, 'even the fucking paper boy'—that's a direct quote—you'll be in violation of the restraining order she's filing tomorrow." Carole opens her eyes.

"That's it?" Will says. "That's all she said?" He's so flooded with relief he starts to laugh, just for a moment. The look on Carole's face sobers him up. She's furious, her teeth clenched so tightly that a band of muscle stands out in her cheek. "See, I thought . . . I wasn't laughing because anything was funny. For a month, almost, I've thought she, Jennifer, I thought she—"

"You slept with this person. You had sex with her."

Will sits down; then he stands back up, puts his hands in his pockets. "Yes," he says.

"She's . . . she's a patient?"

"No," he says. "Was. She was before."

"Before what? Before you fucked her!" Will doesn't answer. "Why!" she says. "Why!"

"Why?"

"All right, how? How could you!"

"I—"

Abruptly, Carole's voice has acquired an edge. "I want a way to understand."

"I'm sorry. You remember I told you about the girl, the one who came on to me?"

"I think you may have understated the case," Carole says, "in that you told me she kissed you." The venom in her voice more than compensates for whatever expression her face lacks.

"She did," he says. "And then I did what I said I was going to. I told her we couldn't continue working together and referred her to another therapist. But she came back. Came to the office, refused to leave. Told me she was sorry and carried on. She even cried, or I thought she did. Anyway, I believed her. I believed her enough to let down my guard. I turned my back for a minute—just to disengage while I tried to come up with a way to convince her to leave without exacerbating the whole mess—and when I turned back around she'd taken all her clothes off. Threatened to, well, to make it appear as if I'd tried to rape her unless I . . ."

"Unless you?"

"Complied."

"Complied."

"Yes. With her intention to have intercourse with me."

"Come on! Am I supposed to believe that—"

"Yes! You are. Because she did. And as it turns out, she was looking for a . . . for revenge."

"Revenge! For what! Revenge for what!"

"I . . . it started when I ran into Elizabeth at the reunion." Will looks away and then back at his wife. "The fact is, when we broke up, Elizabeth was pregnant, and I . . . I wondered was there a chance of her—the daughter—being my biological child. We talked. I said something that offended Elizabeth. I didn't mean it the way she took it—I'm not even sure exactly how she took it, other than badly. Whatever she thought, I just wanted to know, not to interfere. As soon as I read her page in the reunion book and saw the date of her daughter's birth, I . . . I needed to get a fix on it. Needed to know one way or the other. So I asked would she give me a hair sample, so I could have it tested."

"You wanted proof?" Carole says.

"Yes. Something definitive. Otherwise, it would be open-ended. Alive. I wanted to put it to rest."

"But how? How could you if she turned out to be yours?"

"I don't know. I'd have to deal with it, obviously. But it wouldn't be as—I don't think it would be as disturbing as not knowing. Anyway, the conversation got combative. I didn't back down; she got more and more defensive. Clearly, she imagined I was going to . . . to intrude on her life. Or Jennifer's. She even said I was looking for a surrogate for Luke. But, honestly, I don't think that was my intent. Not even unconsciously. I've thought about this a lot. Maybe if the child had been a boy, but I can't see myself drawing an equation—I just don't think that was what I wanted."

"Well, what did you want?"

"I don't know. I'm not sure. It was a mistake to press her, Carole, and I apologize. I was . . . I don't know what I was. Lonely, I guess—at loose ends. And she . . . she went ballistic. Must have then misrepresented my request to Jennifer. Characterizing me as . . . as an asshole, evidently. And Jennifer, who is, well, she probably tends to sexualize every transaction, but in this case she must have determined to possess me in return. In response to Elizabeth's saying I had possessive feelings for her. Jennifer, I mean. Possess me sexually." Carole stares at him, arms crossed, mouth closed. "And I, uh, I couldn't . . . didn't . . . stop it. She didn't tell me who she was until it was over."

"Why!" Carole says. "Why! Why didn't you!"

"I don't know," he says. "After she'd refused to put her clothes back on and leave, I just was . . . I don't know what I was. Struck dumb, basically."

"But not unaffected."

"Not unaffected?"

"As in not unable to perform. I mean, come on, Will, it's not as if a woman can sexually . . . can sexually engage a man without a certain degree of . . . cooperation. A physical willingness."

"Yes. You're—well, you're right. That's true. But that isn't within my conscious moral control. It's not something I can decide whether or not to do."

"So this would be a case of the, the flesh being weak? Is that what you're saying?"

"I guess that's one way to put it."

"Well, do you have anything to say about that?"

"No."

"No?"

"What can I say, Carole? I'm sorry. I'm sorry I was aroused. I didn't do it on purpose."

"Fine. Fine. Great. Swell. That makes it all okay, right? Will can't help it if he has a hard-on, can he?" she says to the wall, the chair, an invisible witness or referee. "Do I get to ask why? Why did you, or a part of you, want to have sex with her?"

"Come on, Carole."

"Why you wanted it enough that you didn't manage to, to control your physical response?"

"I don't know."

"You don't know."

"No."

"Well, think of something! I think you owe me the courtesy of trying to explain, don't you?"

"Well, she was . . . she was attractive. Physically. I said so. She elicited a physical response."

"It's not as if you're deprived at home."

"No." Will shakes his head. "Well, I am. I am in that I never get to make love to someone with a face. Leaving me, what, well, alone, I guess."

"Alone? You? What about me?"

"What about you? Are you lonely, Carole? Because how would I know? You're not exactly a person with her heart on her—"

"Will, you're so involved with, with Luke that—"

"That's too easy! You're projecting your feelings onto me. I don't think I'm any more involved with him than you are."

"He can't . . . Luke can't . . ." Carole shakes her head. "He can't be the end of every argument. He can't be the cause of every problem we have."

"Of course he can't! He isn't. In fact, it's become suddenly clear that from the beginning—long before the accident—my brother was—"

"I never didn't forgive you, Will, for the accident. I forgave you from the beginning. No—that's not right. Forgiving you would imply I'd weighed what had happened and decided you weren't—"

"Carole, you can't just have been automatically saintly. No one is. You've repress—"

"I never blamed you! And I am so sick of this stupid, stupid argument. I always thought of it, and I still do think of it, as something that happened to us. Both of us. All of us."

"So why? Why then? You do have to admit something happened, Carole, something inside you. It wasn't me who, who . . . our sex life wasn't the same as it had been. Right away, it wasn't. The very first time we made love after Luke drowned, it was different. And you were the one who made it different."

Carole opens her mouth, and he sees a tremor in her chin and her bottom lip. "It's not you," she says. "If the accident is anyone's fault, it's mine. Not yours. *Mine*." She says the word with one hand splayed over her breastbone.

Will throws his hands up over his head. "Yours! How is that possible? What kind of upside-down thinking could lead you to believe any of it was your fault?" Carole looks away, her lips compressed into a tight line. "What?" he says. "What!"

She gives up trying to stop the tears. "I can't make myself . . . I know this sounds like what you'd call estrogen logic, but I . . . I can't help feeling that it was, it had to have been a kind of . . . of correction. A realignment. Because of me."

"What are you talking about! I have no idea what you're talking about!"

"Luke was"—her voice catches—"he was perfect, he was good. He was a . . . there was nothing wrong about him. And I'm . . . I was afraid I was being corrected. Punished for, for—"

"For Mitch?" he says. "For my brother's . . . out of some kind of, of cosmic readjustment?"

Carole nods as if what Will said does in fact add up.

"And what about Luke? What about our little boy? In this line of reasoning, why should it be Luke who pays for the realignment?" Will stops pacing to look at Carole. "I mean, unless you have a whole different moral scale for yourself. Unless the rest of us—me, Sam, your friends, your clients and their, their well-meaning, unenlightened parents—unless we all get measured with the mini moral yardstick, the one for regular mortals and their mini virtues and vices. Is that why you forgive me, Carole? Or why forgiving or not forgiving isn't even an issue for you? Because you're on a different plane, a whole other body of water, sailing along smoothly, no waves, no capsizing?"

He stops ranting when he notices the look on Carole's face. An outrage he's never seen before—it's blanched her cheeks and flared her nostrils, so narrowed her usually round eyes that, were he to see this face outside its context, he might not identify it as belonging to anyone he knows. He's so surprised, so intent on her expression, that he doesn't even register that she's seized something from the coffee table, doesn't see her hurl it at his head. Maybe she should have been the one who coached Little League, he thinks absurdly as he stumbles back and trips over his own feet. Then he's on the floor, looking at her through a foggy pink veil.

"Oh God, I'm sorry, I'm sorry, Will. I think I . . . I split open your, your, right above your eyebrow." She has a wad of paper towels and is pressing them to his head. "I think it needs stitches."

"Here," he says. Will uses his own hand to hold the paper towels against his head, pressing harder than she was willing to, to try to stop the bleeding. As he gets to his feet, he sees what it was that hit him, the jar of peanut butter he left on the coffee table when he was talking on the phone with his father, asking him if he was okay with changing their lunch date, seeing each other a week earlier than usual. While talking he'd wandered away from the kitchen, forgotten he was in the middle of making a sandwich. The jar is lying label up, intact. After the Fall is the name of the brand Carole buys, and this strikes him as funny, enough that he starts to laugh.

"Maybe you should start buying Skippy," he says when he can speak, "in the nice plastic jar. Instead of that organic stuff. Then the next time you throw it at me, this won't happen." He's still laughing, he can't help it.

"Shit," she says. "Sorry, sorry, I'm sorry. I'm going to pull the car around. Sam!" she yells. "Samantha! Do you think you can go up and get her, Will?"

The emergency room is its usual purgatory. Will tries not to think of what Samantha might be catching from the little boy next to her, the two of them staring at the overhead TV on the other side of the waiting area, the one tuned to Cartoon Network. Each time the child exhales, a bubble of mucus extrudes from one nostril. He inhales, the bubble deflates, disappears, then reemerges. What it never does is pop.

"I wish you'd thrown it harder," he says; "then I could have been triaged to the front of the line."

"Hmnhh," Carole answers. CNN is on and Will strains to see the time in the lower right-hand corner of the screen, but it's too small to read from where he's sitting. It must be at least midnight, though, because this is the third time they've seen the same tape feed of a distraught Middle Eastern woman holding a man's photograph up to the camera.

"Carole?" Will says. She yawns.

"What is it?" She sits up straight to stretch her arms over her head.

"Marry me?"

He still can't read the time at the bottom of the TV screen, but he can see the digits change before she answers. "I haven't divorced you yet," she says.

Perhaps this is a function of the length of the pause, but Will can't tell whether or not she's being serious. He can't see her face without getting up and walking around in front of her. *You're not serious, are you?* He tries out the question in his head.

"How long do you think it'll take to go through?" he tries instead. Both of them are looking up at the screen rather than at each other.

"That depends."

"On what?"

"Whether it's no-contest or nobody's fault or whatever they call it."

"Fault," Will says. "Fault's tricky."

"Very." Carole retrieves a tissue from her purse and blows her nose.

"You'll think this is ridiculous, but I tend to make pie graphs when I'm assigning responsibility." Will switches the hand holding the paper towels to his head from right to left. "In this case, my brother would get the biggest slice, but then I'd get some, too, and my parents. Jennifer. Maybe Elizabeth. Then there's you."

"Which case?"

"The thing with Jennifer."

"Why am I in there?"

"Because anything that has to do with me and sex automatically involves you."

"Wouldn't there have to be more than one pie?" Carole says after a minute. "One labeled Mitch, the other Jennifer?"

"There could be three. Mitch, Jennifer, and Luke. Drawn on transparencies, so they could be superimposed one over another."

She shakes her head. "Too complicated. Everyone—Mitch, Jennifer, Luke—they're all both pies and slices in other pies."

"Are they?"

"Of course. Take Luke, his drowning I mean. He's a pie, with responsibility apportioned among you, for sailing the boat; Luke himself, for not leaving his vest buckled; me, for renting the house on the lake; my friend, the one who gave me the joint, just in case you were a little hungover, less focused—although I never agreed with you about that. I mean, I didn't notice anything. Then there's the boatrental company, for not, I don't know, issuing warnings, or whatever; the sailing instructor, for not stressing the importance of paying attention all the time; the weather, for being so beautiful; and so on. I mean you can go on slicing smaller and smaller pieces of causation. And aside from being a pie, Luke would also be in the Jennifer pie, if it's true that by drowning he left you vulnerable to involvement with . . ." She trails off.

"It's funny," Will says. "How much of my time is dedicated to helping other people to stop assessing themselves, or situations in which they find themselves, in terms of blame. Judgment. Who did what, and who said what, and what it might mean as far as his or her culpability in the given conflict."

"But?"

"But I do it to myself. To us. I can't let go of the idea that I can figure things out."

"With pie graphs."

"I said it was ridiculous."

Carole looks at his forehead. "Maybe I should go to the restroom for more paper towels."

"No, don't."

"But it's seeping through."

"It doesn't matter. Stay here. Talk to me."

Carole leans her head against his shoulder. "You were sort of right about the different moral yardsticks," she says. "Except you made it sound so smug, and I don't think I am, really. Saying I have two standards—one for me and one for everyone else—it could just as easily be that I give other people the benefit of the doubt, which I don't do for myself."

"Why?"

"I don't know. Maybe because I'm in my own head. With other people I have to correct for not knowing their private experience. As in that old supposedly Native American proverb, the one about having to walk in someone else's moccasins."

The triage nurse comes to the ER door. "Hernandez!" she calls. She crosses the name from the list on the clipboard resting on the counter of the locked service window. Will sees that Samantha has fallen asleep, her legs stretched across the seat where the little boy had been sitting.

"Do we really have to get divorced before I propose?" he asks.

"I guess I might settle for a pre-nup, instead."

"How much?" he says. She's so deadpan, he can't tell what's a joke and what isn't.

"It wouldn't be about money."

"What then?"

"Well, first off, you have to skip your thirtieth college reunion. And your thirty-fifth. Fortieth, forty-fifth. I guess if you haven't kicked the bucket by your fiftieth—you'll be how old, seventy-something?—we can maybe negotiate."

Will holds out his free hand as if to shake hers, but she's not finished.

"You throw out all your ties. Wear only the ones I buy for you."

"Even the paisley ones?"

"Especially the paisley ones."

"Is there more?" Will asks, when she doesn't continue.

"A new dishwasher before you buy even one more antique map.

Also, I think I really do want cable so I can begin my career as a TV watcher. I'm not giving up yoga, but I want to pursue some vacuous activities, practice wasting time. I must be the only person in New York who never saw even one episode of *Sex and the City*. I might even start, I don't know, drinking a glass of wine or two on weekends."

Will nods. "Is that it?"

She shakes her head.

"Well?"

"No more birth control."

Will looks at her. He says nothing, preoccupied with feeling how it feels, their eyes on each other's. Reminded of the old childhood game: Who'll be the first to blink or laugh? Who will turn away?

The idea of Carole pregnant doesn't summon images of a new baby so much as it does a series of fragments, like flash cards, pictures of Luke mostly, Luke before he could talk. Grabbing the cat's tail and laughing when she hissed. Shoving his pacifier into Will's mouth. The way he slept on his stomach, knees drawn under, butt in the air. "I can't," Will says, finally. "I don't think I can do it again."

Carole pulls up one corner of the wad of paper towels to look at the gash. "What if I can't stand not to?"

"I don't know. Is it a deal breaker?"

"Maybe."

He takes her hand in his. "I'm . . ."

"What if I can't stand not to?" she asks him again, before he can figure out what he's trying to say.

"Moreland," the triage nurse announces from the door. Will stands up.

"Aren't you coming with me?" he asks.

"Just let me grab Sam." Carole manages to gather their daughter into her arms without waking her. Her legs dangle down as far as her mother's knees. "Ugh," Carole says. "I never get why it is that kids feel heavier when they're asleep."

They follow the nurse into a small examination room, where she takes his blood pressure and his temperature before saturating the wad of paper towels with hydrogen peroxide in order to peel them away from his forehead. As soon as it's uncovered, the gash opens and begins bleeding again. "Whoa," she says, "what happened here?"

"I threw something at his head."

"I bumped it on the mantel."

They speak at the same instant, and the nurse looks back and forth between them, her plucked eyebrows raised.

"It was a joke," Will says.

"Domestic violence is not something we find funny here in the emergency room."

"I'm sorry," Carole says. "I get a little punchy when I'm tired."

The nurse frowns and turns to Will. "Well," she says, "you picked a good night for a facial. Dr. Cunningham came on at eleven." She tears the paper from around a pad of sterile gauze and tells him to hold it against the split flesh, lifting his hand to his forehead. "You don't have to push so hard," she says.

"A facial?" Carole asks.

"Facial wound." The nurse stands, and they do, too, Will pulling Carole to her feet when she can't rise under the weight of their sleeping daughter. All of them file down the hall, the nurse, then Will, Carole and Samantha lagging behind. "Eyebrows are tricky. They heal up crooked if they're not sutured just so. Dr. Cunningham's a plastic surgeon."

She leaves the three of them in an enclosure made by a white curtain hanging from a U-shaped track in the ceiling. Inside are a bed and a chair. On the orange Formica counter are bandages, alcohol preps, and emesis basins. Carole arranges Samantha facedown on the bed to keep the light out of her eyes. There's only the one sheet, tucked around and under the mattress, so she pulls it out and wraps what she can of it around her.

"Wow," she says, shaking her head. "A good night for a facial."

"I didn't know it went through my eyebrow." Will tries to find his reflection in the stainless steel paper-towel dispenser.

"Hello," someone says, and they both jump, turn around. "Let's take a look."

"Are you Dr. Cunningham?" Will asks.

"Last time I checked." He pulls on a pair of gloves and motions for Will to sit in the chair. "Close your eyes," he says. "Deep. How'd it happen?"

"A jar of peanut butter," Carole says. "Glass. Kind of heavy."

"Didn't break?" he asks mildly, not seeming to infer anything from her answer.

"No."

"Looks clean. Have to trim the dermis. Minimize scarring." He flips up the magnifying lens he's wearing on his own head. "Back in a sec."

"A little weird," Carole whispers to Will after the doctor has left the enclosure, "don't you think?"

"You mean the ponytail? The red clogs? The vampire pallor?"

"His lips are so—he looks like he's wearing lipstick, but I don't think he is, really." Carole strokes Will's hair back, away from the gash. "I am sorry," she tells him. "Does it hurt?"

He shakes his head. "It's going to make a distinguished-looking scar. Dangerously sexy. I can see there'll be times I'll have to cover it with a low-brimmed hat to keep you from going wild." She smiles, but it's not because she thinks what he's said is funny: he can see she's humoring him.

The surgeon returns with a tray of instruments, looks at Samantha sleeping. "Let's go next-door." He grabs a handful of curtain and pulls it aside.

"Numb you up," he says to Will after he's settled him under a light so bright that Will can't help but close his eyes, seeing what looks like lightning striking through a red sky, the veins in his eyelids, he guesses. The doctor's latex-sheathed fingers are cool and sticky on his skin, and the antiseptic smell of Betadine jolts Will back to the delivery room: the white flesh at the top of Carole's thighs stained dark orange, the stuff running down into her pubic hair and onto the white sheets.

The doctor covers Will's face with what feels like paper, a disposable cloth, no doubt. There's a hole in the center, though; he can feel air against his skin, cold where the Betadine is evaporating. "Feel a pinch," the doctor says.

Despite the warning, Will flinches when the needle goes in, and Carole squeezes his hand. "Is it okay if I watch?" she asks, but if the doctor answers, it's with a nod or a gesture, something Will can't see.

"It's not quite as big as I thought," Carole says, narrating what's going on for him. "Maybe an inch and a half. He's not doing the skin yet. He's stitching the muscle together underneath."

Will draws a deep breath, so deep that he feels the cloth lift off his mouth when he exhales. "Carole?" He gives her hand a little shake.

"What is it?"

"I'll try." He waits for her to answer, or even just to squeeze his fingers in return, anxious enough that he forgets to pay attention to the tugging of the sutures.

"Are you . . . do you mean what we were talking about before?" she says at last. He startles at an unexpected ring of metal against metal. The doctor must have dropped an instrument into the tray.

"I'm not . . . I can't promise, but I don't want you to think I'd dismissed the idea. It's just that I—"

"Had to shave some hair," the doctor says, "so I could see. Don't want a jig in the brow."

"I didn't think you dismissed it," Carole says. "I just can't figure out how not to want what I want, you know?"

"I know." Still holding her hand, Will strokes her knuckles with his thumb. "I know."

Suddenly, the cloth flies up off his face. "Want to take a look before I put the dressing on?" the doctor says.

"Can I?"

He points to a door across the hall, on it a little blue sign with the outlines of a man, a woman, and a wheelchair.

Will leans over the sink to inspect his face. Now that the two sides are stitched together in a line, the gash is a little anticlimactic, he thinks. He can count at least twenty stitches, but they're tiny, made with very fine nylon thread. He cups his hands under the faucet for a drink of water, aware of a slight throb as he bends his head down. Whatever was in the needle is wearing off.

Someone knocks on the door, and Will turns off the water. "I'll be out in a minute," he says.

"Can I come in?" Carole's voice asks.

"It's not locked." Will watches in the mirror as she closes the door behind her.

She stands beside him at the sink, and he watches their two reflections. "I wasn't serious," she says, "about the pre-nup."

He nods, starts to rub his eyes, but a stab from the stitched eyebrow stops him. "That blue-colored cloth, the plastic basins. Smell of Betadine. Like being back in the delivery room," he says.

Her reflection nods. "We had that great window when Luke was born. Remember? We could see the top of the Chrysler Building, the sun shining on it."

"I just remember him, and you. Cutting the cord."

Her hair spread on the white pillowcase. One of her feet in his hands, the other in the labor nurse's. After—Luke was in her arms—there was the placenta in its plastic dish. Not formless and Jell-O-y, the way he'd imagined it, but a different thing entirely. Impossible to have predicted so rich a color, or so violent a beauty. The elegant tree of its veins, a perfect symmetry, and the way it gleamed, spilling over the sides of the dish. What is this I'm feeling? he remembers thinking, wondering at the prickling sensation behind his eyes. Then he realized he'd been holding his breath as he stroked a finger over its surface. Hot to the touch, slippery smooth. Something she'd made with her own body. A part of her that felt as she did inside, when he put a finger there, when he touched her.

Carole leans against Will's chest. She puts her arms around him and slips her hands into his back pockets. "Let's go home," she says.

"And go to bed?"

"And go to bed."

"Do you think, in honor of my injury, we could try it face-to-face?"

His hands are on her shoulders, and she looks up at him. "In honor of your injury? Or in apology for throwing things at you?"

"For whatever reason you say. For old times' sake. Because we want to. For the good of the cause."

She puts her arms around him again, pulls him into her, hard, so her pelvis presses up against him. "What cause?" she asks. "Is it a worthy one?"

"It's us. Our cause."

She pushes her face into the front of his shirt. "Okay," she whispers. "Okay, okay," a whisper he knows because he's heard it before.

Overheard it, really, because it isn't an answer; it's the way she talks herself through an unfamiliar task, a challenge she's determined to meet, even if she doesn't know how. *Okay, okay*, he's heard her whisper on the floor of their bedroom, twisting herself into a new yoga puzzle. Or at her desk, computer on, fingers poised over the keyboard, *JavaScript for Dummies* open in her lap. In the kitchen, frowning at the piecrust on the floured butcher's block.

Okay, okay, Samantha watching her mother as Carole advances, step by confusing step outlined by the deceptively titled *Origami Made Simple*, her fingers turning a square of gold paper into a frog, a crane, a tiny cup that, if folded correctly, promises to hold a sip of water.

"Okay?" he says again. She nods against his chest.

"Okay," she says, still whispering. "Okay."

P.S.

Ideas,
interviews
& features ...

About the author

About the book

Read on

Liking Monday Better Than Friday

Sarah O'Reilly meets Kathryn Harrison

Critics have argued that *The Kiss*, an account of your four-year affair with your father, provides the perspective from which all your other books must be read. Would you have been a writer, do you think, if your early life had worked out differently?
I think that there were a *number* of roads leading out of the childhood that I had. I'm not someone who ever planned to be a writer, and I think I could as easily have ended up in a mental institution. But certainly my experiences left me with questions that I needed to answer.

After my mother died and after I had disentangled myself from my father, I had to account for my life and the direction it had taken. Certainly, I wasn't in a place I'd expected to be in from the vantage of being thirteen or fourteen; my life had gone terribly awry and I needed to figure out how and why, and *who* I was. Most people would have had another apparatus for discovering that. For me, the only way I could understand anything was to write about it; it was my means, to use a loathsome word, of *processing* things. So my first three novels, directly or indirectly, were very much about my formative experiences.

But when I wrote *The Kiss*, a work of non-fiction, I think it was freeing to a certain extent. It allowed me to move *beyond* that territory in terms of my writing. That's not to say that there aren't aspects of my life and myself in the fiction I write now – it's just that it's not as claustrophobic as it once was.

You're known for exploring challenging subjects in your work. Is there anything that you wouldn't write about?
Something that bored me. But I don't draw the line anywhere else. I am completely willing to lay open, observe and discuss any aspect of myself – people would say far too willing! I would not do the same to my children or my husband or my friends because I have a relationship with those people that I want to honour, and a sense that certain things are sacred. It's just that mostly I'm not that thing.

You evoke strong critical reactions. Do you enjoy being provocative in your work?
I think that I am, for better and for worse, someone who resents rules. I generally play by them, but you only have to tell me that I have to do something one way for me to want to do it the other. Generally speaking that's not a very useful trait, except on the page. At the time of *The Kiss*'s publication, people were saying that books were invisible, that they didn't matter, so for me there was a kind of gratification in causing a fight. People would say to me, 'I got into a huge argument with my co-workers and it's all your fault!' And I would think, that's fantastic! Having that kind of potency was reinforcing. ▶

> 6 I have no interest in writing nice little books that people will feel tepidly positive about. 9

Liking Monday... *(continued)*

◀ I have no interest in writing nice little books that people will feel tepidly positive about. I would much rather write a book that some people loved and other people hated. There has to be some kind of transaction between you and the reader and I'd prefer to leave people agitated and unhappy than unmoved: at least it means I've somehow gotten under their skin. Why write if you can't do that?

What is your experience of writing? Do the words come easily?

When I think about writing, I am reminded of an experiment that scientists carried out with a pigeon. They discovered that if a pigeon is given one kernel of corn, it will peck a thousand times in expectation of the next piece. Writing is like that: you have moments that are like finding that kernel, moments that are wonderful and transcendent; you know your writing is good and the words just come to you. The rest of the time, the thing is to keep hitting that keyboard, to continue to peck.

Envy is the second of your novels to feature a male protagonist, the first being *The Seal Wife*. Why did you decide to return to writing from a male standpoint in *Envy*?

The Seal Wife showed me that writing as a man could be so much more satisfying than anticipated. But it was only afterwards that I realized that this satisfaction derived from the fact that writing from the position of the romantically or erotically frustrated man who's always in pursuit of a woman who

❛ Writing from the position of the romantically or erotically frustrated man who's always in pursuit of a woman who torments him was really a means of recording and reworking my own childhood experiences with my mother. ❜

torments him was really a means of recording and reworking my own childhood experiences with my mother. I did feel passionately possessive of her, but she was never mine; I did want to penetrate her, not sexually, but I wanted to be inside her, to know her, to break through whatever it was that held me from her. All these are very male desires. So being a man in my fiction allows me to work through those feelings again. It's not a pleasant place to be, but it's familiar!

I read you're scared of twins . . .
I am. I find the idea of identicalness dreadful. I think anything that threatens my sense of having a set and separate identity from other human beings frightens me. Identical twins have a strange symbiosis and there appears to be a very permeable boundary between the two, which makes me anxious. I've heard people say that they'd love to have an identical twin and I think that's the worst idea. I'd hate that. I can't imagine having to live with some kind of double. So I've always found them spooky. But I love staring at them. Whatever manners my grandmother taught me have decayed, sadly.

So you're naturally an observer?
Yes. I really do stare at people. The subway is better than being at the zoo. I find people so peculiar and fascinating. I suppose I eavesdrop on people too. And I routinely and expectantly look in other peoples' medicine cabinets when invited to dinner ▶

6 I routinely and expectantly look in other peoples' medicine cabinets when invited to dinner parties. I mean, how could you not? Don't you want to know what's in there? 9

Author photo © Joyce Ravid

LIFE
at a Glance

BORN

20 March 1961, in
Los Angeles, California

EDUCATED

BA, Stanford University,
1982; MFA, Iowa Writers'
Workshop, 1987

CAREER TO DATE

Worked as an editor for
Viking Penguin for 3
years, 1987–90, first novel
published in 1991; have
published 11 books,
fiction, memoir,
biography. Adjunct
professor at Columbia
University, visiting
professor at Hunter
College in the Fall of 2006,
teaching memoir writing
to graduate students.

LIVES

Brooklyn, NY

FAMILY

Husband, Colin Harrison,
novelist; three children:
Sarah, Walker, Julia.

Liking Monday... *(continued)*

◀ parties. I mean, how could you not? Don't
you want to know what's in there?

What are you currently writing?
I'm working on a non-fiction project about
three murders that took place in a family in
Medford, Oregon, in 1984. Two members
survived and one was going to write a
memoir about what happened, but found
that it was impossible. She couldn't really
immerse herself in this cataclysm that had
destroyed her family so I jumped in and
said, 'I'll do it.' It was her brother who killed
their parents and their sister, so I've been in
Oregon talking to him in prison.

One of my greatest worries about taking
on the project was that he wasn't going to
show up and I'd be left in the anteroom. But
he was willing to talk and he was very open.
We still exchange letters; he's been very
generous with me, tolerated a lot of painful
questioning, beyond the call of duty.

Can you imagine doing anything else?
I've worked alone at home so long I don't
think I'd know how to get dressed in the
morning and go out to work! At the
beginning of my career I would have said
that writing was torture, or, as Flannery
O'Connor said, memorably, that she liked to
have written, rather than liked writing. But
now, at this point in my life, my career, I do
love what I do. I like Monday better than
Friday. It strikes me as an impossible stroke
of good fortune that I get to make a living
doing the thing I love. ■

A Writing Life

When do you write?
Whenever I can: when the children are at
school; between 5 and 7 in the morning; any
other minutes I can snatch.

Where do you write?
In my study, on the top floor of our home.

Why do you write?
I'm addicted to it; it's the only way I know to
explain the world to myself; I love it.

Pen or computer?
Both. I don't use a laptop, so a pen when I'm
away from my desk. It took me some time to
get used to composing on a word processor
and the first drafts of my first eight books
were all in longhand.

Silence or music?
Silence.

How do you start a book?
I wish I knew.

And finish?
I try to apply a rule my grandfather imposed
on me with regard to my arithmetic
homework: make sure you do the last
problem as carefully as you did the first.

**Do you have any writing rituals or
superstitions?**
Many.

A Writing Life (continued)

Which living writer do you most admire?
As someone who works determinedly and who has a lot of stamina, I'm always astonished by how intelligently prolific a writer Joyce Carol Oates is. I love J. M. Coetzee. And I enjoy and respect the work of countless others, but I find it difficult to pick and choose among them. I suppose I feel all our separate voices make a chorus, and that I would miss not having any one of them.

Which book do you wish you had written?
The one I haven't begun yet.

What or who inspires you?
Certain feelings, like fear or longing, push me to write.

If you weren't a writer what job would you do?
Physician or psychoanalyst.

What's your guilty reading pleasure? Favourite trashy reads?
True crime. *Valley of the Dolls*. Tabloids.

Sin Boldly

By Kathryn Harrison

For the first time in my writing life, I have a character for whom I want to plot a return. Naturally, this is Jennifer, the one character in *Envy* whose sole purpose, her *raison d'être*, is to wreak havoc in the lives of others. She is, indisputably, a Bad Girl. Even better, she is a Bad Girl who doesn't get her come-uppance. What's more, her arena is sex. She determines her victim, plots his seduction, effortlessly ruins his life. She suffers no guilt, at least not any her author or audience can perceive, and moves on to the next object of her fleeting attention.

'But why?' an early reader asked me, almost wringing her hands over the turbulence Jennifer left in her wake. '*Why* is she doing this?'

'Because,' I said. Because she can. Because she does. Because that's who she is.

The reader nodded; then she stopped frowning; then she smiled. 'Oh,' she said. 'Right.'

Maybe this is a way of thumbing my nose at the patriarchy, feminism with a sense of humour. (Yes, there is such a thing.) Maybe it's the irresistible lure of the forbidden.

More likely, it has a lot to do with the fact that my life, filled as it is with gratification, lacks excitement. A few years ago, a friend of mine embarked on an affair and destroyed her marriage to a man who was – in her estimation, anyway – decent and law-abiding to a fault. She was a Catholic, and just the previous year she'd been going to Mass every day, tallying up her minor sins and little ▶

9

Sin Boldly *(continued)*

◀ penances in a last-ditch effort to rein in temptation. But once she succumbed, she was flagrantly indiscreet. Still, her decent, earnest spouse was, typically, the last to know. It was my husband who, when he couldn't stand it any longer, took the man out for a drink and told him his wife was cheating on him.

'He used the word "cuckold"', my friend told me later, both relieved and stricken when she reported that she and her soon-to-be-ex-husband had finally had it out. My friend looked at me, rather pointedly, I thought. 'Don't you think that's weird?' she asked me. 'I mean, he's never used that word before. I was surprised he even knew it.' I shrugged, looked away, out the window, anywhere but into her eyes. It was only after the fact that I found out about my husband's telling hers what was going on, and I'd kept the secret. An attorney and an academic, her husband used a lot of words my husband didn't, but the literary, slightly fey and anachronistic 'cuckold' wasn't one of them.

'I just don't understand why she's doing this,' I said a few weeks later, to a mutual friend.

'Of course you do.'

I shook my head. 'No, I don't,' I said.

'She's bored.'

'Still.'

'Come on,' our friend said. 'Look at the stuff you dabble in every day.'

'What? What are you talking about?'

'Shoplifting. Adultery. Murder. Weird sex.'

'Yes, but that's on the page.'

The friend shrugged. 'She doesn't have

6 He used the word "cuckold", my friend told me later, both relieved and stricken when she reported that she and her soon-to-be-ex-husband had finally had it out. 9

that. You don't know what it's like not to be able to act out. You can do whatever you want, whatever you can think of.'

'But it isn't real.'

'It is to you.'

She's right. Everything on the page is real to me. What's more, my characters, over which you might imagine I have control, arrive without warning and behave as they want, without my conscious direction. They steal things, break things, eclipse the people I thought I was writing about, rearrange my plot. They torment others, they hurt themselves, they break the law – all without my permission. Often, their exits – the suicide of my favourite character in *The Binding Chair*, for example – are as unexpected as their arrivals, and leave me bereft. It sounds absurd, but for weeks after that suicide I dragged around in shock, thinking the sorts of things one thinks under those circumstances: *I can't believe it. I just can't believe it. I should have seen it coming. I knew she was depressed.* And it was true. Once I examined her actions, all that the departed character had done and said in the months preceding her death had predicted that she would take her life. And yet, I hadn't known. I loved her, and couldn't imagine the world – the world in which I was immersed – without her.

The cast of each of my novels contains at least one female character (invariably female) that I never intended to be part of the story. Often – in *A Thousand Orange Trees*, *The Binding Chair* and *The Seal Wife* – this character is the heroine, and when she ▶

> ❝ My characters, over which you might imagine I have control, arrive without warning and behave as they want, without my conscious direction. ❞

11

Sin Boldly *(continued)*

◄ arrived in the story I did all I could to
discourage her. After all, she wasn't part of
the book I thought I was writing. But over
the years I've grown more comfortable with
the peculiarities of my job. This time, when
Jennifer walked into *Envy*, I was delighted.
Finally, here was the person who was going
to take this story in hand, and push it places
I couldn't go by myself.

By now I've heard back from a few
readers who know me personally. *Wow*, they
say. *Where did she come from?* Or: *Imagine
that person being part of you.* Because, of
course, she is me, or at least mine. One of
the women I hold within myself, one of the
ones that evens things up in this unequal
world. Mostly suppressed, certainly silenced
in polite company. But not entirely
repressed, because I have a job that requires
input from my id.

As a reader, my interest in sequels has
been limited to children's books – by C. S.
Lewis, Laura Ingalls Wilder, J. R. R. Tolkien,
Enid Blyton – my devotion inspired by the
transgressive characters, the ones who
misbehave, mostly not out of a desire to
wreak havoc so much as an expression of
their personalities. It was Laura whom I
loved in the Little House books; I never
could care for Mary, who didn't disobey or
get her dresses torn and dirty. Some people
aren't cut out for following the rules. Some
people only need hear of a rule to want to
break it. I am one of these.

When I was five or six, I was told never to
write on walls, a thing I hadn't considered
up until that moment. As soon as I had the

> ❝ It was Laura
> whom I loved in
> the Little House
> books; I never
> could care for
> Mary, who didn't
> disobey or get
> her dresses torn
> and dirty. ❞

opportunity to work uninterrupted I pushed aside the very heavy dresser in my room, with the strength born of desire, and with my mother's red lipstick (compounding the crime, as I had been forbidden to touch her cosmetics) I wrote and drew all over the pastel wallpaper that had been hidden by the big piece of furniture. Then I pushed the dresser back into its place and, after doing my best to reshape the worn-down point of the lipstick, put it away as well. It wasn't until we moved out of that house, when I was ten, that the trespass was discovered, a surprise for me as much as anyone else, as I had forgotten what I'd done. This is only one example of my attraction to what is held out of reach. I don't think I'd have lasted a day in Bluebeard's castle. I'd never have been able to wait until he went out of town to see what the key unlocked. It was caller ID, not adulthood, that put an end to my prank phone call career.

So, having completed the novel almost two years ago, I want Jennifer to come back. I miss her – not for the power she wields as much as for the exuberance with which she breaks the rules. 'Sin boldly,' Martin Luther is said to have counselled. In other words, why go to hell for petty crimes? It's Jennifer's swagger that I like, the fact that not only does she not disguise her bad deeds, she brags about them. I wish she'd return and turn another story upside down, but it doesn't feel within my power. Given the fact that she has a mind of her own – or at least her own piece of mine – she'll do what she wants. ∎

> ❛ It was caller ID, not adulthood, that put an end to my prank phone call career. ❜

Have You Read?

*A selection of other books by
Kathryn Harrison*

The Kiss: A Secret Life
'My father takes my face in his hands. He tips it up and kisses my closed eyes, my throat. I feel his fingers in the hair at the nape of my neck. I feel his hot breath on my eyelids . . .'
A searing account of a four-year affair between the author and her father which went on to become an international bestseller, *The Kiss* is a beautiful, honest and shocking account which shatters one of society's remaining taboos.

The Binding Chair
Beautiful, charismatic and destructive, May escapes an arranged marriage in rural China for life in a Shanghai brothel, where, in 1899, she meets Arthur, an Australian. What follows is a compelling account of the lives of two very different women – May and her husband's niece Alice – and the difficulties they face in their quest for independence.

The Seal Wife
Bigelow is a scientist, meticulous and obsessive, a man of tightly coiled passion. Stationed in the tiny frontier town of Anchorage, Alaska, in 1915, he is distracted from his labours when he meets a native Aleut woman, a stitcher of furs, whose muteness calls up in him an almost unbearable longing. An incendiary tale set against the haunting landscape of the Great North, *The Seal Wife* merges the

enchantment of myth with a taut and chilling story of erotic compulsion.

Seeking Rapture: A Memoir
In this witty, touching memoir, Harrison writes of the ties that bind mothers to their children – and the forces that can drive them apart. She ponders the legacy of storytelling she inherited from her grandmother, and peers into the deep well of family history from which she draws inspiration for her novels. ■

IF YOU *loved this, you might like . . .*

Me and the Fat Man
by Julie Myerson

Everything You Know
by Zoë Heller

The Widow's Children
by Paula Fox

Veronica
by Mary Gaitskill

CIRCULATING STOCK ████ UBLIC LIBRARIES
BLOCK LOAN   ษ 14 /03 /11